KATE THOMPSON was born in Belfast ages ago. She came to Dublin to study French and English at Trinity, met her future husband, and became an actress (an award-winning one!) and voice-over artist. She ended up as a dubious femme fatale in a soap opera for nine years, effecting her escape by writing her first bestseller, *It Means Mischief.* Her second novel, *More Mischief,* was followed by *Going Down.* All her books have been widely translated. Kate divides her time between Dublin and the West of Ireland, is still happily married (to the same man!) and has one daughter of whom she is inordinately proud. Incidentally, she is still available for voice-over work because nowadays it's virtually the only thing that gets her out of her attic where she writes.

Also by Kate Thompson

IT MEANS MISCHIEF
MORE MISCHIEF
GOING DOWN

and published by Bantam Books

THE BLUE HOUR

Kate Thompson

BANTAM BOOKS

LONDON · NEW YORK · TORONTO · SYDNEY · AUCKLAND

THE BLUE HOUR
A BANTAM BOOK : 0 553 81298 X

First publication in Great Britain

PRINTING HISTORY
Bantam edition published 2002

1 3 5 7 9 10 8 6 4 2

Set in 11/13pt Baskerville by
Kestrel Data, Exeter, Devon.

Bantam Books are published by Transworld Publishers,
61–63 Uxbridge Road, London W5 5SA,
a division of The Random House Group Ltd,
in Australia by Random House Australia (Pty) Ltd,
20 Alfred Street, Milsons Point, Sydney, NSW 2061, Australia,
in New Zealand by Random House New Zealand Ltd,
18 Poland Road, Glenfield, Auckland 10, New Zealand
and in South Africa by Random House (Pty) Ltd,
Endulini, 5a Jubilee Road, Parktown 2193, South Africa.

Printed and bound in Great Britain by
Cox & Wyman Ltd, Reading, Berkshire.

For my father, Desmond

Prologue

She was sitting on the balcony, as she often did at this hour of the evening. Twilight was slowly creeping up over the garden below, drawing a soft, warm, indigo-coloured pashmina across the lawn. *L'heure bleue.* That was how the French described it. The blue hour. Her favourite time.

Her book – *Jane Eyre* – was lying on the ground at her feet, a crushed petunia blossom marking the place. The *pichet* of red wine on the table beside her was half full. House martins were diving in and out of the eaves, white underbellies gleaming in the last light of the low-slung sun and sparrows were staking claim to dormitories, beating each other up in the process, like small thugs.

Maddie stretched luxuriously, enjoying the comforting, soporific drone of a bee somewhere nearby, surrendering herself completely to the irresistible languor of *l'heure bleue.* She ran a hand down her bare arm. Her skin felt satiny to the touch. It was golden now from days of lying lazily on beaches, and fragrant with the sun-balm she'd rubbed on earlier. There was a pot-pourri of scents in the air this evening. The bee – clearly a workaholic – was buzzing round the lavender that burst exuberantly from a big earthenware pot on a windowsill, disturbing the purple flowers and sending their unique perfume drifting into the dusk.

She'd been like that once – a busy bee: working late, working weekends, working her ass off. In her old life she'd never, ever envisaged herself being lazy. Even her free time had been devoted to a dizzying round of social activity. In her old life she'd never found it easy to sit still.

Her old life. Was this, then, her new? No. She knew she'd have to go back there, to that old life – that other country – and confront her demons. It was ironic, she thought, that her biblical namesake, Mary Magdalene, had been plagued by demons, too. The Magdalene's had been exorcized, but Maddie still wasn't sure if hers had been.

And yet, and yet . . . She'd had no demonic visitations since the evening the nightingale had sung to her. How long ago was that? She had no idea – she'd lost all track of time. Anyway, she didn't want to think about it. She wanted this blue hour to herself: undisturbed, reposeful, utterly sequestered. Maddie picked up the notebook that was her constant companion these days, and reread what she'd written earlier. She'd called her sonnet 'Becoming Madeleine'.

The past's another country. Who lives there?
My loved ones, absent friends, some quick,
    some dead,
Some loving and supportive, some misled.
This renaissance will take some time and care
Especially since I'm healing solitaire:
No soul to help me in my quest to shed
The demonic possessions I so dread
From that time past, that old Real Life
    nightmare.

At least I've left the fast lane. Now I drowse
In deckchairs, dream and drink *pichets* of wine,
Write silly poems like this, and idly browse
Through stacks of books. I think I'm doing fine.
I raise my glass. Good health! *Santé!* Amen
To me at last becoming Madeleine.

L'heure bleue was nearly over. Darkness loomed.
Maddie closed the notebook and reached for her
wineglass. Then she shut her eyes and leaned back
in her chair, wishing that some evening soon she
might hear the nightingale sing its song of ecstasy
again.

9

Chapter One

'What an extraordinary mouth you have. Like a
crushed flower.'

And what an extraordinarily unsubtle chat-up
technique you have, you smooth git, thought
Maddie Godard. A crushed flower! She arranged
her features into a suitably unimpressed expression as she turned to deliver a put-down to the
man who was standing just behind her.

Contrary to her expectations, there was nothing
remotely carnal about the look in his eyes. If
there was a word to fit the expression he was
wearing it would have to be . . . dispassionate. The
withering remark she'd been about to utter never
made it out of Maddie's mouth. For some reason
she suddenly thought it would sound silly, not
withering at all.

'Extraordinary cheekbones, too. Do you mind?'
He leaned closer and briefly traced the contour of
her cheek with a finger, then cupped cheekbones
and jaw between the palms of his hands. Maddie
made to back off. 'Forgive me.' As his hands
left her face he spread them in a conciliatory
gesture. 'I know you must think this extremely odd

behaviour – please don't misinterpret.' He gave her a smile – half apologetic, half amused – and then said: 'I've been experimenting with sculpture, and I find it difficult to resist touching things that I find pleasing.'

'I'm not a thing.' Maddie finally found her voice.

'That's pretty obvious.'

The interested look he gave her invited her to banter back. She ignored it. She was very good at being snooty when it suited her.

The stranger inclined his head slightly, acknowledging that she'd called closure on the conversation. 'I apologize for the intrusion,' he said, looking at her from under his eyebrows. Then he turned and walked away through the crowd of chattering people that surrounded them. Suddenly he stopped and looked back at her with speculative eyes, taking her quite off guard. 'Someone should paint you,' he remarked, before continuing on his way.

Jesus! Maddie resumed her disdainful expression too late, and turned her back on him. She simmered as she leafed through the pages of her catalogue, realizing that her face was hot where his hands had lingered. She hated people invading her personal space! How had she allowed a total stranger to get away with such behaviour? She didn't usually have a problem telling people where to get off if they were rude to her.

And yet . . . if she was to be honest with herself –

she would have to say that the man hadn't actually been rude. His apology had been undeniably genuine, after all, and the way he'd touched her had had a spontaneity about it that had been – well, *disarming*. It had certainly disarmed her enough to make her want to look twice.

She subtly shifted her stance and snuck a look at him over the top of her catalogue. He hadn't advanced more than a few yards across the gallery floor before a little crowd of elegant women formed around him, all air-kissing madly and gushing with delight. The hand that he was extending to a fragile-looking girl looked as if it might crush her fingers between his.

He was a tall man – big might be a better word – and he carried himself well, with relaxed insouciance. A mane of silver-streaked, dark blond hair skimmed powerful shoulders, and there was something leonine about his profile. He had a strong jaw, prominent cheekbones and watchful eyes under heavy brows. Furrows were etched around his mouth and on his high forehead. He wasn't handsome at all.

'Daniel!' A woman standing next to her called out to him, stretching an expensively manicured hand high above the heads of the crowd so that he could see her wave. Maddie ducked behind her catalogue, hoping he hadn't seen her looking. 'It's been an absolute *age*, darling!' The tone was plaintive. 'You really should come back more often.' The woman began to manoeuvre her way through the crowd, ignoring the fact that she'd practically shouldered Maddie aside in her enthusiasm to get to her quarry.

Maddie's jaw muscles clenched, and she fanned herself with her catalogue. She was beginning to realize that she didn't really enjoy these affairs. She must have been to at least five of them in as many weeks, ever since her partner Josh had announced over dinner one night that he'd been neglecting his cultural side. People tended to be rather patronizing about graphic art – but graphic and fine art weren't at totally opposite ends of the cultural spectrum, he'd argued, citing his hero, advertising supremo Charles Saatchi as a prime example of new Renaissance man. There was a latter-day patron of the arts! A force to be reckoned with in the commercial as well as the cultural field.

Charles Saatchi had also made a fortune out of shrewd investment in contemporary artworks, Maddie had thought as she'd sipped her de-caf, but she'd refrained from pointing this out to Josh. He wouldn't like her thinking that there was anything mercenary about his interest.

Later on in bed that night he'd added that it wouldn't do their image any harm at all to be seen at more exhibition openings. Maddie had thought tiredly of the numerous theatrical opening nights and book launches and media parties she'd endured over the past few years just so that Josh could get their names – and that of the advertising

14

agency they represented – into the social columns of the glossier monthlies. Now the glitter of the social round she'd once found alluring was wearing thin, and she was becoming increasingly aware of the hollowness underneath.

However, this exhibition at the Demeter Gallery was one that she genuinely didn't want to miss. It was a collection of recent work by Sara Lennox, a celebrated portrait photographer, and a shot of Maddie's cousin, the actress Maeve Kirwan, was on view. Sara Lennox had asked Maeve to open the exhibition for her. It was customary for a celebrity to say a few words at an event of this type, and Maeve was now a rising star in the film world. Her work had been restricted mainly to theatre and soap opera until a couple of years ago, when she had started to do a lot of work in the UK. Now her career was poised to take off bigtime.

Maddie turned her attention to the photographs that were hung at uniform intervals along the pristine white expanse of the gallery walls, scanning them for the portrait of Maeve. The black-and-white shots were all of female nudes – and breathtakingly sensuous without being in any way explicit.

Sara Lennox's women obviously enjoyed being women. They were all knowing, self-assured in an understated way, and elegantly voluptuous. There was a composure about them that she found arresting, intriguing. Water was a common theme in the photographs. The exterior shots had been taken on sea- or lake-shores, and the contours of the women were mirrored in the geography of their surroundings. The curve of a buttock or breast in the foreground was echoed in the smooth rounded sandstone of the shore, or in the swell of the sea behind. The few indoor shots had been taken in bathrooms or swimming pools, and they featured figures draped in silk made transparent by water, with hair so wet that glistening drops ran down the subjects' bodies.

Maddie wandered from picture to picture searching for the portrait of her cousin until a photograph of a woman floating on her back in a pool with a mosaic floor stopped her in her tracks. The jewel-like tiles of the mosaic shimmered beneath her, and the only ripples on the pellucid water were those made by her hair as it drifted around her calm, beautiful face. She looked utterly at peace. That's where she'd like to be right now, thought Maddie as she contemplated the photograph. Floating in calm water, surrendered to that blissful state of weightlessness.

'Maddie! There you are! Come over here, quickly. A photographer from *Individual* magazine wants a shot of the two of us together.'

Maddie's reverie fragmented as she transferred her gaze from the serene face in the photograph to the fractious one of her partner Josh O'Regan. 'Oh, Josh – you know I hate posing for those things,' she said. 'The last time my photograph was in *Individual* I looked like one of the more

16

cerebrally challenged cast members of *Dumb and Dumber*.'

Josh's voice was testy now, verging on exasperation. 'We can't afford to turn down opportunities of keeping our profile high, Maddie. You know how important it is for the agency.' He took her by the arm. 'Come on. Oh come *on*, gorgeous – it'll only take a minute.'

As Josh led the way across the room, Maddie organized her features into the expression she adopted for these occasions, aware that people were looking at them. She felt stupid and self-conscious as the photographer went about his business, gesturing with an impatient hand for her to look this way and that, and instructing her to smile, smile, *smile*!

She glanced at Josh. He was standing with his head at a rakish angle – green eyes slightly narrowed, sexy smile on his lips – and he had draped a casual arm over Maddie's shoulders in a proprietorial fashion. His handsome face had a Clinique-esque glow, the gloss on his hair was courtesy of Phytologie. His physique was honed and sculpted by rigorous training sessions, he smelled of Aqua di Parma, and his threads were by Hugo Boss. He looked exactly how Maddie knew he wanted to look – like a really happening kinda guy.

Hell. He was right. It *was* important to maintain a high profile. Advertising was a notoriously competitive game, after all. It was just that sometimes she felt as if the circles in which they moved were ever-decreasing. She had three more years before she hit thirty. She wanted her horizons to expand as she got older, not shrink. Suddenly she felt mutinous. She put her hands on her hips, lifted her chin and looked down the lens unsmilingly as the flash went for the last time.

The photographer hung the camera round his neck and extracted a notebook from his pocket. 'Names?' he enquired of Josh in a rather peremptory way.

Beside her Maddie could feel Josh stiffen. 'What's he asking me that for?' he said through gritted teeth. 'That geezer knows my fucking name.' But he kept his cool as he sauntered over to oblige. Maddie didn't bother to follow him. She turned away, and started fanning herself with her catalogue again. Josh would supply her name and address. Or rather her name and professional identity. Maddie Godard: copywriter, the Complete Works Advertising.

Rival media types referred to the agency as the 'Complete Bollocks'. But that was an indication of how paranoid they were. The Complete Works was rapidly becoming one of the fastest-growing advertising agencies in Dublin, and the competition was worried. Maddie had been fresh out of college when she'd approached them about a job, and Josh had used influence with his colleagues to take her on board at once. He had a keen and unerring eye for spotting new talent.

She'd joined them shortly before both her parents had been killed in a car crash. Josh had been there for her when she'd disintegrated, there for her when she was ready to start putting the pieces together again, and now, five years on, he was still there for her. His support had been incalculable. His – and that of her cousin Maeve, who was now her only living relative apart from some distant second-cousin types far away in a remote corner of France. She'd never met them, and because there'd been no letter of condolence after her parents had died, she never wanted to.

A welcome breath of fresh air came from the door of the gallery, which someone had sensibly decided to prop open. There was Maeve arriving now in a swirl of silk, looking so effortlessly elegant that if Maddie didn't like her so much, she'd have every reason to feel jealous of her beautiful, famous cousin. Even amongst the luminaries who were still piling into the gallery space, Maeve stood out. People were gravitating towards her, smarmimg.

Maddie scrutinized this eclectic bunch of opening-nighters. There were genuine bohemians in cheap, eccentrically put together garments; there were self-styled bohemians in expensive rags; there were business types in suits, and there were a few seriously moneyed individuals in genuine-article designer labels. She wondered what category she fitted into, with her expensive haircut and her sharp black trouser suit and her Manolo Blahnik boots.

As she wandered back across the room wearing the bored expression she'd perfected for occasions like this – expressly to conceal her discomfort at not knowing anyone – she met the eyes of the man who'd touched her earlier. He was looking at her as if he could see right through her façade of ostentatious world-weariness, as if she was not really fooling anyone, and as if she certainly wasn't fooling him. She tensed, wondering if he'd seen her posing for that wretched magazine photographer. She found the idea somehow humiliating. He smiled and raised his glass in salute, but she averted her eyes at once, pretending not to have seen.

Just then came the sound of the gallery owner clapping his hands together in an effort to attract the attention of the company. Speeches were about to begin. Maddie watched Maeve stroll in a leisurely fashion towards the top of the room where a long trestle table littered with wineglasses and bottles stood. An expectant hush fell as the actress took a deep breath and began her speech. Maddie had already heard it – Maeve had asked her to listen to it a couple of times because she'd felt too self-conscious to run it by Jacqueline, her long-term partner.

Maeve appeared cucumber cool as she addressed her audience, telling them that by the end of the evening not one of her friend Sara Lennox's photographs should be without a red 'sold' dot.

That big, leonine man was looking at Maeve now with undisguised appreciation, a smile playing around his lips. He obviously fancied himself as some kind of connoisseur of women, Maddie decided. She wished more than ever that she'd been more vocal when he'd annoyed her earlier. All the right adjectives came to her now, when it was too late. Lubricious, nauseating, lecherous, salacious, oleaginous . . .

'Ladies and gentlemen,' Maeve concluded. 'Please join me in a toast to the most inspired photographer of women it has ever been my pleasure to sit for. Sara Lennox!'

Sara Lennox, a forty-ish woman with a halo of wild, golden hair, stepped forward to take her bow, radiating charisma. When the applause finally petered out, she sent Maeve a warm smile. 'I'd like to thank Maeve Kirwan for saying such wonderfully flattering things about me. And I'd also like to take this opportunity to welcome home my brother Daniel. He's come all the way from his retreat in France to be at the opening of this exhibition. I truly appreciate it, Daniel. Thank you.'

There was a stirring in the crowd, and people looked around curiously, eager to put a face to the name. Daniel Lennox, Maddie knew, was a notoriously reclusive – and very famous – painter. She saw Sara blowing a kiss across the room to where the man who'd come on to her earlier was standing. He acknowledged his sister's words of welcome with a brief smile and a nod. Then the applause started again. It reached a crescendo, faded and was superseded by intense speculative chattering as Sara retreated into the crowd.

So that was Daniel Lennox! The man who had taken liberties with her bone structure was the most famous living painter in Ireland! Or rather, she corrected herself as she looked at him with interest, the most famous living *Irish* painter. He hadn't been resident in the country for years.

Maddie had seen a retrospective of his paintings in the Museum of Modern Art, and loved them. She didn't know much about art – unlike Josh, who had boned up bigtime on the subject – but somehow the paintings had spoken to her. They were big canvases – some landscapes, a few semi-abstract portraits – all executed with distinctive panache in vigorous oils. The man responsible for them had a kind of panache, too, she supposed, looking at him again with new interest. Despite his deficiency in the looks department, women were still fawning around him, attracted to the heady aura of his fame. One of the fawners gave a sudden bray of laughter, and she saw him give an almost imperceptible wince. No wonder he was a recluse.

She turned and manoeuvred her way back through the crowd towards the far corner of the room where the photograph of the woman in the mosaic pool was hanging. She wanted to lose herself in that photograph, to visualize herself there, cradled by warm water, serene and uncomplicated. It was no use. The pervasive starling-like chatter of the opening-nighters was too distracting. She would have to come back on another day, when the gallery was less crowded.

'Maddie! Hi!' Maeve was at her shoulder, hugging her.

'Maeve! Your speech was great!' Maddie hugged her cousin back.

'I didn't look too nervous, did I?'

'No. You're too talented an actress for that. Where's Jacqueline?'

'She couldn't come. She's preparing for some politician's annual banquet.'

Jacqueline was a catering demon – very much in demand.

'Great photograph, Maeve.' A man Maddie recognized from a radio arts programme slid past them with a tape recorder, heading in the direction of Sara and Daniel Lennox.

'Thanks, Tony.' Maeve acknowledged the compliment with a flirty smile, and then turned back to Maddie. 'What do you think of it?' she asked.

'I couldn't find it – this place is too crowded.'

'It's right here.' Maeve took Maddie's hand and led her two paces around the corner.

'Wow,' said Maddie. How could she have missed it? It was among the most stunning portraits of the entire exhibition – and one of only a few that were in colour. Or was it? Maddie inspected it at closer range. Actually, it wasn't a colour shot. Hand-tinted in pale inks, it depicted Maeve emerging from the sea like Aphrodite, trailing a length of seaweed behind her and looking straight down the lens with a dreamy smile on her face. There were strands of weed coiled around her legs and tendrils of it clinging like cobweb to her bare breasts. A pale moon hung low over the horizon behind her.

'Well? What do you think?' asked Maeve again.

Maddie shook her head slowly from side to side, mesmerized by the portrait of her cousin. 'It's exquisite, Maeve. It's absolutely ravishing. No – that word's better in French. *Ravissante! Ma cousine est ravissante!*' She gave her ravishing cousin a big kiss on the cheek. 'You must be dead chuffed.'

'I can't deny it. It's a real classic, isn't it? The kind of portrait you dream about.'

'She's photographed you before, hasn't she?'

'Yeah. But only rehearsal shots for publicity. I knew she was the best portrait photographer around, but I never imagined she could dream up a stunt like this.'

Maddie returned her attention to the portrait. 'How on earth do you manage to look so relaxed in front of a camera? I only ever succeed in looking uptight and gormless.'

'It's all down to the photographer, of course. Sara's a genius.'

'She certainly is.' The remark came from a thirty-something bottle blonde, who had insinuated herself through the crowd and was now standing next to Maeve. 'Forgive me – I hope you don't mind me interrupting?' The woman gave Maddie a perfunctory smile, but Maddie could tell that she had barely registered her presence. Her entire focus was on Maeve. 'I just couldn't resist the opportunity of introducing myself to you, Maeve. The name's Darina. Darina Maguire.' She extended a hand. 'I've been following your career with real interest since it took off towards the stratosphere! You're blazing some trail now, aren't you?' Her smile was the most patently insincere one that Maddie had ever seen.

'You're a journalist, aren't you?' Maeve raised an autocratic eyebrow and fixed cold eyes on the woman called Darina Maguire.

'That's right, Maeve,' said Darina, her unacknowledged hand now dangling limply. Maddie noticed that the fuchsia nail polish was badly chipped. 'But I'm branching out. That's what I was hoping I might be able to talk to you about, actually. I've been commissioned to write a series of biographies of celebrity couples – *Irish* couples, of course – and I was hoping you might be able to help me.'

'Really? How?'

'Well. The couple I had in mind for the film-stroke-theatre slot was—'

'Let me guess. Rory McDonagh and Deirdre O'Dare?'

'Spot on, Maeve! I know you were great friends with them when they lived over here, so I thought maybe I could take you out to lunch one day and we could have a chat.' Darina's smile was becoming increasingly unctuous. 'In strictest confidence, of course, if you don't want quotes attributed directly to you.'

'You mean you'd refer to me throughout as – let's see . . . "a close friend of the luvvies who prefers to remain anonymous"?'

Darina nodded enthusiastically. 'Sure,' she said.

'And what's that other famous device journalists use to screen the identity of their *stool*?' continued Maeve. 'Oh, yes! "A source close to the couple hinted that . . ." That's always a useful one, yeah?' Maeve put her head on one side and looked closely at Darina. Her mouth was curved in a smile, but there was no trace of humour in her eyes.

'That's the style! I can tell you read your gossip columns, Maeve!'

'Darina?' said Maeve, adopting an overly cordial tone. 'What makes you think I'd do this?'

'Pardon?'

'Divulge information about my friends to a member of the press?'

'Ah – it's not for the newspaper, now. As I said, I've been specially commissioned—'

'Is the biography authorized?'

'What do you mean?' Darina tried to look uncertain.

'You know what I mean. Have Rory and Deirdre agreed to talk to you?'

'Ah, no, now.' Darina gave a self-deprecating

little laugh. 'It's not an *in-depth* kind of biography, you see. I'm taking a more light-hearted approach. I just want to tell the story of how they got together. How they're coping with their new-found fame and fortune – and parenthood, of course. A human-interest story, you know?'

'Human interest? You mean something along the lines of that feature you did on me in your stitch-up column in the *Sunday Satellite*?'

'Ah. I'm surprised you remember that, Maeve.' The journalist adopted a pseudo-confidential tone. 'Of course – you understand that I wasn't entirely responsible for that. The editor wanted something with a bit more bite, you see. He insisted that I take a more – um – what's the right word? A more *proactive* stance on that piece, d'you know what I mean? And anyway, it's ages ago since that article appeared, isn't it? It must be—'

'Two years and seven months.'

'Well. You must have an amazing memory, Maeve. I have to say that—'

'You don't have to say anything else, Darina, because I don't want to hear it. It may interest you to know that the reason I remember that piece so clearly is because I spent two days with my head under the duvet when it appeared in your paper. I cried myself to sleep every night for a week. I didn't dare show my face in public for a month. I could have sued, Darina, but I knew that would just attract further attention to your nasty little column, and it certainly didn't *merit* further attention. So instead I bit the bullet – hard – and tried to hold my head up as high as I could. There are some very unenlightened members of the public who read your paper, Darina. I'd love to know how *you'd* feel if you received a package through your letterbox which contained something unspeakable, and a death threat which made specific reference to my sexual persuasion? I'm very glad my partner is not here this evening. I'd have difficulty in persuading her not to knife you. Now. What do you think is the likelihood of me contributing to the work of fiction you would like to describe as a "biography" of two of my dearest friends?' Maeve turned on her heel and stalked away. She looked like a queen.

Darina Maguire looked at Maddie and forced a half-hearted attempt at a smile. It came across as more of a grimace. 'Oh, well,' she said. 'You win some, you lose some.' Then she backed off into the crowd.

'Sorry to abandon you,' said Josh, as he rejoined Maddie. 'I ran into Mac.'

'Mac?'

'The art director in Medialink. Who's the tart?' He nodded his head in the direction of Darina Maguire's retreating back. 'I'm sure I've seen her in the Side Bar.' The Side Bar in the Shelbourne Hotel was, on a Friday evening, invaded by various media types. Maddie refused to set foot there. It made her feel as if she was entering a viper's nest.

'She's the journo responsible for the gossip page in the *Sunday Satellite* – you know the one that ruins somebody's life every week.'

' "Who The Hell Do They Think They Are?" '

'Yep.' Maddie followed Maeve's progress across the room with concerned eyes. When she saw her cousin laugh, she breathed easy again. It took more than a scumbag of a hackette to rattle Maeve. In fact, she had probably extracted an amount of pleasure from watching the worm squirm.

Josh had turned his attention to Maeve's photograph. 'Hell. That is one seriously sexy shot. I'd put a red mark on this if I hadn't already gone over budget last time.' Josh had bought what Maddie privately considered to be a rather over-priced acrylic at the last opening they'd been to. 'It's great to see Maeve get her tits out for the lads at last – not just her lezzy friends. Hey, I'd love to catch a load of you looking like that, Mads.' He pulled her towards him, then smoothed her hair back and traced the curve of her ear with his tongue. 'What a shame it is that your gorgeous cousin's a dyke,' he murmured. 'She could make some man very happy.'

Maeve had been joined by Daniel Lennox, who was obviously congratulating her on her speech. Maddie saw him laugh at something she said, and then he scooped up her cousin's hand, turned it so the palm was uppermost, and kissed it.

'So that sleazebag's Daniel Lennox.' Josh gave

her a sudden speculative look. 'I saw him mauling you earlier, darling. Fancies you, does he?' He rested a hand on her buttock.

'Oh, don't be daft, Josh,' Maddie said, wearily.

'What the hell was he doing then?' Josh tilted her chin with his index finger so that she had to meet his eyes. 'You know I don't like to see you being breathed all over by middle-aged men, Maddie. What line did he use? Hm? I bet it was that artist's all-time favourite – "I'd love to paint you". Was that it?'

Maddie flushed. He was almost spot on – *Someone should paint you*, Daniel Lennox had said – and for some reason she felt embarrassed that Josh had been able to hazard such an accurate guess. 'Oh, cut it out, for Christ's sake,' she said, sounding snappier than she'd intended. He shot her a look. 'Sorry, darling. It's just that I'm not feeling too hot.' In fact, she was feeling extremely hot. And bothered now, as well. 'Maybe we could leave now?' she asked hopefully.

Josh glanced at his watch. 'C'mon, Mads. It's still early, and I haven't had a decent look at any of the stuff yet. It would be bad form to leave without looking at a few more photographs. What if somebody noticed?'

Maddie suspected that no-one would notice, and if they did, they'd care less.

'One more drink and then we'll go, OK? I'll get you a fresh one.' He took her half-empty glass and drained it, making a face as he wiped his mouth.

'Christ – you'd think they could rise to something better than mediocre *vin du patron*. Another one of these?' he asked, and then gave her a doubtful look. 'Or maybe you should stick to water if you're not feeling great.'

'I'll have wine, please, Josh,' Maddie said with polite emphasis.

He shrugged, then headed off in the direction of the drinks table. Maddie moved back towards the portrait of Maeve. Her cousin looked so – what was the word? Feminine? No. That was way too weak an adjective. Womanly. *That* was the word that best described how Maeve looked – as if she'd just made love, and was already looking forward to making love again.

Josh had clearly been impressed by the photograph too. Maybe she should buy it for him? His birthday was coming up soon, and a glance at the catalogue told her that she could afford it. She looked towards the drinks table, where he was talking animatedly to the art director of another agency. Then she looked back at the portrait on the wall.

He had to have it. *She* had to have it.

Suddenly Josh was at her elbow again. 'Listen, darling – I got talking to Mac again. He's filling me in on the story behind the La Casita Holidays account. I was right about that new bastard of a marketing manager – fucking stabbed me in the back, he did. D'you mind if I go and get the rest of the story?'

Maddie didn't mind. She was working out how she could let the gallery owner know that she was interested in buying the study of Maeve without giving anything away to Josh. She wanted it to be a surprise. She took a sip of the wine he'd handed her. 'That's OK,' she said, smiling at him. 'Take as long as you like. I know how badly you feel about losing that account.'

Josh gave her a peck on the cheek. 'See you in a while,' he said, and he was gone.

Maddie returned her attention to the photograph. As she studied it she became aware that Sara Lennox and her brother had drifted in her direction. They were on the periphery of her eyeline, and she couldn't help but overhear their conversation. They were discussing the print just around the corner – the one of the swimming pool that Maddie had admired earlier.

'You'll find this hard to believe, Daniel, but that was one of the least arduous shoots. Marie-France was unusually compliant that day. Just look at the blissed-out expression on her face. She took to it like – well, like a duck to water.'

Daniel Lennox laughed. 'Compliant isn't a word I've ever associated with Marie-France, Sara. She was never the most biddable of wives.'

'C'mon, Daniel. Would you really *want* a biddable wife?'

'Well, it would make a change, wouldn't it? I'm getting a little tired of living in white-hot domestic conditions.'

'Is Jeanne still around?'

'No. She couldn't stand the heat either. She'd sulk if I spent too much time in the studio.' Daniel Lennox yawned. 'Fuck. I'm exhausted, Sara. I've been working too hard. I'm going to take it easy now I've finished on the landscape series. Mess around with something else – portraits, sculpture – I don't know quite what yet. I just know I need to move in another direction.'

'I hope your housekeeper's looking after you properly,' said Sara.

Daniel Lennox laughed. 'I love the note of sisterly concern. You mustn't worry. Mme Thibault's the ultimate molly-coddler.' He took a swig of his wine and made a face. 'Jesus – this stuff's shite.'

'Talking of Molly-coddle – how *is* my gorgeous niece?'

'It's working out well this year. She'll come to me for August, while her mother's in the Caribbean.' He looked at his watch. 'Actually, I'm surprised they aren't here yet. I suspect Marie-France is rather pleased about her astonishing physical symmetry being on public view.' He returned his attention to the portrait of the woman in the swimming pool.

'She has reason to be. She's still in great nick,' said Sara, taking a step back from the photograph and looking at it appraisingly. 'Won't Molly find it all a bit embarrassing, though?'

'Find what embarrassing?'

'The fact that there's a nude photograph of her mother hanging in a public gallery?'

Daniel gave Sara a surprised look. 'Oh, come on, Sara. We've never had any hang-ups about nudity in our family.'

'I know that, Daniel. I just thought she might be getting to an age when she'd be more self-conscious about that kind of stuff.'

Daniel Lennox laughed. 'Not at all. The word "embarrassment" doesn't exist in Molly's vocabulary. I just hope she doesn't grow up to be as big an exhibitionist as my ex-wife. You've been looking at that photograph for a very long time.'

There was dead silence for a moment or two before Maddie realized to her astonishment that Daniel Lennox had directed the remark at her.

Chapter Two

She flinched, and then turned to him, at a complete loss for words. He was leaning against the white wall of the gallery, smiling at her, but he said nothing further. Sara Lennox was looking at her curiously. Maddie couldn't believe it. This was the second time she had been reduced to speechlessness by the same stranger within half an hour!

'It's – it's an extremely nice photograph,' she said, with cringeworthy inadequacy.

Both Lennoxes were studying her with identical eyes. She felt like a Thomson's gazelle under the scrutiny of a pair of lions.

'*Nice?*' questioned Daniel Lennox. 'Yes . . . I suppose it is "nice". But I would have thought an advertising copywriter might have come up with a more imaginative adjective.'

'Would you prefer "pulchritudinous"?' she retorted, in what she knew was a pathetic attempt to save face. Something struck her suddenly. How did he know she was a copywriter? She had barely time to register how odd that was when Sara Lennox spoke up.

'*I* know who you remind me of! Just look at you! You could be Maeve's double! Apart from the colouring, of course. Couldn't she, Daniel?'

'Who's Maeve?'

'Maeve Kirwan. You know – the actress?'

'The one who made the speech earlier?'

'Yes.' Sara Lennox rounded the corner and indicated the photograph. 'They're the spitting image of each other, aren't they – even though Maeve is so fair, and you're so dark?' Sara Lennox turned to Maddie with a smile. 'No wonder you found this particular photograph fascinating. It must be like looking at a negative of yourself, d'you know what I mean? You must see the resemblance too, Daniel?'

Daniel Lennox slowly straightened himself and turned to the photograph of Maeve. He scrutinized it in silence for a couple of seconds, and then transferred his gaze to Maddie. She met his eyes square on, determined not to be fazed by him again. Her resolve evaporated as he looked her up and down. She knew he wasn't seeing her as she stood before him in her drop-dead black gear – he was seeing her in his mind's eye as she might look in the photograph, with no clothes on at all. Now she understood exactly what that stupid, clichéd phrase meant. He was undressing her with his eyes.

'You're right, Sara,' he said finally, smiling at Maddie. 'She could be Maeve's *doppelgänger*.'

Maddie picked at a piece of lint on her sleeve,

feeling very ill at ease. She cast around for something to say. 'She's my cousin,' was the best she could manage.

'Maeve is?' exclaimed Sara.

'Well,' said Daniel. 'That explains a lot. How far does the family resemblance go, I wonder? Do you have a mole on the same place, just there on the inside of your wrist?' Unexpectedly he laid a paw on her arm, and turned her wrist so that her palm faced upward. His fingers were cool. Maddie stiffened at the contact, but refused to pull away. He was so obviously trying to rattle her that she was more determined than ever not to let him see how successful he was being. 'Do you want the photograph?' He was examining the texture of her sleeve now, rubbing it between his thumb and forefinger. 'I think you ought to have it. Let me buy it from Sara and give it to you.'

'That's terribly kind of you, but I couldn't possibly allow you to do that.'

'Please. I'm indecently wealthy, and it would amuse me.'

Oh, *please*, Mr Shit-hot Famous Painter Lennox! 'I was going to buy it myself, actually, as a birthday present for my partner,' she said, with a thin smile.

'I've got a better idea!' Sara Lennox interjected. 'Why don't I replicate the photograph using you?'

Maddie's expression relaxed as she turned to the photographer. 'Sorry?' she said. 'I'm not quite sure what you're talking about—'

'I'll set up the same shot with *you* as the subject.

37

Like a mirror image. D'you see how Maeve leans to the left here?' She indicated Maeve's stance with an articulate hand. 'I'd have you lean to the right. And see how Maeve's right hand is trailing the seaweed behind her? I'd have you trail the seaweed using your *left* hand. And the moon! The moon is over Maeve's left shoulder, so I'd have to position you with it over your right. And with you so dark and Maeve so fair – oh yes, Daniel, you must see it too! Hell! I'm getting quite excited about this!'

'I would be too, if I were you,' said Daniel with a laconic smile.

'If you're in agreement, of course,' continued Sara, turning back to Maddie. 'We both stand to get something out of it, after all. I'll have an intriguing companion piece to my photograph of Maeve and you'll have – ' Sara Lennox spread expressive hands ' – well, I can't imagine a more glorious birthday surprise for your partner! Oh – by "partner" you do mean "lover", don't you? I'm never very sure about all this political-correct speak.'

Maddie nodded, still at a loss for words.

'Well, then. Let's do it.'

Maddie remembered Josh's first reaction on seeing the print. 'I'd love to get a load of you looking like that,' he'd said. She had to admit that Sara Lennox's idea was pretty inspired. Then she remembered how much she hated standing in front of a camera.

'I'm not madly photogenic,' she said with an apologetic shrug.

'Yes you are,' said Daniel Lennox. 'When you stop pretending to be somebody you're not. I saw you having your photograph taken earlier. That final shot is the one they should print. But of course they won't. They want shiny happy people in their magazines.'

'D'you want to know a secret, darling,' said Sara Lennox, without a trace of insincerity in the "darling". 'I could make that – ' she looked around vaguely ' – that man over there – do you see the one I mean? With the grotesque tie and the face like a boiled egg? I could make *him* photogenic.'

Her enthusiasm was ridiculously infectious. 'OK,' said Maddie with a slow, complicit smile. 'You're right. It's an interesting idea. Hell – it's an inspired idea!'

'I'll do a limited number of prints, of course, and let you have three. They'll be archival quality, and it goes without saying that they'll be on the best photographic paper.'

'That would be amazing,' said Maddie. Then a thought struck her. Any Sara Lennox photograph would cost her a lot of money. But to set up a shoot with one of the most respected photographers in the country might set her back a small fortune. 'There – um – there might be a bit of a problem, Sara. You're out of my league.'

'What do you mean?'

'I mean financially. I'm not sure I could afford you.'

'What nonsense. I wouldn't dream of charging you – it was my idea to drag you into this piece of whimsy. I'll hang on to the negatives, though. That's my prerogative.'

'Oh – of course!' Maddie felt that little thrill she always got when she came across something perfect – like when she hit on the *mot juste* for her copy, or when she happened upon a sublime pair of shoes. This was turning out to be a very special birthday present indeed!

Sara turned to her brother. 'What do you think, Daniel?' she asked.

Maddie could feel Daniel Lennox's eyes on her again. She took care to keep her gaze directed towards Sara.

'It's an amusing idea,' he said. 'Lends a whole new dimension to the concept of the birthday suit, doesn't it? But I'm sure your copywriter's mind has already made that connection.'

Maddie didn't like his tone. She flashed him a look. 'How do you know I'm a copywriter?' she demanded.

'I saw it in that photographer's notebook. He's a persistent bastard, isn't he? Doesn't take no for an answer. He even thought he could persuade me to let him have a pic for his magazine by showing me what illustrious company I'd be in. Advertising executives, film stars, music industry impresarios – they were all down there in his little black book.

Alongside your name, of course. Maddie Godard, isn't it?'

She looked away from him. 'Actually, the surname's *Godard.*' She pronounced it in the French fashion, rolling the 'r' and leaving the second 'd' silent.

'Happy to meet you, Maddie, I'm Daniel Lennox.' He didn't sound particularly happy and she tensed at his grip as he shook her hand. She'd always thought that artists were supposed to have gentle hands. 'Where did you get the French name?'

Prying git! What business was it of his? 'My father was French,' she said politely.

'That accounts for the difference in colouring between you and your cousin, then,' observed Sara. 'What part of France was your father from?'

'Montpellier.'

'Montpellier? Just down the road from you, Daniel,' remarked Sara. 'Were you born there?'

'No. I've lived in Ireland all my life.'

'Your crowd were responsible for that contentious billboard campaign, weren't they?' said Daniel Lennox.

Maddie resisted the impulse to twist her hair as she went into familiar defensive mode. She was fed up with being quizzed about the Salamander Clothing Company campaign her agency had handled. The violence of the imagery used in some of the above-the-line ads had provoked a lot of controversy. Instead she turned cold eyes

41

on him and adopted the pedantic tone favoured by one of her former English lecturers. 'You are a very fortunate individual, Mr Lennox,' she said. 'You are in the enviable position of earning – as you yourself put it – an *indecently* hefty income from your chosen career in the rarefied atmosphere of the "Art World".' She hoped the inverted commas would register. 'My livelihood is dependent upon a degree of artifice, as opposed to art. I'm afraid I can't afford to be the kind of purist who makes lofty pronouncements about media manipulation.'

'Forgive me,' said Daniel Lennox equably. 'I was unaware that I was making a lofty pronouncement. I thought I was just asking you a simple question.'

Sara Lennox intervened. 'Here. Take my card,' she said, fishing around in her bag. 'Hell's bells – I'm out of them. You'd better take down my number. Have you got a pen on you, Daniel?'

'Please don't go to the trouble,' said Maddie, producing the expensive electronic organizer Josh had given her for her last birthday. 'I'll enter it in this.' She pressed the relevant button, but nothing happened. 'Ah,' she said, 'It looks like the battery's gone again.'

'Sometimes I'm glad I'm a Luddite,' said Daniel Lennox, extracting a fountain pen from his breast pocket. 'Let me write it on your catalogue.'

'Thank you.' Maddie put the organizer back in her bag, feeling foolish. It wasn't the first time the hi-tech gadget had let her down.

42

'When would it suit for me to shoot you?' Sara asked. She was scrutinizing her prospective model in much the same way as her brother had just done, but her look of assessment had none of the sexual innuendo that Maddie had seen in Daniel's eyes.

'When would suit you, Sara? After all, you're the one who's calling the shots.' Maddie returned politely.

'Let me see.' The photographer delved into her bag again. 'More hell's bells,' she said. 'I left my book behind. I'll have to think about this.' A little frown of concentration furrowed her brow momentarily. 'As far as I can remember I don't have much on next week.'

'And neither will you, if things go according to plan,' said Daniel, looking at Maddie with amusement. 'I'm rather sorry I've to go back to France on Tuesday. I'd like to have stuck around for that session.'

Jesus! Maddie wished she could tell the lecherous Mr Lennox to fuck off, but she liked Sara too much to be rude to her brother.

'Papa!' A pretty, dark-haired girl of about seven or eight came charging up out of nowhere. She flung herself into Daniel's arms.

'Molly!' He scooped the little girl up and gave her an enormous bear-hug. They clung together, nuzzling each other and making growly noises.

Maddie found herself smiling, then looked away as Maeve tapped her on the shoulder. 'What plots have you lot been hatching?' she asked. 'I always know when you've been struck by an inspirational idea, Sara, because you wave your hands about a lot.'

Sara filled her in on her latest artistic brainwave, and Maeve's smile broadened.

'What a clever idea! It was this time last year that we did that session, wasn't it, Sara? At around nine o'clock at night. Sam cooked something delicious and I stayed over.'

'Let's do it again! You come out with Maddie, and we'll make an evening of it.'

'I'd like that,' said Maeve. 'Sam's Sara's assistant, Maddie. He's also a wicked chef. I reckon he could give Jacqueline a run for her money. Talking of whom' – Maeve glanced at her watch – 'she should have finished her preparation by now. I said I'd meet her in Meaghers at eight. Want to come?'

Maddie did quite, but she reckoned Josh wasn't ready to leave. He was still all hugger-mugger with his art director pal.

'Maeve? Hey, Maeve!' The man with the microphone was struggling towards them through the crowd. 'I'm really sorry for interrupting, but I've to be elsewhere ten minutes ago and it would be great if I could get a couple of quick words from you before I go. Can we find somewhere a bit quieter where we could talk?'

'For you, Tony, anything.' Maeve turned back to Sara and Maddie. 'This is the man who nominated

44

me for my very first award. So I give good interview in return. Quid pro quo and all that. And just see where quid pro quo got Darina Maguire! Deep doodoo, that's where! Hah! Catch you later, Maddie.'

The cousins exchanged identical smiles as Maeve disappeared back into the crowd.

'Are there more in the family like you?' asked Sara.

'No,' replied Maddie. 'We're both only children.'

'I noticed you used the past tense when you spoke of your father earlier.'

'Yes. He's dead. Both my parents are.'

'I'm sorry. Was it long ago?'

'Five years. A car crash. I'm over it now.'

'They died together?'

'Yes, they did.'

There was something about the direct way Sara Lennox was looking at her that made Maddie want to elaborate. Usually people muttered some clichéd words of sympathy when she talked about the accident that had killed her parents, and then cleared their throats and looked away before changing the subject. Nobody ever considered the possibility that she'd actually *like* to talk about it. Death was a taboo subject as far as most people were concerned.

She took a sip from her wineglass. 'They both died instantly, which helped. Josh – my partner – was sterling at the time. I was out of my mind with grief. Josh took care of everything. He got me put on medication, got me counselling – he even took me away for a week after the funeral to a spa in the West of Ireland so that I didn't have to see anyone, talk to anyone. I don't think I would ever have got my act together if it hadn't been for him.' Maddie looked across the gallery to where Josh was engaged in animated discussion. He threw back his head to laugh at some remark, and she noticed the sideways looks he attracted from women in the crowd. Not only was Josh her rock, her shield, her support – he was also a very sexy, charismatic, *compelling* individual. She sent him a warm look before returning her attention to Sara Lennox, feeling a tiny, smug thrill that she, Maddie Godard, had been lucky enough to land such a covetable boyfriend. 'I still miss my parents, of course. I still talk to them.'

'Of course you do. Talking to the dead often makes a lot more sense than talking to the living.'

'Apart from Maeve.' Maddie looked over at her cousin, who had retreated into a corner of the room with the radio interviewer. 'She's a living doll. She's looked out for me ever since I can remember. We're more best friends than cousins, really. Can you believe she babysat me? She listened to my maudlin tales of teenage crises – God love her! – and nursed me through my first real hangover. She even read my initial cringe-making attempts at writing without sniggering. She's a total star.' Maddie suddenly found herself wondering why she was opening up so un-reservedly to this person who, five minutes ago, had been a complete stranger. She was normally much more restrained around people she didn't know.

'If I hug you any more, baby, I'll get addicted.'

'What's addicted?' The question was asked in a reedy, child's voice.

'It means I'll never want to stop. And then I'll spend the rest of my life just hugging and hugging you, and you'll start to hate me because I won't allow anyone else near you.'

Daniel Lennox had re-emerged from around the corner of the gallery with the child still in his arms. He finally managed to extricate himself from the cat's cradle of her limbs and set her gently down. No sooner had her feet touched the ground than a torrent of French issued from her mouth. Daniel stood smiling at her for a moment or two then gently touched a finger to her mouth. 'Tch, tch, tch, Molly! If you want to be bilingual you must remember that you talk French to your mother, English to your father.'

'Sorry, Dad.' The little girl was skipping from foot to foot. Then she spotted Sara. 'Tante Sara! Hurrah! *Cadeaux!*' And she launched herself into Sara's outstretched arms.

'Hello, my little French poppet!' cooed Sara, kneeling down so that she was on a level with the child. 'How scrummy you look! The presents are at home, sweetheart, but come here with me and look at this beautiful picture of your mother floating in the pool in Saint-Géyroux.' She looked up at Maddie and said: 'Excuse me, won't you? I haven't seen Molly in ages. Give me a call next week and we'll fix a date for your session.'

Sara stood up and led the child round the corner to the swimming-pool photograph. Molly clapped her hands with delight. 'Maman looks so pretty!' she cried.

Maddie felt distinctly awkward at being left on her own with Sara's brother. She cast around for an exit line, but the only one that came to her was: 'Goodbye, then. It was very nice to meet you.' She articulated it in the most cordial tone she could muster.

She was on the verge of turning away when Daniel Lennox gave her a shrewd look and said: 'Nice. It was *nice* to meet you too. Sara's photographs are extremely *nice* aren't they? You're a wordsmith by profession – why do you appear to have such a restricted vocabulary?'

'I don't consider myself to have a restricted vocabulary, Mr Lennox,' she said, with a frigid smile. 'On the contrary – I have a degree in English and Italian, and I speak fluent French.'

To her annoyance, Daniel Lennox laughed. 'A degree in English and Italian! Fluent in French!' He looked hard at her and shook his head. 'Serious credentials. If you ever decide to abandon advertising you'd have other skills to fall back on. You could become a linguist, Maddie.' Something told her that he derived enjoyment from the word 'linguist'. She kept her expression perfectly immobile. She was beginning to hate him. 'But I suspect that you're a media hussy at heart.'

Daniel Lennox looked her up and down for the second time, and she resisted a sudden impulse to send a stinging slap across his face. She could feel his eyes travelling down her black chintz trousers to her smart leather boots and up again to the expensively cut jacket till they met her own eyes. She gave him her best basilisk look, but he just smiled back at her. 'By the way – what's with the "Maddie"?'

'I was christened Madeleine. I didn't think it suited me, so I changed it to Maddie.' Actually, Josh had suggested the change. He had thought Maddie had a sharper ring to it than Madeleine.

'And what made you think you weren't a Madeleine?' He gave another unpleasant laugh. 'Madeleine is redolent of sweetness and *temps perdu*. But of course, you'll have read your Proust?'

'Of course,' she echoed, dismissing him.

'Maman! Viens ici! Regarde cette photo! Comme tu es jolie, Maman!'

A beautiful woman trailing silk and velvet drifted past. 'Hello, chéri. Tout va bien?' she murmured, sending Daniel an ambiguous smile. 'Ah, mais oui – c'est moi, ça!' she said, as she joined Sara and the little girl.

The child looked at her father and gave him a huge, gap-toothed grin. 'I have the best parents in the world,' she said.

Daniel Lennox held out his hand to her. 'Come here, baby,' he said.

Molly took his hand and insinuated her shoulders under his arm, still skipping from foot to foot. 'Hi,' she said to Maddie.

'Hi.' Maddie smiled back at her. 'What's your name?'

'Molly. What's yours?'

'Maddie.' She could feel Daniel Lennox smiling at her, and she hated him more than ever.

'Your expersion looked like Tinkerbell's just then,' declared Molly.

'Expersion?'

'Yeah. You know – your face. Your *expersion* –' Oh! Expression! Maddie tried not to laugh – 'was all cross like hers.'

'In *Peter Pan*?'

'Yeah. You know the bit where Peter locks her in the drawer and she comes out fuming? You looked like her then.'

'Oh! She's the crossest thing ever!' Maddie laughed outright now, remembering the fairy's priceless scowl.

'But you're really pretty when you smile. Who's your favourite girl singer?'

Maddie had never thought about it, but now she gave it serious consideration. She furrowed her brow. 'Christina Aguilera has the best voice,' she said, after a moment. 'But Britney's pretty cool, too.'

'Christina's my favourite, too. My dad's going to take me to see her when she comes to Paris. I can't *wait!*'

Daniel Lennox looked down at her indulgently. 'Molly – that's months away.'

'And he's promised to take me to Euro-Disney again as well. You should see Rocky Mountain Ride. I'm not old enough to go on it yet, but I can't wait for that either. They could easily let me on now. I wouldn't be scared at all, would I, Dad?' Molly had scarcely drawn breath throughout her monologue.

'Not as scared as I would be, baby.'

Suddenly Maddie felt a proprietorial hand on her arm. 'I think it's time we left, Mads, don't you?'

'Oh – hi, Josh.' She was relieved that a getaway opportunity had arisen at last, even though Molly was easily the most amusing person she'd been introduced to all evening. She put her wineglass down and smiled at Daniel Lennox's daughter. 'Goodbye, Molly. It was nice meeting you.'

'Yeah. Hey – know something? I'm not really sure about either of their dress sense – you know, Christina and Britney.' The little girl smiled back at her and started her tap-dance again. 'But Dad loves Britney's latest video. Don't you, Dad?'

'The one where she dresses up as a schoolgirl? Love it.'

Molly gave her father a pitying look. 'Da-ad! That is *so* last millennium. I mean the video for "Don't Let Me Be The Last To Know". The one where she wears practically no clothes at all.'

Maddie steeled herself. 'Goodbye, Mr Lennox,' she said politely.

'Goodbye, Madeleine. It was nice meeting you.' He bowed his head slightly and then turned away, steering Molly back in the direction of her aunt and her mother. Her mind's eye stuck a dagger in his back. What a vile man!

* * *

'Why didn't you introduce me?' asked Josh later in the car.

'I don't think you missed anything by not being introduced to him, Josh. Daniel Lennox is an extremely rude, unpleasant individual.'

'You looked as if you were getting on all right with him.' Josh reached across and took Maddie's catalogue from her. 'I saw him jotting something down on this – his phone number, I presume.'

'No, it's—'

'You didn't seem too put out when he started touching you up, darling.'

Maddie looked blank. 'Touching me up? What are you talking about?'

'Seemed to me he couldn't keep his hands off you. Feeling your arm, pawing your face.'

52

Maddie knew that there was no point in explaining to Josh that Daniel Lennox had been examining her bone structure. He'd laugh out loud. So she said nothing.

'When are you going to ring him, then?' he persisted.

'Look – I wasn't taking down his telephone number, Josh. It's Sara Lennox's number.'

'Oh? Tell me why you want Sara Lennox's phone number.'

'Because . . .' Why? *Why?* She didn't want to ruin his birthday surprise. She couldn't let him know that she'd been arranging a photo session for herself. She thought fast. 'Because I wanted to get that print of Maeve for your birthday, OK? It was already promised to somebody, but Sara's going to do me another one as a favour. I wanted to surprise you with it.'

There was a brief silence. Then Josh said: 'I'm sorry, Mads. I didn't mean to back you into a corner. What a lovely idea.' He put a hand on her right thigh and stroked it. 'Shit – I would have to go and blow the surprise element, wouldn't I?' He looked at her with mournful eyes. 'It's just that I couldn't hack it when I saw the way that geezer was looking at you – I could hardly even concentrate on the La Casita story. You know how I feel when I see you talking to other men—'

'You've got to get over that, Josh. I have to talk to men every day in the course of my work, for Christ's sake!'

'I know, I know – but there was something about that artist bloke. He has one hell of a reputation.'

There was a pause. 'A reputation?'

'Yeah. More mistresses than Picasso, Mac said.'

Maddie looked out of the window. They had stopped at traffic lights and it was raining. She remembered how Daniel Lennox had looked at her when Sara had first commented on her resemblance to Maeve, and how his eyes had travelled down her body. She gave an involuntary shudder.

Josh leaned over and kissed her neck. 'Cold, honey? I'm truly sorry,' he said again. 'About the photograph. I promise I've forgotten what my birthday present is already. I'll pretend I never set eyes on that sexy pic of your cousin.'

And Maddie found herself smiling as he put the car into gear. Maybe it was a good thing that she'd been forced into this double bluff. He really *would* get a surprise on his birthday now, when he opened his present and found it was her portrait under the wrapping, not Maeve's . . .

Josh hung a left and was halfway down a side street when she realized that they'd bypassed her apartment block. Her machinations had distracted her. 'Oh – stop, Josh – go back, please. Or let me out and I'll walk. I'm going to stay at my own place tonight.'

Josh pulled over and looked at her. 'I thought we agreed that you were staying over with me?'

'Look – I'd love to sleep in your bed tonight, Josh, but I'm feeling wretched.' She adopted an apologetic tone. 'I've an early start in the morning – we both have. And we've the pitch for the new account coming up in the next few weeks. We're really going to be up against it – you know how grim it'll get. I really think it's more sensible if I don't come to you tonight.'

'OK.'

He sounded careless, but Maddie knew he was pissed off. She kissed him lightly on the mouth. 'Good night, my love,' she said. 'I'll see you in the morning.' She had her hand on the handle of the passenger door.

'Wait, Maddie,' he said. 'I could do with a proper kiss good night.' He pushed a strand of hair back from her face and proceeded to kiss her thoroughly and expertly. She responded automatically at first, and then, despite her better judgement, with mounting libido. She felt him undoing the buttons on her jacket, and then his hand was inside, pulling at the catch on her bra.

'Not in the car, Josh.'

'Come home with me, then.'

'No.'

His hand slid like an eel under the waistband of her black trousers, and she knew he heard her intake of breath. 'I'll drive you home afterwards. You'll be back in your own bed before midnight, Mads. I promise.'

Maddie lay back in the passenger seat and looked at him. Then she smiled. 'Oh, all right, Josh,' she said.

Chapter Three

The following evening she picked up the phone and dialled Sara Lennox's number. The distinctive voice of Daniel Lennox answered. Maddie resisted the impulse to put the phone back down again. 'May I speak to Sara, please?' she said, trying to make it sound by her tone that she wasn't aware who she was talking to.

'Hello, Madeleine. Hang on a sec.'

He was gone before she could reply, and she felt stupid. It had been silly and childish to pretend not to know who had answered the phone, but she really hadn't wanted to make small talk with him.

A few seconds went by and then she heard Sara's voice in her ear. 'Hello, Madeleine.'

Maddie knew she might as well resign herself to the fact that neither Lennox would ever use her proper name. 'Sara – hello. Is it convenient for you to talk right now?'

'Sure it is.'

'I'm phoning about that photo-shoot?'

'Right. Just let me get my book.' There was the sound of the receiver being set down. Maddie could hear Sara Lennox humming to herself, obviously leafing through the pages of her appointment book. Then her voice was on the line again. 'Are you under pressure to get it done soon?'

'Well, Josh's birthday is on Monday week. Is that cutting it too fine?'

'No. No problem. How does Thursday evening suit you?'

'Thursday's good.'

'I can let you have the prints in time for you to get one decently framed. I'll give you the number of the guy in town who does all my framing for me.'

'That's very decent of you, Sara. Whereabouts are you?'

'It's a bit of a trek, I'm afraid. I'm out beyond Brittas Bay. Do you have a fax?'

'Yes.'

'I'll fax you a map. If you can get here for eight o'clock, we'll try to get going before nine. And if the gods smile on us, the light and weather conditions will be similar to the original. Will you get in touch with Maeve, by the way?'

'Maeve?'

'Yes. Remember? I promised you both supper. It's blissful to dig into good food and wine after an evening shoot when everybody's tired and cold. And if you don't feel like the long haul back into Dublin afterwards – and most people don't – you're very welcome to stay the night. There's plenty of room.'

'Sara, you're being way too generous—'

'Oh, nonsense. I love good food and good company, Madeleine, and I'll need it after Daniel and Molly are gone.'

Maddie thanked God that Daniel Lennox wouldn't be there. The fewer spectators on this shoot the better. 'Sara? I'm not a prude, but I don't particularly like the idea of being leered at. Is the beach secluded?'

'Yes. Very. And don't worry – Sam will wrap you up in a robe at first sign of a fellow human.' Sara Lennox laughed. 'Actually, you might rather like that. He's a very good-looking boy.'

'Um – who's Sam?' Maddie vaguely remembered that Maeve had referred to a Sam.

'Oh – perhaps I should have mentioned that I have a male assistant. Is that going to be a problem for you? Posing nude can feel quite vulnerable, you know. Some women don't like the idea of there being a man around.'

Maddie thought about it for a second, and made her voice sound careless. 'No, I don't have a problem with that, Sara.'

She didn't have a problem with it, but she suspected Josh might if he knew. She suddenly realized how lucky she was that Sara Lennox was a woman. Josh would never have tolerated her posing nude for a male photographer.

'Next thing,' continued Sara in a businesslike fashion. 'Be sure to wear something comfortable and loose fitting on the drive out. And leave off your underwear. Tight clothing leaves crease marks on the skin.'

Maddie knew this from doing photo-shoots on commercials. She ran her mind's eye over her wardrobe. So many of her clothes were tailored and tight-fitting – even the stuff she wore at weekends wasn't really what you'd describe as unstructured. Josh always encouraged her to wear clothes that showed off her shape to advantage. He talked in a disparaging way about those of his female colleagues who had the misfortune to be saddled with rounded figures or bigger than average breasts, saying that they were obviously too lazy to bother about how they looked. To her acute embarrassment, he'd even hinted to a couple of the girls in the agency that they should follow Maddie's example and spend their lunch breaks in the gym instead of sending out to the sandwich bar.

'Would a T-shirt and jogging pants do, Sara?' she asked. She'd done a lot of running in the days before she could afford to join her very exclusive gym.

'Perfect. And make sure to wear slip-on shoes. Keep everything as simple as possible.'

'OK.' She had a sudden thought. 'By the way, Sara – does your assistant do the make-up or will I do my own?'

'You won't need make-up.'

'Oh?' Maddie was taken aback, and rather horrified. The models on the shoots she'd been around had always been meticulously made up. Without make-up they mostly looked incredibly ordinary. 'None at all?' she asked, aware that a slightly desperate note had crept into her voice. Maybe she could get away with a film of tinted moisturizer, a touch of blusher, a clear mascara? Her eyes felt so *small* without mascara!

'Absolutely none.' Sara sounded so scarily categorical that Maddie heard herself give a gulp down the phone. The mascara idea bit the dust. 'Don't fret, Madeleine! We won't be going in close, so there's really no need for slap. Anyway, I hate make-up. I'm convinced it does something to the mindset of the person I'm photographing – it's like a mask for them to hide behind. The less artifice the better, as far as I'm concerned. OK?'

'OK.' Maddie trashed the idea of the blusher. She'd just have to make do with tinted moisturizer. It gave her skin such a subtle sheen that she'd be sure to get away with it.

'So. We're sorted?'

Maddie took a deep breath. There was no going back now. But she was smiling as she replied: 'Looks like it.'

'OK. I'll fax that map off to you later. Oh – hang on – I won't have to, will I? Maeve knows the way. I'll see you at eight o'clock sharp on Thursday evening, then. Do your best not to be late, Madeleine, or the moon will be too high in the sky and the tide'll be on the turn. I'm going to make

60

sure this shot's as near a mirror image of the original as possible.'

'I won't be late. Thanks again, Sara – I'm looking forward to it.'

'Likewise. Bye, Madeleine.'

'Bye.' Maddie put down the receiver feeling excited. She hugged herself inwardly. Josh would be so chuffed! His birthday present was going to be utterly unique.

No sooner had she put the phone down when it rang. She loved the sound her phone made – it had a sexy little gurgle of a ring, not like the shrill, urgent tones of the phones in the agency. Josh was on the other end.

'Sweetheart. Hi.'

'Hi, Josh! Where did you get to after work? I thought it might be fun to take in a movie this evening.'

'Sorry about that. I had to go for a drink with Dim Sum Jim.'

'Oh? Is there a problem?' Dim Sum Jim was the Accounts Director at the Complete Works. He didn't usually socialize outside work unless something awkward needed to be thrashed out.

'Yeah. The Grant & Wainwright pitch has been brought forward.'

Maddie froze. 'Oh no. When's it happening?'

'Next Monday morning. Eleven o'clock.'

'Shit. I don't believe you.'

'That's what I said when I heard. We're going to have to work our asses off this week to get it right in time. The weekend, too. Can you have a look at that script tonight and get it in at bang on thirty seconds?'

Maddie almost sighed, then stopped herself. 'Sure, Josh,' she said.

'It looks like we're going to have to forget about the gig at the Point on Saturday night. The pressure's on, Maddie.'

'OK.' She tried not to sound too disappointed. 'I'd better cancel the table I'd booked for dinner afterwards. Hell – that's the second time I've had to do that in the last fortnight. They're going to start getting pissed off with me at this rate.'

'Jesus, Maddie – get your priorities right, will you? You know how important it is that we land this account after the La Casita fiasco. Your fucking job could be on the line, you know.' He sounded seriously pissed off.

'Yes, I know, Josh. Calm down. It's just that I can't seem to remember the last time we had fun.'

'Last night wasn't bad.'

'I don't just mean sex, Josh. I just seem to be so tired all the time these days – I really could do with a break. So could you.'

'I know, I know. Look, Mads – let's just get through the next week, OK? We can chill all you like then. Take a holiday, maybe. And then there's my party to look forward to.'

Maddie wished he hadn't reminded her. She'd promised to organize a party for Josh on the Sunday night before his birthday, and now that she knew she was going to be working flat out for the next week the idea of getting it together wasn't remotely appealing. Maybe she should ask Jacqueline, Maeve's partner, to come up with some ideas, or even help her with the food. Jacqueline didn't normally work on Sundays, but she might make an exception for Maddie.

Josh's voice brought her back to the more urgent business at hand. 'You'd better get cracking on that script, baby, and then you go straight to bed. You're going to have to be on the ball tomorrow. I'll be needing caffeine hits all night – we'll be in the edit suite till all hours.'

'You poor thing.' She tried to inject her voice with oodles of sympathy, even though she knew she was just as deserving of it as he was. 'Look after yourself, darling – and go easy on the caffeine. You know what too much does to you. See you in the morning.'

'Good night, darling. Love you.'

'Night. Love you too.' Maddie put the phone down feeling miserable. All at once, everything had gone wrong. And Josh mentioning his birthday had only made things worse. At this rate she wouldn't even have a present for him. How the hell was she going to fit in the photo session she'd set up with Sara Lennox? She'd have to cancel it. Next week's schedule would be a killer – they'd be working evenings.

She wandered into the kitchen and poured herself a glass of white wine from a bottle in the fridge. She shouldn't be downing alcohol. It would take a lot of hard work to get the running time on her script down to precisely thirty seconds and she'd need a clear head if she was going to get it right, but the prospect of the week ahead was so grim that she didn't care. She might as well seize any opportunity she could to be good to herself. There wouldn't be that many. In fact, she thought glumly, she'd need to stock up on antacid tablets otherwise she'd end up with another ulcer.

Maddie usually worked well under pressure – she loved the rush she got from the adrenalin – but her workload hadn't let up in months now. Josh's was even more punishing. She wished that her partner found it easier to relax. He was so wound up these days that something was sure to give sooner or later. She added an extra, rebellious splosh of wine to her glass before sticking the bottle back in the fridge and shutting the door with a satisfying slam.

In the sitting room she slid Massive Attack into the CD player to conjure a mellow vibe, then lay back on the couch with the printout of the radio script. She couldn't concentrate on it. She was too preoccupied with trying to work out what to do about Josh's birthday. Maybe she should just book a holiday as a present? God knows, they both needed one. She could pick up some brochures on her way into work in the morning and make subtle hints to the MD about the week off they were due.

But she couldn't get the idea of the Sara Lennox portrait out of her mind. It was such a good idea: original, witty, *special*. Josh *deserved* something special . . .

Then she had a brainwave. Thursday – the night she'd arranged to do the shoot with Sara – was Josh's squash night. He was religious about it – nothing kept him away from his weekly squash game with his mate Baz. He would get himself into the agency at six o'clock in the morning rather than work late on a Thursday evening.

She could do it! She *could* fit in the photo-shoot! And the meal afterwards? She shouldn't – daren't – entertain the idea of a leisurely meal in a week when she should be working her ass off fourteen hours a day. She would just have to turn down Sara's invitation to stay to supper. But how? It would be highly churlish to turn round to the photographer immediately after the shoot and say: 'Right. Thanks a bunch. I'm off now.' After all, Sara Lennox had shown her uncommon generosity. She cast her mind back to the phone conversation they'd had earlier. What had Sara said? *I love good food and good company.*

Good food and good company . . . The idea of relaxing after a long, stressful day with a bottle of wine and a meal that she hadn't had to prepare herself held infinite appeal for Maddie. It seemed ages since she'd been cosseted like that. And not to have to drive home afterwards . . . The notion was blissful.

Oh, hell. She'd do it. She'd stay over at Sara's place and drive into town very early the next morning before the traffic had a chance to build up. She'd be knackered, but it would be worth it. She was going to be knackered all week, anyway.

Maddie knocked back her wine and hoisted herself off the couch, resisting the temptation to go into the kitchen and pour herself another glass. Instead she headed towards her laptop on the dining table. She needed to trim that commercial by at least ten seconds before she could hit her bed.

* * *

They spent the next three days working flat out. Maddie ran between one recording studio where she worked with jingle writers and singers and another recording studio where she worked with voice-over artists. She ran from edit suites where she worked on rough cuts, to the agency where she worked on scripts. When she went home she worked on formulating the Creative Rationale which would outline the campaign. She hated this job more than any of them because it fluctuated wildly from day to day as the campaign evolved and changed shape. At times she wanted to rip the whole thing up when Josh – who as Creative Director of the agency had ultimate artistic control – would slap his hand on his desk and say: 'It's wrong, it's wrong, it's all bloody wrong. We'll just have to start again.'

By the time Thursday evening came she was exhausted, as she'd known she would be. Josh stuck his head round the door of her office at six o'clock as she was packing up. 'Coming for a drink?' he asked.

Maddie looked up from the sheaf of documents she was sliding into her case. 'What about your squash game?' she asked uncertainly.

'Fucking Baz forgot to book the court. I said I'd meet him in Daly's.' Daly's was the pub down the road from the Complete Works.

'Oh. So you're not going to stay on and get some work done instead?' Maddie tried to make the question sound casual.

'No. I'm calling it a day. I'm knackered.' He wandered into the room and sat on the edge of her desk. 'I was all psyched up for my game, and then when Baz called to say he'd blown the booking I just thought: fuck it, I need a break.' He rubbed his eye with a forefinger and yawned. 'Come on. Let's get out of here.' He stood up, helped her into her jacket and slung an arm around her shoulder. It felt as if yet another weight was being added to the ones already there.

'Hell, Mads – I'd love to get trashed,' he said as they descended the stairs.

'Yeah. So would I,' she said automatically. Maddie was actually thinking fast about how to get out of going for a drink. She just couldn't spare the time if she was to get home and changed and out to Sara's place by eight o'clock. She fixed a smile on her face and pitched her voice so that it didn't sound too hopeful. 'Maybe we should hang on till Monday after the pitch?'

'Maybe.'

There was no receptionist to say good night to. She'd already left. The couple passed through the front door and strolled along the canal path, Josh hugging Maddie tighter to him as they went. 'We're going to win this account, Maddie. It's such a simple, uncluttered idea.'

'You're right. There could be awards down the line, for you, Josh.' She looked up at him and he kissed her on the nose.

'And for you, too, clever clogs. How do you feel about promotion?'

Maddie looked at him curiously. 'What do you mean?'

'I've a feeling that it's time for me to set up on my own. You'd come with me, wouldn't you?'

'Well – I – don't you think you're being a bit premature?'

'I've done some sums, Maddie. I reckon this time next year could see us up and running.' He took her by the shoulders and backed her up against the bole of a tree, leaning close into her. 'Maybe we should think about pooling our resources. We could start by moving in together.'

'You mean – *domestically*?'

'Yeah. We've been together for over five years now. I know you've always said you value your solitude, but don't you think it's about time we committed?'

Maddie looked down at her hands. Josh had taken one of them in his and was stroking the palm. 'I don't think it's the right time to talk about this,' she said finally. 'We're so caught up in work at the moment that neither of us is going to be able to think straight about emotional stuff. Let's leave it for a while until this whole thing is finished and we're able to take time out to breathe, OK?' She lifted her chin and looked at him again. To her relief he didn't look too put out.

'OK, sweetheart.' He smiled at her. 'You're right, of course – we've enough on our plates right now. We'll take a raincheck for a week or so, and then we'll talk again.' He brushed her cheek with his lips and stood back from her. 'Come on. Let's get that drink.'

Maddie extracted her car keys from her bag. 'I'm going to take a raincheck on that too,' she said carefully. 'I'm still not happy with the Rationale, Josh. I'm going to head home and work on it for a couple more hours, and then I'm going to have a glass of wine, watch something mindless on the telly and hit the sack.'

'Won't you even come for a quick one?'

'No. You know there's no such thing as a quick one in Daly's.' Maddie was starting to itch to get home. She *couldn't* be late for the shoot, and she'd arranged to pick Maeve up from her house at a quarter to seven.

'Maybe I should stop by later?'

Oh no. Oh God. She forced herself to sound relaxed. 'I'd love that, but I don't think it's a good idea tonight. I really am jaded. Let's leave it till Monday. We won't have the prospect of the pitch hanging over us, and we'll enjoy each other more then.'

'How did you get to be so clever?'

'I ate my greens when I was a kid.'

'So you were one of the good girls.'

'Mm hm.' I still am, she thought.

They'd reached her car now, and Maddie turned to kiss him before zapping the locks and getting in.

'Be prepared for another day in hell,' Josh warned her.

'Yeah.' She gave him a tired smile. 'See you in the morning, darling.' The door closed with a gentle thud, and she strapped herself in. In the rear-view mirror she saw Josh raise a hand in salute as she put the car into gear and took off down the road.

So far, so good, she thought. She'd be home in ten minutes. As she braked at a traffic light a wave of exhaustion hit her. What was she doing, careering off to Wicklow to frolic about stark naked on a beach when she should be getting an early night? The idea that had seemed so inspired four days ago was beginning to take on a nightmarish tinge. She just hoped she wouldn't look too raddled when she stepped in front of Sara

Lennox's camera in three hours' time. Then she slammed the steering wheel with the heel of her hand. She'd just remembered that she'd run out of tinted moisturizer.

* * *

At home she changed out of the suit she'd worn to work, zipped it into a carrier and packed a small overnight bag with basics and a good bottle of wine for Sara. She removed her make-up, discarded her underwear, and shrugged into baggy running pants and a loose T-shirt. Then she grabbed her briefcase and switched on the answering machine, dashing back into her bedroom when she remembered she'd left her contraceptive pill carton on the bedside table.

Maeve was ready when she drew up in front of her house ten minutes later. She emerged with a wonderfully elegant overnight bag in soft toffee-coloured leather – 'A birthday present from Jacqueline,' she said when she saw Maddie's openly covetous expression – and a massive bunch of freesias.

Within minutes the heady scent of the flowers had perfumed the interior of the car, and Maddie started to feel the first stirrings of excitement as they joined the traffic travelling fast along the motorway. She felt as she had used to as a little girl when she and her parents would set off early for their summer holiday in France. She had always had a delicious sense of playing truant, even though her class teacher had been informed in advance that she'd be taking a couple of days off school. She supposed that was what she was doing now: mitching from work. Except the class teacher hadn't been informed this time. The thought gave her a small, illicit thrill.

Prokofiev was playing on the stereo.

'Bit heavy, isn't it?' remarked Maeve as she rummaged around in the glove compartment for another cassette.

'I suppose. It's Josh's. Stick Dido on instead, will you?'

*   *   *

Maddie's Renault pulled up outside a long, low, timber-clad house a little before eight o'clock. There was no answer when Maeve rang the bell.

'Do you think she's forgotten?' asked Maddie.

'Unlikely. We'll go round to the deck.' Her cousin led the way round the side of the house along a sloping path flanked by rhododendron bushes. Maddie could hear the gentle lapping of waves somewhere below them. They emerged onto a blue-washed deck overlooking the sea. Through a wall of glass to her right Maddie could see an airy kitchen panelled in maple wood. There was no-one in the room, but mouth-watering smells drifted out through the open glass panels.

Maeve wandered over to the wooden railings.

'There they are,' she said, indicating the beach below. Maddie joined her and looked down. Strolling along the deserted shoreline were Sara Lennox and a young man with tousled blond hair, bare of foot and bare of torso. A Labrador was performing dance steps at his heels.

'Who's the dude?' asked Maddie.

'That's Sam. Gorgeous, isn't he?'

'Sara's assistant?'

'Also her nephew.'

'Daniel Lennox's son?'

'No. He's their sister's boy.'

'Wow. He's a ringer for Brad Pitt.' She remembered that Sara Lennox had mentioned her assistant was a good-looking boy. She certainly hadn't been lying.

'Hands off, little cousin.' Maeve turned to her with an indulgent smile. 'He's only a baby.'

'Oh?'

'In his second year at college. He's studying photography in Dun Laoghaire, but he's got the best teacher going in Sara Lennox. Kind of puts him at an unfair advantage. He's already had some stuff in a group show in the Rubicon.'

Maddie leaned her elbows on the wooden rail and gazed down at the couple. Sam skimmed a stone seaward, then glanced up, squinting a little against the evening sun, and looked directly at Maddie where she stood on the deck. She straightened up instantly, hoping it wouldn't look as though she'd been spying on them. He raised a hand to shade his eyes and Sara followed the direction of his gaze.

'Hi, Madeleine! Maeve!' she called. 'We're on our way up.'

Maddie waved back and then drifted over to another part of the deck to admire the view.

'It's stunning, isn't it?' said Maeve, settling down on a blue-stained sun-lounger.

'Beautiful. So peaceful.' The beach was deserted now, and there was an atmosphere of utter tranquillity. The sky overhead was streaked a pale tangerine, but otherwise there wasn't a hint of cloud, and the sea was millpond calm. Sara's wish that the gods might smile on them had been granted – the shots of Maeve had been taken on a still, cloudless evening, too.

'Sorry to keep you hanging about.' Sara was breathless when she finally reached the top of the long flight of wooden steps that led up from the beach. 'We went down to the shore for a recce.' She dumped the bunch of sea pinks she was carrying on a sun-lounger and smiled at Maddie. She looked more leonine than ever in the refracted sunlight, her hair a golden halo round her head.

Sam appeared on the deck behind her, followed by the Labrador. The dog gave two or three loud barks but fell silent when Sam gave it a gentle dig with a bare foot. 'Shut up, Karsch,' he said. He looked at Maddie and she made an effort not to colour. The first thing that struck her was that he was the most ridiculously handsome youth she had ever met. The second thing that struck her was that he was about to see her without any clothes on. She found the idea more than a little disturbing.

'Madeleine Godard?' he said, holding out a hand. 'I'm Sam Newman, Sara's assistant.' As she took his hand he glanced at Maeve across her shoulder and smiled. 'Hi, Maeve. Nice to see you again.' Then: 'Wow,' he said, reverting to Maddie. 'I see what you mean, Sara. The resemblance is uncanny. They could be twins if it wasn't for the colouring.'

'Funny things, genes.' Maddie withdrew her hand from his, noticing that he'd held on to it for a beat longer than was necessary. He smiled at her again.

'We'd better get started.' Sara headed towards the kitchen and took a bottle of water and a bottle of white wine out of the fridge. 'I'll stick to water for now,' she said. 'But you might like a glass of wine, Madeleine?' She started to peel the foil away from the neck of the wine bottle.

'Thanks. I could do with some Dutch courage.'

'You won't need it after a while,' said Maeve. 'Sara's just ace at making you relax in front of the camera.'

The cork came away from the bottle with a soft pop, and Sara started to pour wine into glasses. 'The first thing I need you to do, Madeleine – unsurprisingly enough – is to get out of your clothes. Sam'll get you a robe and show you where to change.' She glanced at her watch. 'Have you gone through the checklist, Sam?'

'Twice.'

'Good.' Sara moved to the edge of the deck and looked up at the sky. 'The light's perfect,' she said. 'You might as well bring the stuff down now, Sam, and we'll get started.' She turned to Maeve. 'You stay here and swig Chablis. I'm not having you hanging around making my subject feel self-conscious.'

'Oh – I don't mind Maeve being there!' Maddie had counted on her cousin's moral support.

But Maeve shook her head. 'Sara's right, Maddie. I should stay here.'

Maddie supposed she *was* right. She'd feel like an impostor if Maeve were to get a load of her throwing shapes on the beach, parodying the pose that she herself had struck so effortlessly twelve months earlier. After all, Maeve had been Sara's original muse. Maddie was just the copycat. And an amateur, to boot.

'Come on down as soon as you're ready, Madeleine.' Sara turned and disappeared back down the steps that led to the beach.

'Come with me, Madeleine.' Sam moved towards the sliding doors and Maddie followed him, trying not to trip over the dog he'd called Karsch, who was now sniffing interestedly at her knees. She realized that her eyes were wandering like nomads over his lightly muscled shoulder blades and down the golden skin of his back. They came to rest on the rip on the hip of his denims.

'*Help!*' she mouthed silently at Maeve, but Maeve just raised an amused eyebrow, reached for the glass of wine Sara had poured for her, and settled back on the sun-lounger.

*   *   *

By half-past nine that evening the shoot was finished. Maddie was tired and very cold, but she felt strangely exhilarated. It was as if she had contributed to some astonishing creative process without being aware of exactly how she'd done it.

They'd made a pretty good team, she reckoned. Sam had taken good care of her, making sure she was well wrapped up every time there was an enforced break. As well as a thick towelling robe, he'd supplied a heavy woollen rug and a hot water bottle.

Sara had talked Maddie through the shoot in quiet, unhurried tones, encouraging her all the time. 'That's great, Madeleine – the expression is perfect. Try turning your left shoulder a little more towards me. Terrific – just try not to move your whole body with it. Great.' Click. 'Don't be afraid to look straight down the lens. Challenge me.' Click. 'Beautiful.' Click. 'Lean a little more towards me, OK? But keep your head up. Chin a little higher. Great.' Click. 'Careful – the seaweed's coming adrift from around your hip. Do something about that, will you, Sam?'

A pause while Sam rearranged the seaweed, glancing from time to time at a print of the original photograph of Maeve, which he'd kept close to hand for reference. His brief was to make sure that the physical details of the shoot would be as similar as possible to the one they'd done a year ago. 'OK,' said Sara, when Sam had rearranged the damp strands to his satisfaction. 'One last shot and we're there. Mean the smile. Make it dreamier. Oh, wow – that's the one. Perfect, Madeleine.' Click. 'One more just for the hell of it? Excellent. We're done.'

Sara looked slightly dazed as she raised her head from where she'd been bending over the camera on its tripod. She rubbed her eyes and stretched herself like a cat, then shook her head and laughed. 'Wow. That was fun. How are you feeling, Madeleine?'

Maddie was peeling strands of seaweed away from her breasts and thighs. 'No pain!' she called back. 'Literally! I'm numb with cold!' Then she whipped a long strand of flat weed above her head lasso-fashion and, laughing, flung it as far as she could into the sea. Click!

'Quick – get into this before you catch pneumonia, Madeleine. Oh-oh – jogger alert!' As Sam retrieved the robe from a nearby rock, a lone jogger could be seen puffing tiredly along the sand dunes. The minute he spotted Maddie on the beach below him, he came to an abrupt halt. Then he shook his head, grinning in disbelief, and just about managed a salute before turning and stumbling back in the direction from which he'd just come. Click!

Sam held the robe out for her and she shrugged herself into it. For some reason she hadn't been able to stop laughing. 'Oh – the poor man – how miserable he looked!'

'Until he got a load of you. Seeing you with your kit off has probably made his day.' Sam wrapped her in the robe and deposited a kiss on her cheek. Click! The Hasselblad made its distinctive sound one more time as Sam's arms went round her.

* * *

Back at the house Maddie got into a warm shower and stayed there for a long time, feeling the chill gradually leave her body as the water ran over her. She dried herself with an enormous rough bath sheet until her skin smarted, then got back into the robe Sam had lent her and danced down the corridor to the bedroom she'd changed in earlier.

The room had windows on two sides – one overlooking the beach. Maddie pulled up the casement and leaned out. It was nearly dark now, and the moon's watery reflection shimmered on the sea. The sound of waves reached her, and she knew she would rest well tonight, seduced into

79

sleep by mermaids singing lullabies. She drew the curtains and turned back into the room.

The walls had been painted a pale shade of aquamarine, and the floorboards a rich peacock blue. A rag rug in sea-green was the only floor covering – the sea-green echoed in the cotton counterpane that was draped over the big brass bed. Four photographic prints framed in bleached wood hung on the wall above the bedhead. Maddie knelt on the counterpane and leaned her palms against the wall, examining the prints with interest. Were they the work of Sara Lennox? Somehow she didn't think so.

The subject matter of each photograph was a shell – each one different – taken against a background of blue slate. One was a razor shell, elegant and lethal-looking; another had the smooth, blush-pink curl of a rose petal. The third was as intricately wrought as the turret of a fairy-tale castle, the fourth as delicately whorled as a baby's ear.

As she traced the outline of the fourth shell with her finger, there was a knock on the door.

'Come in.' Maddie glanced over her shoulder as Sam stuck his head into the room.

'Hi,' he said. 'Supper will be on the table in ten minutes.'

'Excellent. I'm starving.' She smiled at him and sat back on her heels. 'Who took these photographs, Sam?' she asked. 'They're not Sara's, are they?'

'No,' he said, taking a step into the room and leaning his shoulder against the door jamb. 'They're mine.'

'Really?' Maddie turned back to look at the framed prints. 'They're beautiful. I'm impressed.'

'Thanks. I'm lucky to have such a genius aunt as a mentor.' He pushed a wing of blond hair back from his face and gave her a disarmingly boyish smile. 'You were great out there this evening, Madeleine. Sara's very happy. If I hadn't gone to the trouble of slaving over a hot stove all day I reckon she wouldn't even have bothered with supper. She'd have gone straight from the beach into the dark-room to develop those rolls. As it is, she'll probably be up at the crack of dawn to get started on it.'

'I'll have to be up at the crack of dawn as well,' said Maddie, making a face. 'I'll need to be on the road back into town before the traffic starts building up.'

'Where do you work?'

'The agency's on Herbert Street.'

'The agency?'

'Yes. I work for an advertising agency. I'm a copywriter.'

Sam shifted his stance so that his back was now leaning against the door jamb. 'Do you enjoy it?' he asked.

'Yeah. I do. But it's tough at the moment. We're working our asses off to have a presentation ready by Monday morning: we're pitching for a new account. We'll probably be working till midnight on Sunday.'

'Is it worth it?'

She shrugged and smiled. 'I hope so.'

'What's the agency pitching for, Madeleine?'

'Please don't call me Madeleine. I'm Maddie, really.'

'OK,' he said, equably. 'Maddie, then.'

'Well, we're trying to win the Grant & Wainwright account – you know – the pharmaceutical giants? They're launching a new line of shampoo, and they want a fresh image.'

'Do you use the shampoo?' he asked. Maddie was slightly thrown. She'd never been asked that question before.

'Well, to be perfectly honest – I don't.'

'That's putting it baldly,' said Sam with a grin. 'Sorry,' he added, registering the rather perplexed expression on Maddie's face. 'I have the most juvenile sense of humour of anyone I know. If my photographic career doesn't get off the ground I could always get a job writing for the *Beano*.'

Maddie returned his smile and tucked her feet underneath her. She realized that her robe was gaping open between her breasts, and she pulled the towelling lapels together, aware even as she did so of the redundancy of the gesture. After all, Sam had already seen all of her that there was to be seen.

'Why don't you use the shampoo?' he resumed.

'Well, I did try it a few times when I heard we

were going to be pitching, but I went back to my old shampoo after I'd satisfied myself that the Grant & Wainwright product was top quality.'

'It must be a tough job trying to persuade the public to buy a shampoo when you don't bother using it yourself.'

'Well, no – it's not, actually.' Maddie found herself on the defensive. 'Every product has something unique about it which will appeal to a certain sector of the consuming public. We're not in the business of conning people.'

'Oh – I'm sure you're not,' Sam said. 'But it must be a bit like being a barrister. You know – having to defend someone even though you may suspect that they're as guilty as hell.'

Maddie didn't like the direction the conversation was taking. 'What's that amazing smell?' she asked, changing tack. 'I've been feeling like a Bisto kid ever since I set foot in this house.'

'It's cassoulet,' said Sam. 'I made it this morning. It's been cooking in a slow oven all day.'

'Wow. Cassoulet's complicated, isn't it? I'm even more impressed. You're obviously a man of many talents.'

Sam responded with an unsettling smile, and during the short conversational vacuum that developed between them, Maddie found herself twisting a strand of her hair round her index finger. 'I'd better get dressed,' she said, finally.

'I'll leave you to it.' Sam slid back through the door and shut it behind him.

Her overnight bag was on top of the chest of drawers – she'd already hung her suit in the small wardrobe. She discarded the robe and rummaged in the bag for her underwear. Jogging pants, T-shirt, toilet bag, make-up case, hair-dryer, stay ups, Manolo Blahniks – one by one she lifted the articles out of the bag until it was empty. No underwear. She'd forgotten to pack any. Hell. She'd just have to survive the next twenty-four hours without it. She was glad that the skirt of the suit she'd brought with her to wear tomorrow was nearly ankle-length. Maddie slipped into her jogging pants and her big, loose T-shirt and went barefoot down the stairs.

Chapter Four

In the kitchen, Maeve was sitting at a long, scrubbed deal table, leaning on her elbows and leafing through a magazine. She looked up when Maddie came through the door. 'Hi! How are you feeling?' she asked.

In spite of the fact that it had been a long and knackering day, Maddie was feeling oddly energized.

'I'm feeling great,' she said. 'That shower must have given me a second wind.' She joined Maeve at the table, which had been set for four.

At the other end of the room – where two armchairs draped in bright throws stood on either side of an Aga – Sam was dishing cassoulet into shallow bowls. The dog Karsch regarded him hungrily from an armchair, a comatose kitten tucked between his paws. Sara was standing in front of a rather dilapidated cupboard which groaned under the weight of a laden wine rack. She was sliding bottles in and out, checking their labels.

'Knock back that white, Maeve,' she instructed. 'I've got some really special red here to go with

Sam's cassoulet. We deserve a treat.' She located the bottle she'd been hunting for and crossed the room.

'Is it from Saint-Géyroux?' asked Maeve.

'Yes. Daniel brought half a dozen bottles over for me. Even the label makes me go all nostalgic.' She put the wine down on the table and smiled. 'It's heaven to think that we'll be there in a week's time.'

'Are you going over on holiday?' asked Maeve.

'No. We're working. I've an idea for a brand new project.'

'Oh? What kind of a project?'

'I want to work on a series of landscapes,' said Sara. 'The terrain in the Languedoc is stunningly beautiful. That's why Daniel chose to live there.' Sara pulled the cork and poured red wine into four clean goblets. 'My brother Daniel lives in France, Madeleine. But of course – you know that. You met him at the opening of my exhibition.'

Maddie took a sip of red. 'Wow,' she said, turning the bottle around so that she could examine the label. It read *Mas de Daumas Gassac.* She remembered that Daniel Lennox had mentioned that he was indecently wealthy. 'This is wonderful. Is it madly expensive?'

'It tastes like it should be, doesn't it? But it's surprisingly cheap. Daniel gets it in the local *caveaux* in Saint-Géyroux.'

Maddie furrowed her brow. 'Saint-Géyroux? Why does that sound familiar?'

'I sent you a postcard from there last autumn,' said Maeve. 'When I was visiting Rory McDonagh and Deirdre. They have a house in Saint-Géyroux.'

'They have a beach house in LA, too, don't they?' asked Sara.

'Yeah, but they like to get as far away from LA as they can whenever possible. They discovered Saint-Géyroux about a year ago. Sara had told me so much about it, Maddie, that I recommended they check it out. They fell in love with the place at first sight. So did I when I went over to visit. It's one of the most peaceful places I've ever been.'

'It's attracting a lot of downshifters,' said Sara. 'Daniel used to be the only foreigner in the village. It's hard to believe that a film star like Rory McDonagh's moved in. You'd better not tell anyone else about it, Maeve,' she warned her. 'Daniel would go ballistic at the idea of his picturesque mountain retreat being invaded by media types.'

'Don't worry, Sara.' Maeve's tone was one of blithe reassurance. 'There's no danger of Saint-Géyroux becoming another Saint-Tropez or Cannes. It's far too sleepy to attract bona fide media types. They'd all die of boredom. And Rory and Deirdre are very picky about who comes to stay because they have to work overtime at being sociable in LA. I'm the only person who has *carte blanche* to go over any time I like. I'm enormously privileged.'

'It sounds like just what I need.' Maddie leaned

her elbows on the table and sighed. 'Josh would never hack it, though. Unless – ' she gave a little smile – 'unless there was a chance of hanging out with Rory McDonagh – or your brother, Sara. Josh likes to be able to name-drop. He got masses of mileage out of the fact that he met Liam Neeson at a dinner party once.' She smiled again and then bit her lip. She shouldn't have said that. She'd just succeeded in making her partner look like some superficial starfucker.

Maeve looked thoughtful. 'I can't see Josh and Rory getting on together, somehow. They're completely dissimilar types,' she said. 'You should look him up when you're over there, Sara. You'd really like him. Rory's one of the most upfront guys I know – real fun to be with.'

Sara Lennox averted her eyes, frowning slightly, and Maddie bit her lip even harder.

There was a fractional, rather embarrassed silence, and then Maeve said: 'Oh. Shit. I didn't mean that to sound the way it did, Maddie. I don't mean to be disparaging about Josh. It's just that Rory and he would have absolutely nothing in common. D'you understand?' She touched her cousin lightly on the arm. 'They just have such different outlooks on life.'

'It's OK, Maeve. No offence taken. I know that Josh isn't the most laid-back individual on the face of the planet.' It was time to change the subject. 'How's Deirdre?' she asked. Maddie had met Deirdre O'Dare with Maeve when the two actresses had worked together on *Ardmore Grove*, an RTE soap. 'She's writing screenplays now, isn't she?'

'Yeah. She's expecting another baby, too, around Christmas time.'

Sam set the last of the dishes on the table, and slid into a chair opposite Maddie. 'To beautiful women,' he said, raising his glass.

Maeve raised her glass back. 'To the chef,' she said. 'This cassoulet smells amazing.'

'To the chef,' echoed Sara and Maddie, and then everyone laid into the food on their plates. Sam's cassoulet was the most delicious thing Maddie had tasted in ages, and the sea air had given her an appetite.

'I've never eaten cassoulet before,' she said when she'd finished. She was wiping her plate clean with a hunk of bread.

'What?' said Sara Lennox in surprise, pouring more wine. 'And you with French parents?'

'Actually, only my father was French. I never lived there. We used to visit my grandparents a lot, though. I spent most of my summers there as a child.'

'I will teach you to make cassoulet some day, Madeleine,' Sam announced gallantly. 'It takes time, but the ingredients are very basic. Carrots, onions, haricot beans, pork knuckles, Toulouse sausage. And lots and lots of duck fat, of course.'

Maddie sat very still, staring at Sam.

'What's wrong?' he asked.

'I don't eat food like that,' she said. 'I have a fat-free diet.'

'Well, you certainly didn't tonight,' said Sam, laughing as he got up from the table and helped himself to another bottle of wine from the rack. 'Are we allowed another *Mas de Daumas*, dear Auntie?' he asked, directing his boyish smile at Sara.

'Oh, why not?' she said, leaning back in her chair and stretching. 'The night is young.'

Actually, the night wasn't that young, thought Maddie, surreptitiously looking at her watch. If she'd been at home she'd have been heading towards bed by now. But she was feeling too sated with good food and too deliciously fuzzy with good wine to care. Sam drew the cork and refilled her glass. She smiled up at him. 'Thanks,' she said.

'Have some cheese,' he said.

'I'm not sure I should,' she said, looking at the ripe Brie on the table.

'Don't tell me you're still feeling guilty about all that duck fat?' he said. 'Go on – be a devil. If you want my opinion, you could do with some fattening up.'

There was nothing salacious about the smile he gave her, but Maddie felt herself colour a little. She'd almost forgotten that Sam was more *au fait* with her physical geography than most people.

'All right,' she said with decision, reaching for the cheese knife. 'I'll work my ass off in the gym next week to get rid of the extra calories.' She gave him a bright smile and helped herself to a wedge of gloriously runny cheese. 'Is this from Saint-Géyroux, too?' she asked, raising her eyes to meet Sara Lennox's speculative gaze.

'Sadly, no. The local deli,' said Sara. The older woman took a sip of wine, still looking at Maddie with interest. 'You really *don't* need to worry about your figure, you know,' she said, 'Sam's right. You could do with putting on a few extra pounds.'

Maddie made an apologetic face. 'I know it sounds really superficial, but appearances are important in the business I'm in. How I look matters. I need to be careful to keep my weight down.'

'I think you look great, Madeleine,' said Sam, lifting the wine bottle to assess the level of *Mas de Daumas.* 'Especially with no clothes on at all.'

This time there was no mistaking the wicked nature of the smile he sent her. Maddie felt herself smiling back, feeling suddenly very aware that Maeve's knowing gaze was on her. She picked up her wineglass and snuck a look at her cousin over the rim. Maeve's eyes held a kind of amused enquiry. Maddie answered with an eloquent look of her own. *Don't be so totally ridiculous, cousin. I don't do toyboys . . .*

Maeve just gave her her best Giaconda smile.

*   *   *

The next morning Maddie was up early. She showered, did a quick make-up job, blow-dried her hair and sprayed herself with scent before slipping on stay-ups, suit and heels.

In the kitchen Sam was standing by the stove with his back to her, cooking rashers in a frying pan. Sara was on the deck beyond the glass wall, looking out to sea through a pair of binoculars. There was no sign of Maeve.

'Help yourself to coffee, Maddie,' said Sam.

'Thanks.' There was a cafetière and a jug of cream on the table. She fetched a mug from a cupboard and poured. The coffee looked frighteningly strong, but she resisted the temptation to dilute it by adding calorific cream. Maddie leaned against the table and inhaled the wonderful cooking smells that were wafting in her direction. She couldn't remember the last time she'd eaten bacon, but the aroma was making her feel ravenous.

'Hungry?' Sam turned round from the stove with a frying pan in his hand and stared at her with an incredulous expression. 'Christ. You look different,' he said. 'What's with the sharp threads?'

'I'm working today.'

'Oh yeah. I'd almost forgotten that you were a Real Life person.' He smiled and moved across the room towards her.

'Christ, you look different.' Sara Lennox had come in from the deck, nursing a mug.

'That's what I said.' Sam dumped a pile of crisp rashers onto a plate. 'I hardly recognized her with her clothes on.' He sent Maddie his wicked smile again, and she returned it. It was difficult to believe that less than twelve hours ago she'd been cavorting stark naked on a beach.

The aroma of bacon had intensified. Sam fetched a bag of rolls from the cupboard and started to split them. Then he gouged out a thick dollop of butter from a dish on the table with a knife and proceeded to slap it onto the bread.

Sara refilled her mug with coffee, added a generous measure of cream, and then sat down at the table, unlooping the strap of the binoculars from around her neck. She handed them to Maddie. 'It's a stunning morning. Go have a look, Madeleine.'

'Thanks.' Maddie took the binoculars and wandered out onto the deck. The sun was dancing on the sea, bouncing off a mass of wavelets that shimmered as far as the horizon. Over the ambient birdsong rose the harsh cry of a gull, and Maddie could just make out the shape of the bird as it wheeled and turned in the bright blue sky. From time to time it would plummet towards the sea, then soar skyward again. She raised the binoculars and focused on the gull as it swooped to the water. Darkly silhouetted against the glittering surface of the sea was an elegant black bird. Its sleek head ducked as the gull dive-bombed, and Maddie kept the binoculars trained on it. 'What kind of bird's that – the one on the water?' she called over her shoulder into the kitchen.

'A cormorant,' called back Sara Lennox. 'Looks like it's damaged its wing – it can't seem to lift itself out of the water, and that herring gull has been dive-bombing it mercilessly for the last half-hour. It's not going to last much longer at this rate.'

Maddie continued to watch the black bird, feeling intensely sorry for it as the gull descended again, screaming shrilly.

Something brushed against her foot, and she looked down. The kitten she'd seen yesterday lying between Karsch's paws was playing with the suede strap of her shoe. She laughed out loud as it stood on its hind legs and swatted with tiny belligerent paws. On the fourth offensive it missed and fell over backwards, whereupon it set on the strap as if it was a mortal enemy, sinking its teeth into it, scrabbling madly with its back legs and digging little needle claws into the soft suede. She couldn't allow it to carry on – her shoe and her stay-ups would be ruined if she didn't put a stop to this fight-to-the-death. She stooped down and picked up the little creature, surprised at how feather-light it was. The kitten wriggled indignantly between her hands for an instant or two before suddenly settling down. To Maddie's delight, it began to purr loudly. She wandered back into Sara's kitchen with the kitten draped over her shoulder, and sat down at the table. Sam was cramming rashers into rolls.

'Oh, look,' said Sara, retrieving a sliver of bacon that had fallen onto the table and giving it to the kitten. 'Carlotta likes you. She normally doesn't bother with strangers. Do you want to take her home with you? I'm trying to off-load as many kittens as I can because her mother's pregnant – again.'

Maddie looked down at the kitten in her lap. It was making a noise like a sewing machine. 'Oh – I'm afraid I couldn't,' she said with genuine regret. 'I live in an apartment, and I'm out a lot. It wouldn't be fair on her.'

Sam put a bacon buttie on her plate. She was on the verge of saying: 'I'm sorry – I don't eat bacon' – and then she realized that she could hardly refuse to eat a couple of rashers after stuffing herself with Toulouse sausage and duck fat as she had done at the same table only hours earlier. Anyway, the temptation was altogether too much. The soft white rolls were glistening with butter, and the rashers were golden and perfectly crisp. Maddie took a bite and thought she had never tasted anything so delicious – apart from last night's cassoulet. She started to wolf down the buttie, feeding scraps of bacon to the kitten between mouthfuls.

Maeve strolled, yawning, into the kitchen. 'What about you, Maeve?' asked Sara. 'Do you want a kitten?'

'I'd love one,' said Maeve, heading in the

direction of the coffee pot. 'But my venerable tub of lard's nose would be seriously out of joint if I came home with competition.'

'Pity,' said Sara. 'I suppose I'll just have to admit defeat and have the fertile feline spayed after her next litter.'

Maddie looked at her watch. 'Bugger. I didn't realize how late it had got,' she said. 'I really ought to head or I'll be late for work. Sorry, Maeve. You haven't had a chance to have anything to eat yet.'

'It's OK,' said her cousin, swigging coffee. 'I'll take one of these with me, if I may, Sam?' She indicated the pile of bacon butties.

'Be my guest,' said Sam, fetching tinfoil from a cupboard. 'Are you sure you won't have another cup of coffee before you go, Maddie?'

'I'd really better not. But thanks anyway.' She turned back to Maeve. 'Sorry to put pressure on you.'

'No problem. I've a load of real life stuff to do today. The sooner I get back into town the better.'

Maddie gently roused the dopy, bacon-sated kitten on her lap before setting her down on the floor. Carlotta gave her paw two quick, cross licks and then tottered over to where Karsch lay dozing in front of the stove. As Maddie brushed kitten hairs off the skirt of her suit her eyes fell on the plate of butties sitting enticingly in the centre of the table. Sam was wrapping two up for Maeve. 'May I take one with me too, Sam? I don't know when I'll next have a chance to get something to eat.'

'Sure.' Humming, Sam tore off more tinfoil and made another food parcel, maintaining eye contact with Maddie as he did so. Maddie couldn't help smiling back at him. What a bold, sexy boy he was!

She took the parcel and stuck it in her bag. 'Thank you for everything, you two,' she said. 'You've been incredibly generous.'

'You're welcome,' said Sara. 'It was fun, wasn't it? I'll get your photographs off to you by courier as soon as they're developed.' She took a sip of coffee, then leaned back in her chair, looking thoughtful. 'You wouldn't mind, Madeleine, if I let my brother have a print, would you? He's getting a copy of Maeve's portrait framed, and I know he'd find it amusing to be able to hang its companion-piece alongside it.'

'Of course you can Sara. Let him have a print, I mean.' Maddie busied herself with the catch on her briefcase in an attempt to cover the state of agonizing confusion she suddenly found herself in. She was actually deeply uncomfortable with the idea, but she knew she had no other alternative than to agree to Sara's proposition. The negatives belonged to Sara Lennox. Categorically. They were hers to do with as she wanted, and she, the subject, simply had no choice in the matter.

The mobile in her case chirruped, and Maddie started fumbling with the catch again. 'Hello, Josh,' she said into her phone when she finally retrieved it.

'I've been trying to get you on the land line

since yesterday evening. Your machine keeps picking up,' he said. 'Were you out last night?'

'No, no – I just went to bed early and didn't want to be disturbed by calls. I forgot to turn the machine off this morning. Sorry. Was it anything urgent?'

'No.' He sounded truculent. 'I just wondered where you were, that's all. I'll see you in work later.'

He'd put the phone down before she could say goodbye. 'I'm going to have to dash,' she said. 'I'm sorry to make such a hasty exit, but if I don't get my ass into town ASAP my partner will start to suspect that something's up.'

'OK,' said Maeve, swinging her leather bag onto her shoulder. 'Let's make tracks.' She gave Sara a farewell hug, and Maddie followed suit. 'Thanks so much, Sara. For everything,' she said.

Then Sam stepped forward. 'It was a revelation working with you. Literally.'

He allowed his lips to linger as he kissed her cheek, and she heard a leisurely intake of breath as he registered her scent. And then Maddie and Maeve disappeared up the stairs to Sara Lennox's hallway with a clattering of heels. 'Goodbye, Maddie,' Sam called after her. 'I can't wait to see how the photographs turn out.'

She turned to give him a final smile, and had to wrench her eyes away. It was like looking at Adonis.

*   *   *

They made good time back to Dublin. Maddie dropped Maeve off at her house, and reached the agency shortly after half-past nine. Josh hadn't arrived yet. She was glad she'd be at her desk when he did.

She poured herself some coffee and started going through the Creative Rationale again, changing details as she went. She was surprised at how fresh she felt – not tired at all, as she'd expected. All that sea air must have blown away a load of cobwebs. She found herself looking at her work from a new, objective perspective, and was delighted to find that it read better than she'd remembered. Maybe she could allow herself to hope just a little that the account would be theirs by this time next week? No, no, no – she didn't want to hex herself.

She was still hungry, she realized. The sandwich bar round the corner would be open, but she hated the surly staff in there. There was the snack bar in her gym, which was only five minutes' walk away . . . No – she felt like something more substantial than the kind of low-cal, 'lite' stuff they served. Then she remembered the bacon buttie that Sam had given her. She took it out of her bag and looked at it. It was cold, of course, but the bacon looked reasonably crisp and she was seriously hungry. She took an experimental bite, and decided that it was still quite palatable.

As she sat there studying the pages and chewing happily, Josh came through the door. He looked wrecked. 'Hi, darling,' he said, kissing her abstract-edly on the cheek as he passed by on his way to dump a file on his desk. 'How's it going?'

'Fine,' she replied, giving him a big smile. He looked as though he could do with some cheering up.

'What are you so happy about?' He ambled over to her desk, rubbing one eye with an index finger. 'Christ, I'm tired.'

'Poor thing. Will I get you some coffee?' She took a large bite of her buttie before getting to her feet.

'I'm not sure I could hack coffee. I overdid it last night and my body's protesting against all the poisons that have been poured into it. What's that you've got – herbal tea? Maybe I should go for the healthy option. Give us a whiff and I'll see if I can stomach it.' He took up her cup and sniffed at the contents. 'Coffee?' he said with surprise. 'You hardly ever touch the stuff, Mads. And what's that you're eating? A bacon sandwich? What's going on?'

Maddie stopped chewing. 'I don't really know,' she said with her mouth still full of bacon and white bread. 'I just had a sudden craving.'

'A craving? You're not pregnant, are you?'

'No, Josh. You know I'm religious about taking my pill.' The alarm function on her phone reminded her on a daily basis.

'Well, that's a relief.' Josh was looking at her curiously. 'You know – there's definitely some-thing different about you. Are you wearing some

100

new kind of blusher? Your cheeks are very pink.'

Maddie went even pinker. 'Yes,' she lied. 'It's a sample from Grant & Wainwright.' She couldn't very well tell him that the roses in her cheeks were due to hearty quantities of sea air.

'Trash it. It looks tarty. And I wouldn't give in to too many cravings for bacon sarnies if I were you. You'll end up looking like Nuala in accounts. Now *there's* someone who could do with an introductory session in your gym.' Josh stretched himself and yawned. He sniffed vigorously, and Maddie looked sideways at him. He was avoiding her eyes. 'Must be getting a cold, as well as everything else,' he remarked in a too-casual way. 'Shit. Maybe I will have some coffee after all. I'm not sure I'll be able to get through the day without a caffeine hit.'

Maddie finally succeeded in swallowing the food in her mouth. She looked at the remains of the buttie wrapped in the paper napkin. It didn't look at all appetizing now. She dropped it into the waste-paper basket by the side of her desk. 'Good girl,' said Josh approvingly. 'No self-respecting über-chick would be caught dead eating anything so proletarian as a bacon buttie.'

'So how come you're feeling so seedy?' she said, fastidiously wiping her lips clean with a tissue. 'Did you go somewhere after the pub last night?'

'No. I just downed too many pints too fast. I'll take it easy tonight and tomorrow. Maybe we should go somewhere quiet for dinner this evening. Just the two of us?'

'Mm. I'd like that. Where'll we go?'

'Somewhere where the waiters will look at me with envy because I'll be sitting with the most desirable creature in the room.' He looked her up and down appreciatively and then reached out a hand to caress the silk jersey of the shirt over her breasts.

'Careful, Josh – Margaret's about somewhere.'

'Fuck Margaret,' he said, taking her nipple between his fingers. Then: 'No bra?' His tone was one of surprise. 'Well, I must say this is a treat. Maybe it's a good idea to leave off your dinky little bras from time to time, darling, even though you wear them beautifully.' He leaned down and ran his tongue down the side of her neck. 'But then, I'm not sure if I fancy the idea of all those middle-aged executives ogling your nipples. They look incredibly prominent under this silky stuff.'

Something in his voice made her wonder if he actually *did* fancy the idea. Maddie moved away. 'I'll get your coffee, Josh.'

'Don't go anywhere, Mads. Feel this.' He took her hand and held it against his groin.

Maddie glanced over her shoulder. 'Stop it, Josh. Margaret could come in at any minute.'

'Like I said – fuck Margaret. Correction. Fuck Maddie. I want to. Now.'

He had reached down and was pulling up the fabric of her skirt inch by inch. Maddie tried to squirm away, but he was holding her too tightly. Then his hand was between her thighs.

'Good . . . stay-ups . . .' His hand slid up further. 'What? No knickers? Jesus Christ, Maddie – what are you trying to do to me? No bra, no knickers – you're going to drive me out of my fucking mind!'

She gave a ragged little laugh. 'I didn't do it deliberately, Josh.' She could feel his fingers exploring her gently as she dreamed up her excuse. 'Oh! I was just so preoccupied with thinking about the Rationale this morning that I completely forgot about underwear – don't ask me why. Oh God!' His fingers were persistent. 'I'm not usually that absent-minded. Jesus Christ, Josh – you must stop. Oh!'

'I think you should be absent-minded a little more often, sweetheart. It suits you.' Josh had taken her by the hand and was leading her across the landing.

'Where are you going?' she asked. Her breathing was shallow now, and she found it difficult to get the question out.

'The boardroom. I've long cherished an ambition to screw you on that table.'

He pushed her through the door and turned the key in the lock. 'Sit up there,' he said, indicating the immense expanse of polished teak. 'And lift your skirt. Do it slowly.'

Maddie sat up on the table, shook her hair back from her face and, looking Josh directly in the eyes with a sexy, conspiratorial smile, did exactly as she was told.

Chapter Five

Three days later they stood up from where they were sitting round the same boardroom table and shook hands with the people from Grant & Wainwright. The presentation had gone like a dream. Josh had sold the idea brilliantly in spite of the fact that he was by then running on empty, fuelled by nothing but caffeine and adrenalin.

'You were sensational, Mads,' he whispered in her ear, before following the G & W suits through the boardroom door. 'Your outline was spot-on. Well done, sweetheart – I'm so proud of you!'

Maddie sat back down at the table and sorted through her paperwork feeling completely drained. It had been one of the most gruelling weekends she had ever experienced. She'd spent the entire previous evening rewriting chunks of the Rationale – as she'd known she'd have to – and her lips were still raw from biting them every time Josh had demanded that yet another change be made. She'd headed home shortly after eleven o'clock, leaving him yelling at a tearful junior for messing about with the artwork, and demonstrating for the fifth time exactly how it should be laid out. He'd been growing more abusive by the minute, and Maddie had been relieved to shut the office door behind her and crawl home to bed. She was used to Josh's behaviour when he was up against it, but she hated seeing him unleashing his aggression on the younger staff members, most of whom didn't know how to handle him.

She'd overheard Nuala from accounts talking about him to Margaret in the office that morning, unaware that Maddie had just stepped into the room. 'How on earth does she stick him?' she'd been saying. 'He must be a deadly ride, that's all I can say. There's got to be something that makes her put up with the way he behaves.'

Maddie had gone very red and had retreated silently through the door. Her immediate impulse had been to stand up for her partner, but she didn't want Nuala to think she'd been eaves-dropping. It wasn't fair! She knew Josh was temperamental, but no-one saw the way he behaved towards her in private. He could be tender and funny and generous and encouraging, and yes – Nuala had been right about one thing – they *did* have a terrific sex life. It was just that he was under so much pressure these days that he was finding it impossible to take things easy.

'Are you coming to Daly's, Maddie?' asked Margaret now, looking at her sympathetically. 'You look a bit knackered.'

'Yeah – I *am* knackered. I just hope it didn't show during the presentation.'

'God, no – you were brilliant back there. You even convinced me – and I think that shampoo's shite. You'd make a bloody good actress, you know. Or a barrister.'

'Thanks, Margaret.' Remembering what Sam had said to her about barristers defending guilty parties, Maddie gave a wry laugh and stood up, returning her paperwork to her case. 'And yeah – of course I'm coming to the pub. I might feel more lively after a glass or two of wine.' Somehow she knew that a glass or two of wine wouldn't help. Endorphins. They'd do the trick. But the only way to get an endorphin high was either by going to the gym and doing a strenuous workout, or by pigging out on chocolate. She'd keel over if she went to the gym, and if she pigged out she'd be going to the gym every night for the rest of the week to burn off calories. A glass of wine it would have to be.

* * *

Daly's was heaving, mostly with media types. There were a lot of recording studios in this part of town, and advertising people who had spent the afternoon laying down tracks on commercials would generally end up in Daly's at around this time of day. As the evening wore on the atmosphere in the pub started to become unpleasant. A rowdy element was beginning to manifest itself, it was almost unbearably warm, and the cigarette smoke had reached a suffocating level.

Josh kept disappearing off to the loo, or to talk shop with other media people, leaving Maddie at one stage to talk to the Account Director on her own for nearly half an hour. Dim Sum Jim was a thoroughly nice guy, but he had an obsession. Bridge. Unwisely, Maddie had let slip that she knew nothing about the game, and Jim obviously felt it incumbent upon him to educate her. He proceeded to do so at length and in such agonizing detail that she wanted to scream at him to stop.

Jim had just finished explaining the tortuous scoring system of the game when she caught sight of Maeve angling her way towards her through the crowd. She resisted the impulse to cheer at the prospect of being rescued, made her excuses to Jim and dragged her cousin into the snug, which had just been vacated.

'Thank God for you. If I'd heard any more garbage about rubbers I'd have keeled over.'

'Rubbers? That suit was talking to you about the comparative merits of condoms?'

'No, you eejit,' said Maddie with a laugh. The thought occurred to her that the last time she'd laughed spontaneously had been days ago, more than likely at some juvenile remark of Sam's. 'Bridge. Sit down and let me get you a drink.' Maddie signalled to one of the bar staff that she needed miniature wine bottles times two. She wished that Daly's stocked decent wine. Those miniatures were so full of chemicals that she always got massive hangovers from them. 'What are you doing in here, Maeve?' she asked, shrugging out of her cashmere cardigan and sitting down across the table from her cousin. 'You don't normally frequent Daly's. I thought Meagher's was where all you luvvie—' She registered Maeve's raised eyebrow and made an apologetic face. 'Sorry: all you thespian types hung out.'

'I was doing some ADR in Moynihan-Russell.' Maeve had spent the past two months working on a film being shot in Wicklow. 'I thought I'd seen the last of that bastard movie, but there's masses of post-synching still to be done. I'll be working on it most of this week.'

'Anything else in the pipeline?'

'My agent's negotiating another film, but that's not happening for ages. It'll be nice to take it easy for a while. I thought I might visit Rory and Deirdre in France. They're spending a month in Saint-Géyroux.'

'Saint-Géyroux? That place is starting to take on mythical proportions in my mind – like some sort of Garden of Eden. Will Sara and Sam be there? They said something about going over soon, didn't they?'

'Yeah.'

'Wow. It'll be a real artists' colony, won't it? I can just picture you sitting outside some unpretentious little café sipping aperitifs and talking about Man Ray and Picasso and Peter Brook and James Joyce.'

'I'll be bringing the latest Jilly Cooper if I do go. I need to chill. I'll be thinking of you at some groovy opening talking about Man Ray and Picasso and Peter Brook and James Joyce.'

'Hell. I really envy you, Maeve. I'd love a break.' Maddie handed over money to the waitress who'd brought their drinks.

'*Sláinte*,' said Maeve, uncapping her wine and pouring. She took a swig, made a face and then leaned back in her chair. 'How did your presentation go, Maddie? It was today, wasn't it?'

Maddie started twisting her hair. 'To be honest, Maeve, I'm so dog tired that I'm almost beyond caring. Josh thinks it's in the bag, but I didn't like to remind him that Reflex is pitching too.' Reflex was the rival agency that had taken over the La Casita holidays account.

'Reflex? Is that the agency that tried to head-hunt you?'

'Yes. *Never* mention that to Josh, incidentally. He'd go apeshit if he knew.'

Maeve was regarding her with an oddly watchful expression. 'How's he been bearing up under the pressure?' she asked.

'He bawled out a junior last night, but he's in good form now.' In fact, Josh had bought drinks all round earlier and apologized to the jaded junior. Maddie had been relieved that both Nuala and Margaret were within earshot when he'd made the apology. Maybe they'd think he was less of a shit now.

A burst of raucous laughter rang out from across the pub. Maeve looked up, and Maddie followed the direction of her gaze. Josh was leaning up against the counter, talking to his friend called Baz. Maddie didn't like Baz. In fact she thought he was a complete scumbag.

'Bit hyper, isn't he?' observed Maeve.

'He always is when we're pitching for an account.'

Maeve looked sideways at Maddie. 'Is everything OK between you two? He's not beaking up again, is he?'

'He promised me he'd stopped, Maeve. As far as I know he hasn't had anything up his nose since we had the last row about it. That was months ago.'

Maeve gave her a cynical look. 'Don't you think you're being a little naïve, Maddie? He's never found it easy to get by at times like this without a little help from his friend Charley. I hate to be the one to—'

Maddie laid a hand on Maeve's arm. 'Please let's not talk about it, Maeve. I really couldn't handle that as well as everything else right now. I'll check it out – I promise I will – but I need a few days to get my own head together, OK? I'll leave it till after his birthday on Monday.' She banged her forehead with the heel of her hand. 'Hell – that reminds me – how's Jacqueline fixed on Sunday night? D'you think she'd do me a huge favour and help with the catering for Josh's bash? The last

110

thing I feel like doing is throwing a party, but the invites have all gone out.'

'I'll ask her,' said Maeve. 'If she's not on for it she'll know someone who can help. How many people are coming?'

'Around thirty.'

'Anyone I know?'

'Um. Not sure. They're mostly advertising types. Oh – Ann Fitzroy! You've worked with her, haven't you? Wasn't she on the soap opera around the same time as you?'

'Mm. We never hit it off, I'm afraid.'

'Oh. Sorry about that. I had to invite her. She does a lot of voice-over work for us.'

'I won't have a problem avoiding her. She doesn't like me either.' Maeve undid the zip on her bag and produced a packet of peanuts. 'Want some?' she asked, tearing it open.

'Better not. I really pigged out at Sara's gaff. I put on two pounds over the weekend.'

'Sara's right, you know, Maddie. You could do with putting on some weight. If you're not careful you could start to look haggard.'

'That's just because I've been working too hard.' Maddie looked down at her tummy and pulled her muscles in. 'I haven't had a chance to get to the gym in ages. If I don't go soon I'll have ballooned so much that Josh won't recognize the sylph-like nymph emerging from the sea in his birthday photograph.'

'Are you going to give it to him at the party?'

'No. His birthday's officially on Monday, so I'll leave it till then. I don't particularly want him to open it in front of a load of people. I'm a bit coy about any of his chums seeing me with my kit off. I hope you don't mind, Maeve, but I told him that I'd bought a print of *your* photograph for his birthday. He was starting to smell a rat so I had to fob him off with some excuse, and that was the only plausible one I could come up with.'

'So he actually thinks he's getting a photograph of me in the buff for his birthday?'

'Mm hm.'

'He's in for a nice surprise, then.'

'Oh, I dunno,' said Maddie with a smile. 'He may be disappointed, for all I know. I think he's always secretly fancied you. He doesn't like the idea that you're "wasting yourself" – as he puts it – on Jacqueline.'

Maeve laughed. 'Jesus. Some people just don't have a clue, do they? No offence,' she said quickly, clocking the expression on her cousin's face. 'I know loads of people who have problems with the fact that I'm gay, Maddie. You've no idea how many of them pretend to be cool about it just because it would be politically incorrect not to be.'

'It's a big male fantasy thing, too, of course,' said Maddie, trying to make excuses for Josh. 'I love looking at those titles on the soft porn shelf in the video shop. You know – *Lesbian Lust, Naughty Threesomes, Girl Guides' Camping Nights* . . .'

'I saw a brilliant one once. *The Highwaywoman*

Rides Again. This highwaywoman went round holding up carriages, pretending to be a man and seducing all the helpless women passengers.'

'Was it sexy?'

'No. It was seriously silly. But at least the highwaywoman was glad to be gay. Most of those films are about lesbians being "cured". You know – seeing the light of day and suddenly becoming hetero after a good priapic shafting by some stud. Jesus – who'd be a porn star! What a way to earn a living . . .'

'I wouldn't mind earning a living as a porn star.' Josh was leaning against the door of the snug looking down at them with his sexy smile. 'How's my gorgeous woman?' he said, dropping a kiss on the top of Maddie's head. 'Hi, Maeve. Sorry to disturb your nice girly chat.'

'I didn't see you, Josh,' said Maddie. 'How long have you been standing there?' She hoped he hadn't heard too much.

'Oh, I came in around Maeve talking about lesbians being cured. I'd love to be the perpetrator, Maeve, if you decide to go for it.' He set a half-full pint on the table, and Maddie noticed that he was a bit unsteady on his feet as he sat down beside her.

She looked at her watch. 'It's getting late, Josh. Do you fancy getting something to eat? We could have something delivered to my place if you like.'

He sniffed. 'You don't want to go home yet, do you? I thought we might hit Lillie's later.'

'Oh, Josh – I couldn't. I really don't feel like going clubbing tonight.'

'Jesus Christ, Mads. We've been working our asses off for weeks. It's about time we had some fun. Come on – let me get you another drink. A glass of wine for you, Maeve?'

Maddie started to tense up. The prospect of having a row with Josh in front of her cousin always made her jumpy. 'OK – maybe one more, but then I really ought to think about heading home.'

Josh gave a heavy sigh. It was enough of a cue for Maeve. 'Let me get the drinks.' She jumped to her feet and gave Josh a bright smile before disappearing in the direction of the bar. Maddie could tell the smile was forced.

'You're being a prize pain in the ass tonight, Maddie.' Josh was looking at her with eyes that he was having trouble focusing.

'I know,' she said ruefully. 'It's just that I'm desperate for a decent night's sleep.'

'If I come home with you you won't get any sleep. I'll keep you up all night.' He stroked her collarbone with a forefinger and let it trail down towards her cleavage. 'D'you know something, gorgeous? I was talking to the G & W Advertising Director while he was laying his paperwork out on the boardroom table this afternoon, and I had a sudden impulse to say to him: "Hey, Murphy. Do you see that beautiful, sexy, clever woman sitting opposite you? Well, I am a very lucky man because she's all mine. In fact, we shagged each other senseless right here on this table a couple of days ago!" ' Josh gave a low laugh and then adopted a more contemplative tone. 'I'm not at all sure I like that geezer, as a matter of fact. He kept staring at your tits.' He turned to her and looked her up and down appreciatively. 'Although I can't say I blame him. You look fab.'

Maddie always took particular care of her appearance on the day of a presentation. A suggestion of kookiness told people that she was a 'creative' type. A touch of sexiness – nothing overt – was permissible, too, and Josh had phoned her before she left for work this morning to remind her to let drop to the clients that she was a Pisces – the sign of creativity and artistic sensitivity – and, more pragmatically, to remind her also to wear her Wonderbra. He'd only been half joking.

'I don't feel fab,' she said, unable to stifle a huge yawn.

Josh pulled her closer to him and kissed her ear. 'Hey. Try and lighten up a bit, Mads – have some fun. It's not like you to be so subdued after a good presentation.' He looked at her askance. 'Or maybe you don't feel it went that well?'

'Oh, no, Josh – of course it went well. It went *stunningly* well, and you were terrific.'

'You think the account's ours, then?' That sniff again.

'Well, let's not jump the gun. Don't forget that Reflex are doing their presentation tomorrow.'

Shit, shit, *shit*. Why in hell's name had she reminded him of that? Josh halted in his exploration of her physical geography, and removed his hand. Then he turned to her and gave her a hard look. 'Thanks for the encouraging words, Mads.'

'Look – I don't mean to sound negative, Josh – honestly. I just don't think it's a good thing to get our hopes up too high. I couldn't bear to think how disappointed you'd be if we didn't win the account.'

Josh said nothing, and Maddie sighed. After a minute she broke the silence. 'Look. Neither of us is having a good time tonight for some reason. Maybe I should just go home by myself.' Beside her Josh stiffened, and she hurried on. 'It makes sense when you think about it, darling. You want to have some fun and I'm just not in the mood. Why don't you make a night of it – head on to Lillie's when you're through here?'

He stood up. 'Good idea, Mads. Funnily enough, I'm through here now. See you.' Leaving his unfinished pint on the table, he got to his feet abruptly, slung his jacket over his shoulder and disappeared through the crowd without kissing her goodbye.

Maddie felt stupid tears rising to her eyes. Hell. She'd blown it. For a minute she debated as to whether or not she should follow him, and then she decided against it. She knew from experience that further discussion would be futile in the mood he was in. Jesus! What a vile week it had been!

Suddenly she craved the sanctuary of her flat more than anything. She stood up, put on her cardigan, and was just picking up her briefcase when Maeve came back with her drink.

'You're not going, are you, Maddie?'

'Yeah. I'm sorry, Maeve – I can't hack this place any more. I'm going to get a taxi home.'

'Has Josh gone to hail one for you? I saw him beating his way out of the door a minute ago.'

'No. I think he's gone to Lillie's.'

'Oh.'

The two women looked at each other. They didn't need to say anything. Maddie leaned over and gave her cousin a kiss on the cheek. 'Good night, Maeve. I'll see you on Sunday. And you won't forget to ask Jacqueline about the catering?'

'Sure. I'll be as persuasive as I can.'

Maddie picked up her smart leather case and prepared to negotiate her way towards the door of the pub.

'Hey – Maddie?'

She looked back at Maeve, enquiry in her eyes. 'Yes?'

'Give me a ring if you need to, won't you?'

'Of course I will. Thanks, Maeve.'

'Bye, Maddie. Take care of yourself.'

There was an expression of fierce concern on Maeve's face as she watched her cousin's retreating back.

*   *   *

Hungover and repentant, Josh apologized the next day. 'Here.' He produced a small gift-wrapped box from his pocket. 'This is for you.'

'Oh, Josh,' she said, looking at it. 'It's *your* birthday coming up – not mine. I don't deserve a present.'

'You should be showered with presents every day, Mads, for putting up with a gobshite like me.'

'You're only a gobshite some of the time,' she said with a smile as he wrapped her reluctant fingers around the little box. 'What's in it? The last time you handed me a box like this I nearly died when I thought how much it had cost you.' The last box had contained a brooch from the Design Yard in Temple Bar.

'Open it and find out.'

As Maddie undid the narrow silk ribbon and stripped away the candy-striped cellophane wrapping paper she felt like a child whose good behaviour was being rewarded with sweeties. She opened the box slowly, with an oddly apprehensive heart and careful fingers. Her intake of breath when she saw what it contained was audible. There, lying on a cushion of midnight blue velvet, was a heart-shaped gold locket. 'Oh, Josh – it's beautiful!'

'Victorian,' he said. 'You'd better get it insured.'

'Oh, Josh – thank you! Thank you so much.' Maddie flung her arms around her lover's neck and kissed him. 'But you're far too extravagant,' she added when they finished the kiss, thumping his shoulder gently for emphasis. 'It must have cost a bomb!'

'You're worth every penny of it, Maddie. I mean it. I don't know what I'd do without you in my life. I'm sorry I was such a shit last night.'

Her head was against his chest and he was holding her so close that he couldn't see her face. If he had, he might have asked her what was wrong, because the expression she wore had something oddly inappropriate about it. There was gratitude there, and love, to be sure. But there was something that wasn't quite right about the relieved way she closed her eyes as he brushed her hair with his lips.

For some very peculiar reason, Maddie Godard was thanking God the box hadn't contained a ring.

*   *   *

On Wednesday afternoon she got a call on her mobile from Sam. Her prints were ready, and he was having them couriered to her.

'The shots are stunning, Madeleine,' he'd said. 'Your boyfriend's going to get the best birthday present of his life.'

She'd made an excuse to leave work early so that she could get back to her apartment in time to intercept the courier. 'It's in your interest, darling!' she said to Josh, flashing him an enigmatic smile as she left the building.

She spent the interval waiting for the prints to arrive wrapping the presents she'd already bought for Josh. A Mont Blanc fountain pen. The new Martin Amis novel. A Hugo Boss shirt. A Wagner opera on CD, a hip flask.

The fax machine started to hum. Jacqueline had agreed to do the catering for the cost of the food only – her contribution to Josh's birthday – and she'd promised to fax through a menu. Maddie had asked her to do all Josh's favourites, and the list of dishes was mouthwateringly eclectic. Thai mussels, quail eggs, paella in croustade, stuffed brioches, Rice Krispie cakes . . .

At around half-past five the courier arrived. Maddie signed for the packet and took it into the kitchen, where she opened it carefully with scissors. Then she took a deep breath and slid out a sheaf of prints.

She stared at the top one, transfixed. The woman in the photograph looked so *other* – and yet it was unmistakably her that was emerging from the waves wearing a smile that would have been spaced-out dreamy if it hadn't been for the hint of challenge in the eyes. Here was a portrait of a woman who was comfortable with her body – and proud of it too. Sara had reproduced the photograph of Maeve with an accuracy that was almost eerie.

The second print and the third were all the same shot – Maddie remembered that Sara had promised her three. But there were six prints in the package. She set the archival quality prints aside and studied the three additional photographs.

One was a shot of her dancing at the water's edge with tendrils of wet hair plastered across her face, flourishing a long, lariat-like strand of seaweed above her head. There followed a shot of her pointing at the jogger on the dunes with her other hand over her laughing mouth. The third print showed her cradled in Sam's arms as he wrapped the robe round her from behind. His chin was on her shoulder and both of them were smiling into the camera as he plonked a kiss on her cheek. In every single one of the prints Maddie looked radiant.

She picked up the phone and punched in Sara Lennox's number. Sam answered.

'Well? What do you think of them?' he asked.

'Oh – Sam! What an amazingly clever stunt to have pulled off! My partner won't be able to believe his eyes!' Maddie was laughing down the phone. 'Is Sara there? I must say thank you.'

'She's not, I'm afraid. But I'll tell her you called.'

'She really is a genius, isn't she? It's almost an exact duplicate of the shot of Maeve.' Maddie looked down at the photographs on her kitchen table. 'It's hard to believe you're not looking at the same person, isn't it? I mean, the only real difference is in the colouring.'

'She captured you with a virtually identical

expression on your face. That's what clinched it. That, and the fact that you mirrored the pose so well. What did you think of the others?'

'They're lovely. Crazy.'

'I put them in for fun. I kept one for myself – the one of me kissing you on the cheek.' She could tell by his voice that he was smiling, and she smiled back, feeling shy but pleased. 'I hope you don't mind?'

'I don't mind,' she said.

'I thought it would be nice for you to have those shots as well. You radiate a real *joie de vivre* in them. They'll be a perfect memento of a day when you were happy.'

What a strange thing to say!

'It's really kind of you, Sam. I don't know how to thank you and Sara enough—'

'No thanks are necessary. Sara's delighted with her companion-piece. And I've got a lovely souvenir of you, Madeleine.'

'Oh – don't say that! You make it sound as if we'll never meet each other again!'

'I hope we do.' That smile again. 'I've to teach you how to make cassoulet, remember?'

'I remember.' The mention of cassoulet triggered a pang of nostalgia. She suspected she'd never learn how to make it. 'Sam? Will you tell Sara I'll phone again to let her know what Josh thought of his present?'

'Josh?'

'My partner.'

122

'Oh yes. Sure I will.'

'Well – goodbye, Sam. And thanks again.'

'You're welcome, Maddie. Goodbye. Take care.'

She put the phone down and put the photographs back into the padded envelope one by one, gazing at them as she did so. The spontaneous shots – the ones she hadn't been aware that Sara had taken – held her attention for a long time.

She stared down at them, comparing the uninhibited woman she saw with the woman who accompanied Josh to first nights and exhibition openings and hip new restaurants. It was as if they were two completely different people.

One was Maddie Godard. The other was . . . Who? Some stranger called Madeleine?

She slid the last print into the envelope, and then she went into her bedroom and locked the photographs in her bureau.

Chapter Six

On Sunday afternoon Jacqueline came round to help Maddie cater for the party and at six o'clock, as if by magic, every available surface in the flat was covered with dishes of food. The fridge was stocked with champagne and Bud, there was new film in her camera and she'd remembered to pre-set the video recorder so that she wouldn't miss the Sunday night costume drama. Jacqueline had brought flowers as well – white lilies, irises, and a glorious jumble of red and yellow roses.

'I know just where to put these,' said Maddie, jamming the roses into a vase and setting it on a small table beneath her latest impulse buy. It was a massive framed reproduction of a painting by Raoul Dufy – a still-life of a vase of vibrantly coloured roses with splendidly gaudy wallpaper in the background. Dufy had called his painting *La Vie en Rose*, and had printed the title in a childlike hand in the bottom right-hand corner. Unfortunately, Josh had hated the print on sight, pointing out quite accurately that it didn't match the rest of the décor in Maddie's flat.

'That looks perfect there,' said Jacqueline,

admiring the roses. 'But you should toss them around a bit more. They look better tousled. Not like these.' She returned her attention to the lilies, which she was fanning out in a plain glass cylinder. 'These can't help looking elegant. Although I'm not sure that lilies are Josh's flower,' she added. 'I'd love to have got hold of a couple of ornamental bay trees to put on either side of the door.'

'Why bay trees?' asked Maddie, filching an olive from a bowl.

'In the language of flowers bay trees are symbolic of glory. More appropriate than lilies for Josh, I'd have thought.'

'Lilies? Ow. I've always associated white lilies with death, Jac.'

'While lilies actually mean purity and sweetness,' said Jacqueline, sending Maddie an oblique smile. 'And I imagine that Josh is about as pure as the driven slush, to quote Mae West.'

Maddie smiled back. 'Yes. But he can be awfully sweet, sometimes. What do roses mean?'

'Red roses are for love, of course. Yellow roses mean jealousy. There are some amazing coded messages you can send when you choose flowers for people.'

'How do you know all this?' asked Maddie.

'Maeve gave me a diary with the language of flowers in it. I have it here somewhere.' Jacqueline retrieved her bag from where she'd dumped it on the couch and extracted a replica of a Victorian journal, bound in calf. 'Roses are seriously eloquent flowers,' she said, leafing through the book. 'They can mean all kinds of different things. Carolina roses mean "love is dangerous"; tuberoses mean "dangerous pleasures".'

'Dangerous pleasures? Wow. That sounds interesting.'

'But if you send somebody an African marigold you're implying that they have a vulgar mind. Pansies – as you would guess from Ophelia's speech in *Hamlet* – are for thoughts, yellow violets are for rural happiness. Shamrock is lightheartedness, which says something about the Irish.'

'What's lightheadedness? I intend to drink bucket-loads of champagne tonight.'

'Larkspur.' Jacqueline continued to flick through the pages. 'Some of the codes are incredibly subtle. A bay *tree* may signify glory, but an individual *leaf* means "I change but in death".'

'You could have great fun with combinations,' observed Maddie.

'Yeah. If you got together a sheaf of oats and oleander you'd be saying: "Beware the witching soul of music".'

'I'll remember that the next time someone sends me a bunch of oats and oleander.'

'And if there's orange blossom in there it implies that "Your purity equals your loveliness". Top it with a pineapple and you're saying "You're perfect."'

'It would make a bonkers-looking bouquet,' said

Maddie, spitting an olive stone into an ashtray. 'What's tranquillity? That's something I've been craving lately.'

'Got any mudwort or stonecrop?'

'Stonecrop? What's that when it's at home?'

'Mm. That's the big disadvantage about most of the plants listed here. Half of them are probably endangered species now. I mean, what in God's name is phlox?'

'Sounds like a cough sweet.'

Jacqueline stuck the book back in her bag and looked at her watch. 'Hell – is that the time? I'd better go home and get changed. What time are you expecting people to arrive?'

'Around eight.'

'Remember to stick some more ice-bags in the fridge. And uncork the red.' She kissed Maddie on the cheek. 'I'd better fly. Don't worry – everything's under control. Take time out to chill.'

'I'll do that,' said Maddie, moving to the hall and opening the door. 'Thanks a million for all your help, Jacqueline. Catch you later – and tell Maeve Ann Fitzroy's not coming after all, so she's safe.'

Maddie turned back into the hallway and headed towards the kitchen to start uncorking the wine. Passing through the sitting room she tweaked briefly at the lilies and then bent over them to inhale their heady scent. The smell was almost too powerful, she thought, shaking her head. She decided she much preferred the sweet smell of the freesias that Maeve had taken to Sara Lennox on the day of the photo-shoot. Then she crossed the room and sniffed at the roses amassed under the Dufy print. She was disappointed to discover that they didn't smell of anything.

The clock in the kitchen read half-past six. It seemed to her that it was the first time in weeks she'd had time to herself – a whole hour and a half! Quickly she uncorked a dozen bottles of burgundy, then ran a deep bath and swished Badedas into a luxuriant froth. She put Chopin on the CD player, poured herself a glass of chilled white wine, lit an aromatherapy candle by the side of the bath, and then she sank down into the warm water, closing her eyes and sighing out loud with relief. She allowed herself twenty minutes to soak, letting music and the scented water wash over her.

Afterwards, she treated her skin to the expensive body lotion that Josh liked. Then she carefully dried her hair until it looked like a length of glossy dark silk, and applied her make-up. Finally she headed for the bedroom to dress, changing the melancholy Chopin Nocturnes for something a little funkier on her way through the sitting room.

She selected her underwear with care. A black Tactel underwired bra with delicate lace trim and matching pants. Sheer black lace-topped stay-ups. High red ankle-strapped heels. Her dress was already laid out on the bed. She'd seen it in the Brown Thomas sale earlier in the year, and on looking at the price tag had decided that it wasn't worth her while trying it on. She simply couldn't afford it – even at its reduced price.

But when she'd described it to Josh over lunch in the Morrison he'd insisted that she go back to the shop and try it. When she'd emerged from the changing cubicle he'd told her that if she paid half, he would pay the balance. She had thrown her arms around him and kissed him right there on the shop floor, and he'd kissed her back, sliding a hand down the red silk jersey that clung to her flank. 'Put it on when we get home,' he'd said.

'But we're not going anywhere tonight,' she'd replied in surprise.

'That's what I mean,' Josh had said.

She slid it over her head now and looked at her reflection in the full-length cheval glass. It was a sensational dress. It was floor length – lean and sleeveless with a low-cut back and a slashed hem. It was spare, it was elegant, and above all it was sexy. She had to admit that she looked good tonight. Streamlined.

As a finishing touch she took the gold locket Josh had given her out of her jewellery case. Then she looked at the clock on her bedside table. It was five past eight. The doorbell rang.

'Hi! It's me!' Maeve's voice came over the intercom. Maddie pressed the buzzer and opened the door to her apartment a minute later to find her cousin standing behind an enormous confection of gold cellophane topped with a spotty blue bow.

'It's an African fertility god,' she said. 'I found it in Mother Redcap's this morning. It's got the most enormous willy.'

'Well, it's not staying in my flat,' said Maddie with feeling, heading towards the kitchen. 'I'm not planning on getting pregnant right now.'

'Am I the first?' Maeve deposited Josh's birthday present on the windowsill.

'Yeah. So enjoy the calm before the storm. What'll you have to drink?'

'Champagne?' hazarded Maeve.

'Be my guest.' With a flourish, Maddie produced a bottle from the fridge. 'Where's Jacqueline?'

'Parking the car. We'll taxi home. Where's Josh?'

'He said something about meeting up with Baz in Daly's.'

Maddie popped the cork and sloshed champagne into a glass for Maeve.

'Baz? I didn't think you liked that geezer. What made you invite him?'

'I don't like him. Josh invited him.' She sent Maeve a resigned look. 'Well – it *is* his party after all.'

'And he'll cry if he wants to.'

The phone and the doorbell rang simultaneously.

'I'll get the door.' Maeve gulped back a mouthful of champagne, then set down her glass and disappeared into the hall.

Maddie picked up the phone.

'Hi, darling.' Josh's voice came rather indistinctly through the receiver. 'Listen – I'm sorry. I've been delayed. Hell – this phone is breaking up. Let me take you outside.' More indistinct muttering before he came back on again. Maddie started to twist her hair around her index finger. 'Ah – that's better. Sorry about this, darling. I'll get to you as soon as I can, OK?'

'Where are you?'

'Daly's. And Baz has just put another pint in front of me. I'm sorry, darling. You know how difficult he is to say "no" to.'

I bet you didn't even try, thought Maddie. She didn't say it.

'So what time do you think you'll be here?' Maeve had come back into the room. There was a sound of approaching laughter from the hall beyond the front door.

'Soon.' She could hear laughter down the phone, too, and then there was a crash. 'Fuck,' said Josh. 'Baz is in serious party mode tonight. I'd better get back to him.'

'Please don't be too late, Josh. I went to a lot of trouble to organize this party for you.'

'Don't sound so pissed off, darling. I'll sink this pint as fast as I can and then I'll come straight over. Half an hour max.'

Maddie looked at her watch. 'Around half-past?'

'Gotcha. Love you. Catch you later.'

Maddie was still twisting her hair when she put

the phone down. She tried to avoid Maeve's eyes, and then gave up.

'Josh?' asked her cousin, sounding careful.

'Yeah. He's running late.' Maddie didn't feel like elaborating.

The doorbell rang again. She bit her lip, got to her feet and went to answer it.

*   *   *

The party kicked in around nine o'clock and Josh and Baz arrived some time later. Maddie hadn't bothered to check her watch once half-past eight had come and gone.

'Sweetheart! I'm sorry I'm late.' Maddie's annoyance with him evaporated when he finally arrived at the door with a smile like a guilty schoolboy and the biggest bunch of yellow roses she had ever seen in her life. There must have been at least forty of them.

'Oh, Josh – they're gorgeous!' She buried her face in them, inhaling deeply before realizing that these roses – like the ones she'd positioned beneath her Dufy print – had no perfume. 'I'll have to put them in a bucket – I've no vases left.'

Josh caught her up in his arms and gave her one of his expert, lingering kisses. From the sitting room behind her came a raucous remark and then someone started up a chorus of 'Happy Birthday to You'. Josh looked down at her with a wicked glint in his eyes. 'You look good enough to eat,' he said. 'I can't wait to get that dress off. Where's the champagne?'

'I've a special bottle for you in the kitchen. Vintage Veuve Clicquot. Don't let anyone else know or they'll all want to have some.'

'They probably wouldn't be able to tell the difference between vintage and non.' Josh followed her into the kitchen. 'Hi, gorgeous,' he said as Maeve turned round from the fridge with a bottle of champagne in her hand.

'Hi, Josh – happy birthday,' she replied, kissing him lightly on the cheek.

'You can do better than that, darling. Wow wow wow – you are looking *good*, Maeve!' Josh pulled her closer and started to nuzzle her neck. Maddie began twisting her hair again.

'Josh?' asked Maeve when she finally managed to disengage herself. 'You and Baz are great mates, aren't you?'

'Sure we are,' said Josh.

'Are you such great mates that you'd allow him to do to you what you just did to me?'

'Ow – Jesus, Maeve! That's fucking gross!'

Maeve gave him a sweet smile. 'Enough said, then?' She turned to Maddie. 'Is it OK to open another bottle?'

'Yeah, sure – but check out the bottom drawer of the fridge.' Maddie went to fetch her special John Rocha champagne flutes from the cupboard. 'There's a really excellent bottle in there. You'll let

133

Maeve have a glass of your Veuve Clicquot, won't you, Josh?'

'But of course. The star of Sara Lennox's show deserves only the best.' Josh's eyes travelled up and down Maeve's body, and Maddie knew by his salacious smile that he was thinking about the photograph he'd seen at the exhibition opening, the photograph he thought he was getting as his birthday present.

'Thanks,' said Maeve briefly. She indicated the bottle she was holding. 'But I'll stick to this, Maddie, and let you two share the special stuff.' There was a sudden rather awkward silence. Then Maeve said: 'I'll go and find Jacqueline. She's going to want to start heating whatever needs to be heated.'

'Jesus,' said Josh in an undertone, eyeing Maeve's ass as she walked out the door. 'I could heat you up, darling. Better than your lesbian pal, that's for sure.'

'I wish you wouldn't say things like that, Josh,' said Maddie, trying to adopt a light tone.

'Sorry, sweetheart. I was just thinking about that photograph. It mightn't be such a good idea to give it to me, you know. I'm not sure Jacqueline would like the idea of her girlfriend's nude portrait hanging on my bedroom wall. Where is it, by the way – and when am I going to see it?'

'It's in the bedroom – and you're not allowed to see it till the morning,' said Maddie with authority. 'It's not your birthday yet.'

'Aw, shucks, Mads,' said Josh, giving her his schoolboy look again. 'Can't I even have a sneak preview?'

'No,' said Maddie. 'It's all wrapped up. Now – open this,' she said. She was just about to hand him the bottle of champagne when the kitchen door opened and Baz crashed through.

'Get your ass out here at once, buddy,' he said. 'Vanessa from Reflex has just arrived and she's wearing something practically topless.'

'No shit!' said Josh, making a beeline for the door. 'She's got the most amazing tits I've ever seen!'

Maddie remained standing in the middle of the kitchen floor with the unopened bottle of champagne in her hand. After a minute or two she pulled the cork, poured fizz into one of her beautiful crystal flutes, and knocked it back.

*　　*　　*

Much later, after midnight, Josh wandered unsteadily into the sitting room with a big grin on his face. He wove his way through the party into the centre of the room, holding something behind his back and then he looked over at Maddie, who was sitting on the couch talking to Maeve. Maddie smiled at him, and he smiled back with raised eyebrows. The raised eyebrows were more eloquent than any words. They said: 'Guess what I'm going to do next', and Maddie felt a

135

sudden ominous rush of apprehension. She knew what he had concealed behind his back before he held it up.

Josh gave a loud cough to attract attention, and someone turned down the music. 'Ladies and gentlemen,' he said. 'My gorgeous bedfellow, Ms Maddie Godard, has bought me something very special for my birthday. Would you all like to see what it is?'

Maddie got up from the couch, feeling drenched with horror. 'Josh – you promised you'd wait till tomorrow!'

'But I'm a good boy, darling, and I keep my promises.' He sniffed twice, loudly. 'Anyway it *is* tomorrow, sweetheart. It's twenty minutes past twelve and it is now officially my birthday.'

This pronouncement met with a fanfare of drunken cheers and another round of 'Happy Birthday to You'. Maddie crossed the room to where Josh was conducting the song.

'Darling,' she said. 'Please don't—'

Josh leaned towards her and kissed her neck. 'Come off it, Maddie,' he said in her ear. 'Maeve won't mind. Anyone who visited the Demeter Gallery will already have seen it.'

'You don't understand, Josh. It's not what you think. It's—'

'And you know what exhibitionists actresses are,' he continued. He wasn't listening to her. 'She'll probably be secretly delighted.'

'Happy Birthday to You' had petered out, and

Josh's audience of party guests were looking at him in expectant silence.

'Josh . . .' began Maddie. What in hell's name could she say?

He smiled down at her. Then he held the parcel aloft with the aplomb of a showman. Slowly, very slowly, he began to strip off the green-marbled wrapping paper. A layer of bubblewrap was revealed.

'Josh . . .' said Maddie again. Then she bit her lip. She'd landed herself in it – there was nothing she could do. Taking a deep breath, she walked back across the room, trying to steel herself for what was to come. She resumed her seat beside Maeve with outward dignity, but inside she was stewing with embarrassment.

'Save me the bubblewrap, will you, Josh?' said Vanessa from Reflex. 'I love popping it.'

'I bet you do, sweetie,' returned Josh with a smile which Maddie knew he thought was urbane. It actually looked like a leer. He was very, very drunk.

He slid his finger under a strip of sellotape and loosened one seam of the opaque plastic covering. Then he ran his hands over it in a leisurely caress until he found another seam. This time he picked at the edge of the sellotape with his nails until he had enough purchase on the tape to peel it away. This he did with maddening deliberation, teasing his audience.

'Oh, come on, Josh. What are you doing?' said Jacqueline. 'We're dying to see it.'

'You've already seen it,' answered Josh, raising a cryptic eyebrow at her and darting a meaningful glance at Maeve. Then he ran his tongue along his upper lip in a manner that was unmistakably carnal as he continued his unveiling of the portrait. He trailed a finger along the third and last strip of sellotape. Once again he found the edge with his nails, and then he paused to survey the expectant faces around the room, letting his gaze linger with a smile on Maddie. She dropped her eyes.

'Don't be upset, darling,' he said gently, and then he tore away the last shred of sellotape with a flourish. The bubblewrap slid to the floor with a sighing sound and Josh held the portrait aloft again, his demeanour even more ostentatiously theatrical. He was so confident he knew who the subject of the photograph was that he didn't even bother to glance at it.

The faces of the guests all looked up.

'*Wow!*' said Baz.

Maeve was the first to speak. 'Oh Maddie – it's beautiful!' she said.

'It's a Sara Lennox, isn't it?' remarked someone else.

'Stunning.' Another voice.

'Gorgeous.'

'Astonishing.'

'Do you mind if I take a closer look, Josh?' asked Maeve.

Josh moved across the floor to her, handed over

the portrait and then leaned back against the dining table, an amused smile playing around his mouth. There was a beat or two as Jacqueline moved to sit on the arm of the couch so that she too could study the photograph. Other guests were craning their necks to get a better look, and there was murmur after murmur of approval.

'It's really weird,' said Jacqueline. 'It's almost like looking at a mirror image of the original!'

Maddie remembered that Sara Lennox had used the very same words. 'Sara described them as companion-pieces,' she explained.

'What a lovely idea!' said another voice behind Maddie. She was beginning to breathe again, feeling her initial embarrassment recede. People were still making appreciative noises, but she sensed that – with the exception of Baz – there was nothing prurient about their interest. 'I'll let you have a copy, Maeve, if you like. She sent me two extra prints.'

'Don't you have your own copy, Maeve?' asked Josh. He was still leaning up against the table, assessing the reaction to his birthday present.

'Well – yes, but it would be lovely to have one of Maddie to keep it company.'

'What are you talking about?' said Josh blankly.

Quick as a flash, Maeve turned to Maddie. 'Doesn't he know?' she said, keeping the pitch of her voice very low. 'I thought you would have warned him before he opened it in public.'

'I didn't get a chance,' replied Maddie in an

equally low voice. 'I tried to, but he wouldn't let me explain. He wasn't meant to open it till the morning.'

'What are you two witches muttering about?' said Josh, with a rather hesitant laugh.

Maddie felt a flash of guilt that Josh was the only member of the entire company who was unenlightened as to the identity of the woman in the portrait. 'I tried to warn you earlier, Josh,' she said, adopting an apologetic tone. 'I *did* try. The photograph isn't of Maeve. It's of me.'

An expression of uncertainty crossed Josh's face, and then he walked over and took the portrait from Maeve, holding it at arm's length and putting his head on one side. For an instant he looked like a little boy who'd been cheated of something, and then his eyes narrowed and he didn't look like a little boy any more.

'Very nice.' His voice had a hard edge. 'Very nice indeed, Mads. You could try posing for *Hustler* next.' There was something oddly formal in the way he positioned the portrait, leaning it up against the wall with its back faced firmly to the room.

There was a moment of absolute silence. Then somebody turned the volume on the CD player up very loud, and Radiohead booted in. It had to be the most welcome blast of noise ever heard at a birthday party.

*   *   *

For most of the rest of the night Josh studiously ignored Maddie, and while she was equally careful to avoid him she tried not to feel too put out. She knew he would thaw eventually. He always did.

Some time in the early hours of the morning the party slid past its best-before date. Since the unveiling of the portrait the evening had been rather strained. Everyone had made a huge effort to look as if they were enjoying themselves, but it was pretty obvious that the enjoyment was forced, and a large proportion of the guests had made their excuses and left shortly after Josh's display of controlled anger.

Now only a few stragglers were left, and the atmosphere had got vaguely surreal. A Fifties clockwork toy train track had been set up in the middle of the room. Someone had given it to Josh for his birthday, and Baz and Vanessa from Reflex were running two tin trains round and round on it, filling them with cargoes of chocolate-covered coffee beans and deliberately staging crashes. Josh was sitting between Maeve and Jacqueline on the couch with his arms around their shoulders, looking lugubrious and talking non-stop into Maeve's ear. He had stuck a yellow rose in his lapel. Jacqueline was asleep. Nuala from accounts was looking through the CD rack, playing Edith Piaf too loudly and singing along with 'La Vie en Rose' and Dim Sum Jim the Account Director was regaling Maddie with further tales of his victories at the bridge table, and offering to teach her the rudiments of the game. When Maddie realized she was giving his proposal serious consideration, she came to the conclusion that she had drunk far too much and that it was time for everyone to go home.

Taxis were ordered and last drinks knocked back. As Maddie went into her bedroom to fetch people's coats she remembered that she'd volunteered to let Maeve have one of her spare Sara Lennox prints.

She unlocked the drawer where she kept her most precious and private things, located the padded envelope which contained the photographs, and returned to the sitting room, extracting a print from the envelope as she went.

'For you, Maeve. They do say that imitation is the sincerest form of flattery.' Maddie kissed her cousin on the cheek. 'By the way,' she added in an undertone, 'I saw Josh coming on to you earlier. I hope he wasn't being obnoxious.'

'Not at all. He was telling me how much he loved you.'

Maddie looked over at Josh, who was lying back with his feet up on the arm of the couch. She badly wanted to be reconciled with him before they went to bed. She tried a smile out on him, and to her relief he smiled back, raising his wineglass at her. Then he extracted the yellow rose from his lapel, kissed it, and lobbed it in her direction. She caught it and, laughing, stuck it in her hair.

Just then Vanessa from Reflex reeled towards

142

the door of the flat supporting Baz, who had his arm slung round her. 'I think Baz badly needs a breath of fresh air,' she said. 'I'm going to try and get him downstairs. We'll wait for the taxi on the street.'

'Are you sharing one?' asked Maddie.

'Yes,' replied Vanessa, with a meaningful smile.

Maddie didn't envy her. 'I'll help you,' she said, as Baz tripped over the train track and lurched floorward. She helped Vanessa lift him to his feet. Each of them tucked a shoulder under his arms to hold him up, and somehow managed to manoeuvre him out through the hall door and into the lift. He'd got very maudlin, and wasn't making much sense.

The taxis were already waiting by the side of the road when they came out, and the drivers exchanged glances, each obviously hoping that the other would be landed with this particular fare. Vanessa climbed into a taxi beside Baz, pushing him along the back seat in an effort to make room for herself. Maddie wondered how on earth the woman could bring herself to go home with someone so wasted, and then she realized that Josh probably wasn't in too dissimilar a state.

Nuala and Jim emerged onto the pavement and got into the second cab, each demanding to be allowed to pay the bill.

'I live further away than you. I should pay it.'

'But I want to make sure you get home safely first. I *insist* on paying.'

'No, no – that's not fair. We should . . .' The door shut behind them and they were off.

Maddie stayed on the pavement waiting for the third cab to pull up, hopping a little from foot to foot to keep warm and feeling a bit incongruous in her silk jersey gown. A light drizzle had started. When the cab arrived she ran back into the lobby of her apartment building, rubbing her goose-bumpy arms. Maeve and Jacqueline were just coming out of the lift.

'Your taxi's here,' she called. 'Hold the lift for me.' Her cousin obligingly kept her finger on the button and the three women exchanged perfunctory embraces.

'Get back up there at once, Maddie – you're shivering,' said Jacqueline. 'Good night – and thanks for the party.'

'Thanks for your help, Jacqueline. I couldn't have done it without you. I'd have been wired to the moon with stress.'

'Give me a ring soon, Maddie, won't you?' said Maeve.

'Sure. And send me a postcard if you do decide to go to – what's the name of that French village again?'

'Saint-Géyroux.'

'Saint-Géyroux.'

'I'll do that,' said Maeve. Then: 'Take care, Maddie,' she added as the lift doors slid silently shut.

Maddie checked her reflection in the mirrored

wall as the lift ascended. There was a smudge of mascara under her left eye, so she wet a finger with her tongue and gave it a rub, then ran her fingers through her hair, shaking away the sleekness to make it look sexier. As an after-thought, she repositioned the yellow rose in her cleavage. The lift announced its arrival on her floor with a gentle chime, and then she was hurrying down the corridor. By the time she arrived in the hallway of her flat she was slightly out of breath. She shut the hall door behind her, registering abstractedly that the smell of cigarette smoke hadn't managed to smother the intense perfume of lilies that still pervaded the place.

'Hi darling,' she said. 'Sorry to have taken so long. Baz was a bit of a handful.' She walked into the sitting room and stopped dead. Josh's back was to her, and laid out on the dining table in a neat row were the photographs that Sara Lennox had taken of her messing about on the beach.

Josh turned and looked at her with dead eyes. 'You fucking whore,' he said.

Chapter Seven

Maddie said nothing. She stood frozen in the doorway, staring at Josh. He took a step towards her. 'You fucking whore,' he said again. Without breaking eye contact he reached out a hand and slid one of the photographs off the table. It was the one Sara had taken of her and Sam as he'd wrapped the robe around her shoulders at the end of the shoot. Josh held it up. 'Who's the stud?' he asked. 'Was he any good?'

Maddie's instinct told her to stay calm. She adopted as casual a posture as her tense limbs would allow her, folding her arms and leaning against the door jamb. 'Josh. Don't be absurd. Sam is Sara Lennox's assistant.' She tried to make her tone sound reasonable, but she was aware that a careful note had crept into her voice.

'He's a good-looking boy.' Josh turned the photograph around so that he could study it. 'A good-looking boy with a cushy job.' He looked back at Maddie. 'I'd have thought that a female photographer who specializes in portraits of naked women would have a female assistant?'

'Sam is Sara's nephew. She took him on as a favour.'

'What a lucky lad. I imagine there are a lot of perks to that job. Like getting to screw his aunt's models.' Josh gave an unpleasant laugh.

'Don't be ridiculous, Josh.'

'I'm not being ridiculous, Maddie. Baz is always going on about how he gets to screw the models when he's off on photo-shoots with his agency. Sampling the merchandise, he calls it. Funnily enough, I've never done it. I had too much respect for you to be unfaithful. Pity it's not reciprocated.'

'Josh—'

'Shut up.'

There was something about the way he said it that made her do just that. He picked up another photograph. 'This is a nice shot.' Josh held up the photograph of Maddie at the water's edge, twirling the long strand of seaweed above her head. 'Look how prominent your nipples are, darling. You were obviously in a state of considerable sexual arousal.'

'That's nonsense, Josh. I was freezing cold. It was the end of the session and I'd spent a long time in the water.'

'If you were freezing cold, my love, why didn't you get straight into your robe? What made you decide to prance around showing yourself off after the session was finished? How many other men were hanging around, getting an eyeful?'

'There was nobody on the beach apart from me and Sara and Sam.'

'Oh? Who's this then?' He held up the third photograph.

'Who?'

'The geezer on the dunes?'

Maddie swallowed. 'Oh – that was – that was just some bloke jogging.'

'You look as if you're having fun. You must have thought it was a hilarious wheeze to flaunt yourself stark naked in front of a complete stranger.'

'Look – I know it seems silly now, but it was just – I was just feeling a bit – well, *juvenile*, you know? It's kind of difficult to explain.' She looked at Josh's face. It wasn't going to be just difficult to explain. She had a feeling it was going to be impossible.

'You're looking very defensive, Maddie.' Josh put the photographs down very carefully on the table and started moving towards her. 'Just take a look at your body language. Arms and legs crossed like that is a real giveaway, darling. I think you're as guilty as hell. I think you're a fucking whore.'

Maddie's arms went up as Josh's fist smashed into her left cheekbone.

*   *   *

Some time later she found herself on the street. It was raining and the pavement was like glass, so she was finding it difficult to run. Her nose was bleeding and she was trying to stem it by keeping her head back and wiping the blood away from time to time using the back of her hand. Her right shoe was missing and the leather sole on the remaining one kept skidding on the wet concrete. As she hobbled along she doubled over awkwardly to the left, trying to reach down and undo the strap which was wound about her ankle. If she got rid of her shoe she might find it easier to run. It was proving difficult, but she'd lose headway if she had to stop to take the shoe off. She had to keep going. She came off her heel and fell on the slippery footpath, landing heavily on her coccyx. She didn't feel any pain. She just hauled herself to her feet and stumbled on. The shoe had come away from her foot now, but its slender leather strap was still knotted round her ankle, so that it trailed after her at every step she took.

She was soaking wet. Her hair was plastered to her face and that, along with the rain in her eyes, made it difficult to see where she was going. Her red dress was flapping around her legs. She grabbed hold of the sodden hem and bunched it up around her hips, noticing as she did that there was blood smeared on her thighs above the line of her stay-ups.

She was vaguely aware that it was the grey hour before dawn – the pale light rimming the horizon told her that. That meant she didn't have much time to get herself ready for work, but she knew she had to see Maeve first.

A car pulled up on her right. For some reason she thought it might be Josh even though he didn't drive a Ford, so she kept on running. The driver had rolled down the passenger window and was leaning across, mouthing something she couldn't make out as he cruised slowly along beside her. She finally allowed herself to look him in the face. It wasn't Josh, it was a taxi driver.

'Stop, love. Get in the car.' She came to a halt and stood there staring at him, water running in rivulets down her face, blood pumping from her nose. Her breath was coming in short, staccato gasps. 'Come on, love. I'm not going to hurt you. I want to help.'

'I can't get in,' she said with what seemed to be crystal-clear logic. 'I don't have any money on me.'

'I don't want your money, love. Get in. I'm taking you to Outpatients.'

'No,' said Maddie. 'I don't need to go to hospital. I want to go to my cousin Maeve's.'

'You need to see a doctor, love. You're hurt.'

Maddie started to cry. In fact she'd been crying since she hit the street – she just hadn't realized it till then. 'Please don't take me to the hospital,' she sobbed. 'I'm fine, really I am. I probably look worse than I am. Nosebleeds always look bad, don't they? Please take me to Maeve's.'

The taxi driver heaved a sigh. 'Another fucking domestic,' he said. 'OK. I'll take you to your cousin Maeve. Get in.'

He threw open the passenger door and Maddie crawled into the seat beside him. She noticed with some surprise that she had started to shake, and she was finding it impossible to stop. 'Thank you,' she said to the driver. 'I'll ask Maeve to cover the fare.'

'Like I said – I don't want money for this ride, darlin'.' He handed her a box of tissues and then released the handbrake. 'Here – better try cleaning yourself up a bit.'

Maddie helped herself to a handful of tissues and held them against her nose, leaning her head back against the headrest and breathing through her mouth. She felt blood slide down the back of her throat and very nearly retched. Keeping the wad of tissues clamped over her nostrils, she took some more from the box and pressed them tentatively against her left cheek. The pain she felt at the contact frightened her. She dropped the tissues to her lap, carefully keeping her eyes averted. She didn't want to look at them.

'Now, love,' said the taxi driver, putting the car into gear. 'Tell me where Maeve lives.'

*   *   *

It was a while before anyone came to the door. The taxi driver waited with Maddie on the door-step until Maeve finally appeared, tying the sash on her kimono and looking as though she was sleep-walking. 'What's going on?' she said. Then she registered the state Maddie was in. 'Maddie? Jesus Christ – Jesus Christ – what happened to you?' Maddie suddenly lost her balance and fell heavily against her cousin. Maeve wrapped her arms around her and shot the taxi driver an urgent look of enquiry over Maddie's shoulder.

'I picked her up on Clanbrassil Street. I wanted to take her to Outpatients, but she wasn't having any of it.' He took a card out of his pocket and scribbled something on it. 'Pat O'Connor's the name. Give me a shout if you need a witness. I'd be glad to help.'

'Thanks. That's decent of you,' said Maeve, taking the card. 'I'd better get her inside. Jacqueline!' she shouted over her shoulder. 'Jacqueline! Come here quickly – I need your help.'

'I've seen a lot of nasty stuff in my time,' said the taxi driver as he got back into his cab. 'But you don't ever get used to it. Whoever did that to her is some evil bastard. Take care of her.' He pulled away from the kerb as Jacqueline came running down the stairs.

'What the hell?' she said. 'Is it Maddie?'

'Yes. Help me get her into the sitting room, then quickly run and get towels and a duvet.'

'Hi, Jacqueline.' Maddie looked up at her with an effort, and noticed that Jacqueline sucked in her breath.

'Fuck,' she whispered. 'Shouldn't she be in hospital?'

'She wouldn't go, apparently. Let's just get her cleaned up and then we'll call Doctor Carr.'

'Please – no. Don't call a doctor,' said Maddie. Her voice in her own ears sounded very far away.

'I'll be all right. I'll have a bath and then I'll be all right.'

Jacqueline and Maeve together supported her the way she and somebody – who? It didn't matter – had supported Baz down the hallway of her apartment block earlier. Earlier? It felt like a lifetime ago . . .

They crossed into the sitting room, and she heard herself make a whimpering sound as the two women laid her down on the couch.

Jacqueline dropped a kiss on her cheek. 'You'll be OK, Maddie. I'll run you a bath now and bring you some tea, OK?'

'Thanks, Jacqueline. I'm sorry to be such a nuisance.'

'Jesus Christ, Maddie. You're not a nuisance. Jesus Christ,' she repeated as, shaking her head, she left the room.

Maeve was kneeling by the couch. She had taken one of Maddie's hands in hers and was stroking her forehead with the other, pushing tangles of hair back from her face. 'Here,' she said, handing her a fresh handful of tissues. Maddie made an apologetic face and handed Maeve the bloody wodge that she'd kept pressed against her nose since getting into the taxi.

'What happened, Maddie? Was it Josh?'

Maddie couldn't trust herself to speak. She shut her eyes and a tear appeared. It hung on her lashes for an instant and then rolled down her cheek, making way for another, and another. She cried silently for a minute or two while Maeve went on stroking her forehead, making little murmuring noises of reassurance. She heard Jacqueline come back into the room, and then she felt a duvet being wrapped around her. She opened her eyes and tried to sit up.

'Take it easy, Maddie. Stay where you are.' Maeve took a towel and rubbed gently at Maddie's hair. 'Bring a basin of warm water, Jacqueline, will you?' she said in a calm, very gentle voice. 'And TCP and cotton wool. Is the kettle on?'

'Yes. And the bath's running.'

'I'm not sure about the bath.'

'What? What do you mean?'

Maeve gave her a significant look as she backed out the door. 'Just bring the stuff. I'll talk to you in a minute.'

Under the duvet Maddie was shivering. 'There's quite a lot of blood,' she said. 'I don't want your beautiful white duvet cover to get marked.'

'I don't give a toss about the duvet cover, Maddie. Now just lie back and try and get warm.' Maeve carried on gently towelling Maddie's hair in silence for a while. Then: 'It was Josh, wasn't it?' she said again.

Maddie looked away.

'Wasn't it?' Maeve's voice was very quiet. 'There's no point in pretending it wasn't, Maddie. You didn't get like that from falling downstairs.'

Maddie nodded.

'OK. Good girl. Here's Jacqueline with some tea. Can you manage to sit up just a little?'

Maddie did as she was told, shifting herself up so that she was leaning against the arm of the couch. She felt like an old woman. She took a look at the tissues she'd used to mop up the blood from her nose. They were spotted with crimson, but they weren't saturated. The bleeding seemed to have been stemmed.

'Take these, sweetheart.' Jacqueline handed her a couple of paracetamol and a glass of water. She swallowed the tablets with an effort. Then Jacqueline put the mug of tea between Maddie's hands.

'It's not too hot for you, is it?' she asked.

'No,' she said, making a face. 'But it's got sugar in. I don't take sugar.'

'Drink it,' said Maeve. 'It'll do you good.'

Obediently Maddie took another couple of sips. Jacqueline had gone out of the room and returned now with a basin of water and a roll of cotton wool. There was a strong smell of TCP. 'I'll make up the futon in the spare room,' she said. 'Feeling any better?' Maddie knew she was trying hard to sound encouraging.

'Yes, thanks,' she lied for her benefit. 'All I need now is a bath.' She saw the two women exchange another look as Jacqueline went back out through the door.

Maeve switched on a table lamp before dipping a hank of cotton wool into the water and squeezing it out. The sound of the water trickling back into the basin was oddly comforting.

'This may sting a little. There now – hold still. Brave girl,' Maeve crooned, as she carefully dabbed at the wound on Maddie's cheekbone.

Maddie flinched involuntarily, then gave a shaky laugh. 'You sound just like my mother used to,' she said. She was starting to ache all over. Until now she hadn't been conscious of her physical state – her body had just been a machine that had performed a useful function in getting her out of a dangerous situation. But the anaesthetic of adrenalin was starting to wear off, and she felt as if her nerve endings were being reawakened one by one. She was aware that her left eye had closed over, and there was a taste of blood in her mouth. Pain flared as Maeve continued to gently wipe her cheek, and Maddie bit her lip.

'I'm sorry,' said Maeve. 'I know the painkillers won't have kicked in yet. You can swear at me if you like.' She helped herself to a fresh swab of cotton wool, dropping the used one on the damp towel by her knees. Maddie could see bright traces of red on it. 'Where else do you hurt, Maddie?' asked Maeve. 'Do you think you're bleeding any-where else?'

'I think I must have bitten inside my cheek. There's a taste of blood in my mouth.'

'Open up.' Maeve positioned the table lamp so that it shone into Maddie's mouth. She squinted and leaned in close, murmuring instructions to

Maddie to angle her head to the left and then to the right. 'Nothing too serious there, I don't think. And cuts on the inside of the mouth heal quite quickly. Anywhere else we might find blood?' Maeve's voice sounded almost too casual as she resumed her gentle cleaning-up operation on the area around Maddie's left eye.

Maddie looked down at her hands and started pleating the pristine white cotton of the duvet cover. 'I think there might be some on my legs.'

'OK. I'll have a look. The cut on your cheek's cleaned up nicely. I still think it's a good idea to call the doctor, though. You might need a stitch or two.'

'No. Please.'

Maeve worked on in silence for a minute. Then she said: 'Whereabouts are the cuts on your legs, Maddie? Are they on your thighs?' Her delivery of the question seemed offhand, but Maddie noticed that a muscle in her cousin's jaw was working, and that she seemed to be concentrating very hard on calculating how much cotton wool to tear off the roll.

'Yes.'

'Inside or outside?'

'Inside. I think.'

Maeve set down the roll of cotton wool. 'Maddie,' she said, very quietly. 'Did Josh rape you?'

Maddie's eyes went very wide as she looked at her cousin. 'No! Josh would never rape me, Maeve!'

Maeve inclined her head. 'He beat you, didn't he?'

'That – that was my fault, really. He found some rather – dodgy – photographs that I'd been stupid enough to leave lying around. It was hard for him – he jumped to conclusions, lost his rag. You know the way he can fly off the handle. He just couldn't hack it. He thought I'd—' Maddie rubbed at the place on her right eye where a tic had started. 'He thought I'd been unfaithful to him.'

'Jesus, Maddie! That doesn't give any man the licence to beat a woman.'

'He loves me so much, Maeve. He couldn't bear the thought of me being with another man. He just went berserk . . .' Then Maddie put her face in her hands and started to sob.

'Sh, sh. There, there.' Maeve took her cousin in her arms and started to rock her to and fro. 'You can tell me about it later. There, now. Cry all you like.'

Maddie let the tears come without bothering to wipe them away. Her head felt as heavy as a stone as she laid it against Maeve's shoulder, and her voice didn't sound like her own. It sounded like the keening of a woman at a rural funeral. She could feel Maeve's hand stroking her hair, and that and the rhythmic rocking calmed her after a while. Her great, racking sobs became sporadic, involuntary shudders, but she still didn't raise her head. Beneath her right cheek she could feel that the thin silk of Maeve's kimono was saturated with tears.

'Maddie.' Maeve's rocking slowed and then finally came to a halt. 'Maddie. I'd like to have a look at your legs. I know you probably just want to go to sleep, but I think it's important that I clean up any other cuts you may have, OK?'

'OK.' Maddie stayed as she was for a beat or two longer, and then she made a huge effort. She opened her eyes and slowly sat up straight. Maeve lifted the duvet and Maddie gave a shiver, wrapping her arms around her knees and hugging herself for warmth.

'We'd better get you out of that wet dress,' said Maeve. 'We don't want pneumonia setting in as well as everything else.' Very carefully she slid the red sheath up above Maddie's knees and over her thighs. 'Can you lift your bum for me, sweetheart?' she said. Maddie raised her hips and Maeve pulled the dress up as far as her armpits. 'Arms up,' she instructed. 'Good girl – that's the way.' Maddie was glad she couldn't see Maeve's face as the dress went over her head. She could imagine the horror in her eyes as they took in the evidence of Josh's assault.

Maeve stood up briskly, threw the dress over the back of the couch and then wrapped the duvet round Maddie's shoulders. 'I'll just have a quick word with Jacqueline. I'll be back in a sec. More tea?'

Maddie shook her head. 'No thanks.' She curled herself into a foetal position on the couch, pulling the duvet tightly around her, and shut her eyes again. Bright spots danced against her closed eyelids and then formed themselves into wavy shapes. She could hear Maeve and Jacqueline talking in low voices outside the door, but couldn't make out what they were saying.

Then Maeve was in the room again. 'Maddie? Can you straighten your legs out for me now?'

Maddie uncurled herself and lay back on the couch. She felt Maeve untie the ankle strap on her shoe and gently slide her stockings down her legs, and then she heard the splosh of water from the basin. The wet cotton wool was cool on her thigh. Maeve worked on the tender skin in silence for a minute or two, and then she said: 'Well, that's that cleaned up.' She sat back on her heels and looked at Maddie. Her gaze was serious and direct. 'I'm going to have to ask you again, Maddie. Did Josh rape you?'

'No! He – we made love.'

'Before or after he beat you up?'

Maddie's voice was very small. 'After.'

'So Josh beat you up and then had sex with you?'

'Yes.'

'And it was consensual? You wanted it as well?'

'Well, not really – but Josh was so upset. He didn't really know what he was doing.'

Maeve bit her lip. 'Look, Maddie – I know this is difficult for you. It's difficult for me, too.' She held up a swab of cotton wool with a rust-coloured stain on it. 'This blood didn't come from a wound on

160

your leg, Maddie. I think it's from an internal tear. That's why I think Josh raped you.'

Maddie started pleating the duvet cover again. She looked up at Maeve and then looked away. Her gaze fell on the beautiful red dress Josh had part-paid for. She'd have to leave it to be cleaned and mended. 'I'd like to have a bath now, please,' she said.

Maeve took hold of her hands and Maddie stopped pleating the duvet cover. 'Look, Maddie. If Josh did rape you then I don't think it's a good idea to have a bath. It means that you'll be destroying evidence.'

'Evidence? Evidence of what? What are you talking about?'

'Oh, God, Maddie. There's no easy way to say this.' Maeve took a very deep breath. 'If you are going to charge Josh with rape it's a help if you can produce a specimen of his sperm. I know the police say that it's a good idea to avoid bathing if you can help it, until after they've seen you.'

The look Maddie gave Maeve was one of total incomprehension. 'I keep telling you, Maeve. Josh didn't rape me. He made love to me. And when he'd finished he told me over and over again how much he loved me.'

'OK, Maddie. For now you don't want to charge Josh with anything. But you may change your mind. In a day or two you might—'

'I won't change my mind, Maeve. Can I have my bath now please?'

*   *   *

In the white bathroom, Maeve helped Maddie take off her underwear. She didn't comment on the broken bra strap, or the fact that her pants were badly torn, but she could not prevent a sharp intake of breath when she saw the raw, red skin on Maddie's shoulder blades, and the gash on the back of her neck. She topped up the bath that Jacqueline had run with more hot water, and added Radox. Maddie had to lean on her heavily as she stepped into the bath, catching her breath as the hot water made contact with her skin. Very slowly she let herself down into the bath-tub, Maeve still supporting her under her arms, and then gingerly she lay back until she was immersed in water up to her collarbone.

'Here's shampoo, soap, sponge, clean flannel. There's a new toothbrush by the basin, and a comb and hairbrush. Would you like me to stay with you?'

Maddie shook her head.

'Fair enough. There are fresh towels in the airing cupboard. Feel free to help yourself to talc, deodorant, anything you like. You can even spray yourself all over with my Vivienne Westwood.' Maeve gave her a bright smile and then her face crumpled suddenly and she turned towards the door. 'Just call if there's anything else you want – OK?'

'OK, Maeve. Thanks,' replied Maddie as the

bathroom door closed behind her cousin. She could hear Maeve sobbing suddenly, and then there was the sound of footsteps quickly descending the stairs and a door shutting somewhere below.

Maddie lay in the water for a long time without moving, staring at the mass of bubbles drifting in the bath. She imagined that she was floating in a soup made of snow. The foam made a faint fizzing noise as it very gradually subsided around her. She felt warm and weightless and drowsy. She let her eyelids close and felt her breathing becoming slower, more measured.

Suddenly she took in a huge gasp of air and sat bolt upright, sending water slopping over the sides of the bath as its surface tension shattered. She tried to shake the image from her mind, but it persisted, lucid and terrifying. Josh's thumb digging hard into the flesh of her left thigh, his hand pushing at her right knee, parting her legs. The seagrass on the floor rough under her shoulders, burning her skin as he hoisted her hips up to meet him. His breath guttural in her ear and a new, searing pain as his teeth gouged into her shoulder. Fingers. And then the worst pain of all as his penis invaded her.

She looked wildly round the room, resisting the image as forcefully as she could, her breath coming rapidly in shallow little gulps. Standing up in the bath, she saw the cake of soap and the flannel that Maeve had laid out for her. She took the soap and started to rub it hard against her body, wincing when it skidded over her grazes. But it was working. The harder she rubbed and the thicker the lather she worked up, the more the appalling picture receded to the dark place in her mind from where it had emerged uninvited.

Her eyes fell on the basket in which Maeve and Jacqueline kept their cleaning products, and she had a better idea. Stretching out her arm with an effort, she located a bottle of Dettol, unscrewed the cap and poured the liquid liberally into the water. There was a nailbrush on the soap dish. She tested it on the palm of her hand. It was pretty heavy-duty – it would help to do the job.

When she had finished scrubbing herself, she shampooed her hair then turned on the shower attachment and let the water sluice over her raw skin. She thought about turning the dial to cold – she'd have to be wide awake for work soon – but she suspected that even a cold shower would do little to invigorate her. Instead she helped herself to a huge fluffy bath sheet, warm from the airing cupboard, and very slowly patted herself dry, sitting on the lid of the loo. So far she had not once looked at her naked body.

Downstairs the doorbell went. She could hear footsteps in the hall, and then voices – Maeve's and Jacqueline's and the voice of a man. She froze, and remained sitting quite motionless for many minutes. Then someone climbed the stairs and knocked on the bathroom door. 'Maddie? It's Maeve. Can I come in?'

'Sure.'

Maeve came through the door carrying a silk kimono. 'Here,' she said. 'Put this on.'

She held it out, and Maddie was just about to slide her arms into the silk sleeves, when she stepped back, shaking her head and pushing the garment away. 'No, no, Maeve – I can't wear that.'

'Why not?' asked Maeve uncertainly.

'It smells of lilies.'

Her cousin made the connection at once. 'OK – no problem,' she said, draping the kimono over her arm and heading towards the door. 'I'll find something else.'

She returned minutes later with a candlewick dressing gown in a very un-Maeve shade of pink. 'I hope you don't mind wearing this,' she said apologetically. 'Jacqueline's grandmother left it behind that weekend we took her to the races. It's been washed, so it's perfectly clean, but it does have a slight lingering smell of vanilla from whatever scent she uses.'

Maddie managed a smile as Maeve helped her into the robe. The faint smell of vanilla was actually rather comforting.

'Wow – matronly!' said Maeve when together they'd done up the buttons. 'Here's a pair of groovy woolly socks to set off your new look.' Maddie sat back down on the loo seat to put on the socks. Maeve was leaning against the door looking down at her. 'Maddie. Jacqueline rang the Rape Crisis Centre.'

Maddie looked stricken. 'No! Why did she do that? I don't want people interfering—'

'Sh, sh. No-one's going to interfere. She made the call anonymously.' Maddie concentrated on adjusting the sock on her left foot. 'They were very helpful and gave her some good advice. One of the first things they recommended was that you should get medical attention. They advised that you should go to the Sexual Assault Unit in the Rotunda.'

'No. I won't go there.'

'That's what I thought you'd say. That's why I asked my GP to make a house call.'

'I told you I'm OK. I don't need to see a doctor.'

'I know *you* feel you're OK. And you're probably perfectly right. But will you see him for me, please? Just to set *my* mind at rest. I'd never forgive myself if there was any real damage.'

Maddie started to put on the right sock. She noticed that a blood blister was starting to form on her big toe where she must have stubbed it, and that one of her toenails was half hanging off. 'Do you have nail scissors?' she asked. Maeve rummaged in a drawer and extracted a little pair of scissors from a manicure kit. 'You said your GP's a man,' remarked Maddie, delicately clipping at the torn nail.

'Yes – but you needn't be afraid that he'll give you a vaginal examination.' On seeing Maddie flinch, Maeve hurried on. 'I checked that out. They positively don't do that on house calls. He's a lovely guy, Maddie. He was very concerned when I told him what state you were in. Please come down.'

'Maeve?'

'Mm?'

'I want you to promise something. If I see this doctor do you promise that you won't make me go to the Assault Clinic, and you won't make me charge Josh with – anything.'

'I won't make you do anything you don't want to do, Maddie. I promise.'

'All right. I'll see him.' Maddie carefully put the scissors back into the case and clicked it shut.

'Good girl. Then you might manage something to eat before we put you to bed.'

'Bed? Why would I go to bed? It's Monday morning, Maeve – I'll have to go to work soon.' The little manicure case slid off her lap onto the tiles as she held her hands up to her mouth, looking at her cousin with anguish in her eyes. 'Oh, Maeve! What'll I do about work? Josh'll be there and I—'

Maeve dropped to her knees so that her face was on a level with hers. 'Maddie – you can't think about going in to work! You're in no fit state to go anywhere. Listen. Jacqueline's made up the futon for you in the spare room. You're going to need some rest. I'd say it'll be at least a week before you're ready to go back to work, and even then you might not feel up to it. There's going to be a lot of stuff to get sorted. You know there is.'

Maddie averted her eyes. 'It's just that I'd feel more normal if I stuck to routine, you know? I'm not sick after all, I'm just a bit . . . We could say I'd had an accident. That would explain the bruises.'

'Maddie, Maddie. It's not going to happen that way. It won't work. You said it yourself. Josh will be there. I don't think you're in the right state of mind to confront him right now, do you?' Maddie bit her lip. Then she shook her head. 'OK. Let's go downstairs,' said Maeve. 'This won't take long. You'll be tucked up under a duvet in no time.'

*　　　*　　　*

Maeve was right. The doctor was efficient and gentle and kind. He suggested that she go to the Sexual Assault Unit at the Rotunda, but he respected her decision when she told him quite categorically that she didn't want to. He mentioned the morning-after pill, but Maddie assured him that she had her contraception under control and that she had no worries on that score. She had taken her pill at the same time as usual the previous morning when the alarm on her phone had reminded her to do so. The doctor took a look at her grazes and warned her that her bruises – and her black eye – would start to look a lot worse before they got better. Maeve's assurance to him that the vaginal bleeding hadn't been copious and that it had stopped by the time Maddie had got to the house satisfied him that she wasn't in any danger of internal injury, but to be on the safe side he gently palpated her belly. He administered a tetanus injection for the bites and scratches, and patched up the wound on her cheek and another on the back of her neck with Steri-strips.

'Do you think you need a sedative?'

'No.'

'Good. They help in some cases, but generally speaking they just get in the way of you getting on with your life. You might want to come by the surgery in a couple of days just so that I can have another look at you – make sure you're healing nicely? Or you might prefer to speak to my colleague, Fiona Price?'

'Thank you. I might do that.' Maddie knew she wouldn't visit the doctor in his surgery. In fact, she'd probably never see him again.

Doctor Carr started putting instruments back into his case. 'I'm glad the damage isn't as serious as it looked when Maeve and Jacqueline first saw you. You gave them an awful fright. But I don't want to minimize the extent of your trauma. That was a nasty beating and you'll need several days' bed rest. Take it easy for a while. Have you family? Anyone you can stay with?'

'Yes – of course. She's staying here. I'm family,' said Maeve before Maddie had time to answer. How right she was. For some reason, Josh often made reference to the fact that Maeve was the only family she had.

'Will there be somebody around to look after her?' Doctor Carr directed the question at Maeve this time.

'Yes. I'll be around. I'm not working for a while.'

'Maeve!' Maddie was indignant. 'You can't do that! You were hoping to go away to France!'

'Maddie – I want to do it and I'm doing it, OK? Saint-Géyroux can wait.'

'But—'

'Don't waste your energy arguing,' said Maeve as she escorted the doctor from the room.

'Goodbye, Maddie,' he said. 'You'll heal up pretty well, I've no doubt. But don't forget about that check-up.'

'Goodbye, Doctor Carr. Thank you.'

Maeve closed the door behind them, but she didn't quite pull it to. Maddie could hear them talking in the hallway. Their voices were low, and it was difficult to make out what they were saying. Then, very slowly, the door began to swing open. Maddie stood up and moved towards it, making sure that she couldn't be seen from the hall.

'It's good that she's got you to look after her,' Doctor Carr was saying. 'She's going to need a lot of support. Is she likely to press charges?'

'It doesn't look like it. Not right now, anyway.'

'Well – it's on file if she needs it. Do you know the perpetrator?'

'Yes.'

'Does he know where she is?'

There was a beat. 'He might guess, I suppose. He's not a fool.'

'OK. Best to be aware of that.'

'Yes. That's what they said in the Rape Crisis Centre.' Jacqueline's voice joined in. 'They asked if she was safe.'

'Well. She's safe here for now.' The doctor's voice grew fainter as they moved down the hall. 'Try to persuade her to visit me in a day or two. And Rape Crisis has a counselling service if she decides she needs it. She's going to need to talk to someone. Be ready to listen if she decides to talk to you.'

'Of course.'

'She's lucky to have you. Some women have no-one.'

Maddie could hear the front door being opened, and farewells being exchanged. She crossed the sitting room to the sliding doors that led onto Maeve and Jacqueline's little patio garden. It was bright now, and the patio was riotous with hanging baskets and containers. Their cat, Senator David Norris, was sitting snoozing in a bright patch of sunlight, oblivious to the sparrows swinging off the bird feeders, and Jacqueline's transvestite garden gnome was winking up at her, wearing his favourite gold lamé ball gown and smiling broadly under his bushy white beard.

He's not a fool. That's what Maeve had said. She started to replay the conversation she'd just heard.

She's safe here for now. Doctor Carr's voice came back to her. *Rape Crisis has a counselling service . . .*

Why were people still harping on about rape? She stiffened as she suddenly felt Josh's finger-nails scrabbling against her vulva, and, shutting her eyes tight against the horrific image, she pushed it right back into the dark recess of her mind where it belonged.

Instead she tried to remember him as he'd looked when he'd gone to make her a cup of herbal tea. He'd been standing in the kitchen doorway, looking down at her with a stricken expression as she lay on the sitting-room floor. 'I'm sorry I had to slap you,' he'd said. 'But you had it coming, Maddie. You deserved it, and I hope it's taught you a lesson.' Then he'd smiled at her. 'You know I still love you, don't you? Jesus, Maddie, I love you so much. I love you so much it hurts.'

Chapter Eight

Some hours later Maddie was woken by the strident sound of a seagull screeching. The sound was coming from the cast-iron fireplace beside her bed: the bird must be perched on the chimney pot. She was dying to go to the loo, but she knew it would take a massive effort to lift herself off the futon. She lay there listening to the raucous squawks for a while, wondering what was aggravating the gull. Then she eased herself very, very slowly out of the low bed and stood up. She was aching everywhere.

Maeve had given her a big white T-shirt to sleep in. The baggy sleeves came down almost to her elbows, and the hem skimmed her knees. She raised it slowly, gazing dispassionately at the pattern of bruises that mapped her legs. They were really rather beautiful, she thought – like a watercolour that had run after being left out in the rain. What had been the subject of the painting? Flowers – to judge by the colours. Pansies and peonies, maybe, and some dark red roses. They'd turn yellow in a few days. Yellow bruises, yellow roses. Josh had tossed her a yellow rose not long before he'd beaten her – the one she'd tucked into her cleavage. What had Jacqueline said a gift of yellow roses meant? Jealousy. Of course.

Maddie tried a tentative stretch, but her body protested at once, sending urgent signals to her brain to stop, and reminding her that getting to the loo should be her priority. She padded across the landing to the bathroom, suddenly realizing that she hadn't a clue what time it was. She wondered whether Maeve and Jacqueline were still in the house – there wasn't a sound from downstairs.

In the bathroom she peed for what seemed like ages, contracting her muscles to stop the stinging flow from time to time. She needed to take it in small stages – her urine was like acid against her raw flesh. She tried to remember if this was the first time she'd been to the loo since she and Josh had had sex, but the sequence of events since then was blurred and hazy. She helped herself to quantities of paper, sucking in her breath as she wiped herself. Then she carefully washed her hands. She was excruciatingly aware that her image was reflected in the mirror above the basin, and some protective instinct warned her not to look at it. But she found herself obeying the same impulse which had made her inspect the bruising on her legs, and she raised her eyes.

She barely recognized the person looking back at her. Her left eye was a slit in her face. It had closed over almost completely, and the swollen flesh around it had turned an ugly, mottled shade of purple. The Steri-strip on the cheekbone just below her eye seemed to be underlining it for emphasis – **black eye**! Her nose was swollen too, and there was a lump on the corner of her mouth that gave it a lop-sided appearance. There were grazes here and there, and her complexion was covered with what she had once referred to in her copy for a magazine advertisement as 'unsightly blotches'. The client had insisted on the word 'unsightly'.

She turned her head a little more to the left, and could just make out the tail of the Steri-strip that Doctor Carr had stuck on the back of her neck. How had she been injured there? It seemed an unlikely place for a cut.

'*How many times did you fuck him, bitch?*' Josh was pulling at the gold locket around her neck – the one he had given her just last week. The chain was digging into her skin as he pulled it tight around her neck and then his hand was on her chest, pushing her backwards. She felt the chain snap as she ricocheted off the wall and banged against the door, sliding down and hitting her nose on the handle, and then she was on her back on the floor and Josh was pulling at her dress.

She was leaning over the basin with her hands gripping the smooth white porcelain, breathing heavily with her eyes shut and feeling bile rise into her mouth. She spat into the basin and then turned on the cold tap and let the water run into her mouth. She sluiced and spat again, then filled the basin with water and very slowly lowered her face into it. She rose for breath then repeated the operation twice before pulling the plug and patting her face dry with a towel. She felt a little dizzy as she let herself out of the bathroom and crossed to the spare room to get her dressing gown. Downstairs the phone was ringing.

'Hello?' Maeve's voice came from the hallway. 'Hello, Josh.' Her tone was formal. Maddie stopped and stood very still. 'No. I'm not working at the moment. Yes, she is. That's right – I rang Margaret earlier to let her know she'd be out sick for a while.'

Maddie moved quietly to the top of the stairs and sat down on her hunkers, pulling the T-shirt over her knees and wrapping her arms tightly around her shins.

'I really couldn't say.' Maeve's voice was even, but very cold. 'No, she's sleeping. Yes, I'll tell her you rang. No, I don't think that's a good idea. I think you have a very good notion why not, Josh. I won't stand in the way of her contacting you if that's what she wants, but I would please ask you to refrain from phoning her here. I don't want to hear your side of the story, Josh. Yes, I know. We all get drunk from time to time.' Suddenly Maeve went from being icily polite to being downright hostile. 'I thought I told you – I'm really not interested. How can you say that? You were *provoked* into pulping your girlfriend's face? An *accident*? Jesus Christ, Josh – I can't listen to this.' There came the sound of a receiver being put down with great force.

Maeve turned away from the phone and started up the stairs, stopping halfway when she saw Maddie crouching on the landing. 'You heard all that?' she asked.

Maddie nodded.

Maeve leaned against the banister. 'He's only just got into work. Margaret told him I'd rung to say you weren't well.'

'What did you tell her?'

'I made it as vague as possible – mentioned that very useful word "virus". Said you'd been taken ill last night and I'd stayed over with you. I also said it was unlikely that you'd be in at all this week.'

Maddie nodded again. 'What time is it?'

'Around half-past two. You've been asleep for over six hours. Feeling any better?'

'I'm still very sore.'

'Come downstairs and have some coffee.' Maeve climbed to the top of the stairs and helped Maddie to her feet.

'What did Josh say to you?'

Maeve looked at her cousin as if assessing how much of the telephone conversation she should repeat. 'Well, he wanted to talk to you. When I told him you were sleeping he said he'd ring back in a couple of hours. I asked him not to – I said I'd leave it up to you to get in touch if you felt like it. Are you warm enough? Let me get your dressing gown.'

She disappeared into the spare room and Maddie started making her way downstairs. Maeve caught up with her as she was going into the kitchen. 'Careful of the puddle,' she said, helping Maddie into the candlewick robe. 'I kicked over David Norris's water bowl on the way to answer the phone. Here – take your socks. Do you want tea or coffee?'

'Tea, please.'

'Are you hungry yet?'

Maddie shook her head. 'What else did Josh say?' she asked.

Maeve looked sideways at her as she filled the kettle. 'He said he'd like me to hear his side of the story. I told him I wasn't interested. He started to say something about a row and an accident – how you'd hit your head on the door and that started your nose bleeding—'

'That's true.'

Maeve flicked the switch on the kettle and turned to her. 'Shit, Maddie. It doesn't account for the other injuries. It doesn't account for the blood on your thighs.' She sat down opposite her cousin at the kitchen table. 'Will you tell me about it? Would it help?'

'I don't know. I don't want you to hate Josh, Maeve.'

'Josh is really a matter of complete indifference to me, Maddie. It's you I'm concerned about. I want to help you to feel better.'

'OK,' Maddie said. 'I'll try. Some of it may not

make much sense. There are – gaps, you know? Blank bits.'

While Maeve made the tea, Maddie told her everything she could remember. She talked for a long time. She told her how Josh had jumped to the wrong conclusions when he'd seen the pictures of her and Sam together – and really, wasn't it perfectly understandable, in a way? Sam was such a drop-dead gorgeous guy. You know, *anyone* seeing those photographs might have assumed that there was something going on between her and the photographer's assistant. Josh had just thought that the best way of reprimanding her was to give her a slap, and somehow, once he'd started, he hadn't seemed to be able to stop. He'd never done it before, and when he'd finished he'd apologized to her, and she'd allowed him to make love to her. Then he'd kissed her and wrapped her in her alpaca throw and gone into the kitchen to make tea for her.

Maeve refilled Maddie's mug. 'Is that when you decided to leave?'

'Yes.'

'Why didn't you stay and let Josh look after you instead of coming here?'

Maddie didn't say anything. She concentrated on stirring milk into her tea.

'Was it because you were scared, Maddie?'

'Yes.' Her voice was very small.

'Were you scared that he might hit you again?'

'No, not really. Somehow I knew he'd finished

179

hitting me. He told me I'd learned my lesson—'

'Jesus!' The flat of Maeve's hand came down hard on the table.

'And said he was sorry he'd had to do it, but I *had* provoked him, after all. And he told me how much he loved me.' Maddie looked at Maeve with entreaty in her eyes. 'He *meant* it, Maeve – honestly he did.'

'I believe you. But what exactly were you scared of?'

'I don't know.' Maddie lowered her eyes again. Senator David Norris had come in through the cat flap and started rubbing himself against Maddie's legs. She reached down and stroked him, running her hand over the smooth apricot-coloured fur and along his soft flank, then toying absently with the tip of his tail.

'Do you remember you told me earlier that you hadn't really felt like having sex with Josh?'

'Did I say that?' David Norris jumped heavily into Maddie's lap and started purring loudly at her, inviting her to go on caressing him.

'Were you scared that Josh might – make love – to you again? Is that why you wanted to get away from him?'

'I don't know.'

The doorbell rang shrilly. Maddie jumped and shot Maeve a look of panic. David Norris slid off her lap. 'Do you think that's him?' she asked in a whisper.

'Don't worry. If it is I won't let him in. I don't

imagine you're ready to see him yet. Am I right?'
Maddie nodded. 'I'll be back in a sec,' said Maeve,
making for the door with a nosy David Norris
trotting at her heels.

She was back in less than a minute with a huge
bouquet of blood-red roses in her arms. 'For you,'
she said, laying them on the table. Maddie looked
warily at the flowers. Then she detached the little
envelope that was pinned onto the cellophane
wrapping and opened it. The logo on the envelope
was that of the flower shop across the road, and
the note inside read, in a florist's careful biro:
'Sorry to hear you're not feeling well. Always, always
remember I love you. Call me if you need anything.
J.' The second 'always' was underlined.

Maddie handed it to Maeve, who read it in
silence. 'What are you going to do?' she asked.

'I'm not sure.'

'You can stay here for as long as you like,
Maddie.'

'I know that, Maeve. Thank you. I really appreciate it. But I'm going to have to get my act
together sooner or later.' It was easy to say. She
knew the big difficulty would be how.

'Don't rush into anything. Don't make any
decisions just yet. Doctor Carr advised bed rest. I
suggest you stay here until you're feeling – and
looking – a bit better, and we'll play it by ear from
then on, OK? His colleague rang, by the way – a
Doctor Fiona Price. She says that you're welcome
to phone her any time.'

'That's very kind of her.' It was evident from Maddie's lacklustre tone that she had no intention of taking up Doctor Price's offer.

Maeve got to her feet and moved to the fridge. 'Now – how about some soup? Jacqueline made some excellent vichyssoise. And there's Cooke's tomato bread and a Brie that needs to be eaten today.'

Maddie still didn't feel like eating, but she wanted to make Maeve happy. 'That sounds good. Thanks, Maeve. Thanks for everything.'

* * *

Maddie spent most of the next three days in bed. She slept a lot during the daytime because she found sleeping at night difficult. Her mind would go into a spin as soon as she turned off the light, and what she had taken to referring to as 'the incident' with Josh would start playing like a video-tape on a loop over and over again in her head. She would lie there in a state of constant wakeful-ness, stiff with apprehension and drenched in sweat, jumping every time she heard a noise out-side her window or a footstep on the stair outside her door.

She took to leaving the bedside lamp on all night because, for the first time since she was a very small child, she found she was afraid of the dark. She kept remembering what Doctor Carr had said. *She's safe here for now.* What would she do when she returned to her own flat – when she no longer had the security blanket of Maeve and Jacqueline's presence in the next room? How was she going to handle Josh? She'd have to face him sooner or later. And if their relationship had broken down irretrievably, how was she going to face him at work? She couldn't think about it – it was all too confusing. She just wanted everything to be back to normal.

In the mornings, Maeve would quietly open the door and feel glad when she saw her cousin lying comatose on the futon. She didn't know that Maddie was sleeping the sleep of exhaustion, that she had finally shut her eyes after spending the entire night in hell.

*   *   *

On Thursday she woke around lunchtime as usual, and made her way down to the kitchen. Maeve was sitting at the kitchen table, reading the *Irish Times*. There was a half-full cafetière in front of her.

'Hi! How are you feeling? Did you sleep well?'

Maddie hadn't told her cousin that she was too frightened to sleep at night. She didn't want Maeve to ask what she was frightened of. She didn't want to hear Maeve use the 'R' word again. She managed a smile. 'Oh – so-so. I'm not hurting anywhere near as much.'

'Good. I was going to suggest a follow-up visit to Doctor Carr might be—'

'No. Honestly, Maeve, I'm feeling fine. I don't need to see him.'

Maeve shrugged. 'That's absolutely your prerogative, Maddie. Want some coffee?'

'Mm. Please.' Maddie helped herself to a clean mug from the draining board and looked for a cloth to dry it with. 'Did Josh call yet?' He'd taken to phoning two or three times a day. Maddie still hadn't spoken to him.

'Yeah. Around eleven o'clock. He said he'd ring again later. I told him not to bother. And I told him to stop wasting money on flowers. Three days in a row is a bit excessive by anyone's standards.'

Maddie looked at the roses that stood in a big white vase on the kitchen dresser. She hadn't been able to bring herself to trash them, as Maeve had suggested, or send them to the local hospital. Neither had she been able to send back the tousle-headed chrysanthemums which had arrived on Tuesday and which now dominated the sitting-room mantelpiece, or the elegant sheaf of irises which had taken the place of Maeve's Swiss cheese plant on the hall table the previous day. She poured coffee into her mug, and moved over to the kitchen window to look out at the gaudy patio. Geraniums were nodding their bright pink and red heads as if they were listening to some particularly funky piece of music and various provocative-looking items of Maeve and Jacqueline's underwear were waving on the line like lacy pennants. Small white clouds scudded fast across the bright blue canopy of the sky. An uncharacteristically kittenish Senator David Norris was chasing begonia dead-heads which had been caught up in an eddy of wind in the corner of the patio. Maddie suddenly ached to get out of the house. She realized that she was beginning to feel like a prisoner. 'I'd really love a walk, Maeve. I haven't had a decent blast of fresh air for ages. D'you think we might manage a stride up the Pigeonhouse Pier today? If I cover up my bruises with make-up and put on a pair of shades I don't think I'll feel too self-conscious.'

'The forecast's not that great. It's very windy out, and there's rain on the way.'

'I don't care. I wouldn't mind getting blown about a bit.'

'All right, then. But you can't go out in Jacqueline's granny's dressing gown. I'll lend you something, if you don't mind looking like a hippie cast member of *Hideous Kinky*. Or maybe I should run by your place and pick up some of your own stuff for you to wear?'

'Oh.' Maddie didn't like the idea of Maeve going into her apartment without her. It would still be in a mess. There were things she didn't particularly want her cousin to see. She seemed to remember that there was a broken wineglass on the floor, and that a couple of chairs had been turned over. She suspected that there might be bloodstains on the carpet and on the paintwork by the door. The locket with its broken chain would be lying around somewhere, and her other shoe, and a candlestick which Josh had used at one point to— She froze the image instantly and pushed it, pushed it away.

'I'll go now if you like,' volunteered Maeve.

'What about keys?' Maddie was still reluctant.

'I have your spares. You gave me a set last time you got locked out, remember?'

There was no way round it. She was going to need her own stuff sooner or later. 'OK – thanks, Maeve.' Maddie sighed. 'Maybe I should make a recording of myself saying thanks so I can just play it back to you non-stop. Are you sure you don't mind?'

'You know I don't. What clothes do you want?'

'Something loose, please. That T-shirt and the jogging pants that I wore out to Sara Lennox's are in the airing cupboard. Root around as much as you like.' She remembered her bruises. 'And could you bring me my make-up bag? I think it's in the bathroom.'

'Sure. And by the way, Maddie?'

'Yeah?'

'Don't answer the phone while I'm gone, OK? I'll turn the answering machine on.'

'OK.'

'I'll be back as soon as I can. Forty-five minutes should do it.'

*   *   *

In the bathroom real life seemed to recede. It was Maddie's favourite place these days. She soaked in the bath for fifteen minutes, soothed by the gentle plip! plip! of the dripping hot tap. Then she reached for the soap – resisting for the first time that week the temptation to use the nailbrush on her skin or slosh Dettol into the water. She did use a flannel, though – and she used it quite hard.

As usual when she stepped from the bath her skin was raw and smarting. She dried herself off and then rubbed herself all over with E45 lotion, which relieved the stinging a little. The bruises on her body looked more than ever like an abstract painting, with an extraordinary shade of muddy yellow creeping in amongst the blues and purples, as she'd known it would.

In the kitchen she made herself tea and toast. There was pâté in the fridge, and she was hungry today. Then she took a look through Maeve's and Jacqueline's CD collection. She wanted to listen to something light and classical that would mirror the blue-sky day that danced beyond the window. She would be going out into the world today for the first time since she had last seen Josh.

The opening strains of Mozart's Fortieth had just burst over the speakers when the doorbell rang. Maddie tensed, and then looked at the clock on the kitchen wall. It was just after three – the time Josh's flowers tended to arrive every day. She moved cautiously towards the front door. 'Who is it?' she called.

'Flowers for Ms Godard.'

She was right. More flowers from Josh. At this rate there'd be nothing left in the house to put them in.

The first thing she saw was a mass of gladioli. The second thing she saw was Josh's face. She tried to slam the door shut, but he anticipated her. The door swung back into the hall, nearly knocking Maddie off her feet, and then Josh was in the house. Maddie scampered down the hallway to the kitchen as he turned and calmly shut the door behind him, then strolled after her. She ran round to the other side of the kitchen table. It was the only barrier separating them.

'Go away. Go away, Josh. Go away.'

He set the flowers down on the table and smiled at her. It was the smile that said *I'm sexy, I'm charming, I'm fucking irresistible*, the smile he reserved for clients during a presentation. She'd witnessed women – even ice-queens in Prada – get very flustered indeed when he used that smile on them. 'Maddie,' he said. 'Maddie. I'm not going to hurt you. Believe me, OK?' He paused, then shrugged his shoulders and sent her a vaguely apologetic smile. 'So I slapped you. It'll never happen again, I swear it. I love you. I just want you to be happy.' He took a step to his right as if to come round the table to her and when he saw her immediately mirror his move he stopped and held up his hands in a conciliatory gesture. 'Look – I can understand you're feeling a bit nervous. You did a terrible thing, deceiving me like that, Maddie. But I forgive you. Shit, I forgave you that night, didn't I, when we made love? I didn't have to touch you ever again. I could have walked away and left you. But I didn't want to do that, Maddie, because in spite of everything I still love you.' He was smiling at her and his voice was very gentle. Maddie clutched the candlewick dressing gown more tightly around her. 'And I know you still love me. You wouldn't have allowed me to make love to you on Sunday night if you didn't.'

Make love. They were the words she'd used to describe what had happened between them to Maeve. But they sounded odd coming from Josh's lips. Unconvincing. She remembered how he'd bludgeoned his way inside her, and the pain. 'You hurt me, Josh,' she said through very dry lips.

'I know I did, darling, and I've apologized for it. I've just promised you that I'll never slap you again, haven't I?'

'I don't just mean that. I mean you hurt me when you – when you had sex with me.'

Josh raised an eyebrow and gave her a rather sceptical look. 'Oh, come on, Maddie,' he said. 'I *know* you, remember? I'd like to think I know you better than anyone. You've never objected in the past to a bit of rough stuff. You *enjoy* playing games. Don't pretend to me you don't.'

'That wasn't a game, Josh.'

'I think you're being a bit melodramatic, darling.' He folded his arms and narrowed his eyes at her. 'Would I be right in thinking that you and Maeve have been analysing things from a comfortably feminist perspective? Feminists don't have any truck with sex games, do they? Feminists think they should be on top. Feminists demand orgasms as a basic human right, for Christ's sake!' He gave a laugh which sounded more like a bark. 'Come on, Maddie, lighten up. A little bit of sexual experimentation never hurt anyone. Think how dull life would get if we all started having to be politically correct in bed as well as at work. Where's your sense of fun gone, darling?' He flashed her another smile and then looked down at the flowers on the table and started fiddling with one of the blossoms. 'I suppose you'll be accusing me of rape next.' Without raising his head he looked at her suddenly from under his eyebrows. It was a hard look, a look of assessment, but there was also something guarded about it. It was the first indication she had that there might be unease there. 'Won't you give me a kiss to show me everything's all right?'

'No, Josh.' To her relief, she heard Maeve's key in the front door. 'Go away now, please.'

'Of course I will if that's what you want. But

when you need me I'll be there. I'll be waiting for you, Maddie. I still love you. And you know you love me.'

'Hi! Sorry. I was a bit longer than I thought,' came Maeve's voice from the hall. She walked into the kitchen swinging carrier bags. 'I ran into—' She stopped dead when she saw Josh. 'What the fuck are you doing here?' she said. 'Get out. How *dare* you come into my house without my permission?'

'Oh – hi, Maeve. Maddie let me in,' came the smooth reply. 'But I'm going now.' He tried laying a friendly hand on Maeve's shoulder as he passed by her, but she shrugged it off. 'Thanks again for the birthday present. I have to say that a priapic fertility god was the last thing I expected to receive from a couple of lesbians.' At the kitchen door he turned. 'I'll talk to you soon, Maddie,' he said, blowing her a kiss. 'And don't forget we've a party to go to this weekend, if you're feeling up to it.' Then he disappeared up the hallway and the two women heard the front door close behind him.

There was a beat before Maeve spoke. 'Did you really let him in, Maddie?'

'No! I couldn't stop him!' She sat down abruptly on one of the wooden kitchen chairs. She was gulping air and had started to shake violently.

'Fuck him! Fuck him! How dare he do this to you!' Maeve dropped the bags she was carrying and went to wrap her arms around her cousin.

'It's OK – I'll be OK.' Maddie was trying very hard not to cry. She didn't want to fall to pieces all over again. If she did, she somehow felt that she'd spend the rest of her life picking them up.

'You know the craven fucking *bastard* must have seen that my car was gone?' Maeve was incandescent with rage. 'He wouldn't have done this if he thought I'd be here.'

'Josh isn't a bastard, Maeve, honestly he isn't. He – he really cares for me. I know it's hard for you to understand. But he doesn't deserve to be called that, he really doesn't. He's – he's – oh, I can't begin to explain. It's a stupid love thing.' Knowing she was sounding lame, Maddie shut up and looked down at the table.

'OK, OK. I promise I won't call him a bastard again until I hear you doing it.'

They let a few minutes go by in silence. Then: 'Shall I make some tea?' asked Maeve quietly.

Maddie let out a huge, shuddering sigh. 'Tea? Fuck tea. I want a drink.' She let go of her cousin, buried her face in her hands for an instant, and then shook her head. 'What berk came up with the bright idea of *tea* as an antidote to shock? No offence to you,' she added, thinking of the vast quantities of the stuff she'd consumed since Sunday night.

'I couldn't agree more.' Maeve pushed a lank strand of Maddie's hair back from her face before going over to the fridge. 'While I was forcing all that tea on you that night – morning – the doctor came, I was swigging out of the Jameson bottle every time I left the room.'

'Hypocrite.' Maddie found she could manage what passed muster as a smile.

Maeve dumped a bottle of white Rioja on the table and handed Maddie a corkscrew. 'Open that,' she said, going to fetch glasses from a shelf. 'There are olives and stuff in the cupboard – help yourself. I suppose I should put these in water,' she said, indicating the gladioli that Josh had left on the table. 'This place is going to start looking like the Botanical Gardens at this rate. Do you still feel like a walk?'

'Oh, God, yes – more than ever. I badly need to feel wind blowing through my brain. I can understand now why some people are attracted to the idea of trepanning.' As Maddie started to strip the foil from the neck of the wine bottle she was glad to see that her hands were at least steady enough to do the job without botching it.

'Right. We'll have a quick drink before we go, and then lots of long drinks when we get back.' The phone went in the hall. 'Shit, Maddie – you've got to stop jumping every time you hear the phone. Here – fill these.' She put two enormous long-stemmed wineglasses on the table and went out into the hall.

Maddie did as she was told, and then took a long gulp of the cold, straw-coloured wine. From what she could hear of Maeve's phone conversation her cousin was obviously talking to her agent, and

Maddie guessed that this was only the beginning of what could be a long conversation. She might as well take her wine out to her.

Maeve was sitting cross-legged on the floor in the hall, chewing at the nails of her left hand and leafing through the pages of her Filofax with her right. She gave Maddie a grateful look and the thumbs-up as she took the wineglass from her, then covered the mouthpiece with her hand. 'Thanks,' she whispered. 'This might take a while.'

Maddie wandered back into the kitchen and picked up the *Irish Times*. Sipping at her wine, she scanned the front page. There was nothing worth reading. On the inside pages the first headline she saw included the word 'rape'. She shut the paper immediately and dropped it onto the floor. The carrier bags were still lying where Maeve had dumped them.

Her clothes. At last she could stop sloping around in pink candlewick.

She knelt down on the floor beside the bags, picked one of them up and looked into it. It contained clean underwear – lots of it – her make-up bag and – sweet of Maeve to think of this – her Chanel 19 and the book she was currently reading. Maeve must have found it on her bedside table. The second bag – one of the big paper ones from Habitat – had in it her sweat pants, a selection of T-shirts, and her leather coat. Her runners were in there too, and – sweetest thought of all – the

194

ancient panda she'd had since she was tiny. Her parents had given it to her one Christmas, and she'd christened it Bassa. 'Bassa' had been her toddler-speak way of saying 'thank you'. She hugged the panda to her before she started on the third bag.

There was some rectangular object in there, wrapped up loosely in lots of newspaper. Maddie couldn't think what it might be as she started pulling away the layers. The final layer was of green marbled paper. It was the gift-wrap she'd used for Josh's birthday presents.

Now she knew what the parcel contained. It was the Sara Lennox photograph. Josh must have left it behind in her flat that night. She didn't really find that surprising. What she *did* find strange was that Maeve had bothered to bring it back here. Maybe she should put it back in the bag. She didn't really want to look at it again. But some perverse instinct made her fold back the wrapping.

She went very cold. The glass protecting the photograph had been broken, and only a few shards remained attached to the frame. The photograph itself had been slashed – not randomly, but with extreme and calculating discretion. Deep scores had been made across Maddie's pudenda, across her breasts, and across her face. The word WHORE had been neatly printed at the top of the photograph in red ink.

She stared at it for a minute or two and then carefully wrapped it up again. She could hear

Maeve coming down the hallway. Maddie didn't move, and she didn't say anything. She just stayed kneeling on the kitchen floor with the makeshift parcel in her hands.

Then she looked up to where Maeve was standing in the kitchen doorway. She had never seen her cousin look so stricken. 'I didn't mean for you to find it. I'm sorry. I didn't want to leave it in your flat – I was going to trash it, and I knew that our bin would be a safer place for it than yours. If I hadn't been so fazed by Josh being here I'd have disappeared it by now.'

'It's OK, Maeve,' she said. Her voice was surprisingly calm. 'It's probably better that I did see it. Can we go for that walk now?'

* * *

Maddie didn't even wait until Maeve had finished parking the car on the road that ran down to the pier. She slid out of the passenger seat while the engine was still running and faced full into the wind with her head back and her arms outstretched, drinking in great greedy gulps of air.

Maeve joined her, struggling to get her arms into the flapping sleeves of her jacket. 'Wow – look at that,' she said, pointing towards the waves that were leaping up against the side of the pier, sending cascades of spray skidding over the uneven paving of the walkway. 'I've never seen the tide so high.'

Maddie linked arms with her cousin and they aimed for the pier, heads down against the wind. She was glad to see that there weren't many people about. She had camouflaged her bruises as best as she could with heavy make-up and she was wearing very dark sunglasses, but she still felt conspicuous. She kept the collar of her coat up around her chin. It was a tailored black leather coat with a sheepskin collar, and it looked very odd with her runners and sweat pants, but she really didn't care. Anyway, the few people she passed didn't give her a second glance. They were too intent on getting the benefit of a brisk walk on a blustery day, striding along in their anoraks and walking shoes, chests out and arms swinging.

For a while Maddie and Maeve walked without saying anything. To the right of the pier the open sea was being whipped by the wind into a mass of skittish white horses; to the left, in the shelter of the harbour, the movement of the water was swollen and sluggish. The surface of the sea there looked like the smooth flank of some giant beast rolling over in its sleep.

A wave pounced over the pier wall and landed a couple of feet away from them, slapping against the slabs with a sound like wet silk, and making them jump sideways. The sound reminded Maddie of a CD she had at home – a recording of ocean waves that she played when she was having trouble sleeping. She thought about her own bed, and wondered when she would next sleep in it. She thought about her flat, and pictured it as it had been when she'd last been there. She knew it was time to go back.

'Will I have a lot of cleaning up to do?' she asked suddenly.

'What?'

'At home. What kind of shape's the flat in?'

'Oh.' Maeve looked at her and hesitated. Then she said, 'Actually, you won't need to do anything.'

'What do you mean? Things were pretty chaotic after the party.'

'It's pristine now.'

'No signs of – the rape?' In her confusion she'd used the word without meaning to, and before she could stop herself. She slid a glance at Maeve, but her cousin's expression was unreadable.

'No. Josh must have cleaned everything up.'

Maddie stared at her, aghast. 'Ugh,' she said. For some reason she found this news more upsetting than if the flat had been in the same shambolic state as when she had staggered out through the door at dawn on Monday morning, with overturned chairs, smashed wineglasses and bloodstains on the walls and floor. The thought that Josh could have done what he did to her and then calmly gone around cleaning the place up afterwards was deeply disturbing. She shook her head and increased her pace, as if by moving faster she could put more distance between herself and the unpleasantness of what she was hearing.

'Maddie – you're going to exhaust yourself,' warned Maeve, struggling to keep up.

'No I'm not – I need to do this.'

They walked on in silence again for a while, and then Maeve said, 'I listened to your messages. I hope you don't mind.'

'Were there many?' Maddie tried to make the question sound casual.

'Yes. There were one or two from work – nothing important I don't think. And a couple of social ones – I wrote them all down for you.' Maeve cleared her throat. 'There were quite a few from Josh.'

Maddie pulled her coat collar up higher and then stuck her hands in her pockets. 'What did he have to say?'

'He rambled on a bit. Mostly stuff about how much he loved you and how he – forgave you.' Maddie could tell that Maeve had difficulty in getting out the word 'forgave'. 'Asking when you were coming home, wondering when you'd be back in at work. I wiped them. Is that OK?'

Maddie wasn't sure whether it was or not. 'That's OK,' she said finally, and then added: 'Any faxes?'

'No. Someone had been trying, but the display read that you were out of paper. I'd have put in a new roll for you, but I didn't know where to find one. And of course, I couldn't check e-mail for you.'

'Letters?'

'Bills. I thought they could wait till you got back.'

A wave surged up on their left, sending water swilling across the pier. 'Maeve?' Biting on her lip, Maddie turned to her cousin. This was a question she'd been putting off asking. 'You know the other photographs I told you about – the ones that Sara took of me after the shoot? When you went to the flat, was there any sign of them?'

'No.'

Maddie sucked in her breath. 'OK,' was all she said.

A stout man with a military gait marched past them, heading back along the pier in the direction they'd come. 'Srennyay!' he announced, as if issuing a command.

Maeve nodded sagely at him and then said: 'Did he say "There's rain on the way" or "It's a splendid day"?'

'Both, probably. It's glorious now, but look over there.'

Black clouds were banked up steeply on the horizon, in dramatic contrast to the bright blue and white of the sky immediately above.

They were coming to the end of the pier. 'Let's have a breather before we go back,' suggested Maeve. 'I'm knackered.'

'Sorry. I suppose I did take it at a bit of a lick.'

They sat down side by side on a wooden bench beneath the lighthouse. Maeve took some chewing gum out of her pocket and offered Maddie a stick.

They rested there with the sun on their faces, watching a cormorant bobbing up and down on the sea.

After a while Maeve said, 'Maddie? Have you thought any more about what you're going to do?'

'About the future, you mean?'

'Yes. More specifically about Josh.' Maeve turned to look at her, putting a hand up to shade her eyes from the sun.

'He still loves me, Maeve.'

'That's not a good reason for staying with him. Do you still love him?'

'I don't know what I feel about him now.' Maddie shut her eyes and bit down hard on her chewing gum. 'This is difficult. I don't know what I'd do without him.'

'I think you should be very, very careful, Maddie.'

The sun had disappeared behind one of the woolly white clouds. It was quite cold in the shade. Inside her coat pockets, Maddie's hands were clenched into fists. 'The thing I'm dreading most is going back to work and having to pretend that everything's normal. I'm not sure if I can handle that.' She could hear her voice starting to shake.

There was a pause. Beside her Maeve was pleating the silver foil of her chewing-gum wrapper into a miniature fan. 'You may not have to go back.'

'What do you mean? Do you think I should quit?'

Maeve turned to her and looked at her with serious eyes. 'You're going to find this out sooner or later, and it's probably better that you hear it from me. It looks like the agency's going down the tubes.'

'What? The Complete Works?'

'Yes. You didn't win the Grant & Wainwright account. Reflex did. I ran into that woman who was at your party – I couldn't remember her name—'

'Vanessa?' Maddie's nails were digging into the palms of her hands.

'That's right. She asked me how you were after hearing the bad news, and whether you were going to reconsider the offer that Reflex had made that time they tried to headhunt you. I told her you knew nothing about it, and she immediately asked me not to breathe a word to anyone. She'd been pre-emptive, and was seriously embarrassed that she'd let anything slip. It won't be official until tomorrow.'

Maddie bit her lip. 'Shit,' she said. 'No wonder Josh was up to ninety about winning that account. He must have known we were in trouble. This'll break him.'

'I'm sorry you had to hear it from me.'

'No, no – you were dead right to tell me. I'm glad I heard it from you,' Maddie said. Very slowly she unclenched her fists and withdrew her hands from her pockets. She took the gum out of her mouth and wrapped it in its foil. Chewing gum seemed too casual a thing to be doing when her whole world was in upheaval around her. She wished she were a smoker: she would have loved to light up a cigarette. She turned uncomprehending eyes on her cousin. 'D'you know the strangest thing of all, Maeve? I know I should be on the floor – I should be devastated – but all I can feel is a weird sense of relief. Why is that, do you think?'

Maeve met her gaze with absolute candour. 'You won't have to face Josh,' she said.

Maddie nodded. For a split second tears threatened and she averted her face. Then, abruptly, she got to her feet. 'I'm not going to think about it now,' she said with determination. She looked out beyond the lighthouse to the horizon. 'We should go. We're going to get pissed upon.'

Minutes before they reached the end of the pier they felt the rain on their backs. They ran for it, piling into the car breathless and dripping. Maddie wiped her face with her hands. Her skin tasted of salt. In the distance, striding purposefully towards the horizon, she could just make out the bulky outline of the intrepid walker who'd greeted them earlier. In a funny way, she envied him. At least he knew where he was going.

Maeve turned on the headlamps and pulled out from the side of the road, switching the windscreen wipers to full tilt. 'I'm starving after that,' she said. 'I'm not going to be able to last till suppertime. Maybe we should stop off somewhere on the way home and get doughnuts.'

'Yes,' said Maddie. 'Jam ones.'

They didn't notice the car that pulled out after them. The driver hadn't bothered to turn on his headlamps, or to indicate. It was the low, black BMW that belonged to Josh.

Chapter Nine

The following evening Maeve and Jacqueline drove her home. They both came up to the flat with her, at Maeve's insistence. Earlier in the day Jacqueline had done a shop, and there were fresh flowers in a vase.

'You're fantastic, Jacqueline. I wouldn't have come through this week if it hadn't been for you and Maeve.' Maddie slung her carrier bag of clothes onto the couch. 'Christ, I'll be really glad to wear something other than sweat pants and T-shirts. How do I look, anyway? Can I start touting for a job next week?'

She took off her sunglasses and looked at herself critically in the mirror on the sitting-room wall. Her bruising had subsided very slightly, but the foundation she'd applied in a thick layer still didn't quite conceal it. She'd made up her right eye with a rather revolting mauve eye shadow which Maeve had found for her amongst her theatrical stuff. Now it matched the left one, which was a dramatic shade of purple.

'A bit *Moulin Rouge*,' remarked Maeve. Maddie saw her cousin's eyes slide towards the shelf where her answering machine lived. The red light was blinking nervily. 'Are you sure you don't want me to stay with you tonight?' she asked. It was about the sixth time she'd asked that question.

'I'm positive. It's sweet of you to offer, but I have to take a deep breath and just do this by myself.' She knew she needed to be on her own, in her own environment. She remembered her flat as it had looked when she'd abandoned it in such a panic less than a week ago. The first thing she'd done when she'd come through the door had been to look sideways through her dark glasses at the place on the wall where her blood had been smeared, but there was no longer any trace of it. In a way her living space had been defiled as well as her body. She wanted to repossess it.

Maeve looked at Maddie and relented. 'All right. If you need me, give me a ring – any time. I mean that. If you want to ring me at three o'clock in the morning just do it, OK? Or try Jac's mobile.'

'Not yours?'

'It's "on hold in dispatch". I sent it to be repaired weeks ago and the efficiency-challenged individuals in the dispatch department still haven't sent it out. Can't say I miss it, though. I hate the bastard thing.'

Then Maeve sucked in her breath and said, 'Maddie, I really don't want to alarm you unnecessarily, but I need to ask you this. Does Josh have keys to your apartment?'

'Oh,' Maddie looked uncertain. 'Oh. I'm not sure.

He had a load cut for me after I had to fork out all that money to the locksmith. I gave you your spare, Maeve, and I know I left a spare in the office, but I don't know if Josh kept a key for himself.'

'In that case, will you make sure you put the security chain on when we leave? Just to be on the safe side.'

'Of course I will. I always do that anyway.'

Maeve and Jacqueline started to move towards the door, looking reluctant to leave. 'There's a load of those individual meals from Marks in the fridge, by the way, Maddie,' said Jacqueline. 'I didn't think you'd want to be bothered cooking for yourself for a while.'

'Any pasta dishes?' asked Maddie, trying to sound bright.

'Yup. There's one with prawns.'

'Excellent. Pasta's just what I feel like.'

'You're not the only one who couldn't be bothered cooking tonight,' said Maeve. 'I know it's my turn, Jacqueline, but let's eat out. We haven't done it for ages.'

Jacqueline shrugged. 'OK. Let's go somewhere posh. I deserve a treat after doing all the cooking last week. Do you want to come with us, Maddie?'

The prospect of sitting in the comfortable ambience of some classy restaurant having dinner served to her and drinking good wine with her friends was very seductive. Maddie thought for a second or two and then she shook her head. 'No. If I have dinner with you it'll be a form of procrastination. I've got to get on with real life.'

She took a deep breath and tried to smile. 'You must go away now,' she said, pushing them out the door. 'I'm not being ungrateful, but you've been so good to me it makes me feel like crying. Go away at once before I start to blub.'

'OK then.' Maeve kissed her on the cheek. 'Bye, Maddie. Take care. Give us a ring soon.'

'Take care of yourself.' Jacqueline was smiling, but Maddie was extremely aware of the concern in both women's eyes.

'I will,' she said, watching them go and then shutting the door behind them. She fastened the security chain and turned the key in the Chubb. 'I will take care of myself,' she repeated, fiercely.

She moved to the sitting room and stood for a minute or two in the doorway, leaning against the jamb and rubbing her thumb over the smooth, flat surface of the jade worry stone she kept attached to her key-ring. She scooped up the small pile of mail that had arrived in the morning post and walked towards the kitchen, tossing her letters onto the dining table and not looking at the answering machine.

Josh had been thorough. Her kitchen resembled a set in a television commercial for some household cleaning product. The floor shone. Work surfaces gleamed. Everything had been tidied away in its proper place. It was as if by putting everything away so meticulously he had been laying claim to her – trying to prove to her how well he knew her. It must have taken him hours.

She found herself speculating when he might have done it. At dawn that Monday, just after she'd left? It seemed unlikely, somehow. She remembered that Maeve had mentioned he'd just got into work when he made that first phone call later in the afternoon. Maybe he'd slept here? Or maybe he'd come back and let himself in? The thought alarmed her. *Did* Josh have keys to her apartment?

She went back into the hall and stuck her key in the Chubb. If Josh did have a key it would make it more difficult for him to gain access to her flat if there was something obstructing the keyhole. The security chain would stop him anyway, but she wanted to make doubly sure. As she walked back towards the kitchen she wondered if she was being paranoid. Then she remembered the way he had forced his way into Maeve's flat yesterday afternoon and decided she wasn't.

She opened the fridge door and took out a bottle of wine, noticing that there was still champagne left over from Josh's birthday party. As she poured herself a glass of white burgundy she wondered when she'd ever feel enough like celebrating to open a bottle of champagne again. When life got back to normal. That's when she'd feel like celebrating. And the quickest way of getting back to normal was by doing routine things. She went back into the sitting room. Maeve had mentioned that the fax was out of paper. She fetched a new roll and inserted it in the machine. That was a routine thing to do. Then she hit the playback button on the answering machine. It was time to deal with her messages. Another routine thing. The tape took a while to unwind. She thought about all the e-mail that must be waiting for her, and decided that she'd put off accessing it for a while.

All the most recent messages on her machine were from Josh.

'I'm sorry, Maddie. How many times do I have to say it? But what you did would be a test of endurance for any man. I just couldn't handle the fact that you behaved like a common whore behind my back, and common whores get what they deserve. Having said that, I still love you. I'm sure you're keeping tabs on your voice mail. Phone me.' *Thursday. 6.30 p.m.*, said the automated voice.

'Why are you playing so hard to get, Maddie? Most whores go out of their way to make themselves available.' *Thursday. 11.50 p.m.*

'I'm sorry for that last message. It was below the belt.' His voice sounded slurred. There was a pause, and then a sniff before he resumed. 'By the way, if there are any other copies of those photographs in existence, perhaps you'd be good enough to ask your pal Sara Lennox to destroy them along with the negatives? Love you.' *Friday. 1.15 a.m.*

'When are you coming home, Mads? You can't stay with your cousin for ever – you have responsibilities to face up to. And we'll need you back at work soon – we'll be hearing about the G & W account any day now. I love you, darling,

very much. Please don't lose sight of that.' *Friday.*
9.49 a.m.

'Maddie, Maddie – get in touch. I'm feeling
wretched. It's been a fuck of a day. I love you,
darling.' His voice contrived to sound tired
and concerned at the same time. 'I'm worried
about you, you know? I'm not sure you're thinking
straight. Talk to you later.' *Friday. 4.15 p.m.*

The tape finally stopped. The answering
machine made its usual noises, and then the un-
blinking red light appeared. Maddie looked back
at it with unseeing eyes.

She jumped when the phone rang. She backed
away from it immediately, keeping her eyes fixed
on the machine as if it was some small, vicious
animal that might harm her if she looked away.
The answering machine picked up. 'Maddie?
Maddie – I know you're there. Please pick up the
phone, Mads. Please talk to me. Maddie. I need to
talk to you. I badly need . . .' In the middle of the
sitting room Maddie paused. Josh had started to
weep down the phone. She had never heard him
cry before. She thought that never in her life had
she heard anything quite so heart-rending. 'I badly
need to talk, Mads. Something awful's happened.
Please. I know you're on your own there. We can
talk in private. Oh, God, Maddie – don't tell me
I've lost you as well.'

His sobs were pitiful. Maddie found herself
moving towards the phone. She picked up the
receiver.

211

'Josh?'

'Maddie – Jesus. Thank you. Thank you. Oh, God – it's so good to hear your voice.'

'What is it, Josh?'

'The agency's gone under.'

'I know.'

There was a pause. 'What? How could you know?'

'Maeve ran into Vanessa yesterday. She accidentally let it slip.'

'You mean you knew and you didn't get in touch?'

'It was classified information, Josh. I—'

'You fucking bitch,' he said. He wasn't crying any more. 'You might have warned me. I had to hear it from Jim, of all people. I had to—'

Maddie put the phone down. It rang again almost instantly. 'You bitch. You fucking—' began Josh. Maddie lunged for the volume control on the answering machine and turned it right down. She was shaking. When the incoming message tape cut out she took the phone off the hook before it could ring again.

She felt a sensation which had become familiar to her in the past week. Her skin crawled damply and her breathing quickened. She could feel sweat starting to meander slowly down her ribcage. Her fear was so all-pervasive she could almost smell it.

Maddie grabbed the phone and punched in Jacqueline's mobile number with shaking fingers. There was a beat. Then, from the kitchen, came the sound of an electronic melody. The 'Dance of

212

the Fairy' – Jac's signature ringing tone. Maddie moved like an automaton towards the kitchen. The sound was coming from a reusable Marks & Spencer bag that the caterer had left hanging on the back of the door. She'd forgotten her phone. With mounting panic, Maddie pressed Maeve's home number. She'd just have to leave a message on the landline.

'Maeve? It's Maddie. I'm feeling a bit scared. Josh has been on the phone and he turned very abusive. I'd be really glad if you could ring me when you get in. Will you do that, please? As soon as you get in. Thanks.'

Maddie suddenly realized she was shivering. Quickly she crossed the hall to her bedroom, wondering if she should run a bath. Maybe she should just get into bed and get warm under the duvet? Then she remembered that she and Josh had made love on those sheets the night before his birthday party. She didn't want to lie on them again – she'd have to change them, and she didn't have the energy right now. She stripped off the T-shirt she was wearing and ransacked her chest of drawers for something warm to put on. The only thing she could find was a tight-fitting polo-neck in slate-grey cashmere. Why didn't she have anything big and baggy and comfortable to wear?

As she stripped off her T-shirt, a little trickle of gold on top of the chest of drawers caught her eye. She picked it up. The fine chain fell in a glittering loop between her fingers, reflecting the evening sunshine which was slanting in through the bedroom window. It was the chain she'd worn on the night of Josh's birthday – the one that had broken when he'd pushed her back against the sitting-room wall. Where was the locket? She looked down at the floor to see if it had been knocked to the ground, but there was no sign of it. Clenching the chain in her fist, she went into the bathroom and dropped it into the litter bin under the wash-hand basin. Then she continued dressing.

As she pulled the jumper over her head, the phone rang again. She remained standing stock still for a couple of seconds, then moved with a cautious tread into the sitting room to listen to the message. No voice came over the speaker, but she knew there was someone at the other end of the line. The silence lasted a long time before the connection was broken.

Maddie stood in the middle of the floor for a minute or two, uncertain what to do and feeling incredibly alone. She wished she had gone out with Maeve and Jacqueline. She wished she had never come home. Her flat didn't feel like home any more – it felt like a prison. She looked round the room with new eyes, seeing furniture which suddenly seemed unfamiliar to her, and which was utterly devoid of character. She realized that there was very little in her apartment that she hadn't seen in half a dozen other stark, tastefully furnished flats she'd visited in the last year. This wasn't a home. It was a space for living.

The only purely decorative item in the room was her Dufy reproduction. With her index finger, she traced the title over and over again. La Vie en Rose. *La Vie en Rose.* Then she picked up her glass of wine from the table and moved to the sofa. Despite the cashmere pullover she was still feeling very cold. Yesterday she had thought that she was healing. Now she was feeling like an old woman again. Hell. She had to find energy from somewhere. She had to force herself to think hard, and take some sort of action. She couldn't sit in her apartment like a hostage, waiting for something to happen. Waiting for *what* exactly to happen? She wasn't sure. She only knew that she was terribly frightened, and terribly confused.

She stood up again and started to walk around her sitting room, as if pacing the floor would help galvanize her. It would be a couple of hours before Maeve got home. Was there anyone else she could ring and ask for help or advice? For some strange reason she thought of Sara Lennox, and then dismissed the idea. She'd only met the woman a couple of times. There were plenty of other people she knew who would be only too willing to help her out. But if she were to approach any of her other friends she would have to explain what had happened between her and Josh, and she didn't want to do that. Maeve and Jacqueline were the only people who knew – who would ever know – what had happened that night.

As she paced to and fro she was aware that her

breath was coming faster and that the tight cash-mere pullover was damp with sweat under her arms. Terrified that she might be about to ex-perience another flashback, she flailed mentally, trying to think of something that would distract her. Music? Sometimes music helped. She ran a finger along the CDs in the rack. Mozart. The Mass in C minor. She inserted the disc with clumsy fingers, pressed play, and the Kyrie soared out through the speakers.

Maddie lay down on the couch and closed her eyes, keeping her breathing deep and even. Very gradually she felt the tension leave her body. She lay there limply for several minutes until the Mass launched into the more strident notes of the Gloria. Then she opened her eyes again.

The doorbell had rung. It wasn't the street doorbell – it was the one on the door of her apartment. Maddie didn't move. It rang again, and then she heard the sound of a key being inserted into the lock.

She ran into the hall, swinging round the sitting-room door and knocking her hipbone hard against it as she did so. Her key was still in place on the inside of the Chubb. 'Go away, Josh!' she shouted.

The sound of his key rattling in the lock stopped suddenly. 'Maddie? We have to talk. Let me in, will you?'

She squatted down on her hunkers in the hall, not taking her eyes off the keyhole. 'No.'

'Come on, Mads. I'm sorry I flew off the handle

earlier.' A pause. 'Act your age, darling. Be a good girl and let me in.'

This time she didn't answer. She wound her arms around her shins, leaning her chin on her knees, and rocked backwards and forwards.

'Christ, Maddie – where's your heart? I know we had a row, but can't you forgive me the way I forgave you?' There was the sound of lift doors opening down the hallway, and people laughing as they emerged. Then she heard Josh say brightly: 'Hi! Lovely evening isn't it?' There was an indistinguishable reply, and then a door was shut across the hall. Maddie's heartbeat slowed fractionally. The knowledge that her neighbours were in was infinitely reassuring to her.

When Josh spoke again his voice was perceptibly lower. 'Look, Maddie – we don't have to do anything physical tonight if you don't want to, OK? I just want to talk to you.' There was a long pause, and then she could hear him begin to pummel the wall lightly and rhythmically with his fist. 'Shit. I can't believe that you could be such an unfeeling bitch. How can you do this to me on the day I lost my job?'

'Stop it, Josh, and go away. I lost my fucking job too, you know.'

'I know, I know. I'm sorry.' There was another long pause. Then: 'Look Maddie – won't you please let me in? I can't talk to you from the other side of a door.'

'No. Go away.'

'Please, Maddie. I just need an opportunity—'

'Fuck off, Josh.' It was the first time she had ever said those words to him. She had never dreamed that she'd be capable of it. And she had never dreamed that she could issue the command with such authority, such force. Such passion. More than anything, she wanted Josh O'Regan out of her life now.

She could almost feel him thinking before he eventually said, 'OK. But you're not making this easy for either of us, Maddie. You know we'll get together again before long. You're just wasting time now. I'll phone you tomorrow.'

Not many seconds later she heard the lift doors slide open and then close again. She turned her face to the wall, resting her cheekbone against her knees, and started to weep.

*　　*　　*

It was dark when she woke. She was still curled up in the same position with her arms hugging her shins and her head on her knees. The skin on her face felt stiff with dried tears. Moving was difficult. It was as if her limbs had been clamped.

Something had woken her – she wasn't sure what. She lifted her head and saw an object glinting on the floor of the hallway. For some reason she thought it must be the locket that had gone missing. It was only when she stretched out a hand and made contact with the jade worry stone that she realized it was her key gleaming in the refracted light from the corridor outside. The door to the flat was open. It was only open the fraction that was permitted by the restraints of the security chain, but a small, surreptitious sound told her that someone was working on the chain.

She heard herself scream at the same time as the phone started to ring. Bolting into the sitting room she lunged for the phone before the answering machine could kick in. 'Maeve? Thank God – thank God it's you. Can you come now, please? Come quickly. Josh is at the door.'

*   *   *

The next day Maddie woke up feeling groggy from the sleeping tablet which Maeve had insisted she take the previous night. Her memory of events after she'd screamed down the phone was hazy. Josh had disappeared, and Maeve and Jacqueline had come over as fast as they could. Maeve had made up a bed for herself on the pull-down couch, but had told Maddie that she had no intention of going to sleep. 'I'm really not tired,' she'd said. 'And I never need much sleep. I'm quite happy to stay up if you give me a good book to read.'

Maddie emerged from her bedroom into the sunlit hall to find a strange man in overalls working on her front door. 'Lovely morning!' he said cheerfully, as she sidled towards the kitchen, pulling her robe tightly around her. She didn't want to know that it was a lovely morning. She didn't care what kind of a morning it was.

Maeve was in the kitchen. She was dunking a tea-bag in and out of a mug and looking very thoughtful. She looked up when Maddie came in.

'Who's the geezer in the hall?' asked Maddie, shutting the door behind her.

'I'm having your lock changed.'

Maddie just nodded.

'What kind of tea do you want?' asked Maeve with an attempt at brightness. 'There's about twenty varieties of herbal in there. I'm having peppermint. It tastes like shit.'

Maddie sat down at the table. 'No tea, thanks. I'd love a cup of coffee.'

'I didn't think you drank coffee?'

'I keep it for Josh.' There was a half-full packet of Lavazza at the back of one of her cupboards. 'What time is it?'

'Twenty to one. Sit down, Maddie. Let me do this.' Maeve took the coffee from her and filled the kettle.

'Twenty to one? *Another* morning vanished without trace.' Maddie put her head in her hands. 'Oh, fuck, Maeve – what am I going to do? Everything's gone wrong.'

Maeve spooned coffee into a cafetière. 'You still have the option of getting the police involved, you know, Maddie.'

'No.'

'I think you're crazy not to.'

Maddie looked up at her cousin with blank eyes. 'Why is he doing this to me, Maeve? What's got into him?'

Maeve looked very serious. 'I think he's unhinged. You're not dealing with a rational person here. I think he's dangerous, and I think you need to get away. I phoned Deirdre O'Dare and asked if you could take the slot I'd earmarked for myself in Saint-Géyroux.'

'What? You can't do that, Maeve!'

'Of course I can.'

'No, no – then *I* can't do it! I can't commandeer your holiday!'

'Listen to me, Maddie. You need to go somewhere quickly and you need to go somewhere far away. Saint-Géyroux's perfect.'

There was a pause. Maddie twisted her hair. Then: 'What did Deirdre say?' she asked.

'I haven't talked to her yet. It's still night-time in LA. I left a message on her machine asking her to call me back when she gets up.'

'Fuck it, Maeve. I can't let Josh do this to me! I can't let him drive me off to another country! I'd be wimping out, bigtime.' Maddie stood up from the table and moved across to the kitchen window.

'You're not wimping out. If you're not prepared to tell the police about that bastard, you have absolutely no protection against him. You'll be running scared anywhere you go in Dublin. By the way, is it OK to call him a bastard now it's official?' Maeve raised her eyebrows in enquiry, and Maddie gave a rather wan smile and nodded. 'Anyway – what have you got to stay for?' continued Maeve. 'You've been saying for ages that you need a holiday, and now you've no job to keep you here.'

Maddie was beginning to find her cousin's authoritative tones very seductive. Maeve was right. She badly needed a break. But some perverse streak in her caused her to flail around for more excuses. 'I need to find a new job.'

'Reflex will take you on any time, you know that.'

'But running away's not going to solve anything, Maeve, even if it's cool with Deirdre that I stay. What about when I come back?'

'We'll deal with that when we have to. The most important thing right now is for you to get yourself together. You're in rag order – physically and mentally.'

Maddie couldn't really conjure up any more reasons not to go. Every time her cousin opened her mouth she seemed to remove another obstacle. 'Hell's bells. I envy you your powers of persuasion, Maeve. You'd be a demon at a presentation.' She took another sip of coffee and then put her mug down. It was almost as if the thud it made as it hit the table decided her. 'OK,' she said. 'I'm going. That is, if Deirdre'll have me.'

'Excellent. You're doing the right thing, you know.'

The phone rang, making Maddie jump as she always did these days. The two women waited for the answering machine to pick up. 'Hi? Maeve? It's Deirdre,' came a voice from the sitting room. Maeve started moving towards the door. 'Have you moved house or something? I don't recognize the phone number,' continued Deirdre. 'Well, here I am returning your call. It's about five o'clock in the morning and we've just come in from some nobby LA do. Actually, we should have been tucked up in bed an hour ago, but we decided to go for a swim and watch the dawn come up. That's the brilliant thing about living on a beach. Anyway, I'm glad you rang because I wanted to talk to you about—'

'Deirdre!' As Maeve picked up the phone in the sitting room, the answering machine shut off. 'Thanks for getting back. How are things? Good. Good. Rory? Good. Aoife? Excellent. In other words, life couldn't be better? Yup, yup – we're fine. Now, listen to me . . .'

Maddie stared out at the view through her kitchen window, noticing that the glass was smeared with city grime. There was an apartment block identical to her own directly opposite. She'd tried to grow geraniums in pots on her windowsill once, but they'd all died. The pots were still there, with dead geranium stalks sticking out of them. She noticed for the first time that the ledge was thick with pigeon droppings.

Maeve came into the kitchen. 'Maddie?' she said. 'Deirdre says it's cool for you to stay. Will you have a quick word with her?'

'OK.' Maddie headed towards the sitting room. At the door she turned to her cousin, biting her lip. 'Shit, Maeve – I hardly know her!'

'That's immaterial. Deirdre's got a big heart. I told her you were going through a messy time – don't worry, don't worry – ' (this at Maddie's appalled expression) ' – I didn't elaborate any further than that. She says you're to go over whenever you like.'

'But I – I – oh, God!' Maddie shook her head and threw up her hands. Then: 'Oh, *God*!' she repeated. 'I'd better not run up her phone bill any more.' She ran into the sitting room and picked up the phone. 'Hi, Deirdre,' she said.

'Hi, Maddie! We met once before, remember? After some opening night in Meagher's – ages ago. I remember you quite distinctly because you were wearing the most divine frock, and my husband made some appreciative remark about you and I was madly jealous.'

'Oh!' Maddie was slightly taken aback by the other woman's candour.

'Anyway,' continued Deirdre. 'It's fine by me, your coming to stay.'

'Are you sure, Deirdre?'

'I'm absolutely sure. I'd love to have a chum to do girly stuff with in Saint-Géyroux. It might get Bianca off my case.'

'Who's Bianca?'

'The local socialite. You'd better introduce yourself sharpish – she's got the keys to our gaff.'

Maddie sounded uncertain. 'Won't you be there?'

'Maybe, maybe not. We intended to get over next week sometime, but things are a bit up in the air at the moment. You're perfectly welcome to make yourself at home, though, whether we're there or not.'

'Oh, God, Deirdre – I don't know how to thank you.'

'Fiddle-dee-dee. A bottle of plonk will suffice. Now – I'm afraid I'm going to have to go. Rory's out on the deck looking as if that sunrise belongs exclusively to him. I think he's doing it deliberately, and it's irritating the hell out of me.' She didn't sound remotely irritated. In fact, she sounded as if the sight of Rory McDonagh watching the sun rise somewhere over Los Angeles was pretty damn special.

'Oh – OK, Deirdre. I'll see you soon, then?' There were dozens of Saint-Géyroux-related questions that Maddie wanted to ask, but she knew she couldn't keep Deirdre on the phone any longer.

'Mm hm. I'm looking forward to it. We could have a lot of fun, Maddie. Bon voyage!'

'Thanks, Deirdre. 'Bye.'

Maddie put down the phone and wandered back into the kitchen feeling dazed. Everything was happening so *fast*.

Maeve set two refills of coffee down on the table and picked up the Golden Pages from where it lay by the kitchen phone. She flicked through the directory until she found the travel agents' section. 'Now,' she said. 'How soon can you leave?'

'Whenever there's a flight available, I suppose,' Maddie said numbly. She took a sip of strong black coffee. 'But what about you, Maeve? Won't you be coming too? You were so looking forward to your break in Saint-Géyroux.'

'You're priority. I can go another time. Anyway, Jacqueline went into a huff when I told her I was thinking about going over. She's taking time off at the end of the summer. We'll make the trip together then.' Maeve ran an index finger down the columns of travel agents. 'There's an agent on Camden Street that I used last time I went over. They'll work out the connections and fax through an itinerary. You'll probably have to spend some time hanging around Gatwick.'

'That's OK. I'll get a lot of thinking done.' She twisted a strand of hair with listless fingers. 'Whereabouts exactly is this place, Maeve?'

'Saint-Géyroux? Well, your father was from Montpellier, right?'

'Yes.'

'Saint-Géyroux's literally a bus ride from there. Have you a map of France anywhere?'

'Mm. There should be one in the sitting room. I'll go and get it.'

She went into the sitting room and made straight for her bookshelves. The atlas she took down had a layer of dust on it, and she wiped it away with the sleeve of her robe. As she turned to go back into the kitchen she stopped dead.

'Maeve?' she called in a small voice. 'Can you come here?'

'Yeah. What is it?' asked Maeve, coming through the door.

'Look.' Maddie pointed at the fax machine on the shelf. It was quietly extruding fax paper, and several curling pages had already snaked onto the floor.

Maddie could see her own face looking up at her. It was a photocopy of the shot Sara Lennox had taken of her when she'd laughed at the jogger on the beach, and it had been defaced in much the same way as Josh had defaced her birthday photograph, with black lines scored over pudenda, breasts and face. A speech bubble had been drawn coming out of her mouth, and Maddie could just make out the words that were neatly printed inside it. It read: 'I AM A WHORE. I DESERVE WHAT I GET.' Another page was slowly emerging from the fax. It showed Sam's face, with his cheek against hers. A lewdly waggling tongue – similar to the Rolling Stones' logo – had been carefully drawn protruding from his smiling mouth. There were two speech bubbles on this page, but Maddie turned away. She didn't want to read what they said.

'OK,' said Maeve, briskly. 'I'll deal with this. You take that atlas into the kitchen and find out where Saint-Géyroux is. Then we're going to phone the travel agent.'

Maddie made her way back into the kitchen and sat down, setting the atlas on the table in front of her. She didn't bother to open it. She knew her hands were shaking too hard to turn the pages.

* * *

'We're going shopping,' Maeve said the next day. 'I had a look in your wardrobe while you were in the shower, and you have absolutely nothing that is suitable for June in a small village in the South of France.'

'I'm not going to be able to afford much. I'm not sure when I'll be earning again.'

'Go to the old fish market.'

'The arcade on George's Street?'

'Yeah. You'll get some fab retro stuff there. I got that frock I wore to Josh's party there for half nothing.'

'What? That sexy little chiffon number?'

'Yup.'

'But I heard you telling Vanessa it was English Eccentrics!'

'I lied. Do you think I fooled her?'

Maddie gave her cousin an indulgent look.

'I know,' confessed Maeve. 'I can be an appalling snob. But it's hard to admit that you're wearing a second-hand gúna when you're sitting beside someone whose Versace label is showing.'

'Maybe she just sewed it in,' said Maddie. 'Maybe she got her frock in the fish market, too.

Anyway, if you think about it, it's pretty cool to wear second-hand gear given that you can afford the real thing now. Very fuck-you.'

'So. We'll buy you a load of fuck-you stuff to wear in France.'

'That would really get up his nose, wouldn't it?'

'Whose nose?'

'Josh's. He liked me to look structured. He always encouraged me to wear clothes that set off my shape to advantage. He said it reflected a disciplined approach to life.'

'Jesus!' Maeve raised her eyes to heaven. Then she took Maddie by the hand. 'Come with me,' she said, leading her through into the bedroom and flinging open the wardrobe door. 'Just look!' she said, sweeping a dramatic hand along the rail and setting hangers jangling. 'Look at the labels! Sonia Rykiel, Jil Sander, Jean Muir . . .'

'They're all sale purchases, honestly,' said Maddie apologetically. 'I never fork out the full amount for anything if I can help it.'

'Now picture this,' said Maeve. 'This time next week you could be sitting on the *terrasse* of a café looking like a land girl, drinking *vin du patron* and reading some splendidly frivolous book.'

'D'you know something, Maeve?' said Maddie, taking a step back from the wardrobe and surveying its contents with a critical eye. 'Apart from having nothing suitable for holidaying in the French provinces, I just realized last night that I've nothing really *comfortable* to wear. I'm going to get rid of most of these clothes.'

Maeve flashed her a look of conspiracy. 'Shall we do it now?' she asked.

Maddie knew her cousin was working overtime to keep her diverted. She could have hugged her. 'Yes. Let's,' she said. The first thing she took out of the wardrobe was her tailored tux. 'That's going,' she said, throwing it onto the bed. 'And those black chintz trousers. And that skirt. It makes me feel as if I'm hobbled when I walk in it.'

Maeve sucked in her breath. 'Holy shit. That skirt cost a bomb, didn't it, Maddie? You're going to make a fortune from the swap shop.'

'That skirt was a present from Josh. It's going to Oxfam. I don't want any money for it.'

Maeve gave her an uncertain look. 'Oh. What about this?' she asked, holding up a sharply cut suit on a padded hanger.

'That can go to Oxfam too,' said Maddie.

'But it's a Louise Kennedy!'

'I don't care.'

'Shit, Maddie. Don't you think you should be a bit more rational about this? As you said yourself, you're not going to have an income for a while. Don't you think you should make two separate piles – one for Oxfam and the other for the swap shop? You could make a few bob from any designer stuff you have.' Maeve riffled through the clothes on the rack. 'I mean, look at this.' She held up a very plain, classic black dress with a Betty

Jackson label. 'You may have got it cut-price in a sale, but it's in great nick. They'd stick a price tag of fifty quid on that in the swap shop, and you'd get around half. You could make at least five hundred quid out of this lot.'

'No, Maeve. I'd rather they went to charity. These clothes are like big mistakes. D'you know what I mean? *Someone* might as well benefit from the mistakes I've made in my life—'

'Maddie. You haven't made mistakes. You're not to start blaming yourself.'

'I made a mistake with Josh. And I made the mistake of thinking that I was someone I'm not.' She sat down on the bed. 'I'm going to start all over again. I'm going to reinvent myself.'

Maeve smiled. 'Well. I think that's very brave of you.'

'I'm not sure it *is* brave. It's just something I have to do.'

Maeve gave Maddie a thoughtful look. Then suddenly she laughed. 'Way to go, girl!' she said. 'Hey – this could be fun! What else is in here? Oh! I don't think I've ever seen you wear these before. These are perfect for France.' She had retrieved a crumpled outfit from the very back of the wardrobe. White linen Capri pants and a matching top. She held them out, assessing with a critical eye, and then gasped and affected a shocked expression as she registered the label. 'What! Marks and Spencer! Not Comme des Garçons? Not Equipage? Not DKNY? Yeuch!'

She thrust the offending items of clothing into Maddie's hands.

Maddie looked at the Capri pants with a puzzled frown, trying to remember their provenance. 'When did I buy these?' she wondered. Then it hit her: 'Of course! It was yonks ago. The only time I wore them was to dad's fiftieth birthday, just before he died. Josh hated them.'

She recalled now with perfect clarity the day she'd bought the outfit. It had been a glorious sunny day in late June: she'd had lunch with a girlfriend on the terrasse outside Fitzers on Dawson Street and they'd gone impulse buying later, feeling a bit giggly and nicely fuzzy from the wine they'd drunk over lunch. She'd bought a silly night-shirt with a picture of a panda on, and a pair of flowery flip-flops, and a T-shirt with 'Don't Judge a Girl by her T-shirt' in wavy lettering on the front (where were all those frivolous garments now? she wondered), and when she'd tried on the Capri pants and white top in Marks and Sparks, her friend had said: 'Oh, yes, Maddie! They look great on you!'

And later on that evening Josh had called round to take her to a friend's barbecue. 'Been shopping?' he'd queried when he saw the carrier bags strewn on her bed. 'Yes! Get an eyeful of this,' she'd said, producing her pristine new ensemble with an enthusiastic flourish. 'Aren't they sweet? I thought I'd wear them this evening.' Josh's eyes had narrowed as he registered the M&S carrier

bag. 'Darling,' he'd said. 'You are not –
emphatically *not* wearing chain store threads to
Julian's.'

'But it's just a barbecue!' she'd protested.

'It is not "just" a barbecue,' he'd remonstrated
with exaggerated patience. 'It's an extremely
valuable networking opportunity, and you are an
extremely valuable accessory, sweetie-pie, whether
you like it or not.' Ignoring her mutinous look,
he'd pulled her into him and kissed her on the
nose. 'Anyway, white makes you look at least half a
stone heavier than you are. You look much better
in black. Svelte.'

Maddie had started to twist her hair, reconsider-
ing. 'OK. You're right. But what *will* I wear, then?'
she'd asked uncertainly. Josh had given her a long,
assessing look as he had done her thinking for her,
that assessing look she always found such a turn
on. 'Let's see. That skinny black top. Your Diesel
jeans, that silver belt, those black leather boots.'

'Boots in this weather!' she'd protested. 'I
thought a pair of funky sandals—'

'Boots,' he'd said. 'And that black thong I
bought for you. I wouldn't mind a replay of last
weekend's raunchy little scenario when I take you
home tonight.' He had pulled her even closer and
run his hands over her buttocks. 'Do you remember, Maddie?'

And she had smiled as she remembered, and
allowed herself to be fondled, and then she had
gone obediently to the wardrobe to fetch the

garments he'd specified. And now she looked down at the crumpled white linen in her hands and repeated in a toneless voice: 'He really hated them.'

'Then they're definitely going to France with you,' said Maeve, taking Capri pants and top from her and throwing them into the laundry basket. The jangling noise of hangers resumed as she carried on riffling through the wardrobe. 'Oh! What about this?' She held up a sea-green satin cheongsam.

'Chuck it.'

Maeve looked at her dubiously. 'Actually, I think you should keep this, Maddie. You've always looked sensational in it. It's one of the sexiest things you have.'

'I don't ever want to look sexy again.'

'Hell – I know you think that now, Maddie, but there's going to come a time when you'll change your mind. I don't know how long it'll take, but it will happen. I'm absolutely sure of that.'

'*I'm* not.'

'Oh, don't let him *do* this to you!' pleaded Maeve. She sat down beside Maddie on the bed and took hold of her hand. 'Listen to me. If reinventing yourself by trashing your entire wardrobe is an act of courage, then holding on to this dress is – well, it's an act of faith.' She held the cheongsam out to her cousin. 'Hang on to it, please? Do it for me. I want to know that you're going to come through this. I want to know you're going to wear a dress like this again some day, because otherwise Josh has won.'

Maddie took the dress reluctantly. 'OK. I'll keep it.'

'And you've to let me know when you wear it again. Is that a promise?'

'That's a promise.' Maddie hung the dress back in her wardrobe.

'You won't regret keeping it – I'm sure of it. Now – where's the partner to this?' Maeve picked up a sandal from the floor of the wardrobe. It was of soft red leather with a high, slender heel and a long, narrow ankle strap. As soon as she held it out, she realized what she had in her hand. 'Oh, Jesus, Maddie – I'm sorry. It's in my house, isn't it?'

Maddie nodded. 'It's OK. I'll bin it.' She stooped down and picked up the sandal from the floor. 'By the way, Maeve?' she said on her way out the door. 'Maybe you'd get rid of that red dress I left in your house?'

'I'll need to have it cleaned before I send it to Oxfam,' said Maeve carefully. 'Mended too. And I'm actually not sure it can be.'

'That's OK,' said Maddie. 'I want you to burn that one.'

*   *   *

The next day Maeve booked Maddie on a flight to Montpellier on Thursday, leaving the ticket open-ended so that Maddie could stay for as long as she felt she needed. She also retrieved her cousin's bits and pieces from the Complete Works, telling Maddie's former colleagues that the reason she was unable to pick them up herself was because she was still down with a nasty virus. Maddie felt bad about not going back to the agency to say goodbye. She had spent the last five years of her life working there. But she couldn't run the risk of bumping into Josh.

On Tuesday after another pacy walk along the Pigeonhouse Pier with Maeve, they arrived home to find that a bulky manila envelope had been pushed through her letterbox. It contained the keys Josh had appropriated with a note attached which read: 'You're still behaving very childishly, Maddie. Don't you think changing the lock is a bit over the top? It won't be long before you'll be begging me to visit you. In case you've forgotten what we had going between us, have a look at the enclosed. I still love you. Josh.'

'The enclosed' was a bunch of printed-out e-mails which Maddie had written to Josh quite early on in their relationship. A lot of them contained explicit references to their lovemaking, and how good they had been in bed together. Maddie hadn't held much back, and some of the letters were seriously raunchy. Josh had used a text-liner to highlight these passages in a lurid shade of purple. Weeping with humiliation, Maddie consigned the pages to the bin.

Her fax had been disconnected since Monday afternoon when Josh had sent the copies of Sara's photographs, and she never answered the phone now. It rang dozens of times in the day. The volume on the answering machine was turned down, and Maddie would retreat to her bedroom so that she wouldn't hear anything when Maeve played the messages back.

She knew that Maeve wasn't erasing any of them. Maddie had a suspicion that she'd held onto the obscene faxes, too, in case they were required as evidence. She had even questioned the wisdom of Maddie binning the bundle of e-mail letters, but had backed down immediately when her cousin had turned on her, screaming that no-one – *no-one* – would ever see those letters, even if Josh went as far as murder.

Maeve had sought the advice of the gardai regarding Josh's behaviour. She sat Maddie down on Tuesday evening and told her what they'd said. Maddie had gone into a panic when the guards were mentioned, but Maeve had reassured her that she hadn't touched on the rape.

'How could you think I'd go against your wishes, Maddie? My own instinct would be to report him, but it's none of my business if you choose not to.'

'I just can't, Maeve. I couldn't do that to him. I know he's being a bastard from hell, but we had a good relationship once – you know we did. I spent five years of my life with him – I couldn't bear for him to maybe end up in jail.'

'OK. You won't charge him with rape in case he goes to jail. But it's unlikely he'll go to jail for stalking you. Couldn't you at least put in an official complaint that you're being seriously harassed? It could only do some good. He might get off your case if he knew the guards had been approached.'

Maddie looked uncertain. 'Look – I'm going away soon. Let's leave it until I come back, OK? If he's still bothering me then, I'll think about doing something to try and stop him.'

' "Bothering" is a pretty mild term for what he's doing to you, Maddie.'

'Maeve – you're putting me under pressure. Let's leave it.'

Maeve acquiesced with a sigh. 'OK. Let's just try and get through the next couple of days.'

*   *   *

The following day over breakfast Maeve suggested that it was about time they took a trip into town to buy clothes for her holiday. Maddie hadn't wanted to leave the flat, but she knew she had to. Shopping for clothes was a *routine* thing to do. It was yet another step towards getting her life back to normal.

'And when we've finished doing that I'm going to drag you off somewhere for a drink,' announced Maeve. She registered the expression on her cousin's face. 'Having a drink is another *normal thing* to do, Maddie, and I'm going to encourage you to do as many normal things as I can before you go away. With a bit of luck, by the time you come back, *everything* will be back to normal, and we can put these last hellish few weeks behind us for ever.'

Maddie looked so insecure suddenly that Maeve took her hand between her own. 'I don't want to bully you into behaving normally, Maddie. If that's not the way you want to handle this, I'm not going to force you.'

'You're not bullying me. You're dead right, Maeve. It's just that some days are more difficult than others.' She'd had another flashback the previous evening, and hadn't been able to get to sleep for hours afterwards. She still hadn't said anything to Maeve about them.

As she stood up and reached for the breadknife she suddenly went rigid. Josh was turning her over and was thrusting himself into her from behind. One hand was round her throat, the other on her mouth pulling her head back until she thought her neck might break. It was impossible to breathe. She heard herself trying to say 'Please', but no sound came. Finally she managed a huge, shuddering gasp of air, shaking her head violently from side to side.

'Maddie? What's wrong? Are you all right?' Maeve's voice came from a distance. Maddie found herself sitting down again, the breadknife clutched tightly in her hand, her breath coming raggedly. She would never get used to them –

never immunize herself to the horror of those images which came alive without warning before her mind's eye.

'I'm fine,' she said with an unconvincing smile. 'I just had a cramp. I'll be all right in a minute. And yes – I'd love to go for a drink later.'

Maeve was looking at her with a concerned expression. 'Maddie? You know I'm not under-estimating what you're going through, don't you? If you feel that weeping buckets or smashing a window or telling me to shut the fuck up is what's appropriate, I'll understand, you know.'

'I know you will, Maeve. That's why you're my friend. Now, shut the fuck up.' She was amazed that she could actually manage a smile.

* * *

In Jenny Vander, a retro clothes shop in the old fish market, Maeve rummaged through the rails of clothes while Maddie looked on, trying hard to show an interest she was far from feeling.

'What about this?' asked Maeve, holding up a little Forties dress in pale rose silk crêpe de Chine. It was gossamer light and had small doves embroidered on the bodice. Maddie made a face. 'Not really me, is it? But then I don't really know what *is* me any more, do I?'

'Try it on, Maddie. It'll be hot in France – you'll want to bring really lightweight stuff. Here – try these as well.' Maeve hung a couple of Fifties cotton sundresses on the hook in the changing cubicle. One was in a floral print with a tight bodice and a full skirt, and the other had yellow and white stripes and a boat neck with a white collar. It was very Audrey Hepburn.

'How much?'

'Thirty quid for the stripy one and thirty-five for the flowery one.'

'Shit. Is that all? Maybe I could afford something else?'

'I'll root a couple out for you to try. Do you trust me?'

'You know I do.'

Maddie got into the crêpe de Chine dress while her cousin continued to search through the rails of clothes. When she emerged from the cubicle, Maeve looked at her and smiled. 'You look about fourteen,' she said.

'It feels kinda weird. Girly.' She looked at the price tag attached to the sleeve and gave a theatrical gasp. 'Uh-oh. This one's expensive.'

'How much?'

'Forty-five.' She smiled.

'Go for it, Maddie. Take all three. And this one too.' Maeve handed her a yellow-sprigged cotton with buttons down the front. Maddie looked at it rather dubiously. 'You said you wanted to reinvent yourself,' Maeve reminded her. 'This stuff is a million miles away from the kind of stuff you used to wear for Josh. And just think how it'll feel in France, strolling through olive groves and vineyards in your little gúnas with the sun on your face, picking ripe figs and doing all that country shit. You'll look like Juliette Binoche in *Chocolat*.'

'Actually, I'll look more like that advertisement for low fat spread that I worked on a couple of years ago.' Maddie took the dress from Maeve. 'This is quite sweet.'

'This kind of stuff always looks better on. Try it. And these.' She slipped a couple of little cardigans off their wire hangers. 'You'll need something for when dusk falls and you're listening to the cicadas while sipping the local wine, sitting out under the fig trees and—'

'OK, Maeve. You've painted a very appealing picture. I'll take the lot. What'll the damage be?'

Maeve checked the price tags and did some quick mental arithmetic. 'Around a hundred and seventy-five quid if you take the cardigans as well.'

Maddie gave a wry smile. 'That's less than Josh paid for that skirt I sent to Oxfam.'

'All right!' said Maeve. 'Let's try some more.' She resumed her assessment of the garments on display, critically rifling through frock after retro frock. And this time, Maddie joined in.

*　　*　　*

On their way home they stopped off in Fallon's pub on the Coombe for a drink. Maeve had suggested somewhere in Temple Bar and had kicked herself when Maddie reminded her that it was a regular haunt of Josh's.

Maddie was glad they'd chosen Fallon's. The atmosphere there was relaxed and easygoing. Most of the pubs in Temple Bar were mercilessly hip; Fallon's was unpretentious and cosy and had resisted the relentless trend toward 'Oirishification'. And the staff there were friendly – not self-consciously cool or ostentatiously superior.

It was just after three o'clock and there were very few in. A couple of middle-aged women had laid claim to the snug, and an elderly man sat propped up at the bar. The barman was leaning against the counter, reading the *Evening Herald*.

Maddie surprised herself by following Maeve's example and ordering a pint of Guinness, which was something she rarely drank. They made themselves comfortable at a table under the window. Motes of dust were dancing in the rays of the afternoon sun which streamed in on top of them, and Maddie felt tension very gradually seeping from her body. As long as she was here in Dublin she would feel the need to be vigilant, but for the first time in ages she was experiencing a state verging on relaxation.

Maeve's mobile chirruped, and she excused herself and took it outside. Maddie remained sitting in what could only be described as a pleasant torpor, watching the progress of the motes in the sunlight and enjoying the fact that her mind was quite blissfully blank.

'That was Deirdre,' said Maeve, on her return a minute or two later. She tucked her mobile away in her bag and sat back down beside Maddie.

'Deirdre O'Dare?' Maddie immediately felt tension begin to atrophy her limbs. She sat up straight. 'Is there a problem?'

Maeve made an ambiguous face. 'Not really,' she said. 'But they've been delayed in LA for a few days. They were hoping to have arrived in France at the weekend, but there was a glitch – Rory's agent had lined something up for him that he couldn't get out of. Deirdre says she's not exactly sure when they'll get there, but that they'll definitely be arriving some time next week.'

'Oh.' Maddie couldn't help sounding dismayed. 'What should I do in the meantime? Should I postpone my flight?'

'Absolutely not.' Maeve was adamant. 'Deirdre was going to contact someone in Saint-Géyroux and ask them to pick you up, but I had a better idea.'

'Oh?'

'I said I'd ring Sam.'

'Sam? Sam Newman?'

'Yeah. He and Sara will be there, remember? I thought it would be nice for you to be picked up by someone you knew.'

'Oh, Maeve – I couldn't ask them to come all the way out to the airport!' Maddie was beginning to think that this odyssey was jinxed. 'They've already been so kind to me – I'd feel like some

244

awful kind of grasping nuisance. Isn't there a bus that goes directly to Saint-Géyroux?'

'It only runs twice a day. But if you make your own way to Gignac – that's the nearest town to the village – they can meet you there, no hassle. I've done it. You just take the *navette* from the airport to the bus station in Montpellier and get on the bus to Gignac. Sam picks you up on the esplanade, and within ten minutes you'll be bang in the centre of bustling downtown Saint-Géyroux.'

'It's really that simple?'

'It really is that simple.'

Maddie sucked in her breath and let it out in a long sigh of relief. 'Actually, it's very reassuring to know that there are at least two people at the other end who aren't complete strangers.'

'Three.'

Maddie gave her cousin a look of incomprehension. 'Three?'

'You've met Daniel, haven't you? Sara's brother. I saw you talking to him at her exhibition.'

Maddie made a face. 'Yes. I'll steer clear of him. He's the rudest man I ever met.'

Maeve looked surprised. 'Did you really think so? I thought he was quite charming. And he's incredibly sexy. Even I could see that.'

'Daniel *Lennox*! Sexy! He's middle-aged and he looks as though he works on a building site.'

'That's what I mean.' Maeve raised her eyebrows at Maddie and smiled. 'Like a bit of rough with a lot of *savoir-faire*.'

Maddie shook her head. 'Not my type at all.'

'Excuse me?' The barman raised a hand to attract attention. They looked up simultaneously. 'Is one of you Maddie Godard?'

'Yes. That's me.'

'There's a phone call for you.' He indicated the pay phone on the wall next to them.

Feeling puzzled, Maddie automatically got to her feet and picked up the receiver.

'Don't talk to him, Maddie!' blurted Maeve, suddenly making the connection that Maddie had failed to make.

She was too late. Josh's voice was already in her ear.

'How many times did you fuck him, whore? Did you bend over for him like you used to for me? Did he fuck you doggie-fashion like the bitch you are?'

*   *   *

At one o'clock the following afternoon in Gatwick airport, Maddie boarded the flight to Montpellier.

Chapter Ten

Maddie emerged from the air-conditioned atmosphere of the Aéroport Montpellier Méditerranée into a hot, blue-sky afternoon and boarded the *navette* – the airport bus – which would take her into the centre of town.

As the bus sped towards Montpellier, she studied the passing landscape. She tried to remember what age she'd been when she'd last visited this part of France. It had been shortly before her grandfather died, so she supposed she'd been around sixteen. There were a lot more industrial parks flanking the motorway now, and anodyne office buildings constructed from pale concrete and steel.

As they drew nearer the city, elegant constructions of glass, with plazas and fountains and sculptures began to appear. These in turn gave way to gracious boulevards shaded by mature plane trees, which led into the old part of the city where the bus station was. Here the streets were narrow and winding, and things were more rundown. Once-elegant apartment buildings had fallen into varying states of disrepair, with crumbling stucco and dangerous-looking wrought iron balconies laden with pots containing bright geraniums. Laundry hung from windows.

She got out of the *navette* at the station and made her way straight to bay seventeen, where Maeve had told her the bus to Gignac would be waiting. There were half a dozen people already on the bus, and as more people boarded Maddie realized that they all seemed to know each other. When he wasn't hurling abuse at the kamikaze mobilettes swinging carelessly in and out of the traffic, even the driver joined in the chat. Maddie learned that Monsieur Béraud's beloved dog had died, that Mme Minot's son had landed a wonderful job in Boston, and that Régine Thibault had dislocated her shoulder.

They travelled along the dual carriageway for several kilometres, heading north away from the city. When they eventually turned off, negotiating recently built roundabouts, the landscape changed. The barren terrain that had been carved up to build the motorway became more lush. The scorched ochre earth was stippled with leaf green where they passed vineyards; terracotta tiled roofs of farmsteads rose above clusters of dense, dark cypress trees, and wooded hills stretched towards a blue horizon lightly streaked with pale traces of candyfloss cloud.

The bus stopped at three or four small villages before the driver turned his cheerful face to her and said: 'Gignac, Mademoiselle.'

Thanking him, Maddie climbed down onto the footpath and hefted her bag up onto her shoulder. 'Mademoiselle!' A call came from inside the bus, and through the window she saw an elderly woman waving at her. 'Vous avez oublié votre sac, Mademoiselle,' she said with a smile, as she passed down the bag containing the airport shop vodka that Maddie had bought as a present for the McDonagh–O'Dares.

'Oh! Merci! Vous êtes très gentille,' said Maddie, smiling back. She watched as the bus took off down the street, and then looked around her.

She had been set down on a quiet, tree-lined esplanade. Across the road from her were three or four small cafés which shared access to a long, narrow terrasse where tables were laid out under a green awning. This was where Sam had arranged to meet her.

She crossed the road and wandered down the long terrasse, looking out for her lift. There was no sign of him. In fact, there was hardly anyone around. A couple of dark-haired blokes sat nursing beers and lolling back ostentatiously in their chairs with their tanned bare legs outstretched. They eyed her with interest as she walked past, so she made for a table at the opposite end of the terrasse. A stout elderly woman was resting in the shade of a plane tree, fanning herself with a magazine, and a man wearing very dark sunglasses was reading a newspaper, a pastis on the table in front of him. She glanced at him as she passed, and then she took a second look. The newspaper was the *Irish Times*, and the man behind the paper was Daniel Lennox.

She hesitated, but he hadn't seen her, so she went on by with her face averted. She knew it was childish of her, but she really didn't think she could handle him right now. She extracted her magazine from her airport carrier bag and sat down at a table some distance away, hoping that Sam wouldn't be long.

A waiter came over and she ordered a beer. She felt rather foolish sitting by herself, gazing intently at the magazine she'd already skimmed twice from cover to cover while someone she knew was sitting just half a dozen tables away from her. She sensed that she was still being scrutinized by the two dudes she'd passed by, and this made her feel even more uncomfortable.

The waiter approached with her beer. There was something too polite about the way he presented it to her, and about the tone of his voice when he addressed her as *Ma'mzelle*, and she was glad when he turned and walked away with an arrogant swagger. When he reached the dudes, he paused, and they exchanged low words. Maddie lowered her head and kept her eyes locked unseeingly on the text of the cinema review she was pretending to read, hearing laughter ring out at the other side of the terrasse. There was something nasty about the laugh that reminded her of Josh and the way he used to laugh with his awful friend, Baz. She'd wondered sometimes about what provoked that laugh, and she'd worked out without too much difficulty that it was the way they used to laugh when they were observing women. The laughter from the other end of the terrasse came again, and Maddie found herself hyperventilating. Quickly she adjusted her posture, leaning her elbows on the table and hiding her expression behind the magazine. There was nothing she could do about her body language – shoulders hunched, one leg wound tightly round the other – but she couldn't allow anyone to see her face as the demon possessed her.

The flashback was brutal, but, mercifully, it was brief.

Afterwards, she took time to regain control of her breathing, adopt a more relaxed demeanour, and resume her mask. She tried to take a sip of her beer, but by the time the glass met her lips her hand was shaking so much she had to put it down again. Instead she sought refuge once more behind the screen of her magazine.

When she lowered it and raised her eyes again some minutes later it was to find Daniel Lennox looking directly at her with an interested expression on his face. He was leaning back in his chair with his newspaper folded on the table in front of him and he had taken off his shades. He raised his glass. 'Hello, Madeleine,' he said.

'Oh, hi!' she answered, with a feeble attempt at injecting a note of surprise into her voice. She was glad that her sunglasses were nearly as dark as the ones he'd been wearing. 'I didn't know it was you behind the paper.'

'It's shocking really, how few people read the *Irish Times* in Gignac,' he remarked, getting to his feet unhurriedly. 'A lot of them actually read *Midi Libre* or some other French rag. Hard to credit, isn't it?' She'd almost forgotten what an insufferable git he was. The muscles in her jaw stiffened as he moved towards her, smiling and holding out his hand. Hell. Oh – *hell*. Why did he have to be the first person she'd run into in this rural retreat? She took his hand and smiled politely at him. It crossed her mind that this man couldn't extort a genuine smile from anyone who wasn't lionizing him. As their hands made contact, Daniel leaned down and kissed her in the continental fashion, once on each cheek. She wasn't prepared for the third kiss which he planted to the left of her nose, and she found herself flinching. He looked at her with some amusement. 'You've forgotten, haven't you, that only Parisians confine themselves to two kisses? We Southern peasants are more demonstrative. We like to steal three. An intimate might even expect four.'

He sat down beside her and raised a hand. 'Encore un pastis, Olivier, s'il vous plaît,' he called to the waiter. 'Et un demi pour Madame.'

'D'accord, Monsieur Lennox. Tout d'suite.' This was accompanied by an obsequious bow, and

Maddie noticed that this time the waiter didn't meet her eye.

'I told Sam I'd pick you up. It's the last day of Sara's stay here, and she wanted him to help pack equipment. He was very cross at not being allowed to meet you off the bus, but I reassured him by promising that we'd meet up by the river on the way home. Maybe have a swim.'

Something lurched ominously in Maddie's heart. She started to twist the end of the long silk scarf she'd bought to cover the gash on her neck. 'I thought Sara was staying here for the rest of the month?'

'She's decided to head north. There's some phenomenal countryside that was flooded in the Picardie region recently, and she wants to get shots.'

'Is Sam going with her?'

'No. He was vociferous in his objections for some reason, so Sara let him off this time.'

Thank God. At least there was *someone* here with whom she had some rapport. She cringed at the thought of being stuck in a remote French village with this man she hardly knew – and really didn't want to know any better.

Daniel stretched his long legs out underneath the table, and she shifted her stance imperceptibly in case his foot might make contact with hers. 'Sara tells me that you're here for some peace and quiet?'

'Yes.'

'Then you've come to the right place. Saint-Géyroux's a seriously sleepy town. The only major event of recent history is the war being waged over the new rubbish-disposal system.'

'Really?' She made an effort to sound interested.

'Mm. The local *mairie* has introduced a wheely-bin system and the villagers don't like it. Merci, Olivier.' The waiter had reappeared with their drinks on a tray. 'They spend a lot of their time surreptitiously pushing bins around the streets at night. No-one wants a *poubelle* parked outside their door with half the neighbourhood's stinking rubbish crammed into it. You've lost a lot of weight.'

'What?' Maddie didn't like the personal tone of the remark. What business was it of his whether or not she'd lost weight?

'You've lost a lot of weight. It doesn't suit you.' He was regarding her with analytical eyes. Maddie had seen that look before. It was the way Sara Lennox looked at people, too, but Sara's eyes didn't have that knowing glint that her brother's held – that glint that seemed to say 'I am so fucking superior to you.' 'Maybe Sam could rustle up a few square meals for you to fatten you up. He's been indispensable since Mme Thibault banjaxed her shoulder.'

Who was Mme Thibault? The name sounded familiar, somehow. Daniel Lennox pre-empted her question.

'Mme Thibault's my housekeeper. She dislocated her shoulder two days ago and she's staying with her sister here in Gignac to recuperate. I'm lost without her. I might try bribing Sam to stay on and cook for me until she's mended.'

He leaned back in his chair with his arms folded behind his head and allowed a silence to fall between them. He didn't seem to find the silence at all uncomfortable, but it fazed Maddie badly. She tried to think of something to say.

'So. How's the painting going?' She yelped inwardly. God! What a banal question to ask of a major artist!

'All right,' he replied, affably enough. 'I'm working on a series of portraits at the moment.' There was a beat. Then: 'Sam tells me you've lost your job?' he said.

'That's right.'

'Are you very upset about that?'

'No. I'm not at all sorry, actually. I realized that I hadn't been enjoying it really, not for ages. I'd been with the same agency for five years. It was time for a change.' As she spoke the words she was amazed by the confidence with which they rang out. It seemed to her that it was the first honest observation she'd made about her career in a long, long time.

'What are you going to do?'

'I'm not sure. That's why I came here. So that I could have time to sort myself out.'

Silence fell again. Maddie reached for her beer

and pretended to be riveted by the performance of a sparrow pecking at crumbs beneath the adjoining table.

'Daniel! Hi!' A sexy female voice rang out across the terrasse.

'Bianca! How are things?' Daniel Lennox rose to his feet.

'Fine, thanks.' A striking-looking woman somewhere in her mid-thirties was making her way towards them between the tables. She wore palazzo pants in fluid white silk with a white shirt knotted at the midriff, and a snowy white Highland terrier strutted importantly at her heels. The eyes of the two dudes on the other side of the terrasse followed her appreciatively as she moved towards their table. She was carrying a basket of groceries which she dumped on a chair before air-kissing Daniel four times.

'Do you want to join us? This is Madeleine Godard, by the way. Madeleine, this is Bianca Ingram.' Daniel held out a chair for her before resuming his own seat.

'Hello, Madeleine. Pleased to meet you. You must be the friend Sam was expecting?' said Bianca, smiling at her with her teeth. Maddie suspected that the older woman had calculated her age, her dress size and her sex appeal quotient in a single glance.

'That's right,' said Maddie, smiling back.

'How did you know that?' asked Daniel.

'I ran into Sam earlier. Anyway, I know everything that goes on in Saint-Géyroux,' said Bianca. The smile she bestowed on him contrived to be both knowing and coquettish. 'Here – have a nectarine,' she said, taking one from a paper bag, polishing it on her pristine sleeve, and biting into it herself before handing it to him. 'Would you care for one, Madeleine?' she asked, setting another one down in front of her without waiting for an answer. Then she glanced at her watch. 'I'm afraid I mustn't linger. I'm expecting guests for dinner tonight and I've masses of shopping still to do.'

'Why am I not one of your esteemed guests?' asked Daniel, taking a cigarette from a packet of Gitanes and tapping it against the box.

'I invited you, Daniel. You said no.'

'Did I? That was before Mme Thibault dislocated her shoulder. Can't I change my mind?' Daniel lowered his head and lit his cigarette, regarding Bianca from under his eyebrows.

'At such short notice? You are incorrigible.' A sexy little purr of laughter came from somewhere low in Bianca Ingram's throat.

'Please. I should be taking advantage of any offers of square meals that come my way while my housekeeper's out of commission.'

Bianca relented. 'Oh, all right. Sara and Sam are coming, and so are you, Madeleine. That is if you want to. I mentioned to Sam that I needed to make up numbers now that the McDonaghs can't make it, and he came up with the bright idea of inviting you.'

'Oh! I —'

'You're staying in Rory and Deirdre's house, aren't you?' she continued blithely. 'I have their spare key. You can get it from me this evening when you come for dinner.'

It was *fait accompli*, then.

'You're very kind. Thank you.' Maddie was at a bit of a loss. She would have loved to have spent the evening on her own, unpacking the few things she'd brought with her and just taking it easy. She wasn't feeling remotely sociable, and if she was finding small talk with Daniel Lennox difficult, dinner party conversation would be a nightmare.

Bianca's dog was snuffling around at Maddie's feet. 'Dora Maar! Sit!' commanded Bianca. Maddie wondered why the dog's name sounded familiar, and then remembered that Dora Maar had been one of Picasso's mistresses. Ma'mzelle Maar chose to ignore Bianca and continued to sniff interestedly at Maddie's ankles.

'That bitch could do with a firm hand,' said Bianca, glancing down at Dora Maar, and then smiling up at Daniel through flirtatious lashes. She took hold of his wrist and squinted first at her own watch and then at his, letting a finger brush against his palm as she did so. Maddie noticed that there was dried paint under his nails. 'Oops,' said Bianca, getting to her feet with a flurry of white silk. 'My watch is running slow. I'd better fly. See you both around eight.' She gave Maddie a sudden curious look. 'Do you know – I'm certain I've seen you somewhere before.'

'Oh? I wonder where we might have met?'

'It'll come to me later. It always does,' she said. 'Come, Dora Maar.' This time the dog obeyed her.

Daniel watched her flutter away and then he drained the pastis in his glass. 'Drink up,' he said. 'We should think about making tracks, too.' He turned to her suddenly and gave her a shrewd look. 'Do you really want to go tonight?' he asked.

'Not really,' she found herself saying, watching his fingers as they ground out the cigarette in the tin ashtray on the table.

'We'll get a bloody good dinner,' he said, stretching himself lazily. 'Unless Bianca's on a diet again. She has an unfortunate penchant for *cuisine minceur*.' Maddie found herself looking at the gap between buttons where his shirt stretched across his belly. He followed her eyeline. 'I know. *I* can afford to lose weight, but *you* can't, Madeleine. Maybe you could do us both a favour by stealing food off my plate this evening.' He bit into the nectarine which Bianca had given him, and then he stood up and swung her bag onto his shoulder. 'Don't forget your nectarine,' he added. 'Or don't you want it?'

'I'm not really hungry.'

'Keep it for later, then.' He picked up her plastic carrier bag and dropped it in.

'I'll take that,' offered Maddie, but he ignored her and strode off across the terrasse, adroitly

259

managing to handle her bags and dispatch his nectarine at the same time. She found it difficult to keep up. 'What'll I do until it's time to go to Bianca's?' she asked, feeling agonizingly inadequate. 'I've no way of getting into where I'm staying.'

'You can come to my house,' said Daniel.

'I don't want to get in the way—'

'You couldn't get in the way in my house even if you tried to,' he replied with equanimity. 'It's vast. Hell – you could even live there and I wouldn't notice.'

They made their way down the road to a battered deux-chevaux that was parked on a nearby square. It was the only car there, and had obviously been parked with a complete disregard for restrictions. Daniel threw the bags onto the back seat, and Maddie reached for the door handle, thinking it was odd that a wealthy man like Daniel Lennox should be driving such a beat-up car. But then, it was *de rigueur* for artists to be eccentric and unpredictable. She supposed it was his ostentatious way of showing a lack of interest in material things. She pulled the door open and found herself looking in at the steering wheel. She'd opened the driver's door by mistake.

'Excellent. It'll make a change to be chauffeured,' remarked Daniel. He tossed her the car keys and got into the passenger seat.

Maddie made an automatic grab for the keys as they flew across the bonnet.

'Oh – I didn't mean to do that,' she said, leaning into the car and addressing him over the steering wheel. 'I mean, I just opened the left-hand door because I thought it was the passenger door. I'm not used to left-hand drive.'

'Well, you might as well get used to it,' he replied. 'Get in. I'll give you directions.'

She fingered the car keys, stalling for time. She didn't feel comfortable about driving an unfamiliar car on the wrong side of the road. She had only ever driven on the left-hand side of the road one summer in the States years ago, when she was a student. Any time she and Josh had holidayed together, he had done all the driving. 'What about insurance?' she hazarded.

'You're covered.'

Again she hesitated fractionally, but she knew it was important not to wimp out. She'd have to give it a go. She slid into the driver's seat feeling awkward, started the engine and put the unfamiliar gear lever into what she hoped was first. The car stalled immediately.

'You haven't driven a deux-chevaux before, have you?' he asked.

'No,' she confessed.

'OK. Let me explain how it's different.'

He gave her a simple rundown on how the gears worked, and when she got the car going she drove around the square a few times for practice before setting out through the streets. Her progress was rather jerky, but she resisted the impulse to ask

Daniel to take over. He didn't talk much as she drove except to tell her where to turn, and she was glad of this because she needed to keep her concentration fixed on the road. It was hot in the car, and she knew that her face had gone very red and that sweat was starting to show on the underarms of her dress.

Beside her Daniel Lennox seemed enviably cool. He had pushed the passenger seat as far back as it would go in order to accommodate his long legs, and there was nothing about his body language to suggest that he was in any way fazed by her driving, even when she nearly went into the back of a double-parked Merc.

Once they were out of the town her confidence increased and she allowed herself to take in some of the passing scenery. Daniel filled her in on the local geography.

'This is the scenic route,' he said. 'We're going the long way round. I thought you might like to know where to go if you want a swim. That river you see there is the Hérault. There are some beautiful spots for swimming along the river, but if you're on your own it's probably safer to go to the creek by the pont du Diable, on this side of Saint-Jean-de-Fos.'

'The pont du Diable? The Devil's Bridge?'

'It's the oldest medieval bridge in France. It lies on the path of one of the old pilgrimage routes to Saint-Guilhem-le-Désert. Old Guilhem was a staunch defender of Christianity way back in the ninth century. He went so far as to get his nose cut off by a wild Saracen in the process of defending it. Christianity, that is – not his nose. Charlemagne gave him a piece of the true cross as a reward, and I imagine Guilhem's ma gave him a piece of her mind.'

The bridge they were approaching was twentieth century. 'Where's the pont du Diable?' she asked.

'Over there.' Daniel Lennox indicated an area slightly below them. The old bridge lay beneath and to one side of the one they were about to cross. 'The local boys dive from the ramparts in a very ostentatious display of machismo.' He looked at her and smiled. 'Needless to say, I've never done it. Hang a right here and pull over. We'll see if Sara and Sam are here yet.'

Maddie negotiated the right-hand bend and pulled up by the side of the road where a number of cars were parked already. She got out of the car, relieved to feel a breeze move the silky crêpe de Chine of her frock against her sticky legs, and followed Daniel over to the rampart. He stood looking down at the river far below. It was turbulent and green, and swirled over dangerous-looking rocks into a wide creek where it rested calmly before continuing its journey further downstream. A couple of people were swimming in the creek and others were stretched out on the shores on either side, taking it easy in the late afternoon sun.

Maddie felt dizzy as she looked over the bridge. It was a long way down. 'Do boys really dive from here?' she asked.

'Yeah,' said Daniel, sitting astride the rampart. 'Their street cred depends on it. Some poor bugger ends up rather uncoolly splattered across the rocks every summer, but it doesn't put them off. Look. There goes one now.'

A lean, brown-skinned youth in baggy swimming shorts had just sauntered across the bridge and vaulted onto the rampart. He stood poised there for a moment or two with his hands on his hips, laughing and joking with his friends before casually turning round and preparing to dive. As he hurled himself into the air, Maddie found herself grabbing hold of Daniel Lennox's arm and hiding her face in his sleeve.

'Jesus Christ!' she said.

There was the distant sound of a splash from below.

'It's OK – he made it. You can look now,' said Daniel, leaning over the parapet.

Maddie let go of his shirt sleeve and made herself look over the wall. The boy surfaced, waved up at his friends and then struck out for the shore.

'Maddie! Good to see you!' A beautiful young man in swimming shorts was walking towards them along the bridge. It took her a moment to identify him.

'Sam! Hello!' Feeling self-conscious, Maddie

held up her face for the ritual three kisses. 'I didn't recognize you for a minute there. You've cut off all your hair.'

His floppy fringe was gone, his hair now close-cropped and sun-bleached. He was tanned and fit-looking and had more than ever the appearance of a golden Adonis. 'Yeah,' he said, smiling down at her. 'Sara did it. She said I was beginning to look like a boy band wannabe. Anyway – you're hardly one to talk. Can this be the same woman I last saw wolfing down cassoulet and bacon butties? You look like a heroin-chic model displaced from the Forties. Since when did you start dressing retro instead of minimalist?'

Maddie made a rueful kind of face. 'I just thought it was time for a change,' she said. 'Where's Sara?'

'Down there,' he said, indicating the shore below. 'Grabbing as many rays as she can before the sun goes down. Packing her kit took longer than usual. She keeps accumulating more equipment that she swears she can't do without. Did Daniel tell you she's off up north in the morning?'

Maddie nodded. 'Yes. I'm sorry I won't get to see more of her.'

'I take it you're not ready to quit the beach?' asked Daniel. He was sitting on the parapet leaning back on his elbows with his legs stretched out in front of him. Maddie felt queasy when she thought of the drop behind.

'Not yet,' said Sam. 'There's a shot I want to get,

and I have to wait for the right light. It's a good thing you dropped by. Sara wants to get away before seven and she'll be stuck for transport. Can she take the car? I'll let you have the bike back.'

'Sure,' said Daniel, getting to his feet. 'How will you manage?'

'I'll walk into Saint-Jean-de-Fos and call in on Dominic and Françoise. They're going to Bianca's dinner party tonight, so I can bum a ride with them.' Sam turned his heliotrope-coloured eyes on her. They seemed bluer than ever against his tanned face. 'Would you like to come to dinner tonight, Madeleine? I suggested to the hostess that she include you. She's always anxious to meet new arrivals in the village. Say yes.'

'We've already said yes,' said Daniel. 'We met Bianca in Gignac.'

'You're coming too?' Sam looked surprised. 'I thought you were going through one of your emphatically anti-social phases?'

'No-one else is going to cook for me.'

'You're a lazy bollocks, Daniel. It's about time you learned to cook for yourself.'

'This dog's too old and knows too many tricks already. I couldn't be bothered learning new ones. Can you manage without your stuff for a couple of hours, Madeleine?'

'Sure.'

'Then give Sam the car keys, will you?' said Daniel.

Maddie handed the keys over to Sam, feeling

puzzled. If Sara was taking the car, how were she and Daniel expected to get home? He'd told her that Saint-Géyroux was another six or seven kilometres away.

'Why don't you stay for a swim?' asked Sam.

Maddie looked uncertain. She'd have loved a swim, but she didn't fancy the idea of having to change on the shore. She hadn't bothered to disguise the remaining bruises on her thighs with make-up. They were barely discernible now, but *she* knew they were there. The irony of the situation wasn't lost on her. Here she was, reluctant to even change into a swimsuit in front of a man who'd seen her emerge stark naked from the Irish Sea.

Daniel was looking at her with a hand shading his eyes. She could not read his expression, but she had the sensation once again of being analysed. 'It's a bit late in the day for a swim,' he said. 'The sun'll be going off this side of the river soon. Come down tomorrow morning instead.'

'OK. I might do that.'

'Get the gear, Sam, will you?'

Sam took off in the direction of the path which descended to the beach. At the far end of the shoreline Maddie could just make out the figure of a woman standing at the water's edge, waving at her. It was Sara Lennox. Maddie waved back. 'Tell Sara I said hi,' Maddie called after Sam, and then she turned to Daniel. 'How do we get to Saint-Géyroux?' she asked.

'On the bike,' he replied. Maddie looked

dubiously towards an ancient pushbike chained to a post at the top of the path. Daniel Lennox laughed. 'Not that one. That one,' he said nodding his head in the opposite direction.

The sunlight that bounced off the chrome fittings dazzled her. There, parked across the road between a red van and a Volkswagen, was an electric blue Harley-Davidson.

Chapter Eleven

'Have you ridden pillion before?' he asked.

Maddie nodded. 'A long time ago. I had a boy-friend at college who had a Honda.' She looked at the bike. It was seriously glamorous. She'd heard someone once describe Harley-Davidson as the Rolls-Royce of motorbikes. 'It was pedestrian compared to this, though.'

'You look a bit unsure. Would you prefer to wait and go back in the car with Sara?'

He couldn't know that it wasn't the machine Maddie was fazed by. It was the prospect of imminent and unavoidable close physical contact with a man. Maybe she should join Sara and Sam on the beach after all? Hell! There was a time when to be offered a ride on a Harley would have thrilled her, but now she was actually trying to find a reason to back down! What had *happened* to her?

Don't let him do this to you, Maddie. Otherwise Josh has won. She remembered what Maeve had said to her in her bedroom last Monday, when she'd urged Maddie not to trash her satin cheongsam. Maeve was right. The more she shied away from life, the more Josh was exercizing his influence over her. She couldn't let what he'd done to her prevent her from living the way she wanted to. She was determined to regain control.

She took a deep breath. 'I'll go with you, Daniel,' she said. 'Thanks.'

'Good. It's more fun than the deux-chevaux. I only use that when I have to.'

'When it's raining?'

'No. When I have to pick up people with baggage. Like you.' He looked at her and for some reason she got the impression that he was referring to emotional rather than physical baggage. She turned away and looked back down at the river. 'It doesn't happen very often,' he continued, taking a band from the pocket of his jeans and tying back his hair. 'I don't get many visitors. My small daugher, my nephew and my sister have been the only arrivals since last summer. The deux-chevaux is really for Mme Thibault. She uses it as a run-around. You can borrow it if you like – there's a pushbike around somewhere too.'

'Thank you. That's very generous of you.' It *was* generous of him, she thought, realizing rather uncomfortably that she was beholden to him now. The man deserved more than a perfunctory thank you. She made an effort to sound a little more obsequious. 'And thank you for coming into Gignac to pick me up. I feel guilty about putting you to so much trouble.'

'You haven't put me to any trouble at all.' He

gave her an unexpectedly warm smile. 'That is, apart from the fact that you wasted around ten minutes of my time this afternoon because you didn't want to come over and sit down beside me.'

Maddie flicked a small insect off the skirt of her dress, wishing that she hadn't tried to avoid him at the café in Gignac. She was spared the necessity of a reply by the arrival of Sam, who was coming back up the path swinging a couple of helmets.

'That was quick,' said Daniel. 'You're a sickeningly fit bastard, aren't you, Sam? You make me feel incredibly middle-aged.'

'You *are* middle-aged. An irascible middle-aged git,' said Sam amiably.

'Irascible. Good word, that. How do you say it in French?'

'Irascible,' said Maddie, elongating the second 'i'.

Daniel looked down at her with amused eyes. 'I'd forgotten you were multilingual. It could be very useful having you around. You could translate for me as well as chauffeuring me. My French has always been execrable. See you at Bianca's, Sam.' He turned and strolled across the road. Then: 'Put your helmet on, Madeleine,' he added over his shoulder.

'Enjoy the ride, Maddie,' said Sam.

'Thanks. See you later.' She returned his smile, then followed Daniel to where the Harley was parked. He slung his leg easily over the machine

271

and Maddie climbed up behind him, pulling the visor down over her face.

'Don't you like the feel of the wind in your face?' asked Daniel. 'I seldom wear mine down.'

He turned the key in the ignition and the Harley purred and pawed the ground. The purr became a growl as the machine leapt up the road. Maddie could feel herself sliding forwards. To avoid making contact with Daniel's body, she reached behind her and grabbed hold of the back-rest, clinging onto it with both hands. She felt like a small monkey riding on the back of a sleek beast.

The journey was a short one – not much more than five minutes – but it left her feeling breathless. As they veered along the winding roads that led to Saint-Géyroux the countryside was a hazy blur lit up by the occasional vibrant flash of hot pink and red oleander blossoms. Her silk scarf streamed out behind her, and she found herself thinking ominously of Isadora Duncan. At last the Harley pounced over the breast of a hill, slowing dramatically as they hit the outskirts of the village, and Maddie was able to relinquish her grip on the back-rest. She sat back and looked about her.

They were travelling at a sedate pace along a street so narrow that it would have been impossible for two cars to pass at once. The street was flanked by massive, ancient houses constructed from great blocks of warm yellow sandstone and roofed with terracotta tiles. No two houses were the same. Each had its own unique brand of architectural whimsy – although there was nothing frivolous about these residences. They were as solid as the citizens who'd built them.

They pulled up in front of a huge pair of ancient oak gates set into a high whitewashed wall overgrown with ivy. This house was at right angles to an even narrower side street. Maddie looked at the street sign on the wall opposite. 'La rue du Jujubier. Great name!' she said, trying to sound conversational. 'What's your street called?'

'La rue des Artistes,' said Daniel, producing a heavy-looking iron key from a bunch that hung from his belt, and unlocking the gates.

'I don't believe you!'

'Strange but true. If I were easily embarrassed it might be a problem, but it's not. Some people assume that I'm a pretentious wanker who chose the house because of the address.'

'Did you?' Maddie was foolish enough to ask.

'What do you think?' he replied, not bothering to wait for an answer. He pushed open one of the big gates and gestured for Maddie to go ahead of him.

She found herself in a courtyard full of tangled greenery. Vines snaked upwards to where the blushing faces of clematis and the surprised, violet-rimmed eyes of passion flowers stared down at her. A fig tree grew in a corner, and she could just make out the pendulous purple fruit gleaming among its branches. Pots were everywhere. Pots of

273

fuchsia with the most voluptuous blooms she had ever seen, pots of violently clashing red and pink geraniums, pots with exotica she couldn't identify.

The sound of water splashing to her left made her turn. In a hollow in the wall was a well surrounded by a carpet of moss. Water ran into it from the open mouth of a disintegrating gargoyle which leered down from a stone alcove above. Somewhere in the courtyard a dove was cooing. Maddie stood absolutely still, and felt serenity envelop her. 'It's like a sanctuary,' she whispered.

'Yes, it is.' Daniel Lennox had shut the heavy gates behind him and was leaning against them, observing her.

She turned to him and smiled.

'Well. That's the first genuine smile I've ever had from you. It's a good feeling,' he said. Then he narrowed his eyes and she felt her smile fading. 'I seem to remember telling you once that someone should paint you, Madeleine. Maybe *I* should. Would you consider sitting for me while you're here in Saint-Géyroux?'

She was completely taken aback. 'If you like,' she found herself saying. Feeling self-conscious under his scrutiny she turned away from him again, crouching down to examine a cluster of yellow violets that were growing in a stone trough at her feet. Yellow violets – what had Jacqueline said they represented? *Rural happiness . . .*

'Think about it first,' he went on. 'It's not a commitment to be undertaken lightly. It's bloody hard work. You get bored out of your mind and very, very stiff.' He moved across the courtyard and started up a flight of steps which led to another heavy oak door. This one had a stained-glass panel with an intricate wrought-iron grille covering it, and there was elaborate carving on the scarred oak. 'Come on in.'

'How old is this house?' asked Maddie, following him up the steps.

'Eighteenth century. It was built by a wealthy merchant. It was falling down when I bought it. Some of it still is.'

They passed into a hallway with a number of massive doors leading off it and one of the biggest fireplaces Maddie had ever seen. The ceiling was high and vaulted, and covered with elaborate plasterwork, some of which had crumbled away completely. The walls were embossed with a delicate tracery of vines and leaves, and a coat of arms had been worked in stucco on the chimney breast.

Moulded plaster faces gazed down impassively from archways and alcoves, their necks tapering gracefully back into the peeling walls. Most of the faces were expressionless, their features eroded by the centuries, but there was a jolly-looking man's head in a prominent position high on the stairwell. He was wearing a hat that looked like a pineapple, his smiling mouth had been painted fire-engine red, and he had been given two bright spots of pink on his cheeks.

'That's Molly's work,' said Daniel, following the

direction of Maddie's gaze. 'That face is supposed to be a likeness of the merchant who commissioned this house. I think he'd approve of what Molly's done to him. He looks as if he had a sense of humour, doesn't he?'

Maddie smiled back at the clownish plaster face and nodded. She remembered the little girl she'd seen at the Demeter Gallery, and the way father and daughter had exchanged bear-hugs.

'His wife's in the billiard room upstairs,' added Daniel. 'She's a stunner. I didn't allow Molly to mess about with *her*.'

Beyond the most impressive of the archways a wide stone staircase curved up to the first floor of the house. Halfway up it divided in two, and on the wall where it branched hung a huge, unframed canvas which she recognized at once as the work of Daniel Lennox. She had seen a similar piece in IMMA – the Museum of Modern Art in Dublin. It was a representation in oils of a river at night, the turbulence captured in bold strokes of murky blues and greens so dark they looked almost black.

Maddie slowly turned through three hundred and sixty degrees. 'This is the most beautiful house I've ever been in,' she said.

'Feel free to explore,' said Daniel Lennox, taking the stairs two at a time with an easy stride. 'I won't offer to give you a guided tour. It's always more interesting to discover a place by yourself without someone droning on in your ear. You can wander anywhere you like – except for here.' He indicated the right-hand branch of the staircase, and paused to look down at her. 'This is my private domain.' Then he gestured towards a door on the first floor. 'There's a balcony off the billiard room,' he said. 'Join me there for a beer if you like, when you've finished.'

'Thank you,' she said.

She spent a long time roaming around the house. It was huge. On the ground floor there were five vast reception rooms – including a library where floor to ceiling shelves were stacked haphazardly with thousands upon thousands of books and a grand piano stood imposingly on a low platform. All the rooms contained items of heavy, ancient furniture which looked rather lost in the acres of space they inhabited. There were threadbare Turkish rugs strewn across the stone-flagged floors and hanging on the walls, and Turkish cushions on the couches and armchairs.

Maddie got the impression that the downstairs rooms were rarely used. They were all dark and rather gloomy. She supposed they might look more cheerful in winter with fires burning in the enormous grates, but there was a distinctly chilly feel to them now, even though there was still heat in the sun outside. The exception was the kitchen, which was obviously the housekeeper's territory. It was a big, whitewashed room with a high ceiling, a black, cast-iron range, a huge refectory table and a sofa like a sinking boat. An old clothes horse was hung with bunches of dried herbs, and vegetables were heaped in a china basin. The shelves were laden with bottles and jars and assorted crockery, the cupboards were crammed with cast-iron pots and earthenware dishes, and utensils hung from iron hooks. A broom stood propped up in a corner with a rose-patterned apron draped over it. Mme Thibault's, she supposed.

She made her way back through the cavernous entrance hall, very conscious of the echo that rang out as she walked, and then climbed the left-hand branch of the staircase. The rooms on this storey were probably bedrooms. They were big rooms, too – as big as the ones downstairs, to judge by the distances between the carved oak doors. All the doors were shut, and she didn't want to pry. But the doors on the corridor above stood open, revealing plainly furnished interiors, whitewashed walls and unplastered ceilings. The terracotta roof tiles were supported by wooden beams – whole boles of trees so ancient their dark timber was pitted with the traces of long-deceased wood-worm.

At the end of the top corridor stood a partition hung with a moth-eaten Chinese silk rug. She pulled aside the heavy fabric to reveal a door constructed from unpainted plywood and fitted with a plain chrome handle. The door didn't budge when she tried it and she guessed, going by the rather tortuous geography of the house, that it must lead to the top floor of Daniel Lennox's private apartments.

On her way back down the stairs, curiosity drew her gaze to where the stairs forked to the right. The tall doors that led to the painter's domain were firmly shut.

Following Daniel's directions, she found herself in the billiard room. A plaster panel over the door featured the moulded head of a woman whose sensual mouth bore the hint of a smile. Tendrils of hair coiled over her shoulders. Maddie supposed that this was the wife of the jolly merchant she'd seen downstairs. This room was more conventionally furnished than the others: it contained a hi-fi system, a television and a pool table, and a long oak sideboard stocked with glasses and bottles. Videos and CDs were piled untidily in a rack on the wall. A glance told her that most of the videos were children's. She noticed a framed photograph of Daniel's daughter on the mantelpiece. The little girl was running towards the camera with her arms outstretched and her hair flying.

Suddenly she stopped in her tracks. A great grey dog was standing on the balcony beyond a set of open french windows, looking at her with its ears pricked up. It began a low growl.

Maddie took a step backwards, and then she heard Daniel Lennox's voice. His hand moved from where it had been resting on the arm of a garden chair with its back to her. 'Shut up, Pilot,' he said, grasping the dog by its thick leather collar. He glanced over his shoulder. 'Come on out,' he said. 'Pilot won't hurt you.'

Maddie walked out onto the balcony with a hesitant tread.

'Lie down,' said Daniel. The dog obeyed without hesitation, looking up at Maddie with watchful yellow eyes. Maddie looked back at him, then crouched down and stroked the top of his head with a tentative hand. The smooth, short hair felt like velvet under her palm. She caressed his ears with more assurance. 'What kind of a dog is he?' she asked.

'He's a Weimaraner. A kind of pointer.'

'He's very beautiful.' Maddie took a proffered paw, and let her other hand run over the dog's glossy back. 'What a strange colour his fur is! You'd swear there was purple in there somewhere.'

'It depends on the light. The colour often reminds me of a heather-covered mountain in Ireland.'

His painter's eye had identified the shade with effortless accuracy. 'That's bang on,' she concurred. 'He looks like Croagh Patrick on a hazy day.'

Daniel Lennox gestured towards the french windows. 'Help yourself to a beer. You'll find a fridge in the armoire in the corner of the billiard room.'

She relinquished Pilot's paw, then rose to her feet. The glass-fronted fridge set into the armoire was stocked with cans of beer and white wine, and a couple of bottles of champagne. She helped herself to a can of Stella, pulled the tab and then went back out onto the balcony, sitting down on a cane chair to the left of the french windows. 'It's hot,' she said, putting the can to her lips and drinking deeply. She hadn't realized how thirsty she was.

'Why don't you have a swim?'

'What? Go all the way back to the river?'

'No. I mean in the pool downstairs.'

'What pool?'

'The pool in the basement.'

'You have a swimming pool in your basement?' How had she missed it?

'Well, it's actually in the old cellar, or *cave*,' he replied. Her curiosity must have been obvious, because Daniel Lennox went on to elaborate. 'It's easy to miss. The door's hidden away under the staircase. My ex-wife was too lazy to go all the way to the river to swim, so I had it converted into a swimming pool for her. I'll show you, if you like.'

'Thanks – I'd love to see it. But I think I'll skip the swim. My togs are in my bag in the car.' She was glad of the excuse.

'We don't usually bother with togs,' said Daniel, getting to his feet.

Maddie said nothing.

He led the way back through the billiard room and down the stairs. Pilot followed him, his claws clicking against the stone steps. On the left-hand side of the staircase was a low door. Daniel had to stoop to go through, and as he did he reached for a light switch on the wall beside the door, and turned the dimmer up.

The steps down into the *cave* were steep and uneven, worn away by the passage of centuries of feet. Maddie took off her dark glasses and hugged the cold, slightly clammy wall on her left as she followed Daniel down to the poolside.

The pool was lit by small spotlights set into the vaulted brick ceiling. Its surface was perfectly still, and through the pellucid water Maddie could see a gleaming mosaic depicting Aphrodite rising from the waves. Maddie looked down at the face gazing up at her. This Aphrodite was the woman she'd seen at the Demeter Gallery – Daniel Lennox's ex-wife, Marie-France. She recognized the curve of her sensual mouth, the gleam in the sleepy, sloe eyes and the lustrous coils of hair.

There was an echo when he finally spoke. 'My ex-wife fancied a similarity between herself and the goddess of love. I'm afraid I rather over-indulged her in those halcyon, faraway days when we first moved in here.'

Maddie remembered the photograph of the serene woman floating in the swimming pool.

'That photograph – the one of your wife in the swimming pool that I saw at Sara's exhibition – it was taken here, wasn't it?'

'Yes it was.' There was silence between them for a moment, and then Daniel said: 'Well, if you're not going to dive in we might as well go back outside.'

She preceded him back up the steps and waited while he turned down the dimmer switch. The *cave* disappeared back into darkness. Not a glimmer of light fell on the veil of black water covering the face of Marie-France Lennox.

There was a dull thud as he pulled the door to behind him. 'Now you know where the pool is,' he said. 'Feel free to come and use it any time you like.'

'I wouldn't want to disturb you.'

'I told you before. It's difficult to disturb somebody in a house this size. Anyway, I spend most of my time in the studio on the top floor of my apartment.'

'But – I'd have to ring the bell, you'd have to come to the door—'

'I'll leave it unlocked. Just walk straight in.' He looked at her evenly. 'But don't feel you have to make excuses, Madeleine. If you don't want to use my pool, don't use it.'

Pilot had raced ahead up the stairs and was standing waiting for them where the staircase branched.

'Do you use it a lot?' asked Maddie, just for something to say.

'Sometimes at night when I finish work. I prefer to swim in the river. What happened to your face?'

'I beg your pardon?'

'I'm sorry. I don't mean to be rude, or to make you feel self-conscious.' He gave her another perfectly level look and Maddie found herself turning her face away. 'There's no need to be self-conscious, Madeleine. The bruising's almost gone, and you've been clever with your camouflage. I'm probably the only person who'd notice it.' They had passed through the billiard room and reached the balcony again, and Maddie put her sunglasses back on. 'That little scar beneath your eye is what made me look twice. It wasn't there the last time I studied your face – which was pretty closely, as you may recall.'

Maddie leaned over the wall of the balcony and regarded the terrasse below. 'I was in a car accident,' she said, in a toneless voice.

'I see.' Daniel Lennox handed her her beer and then picked his own up from the table and joined her in her survey of the garden. She could tell he wasn't going to put pressure on her to elaborate, but somehow she knew he didn't believe her about the accident.

They looked at the garden in silence for a few minutes. It was the first time Maddie had felt comfortable to be silent with him. The sun was quite low in the sky now, and shadows were starting to stretch across the grass, but the evening air was still warm. Cicadas were humming, and swallows swooping and diving in their ritual evening quest for insects.

Daniel Lennox raised his can of Stella to his mouth, and as he did so his sleeve brushed accidentally against Maddie's bare arm. She flinched involuntarily and shifted slightly to her left, hoping that he hadn't noticed. Suddenly she was uptight again, flailing around for something to say. 'Your house is amazing,' was all she could think of.

'Thank you. It's a bit of a mess, really. Marie-France was responsible for most of the décor, but she took a lot of stuff with her when she left, and I couldn't be bothered to replace it or redecorate the joint. Bianca's always nagging at me to give it a face-lift, but I rather like the idea of it crumbling away.'

'Like Gormenghast.'

'Yup.' He drained his beer. 'Are you ready for another one?' he asked.

'No thanks.'

He disappeared through the french windows and came back with a fresh can for himself.

'How many rooms are there?' asked Maddie. 'I lost count.'

He paused for a minute, doing calculations in his head. 'Do you know, I'm not absolutely certain,' he said with a laugh. 'Far too many for one person, that's for sure. But I bought it on the premise that I needed a lot of spare rooms for visitors. I was a lot more sociable then than I am now – or rather, Marie-France was.' He moved to the chair he'd been sitting in earlier and sat down in it, swinging his legs up onto the table in front of him. 'She liked to entertain a lot – there were always strange faces around. You needed to come here, didn't you Madeleine?'

'What do you mean?' He had a totally disconcerting line in non-sequiturs.

'You needed to come here. To Saint-Géyroux. I hope you find what you're looking for.' There was nothing insincere about the smile he sent her. It made Maddie want to burst out weeping.

Suddenly Pilot jumped up and ran off through the billiard room. Maddie could hear his claws clicking against stone again as he descended the staircase.

The voice of Sara Lennox floated up through the house. 'I'm back,' she called.

Maddie finally broke contact with Daniel Lennox's relentless artist's gaze, and went to greet her.

Chapter Twelve

Shortly after seven o'clock Maddie went upstairs to dress for Bianca's dinner party. The room she elected to change in was spartanly furnished with a carved wooden *bateau lit*, a table, a chair with a woven straw seat, and a cupboard for clothes. A raised alcove in one of the whitewashed walls housed a row of books and a vase containing dried hydrangeas. The small window was draped with a length of white muslin. It overlooked the street three storeys below, and Maddie could plainly hear the ringing voices of the villagers bouncing off the tall houses on either side of the narrow thoroughfare as they indulged in end-of-the-day gossip. The word *poubelle* was a recurrent one, pronounced in tones that even Sarah Bernhardt might have found over the top.

When she opened her bag to unearth a clean frock, she found that Maeve had carefuly rolled up her sea-green cheongsam and slipped it in at the top. There was a note pinned to it, along with the tiny matching purse that Maddie always carried when she wore the dress. The note read – in Maeve's elegant handwriting – 'Good gracious.

How did this get in? Seriously – you don't *have* to ever wear this again, Maddie. I just thought I'd put it in in case you *wanted* to. And it's just as well I helped you pack – you nearly forgot Bassa. Love, M. XXX.' Maddie smiled. She'd been in such a hurry to leave Dublin that she had neglected to pack her battered panda. Maeve had rolled him up in the satin dress. Maddie kissed the bear's nose and then put him carefully back in the bag.

She wasn't sure what to wear to Bianca's party. She had a feeling that whichever of her new second-hand frocks she picked, she'd look very underdressed. But she wasn't going to wear the cheongsam. In the end she settled on her plain white linen Capri pants and matching top.

She showered in the little bathroom next door to her bedroom, and re-camouflaged her bruises. Then she located her bag of airport purchases. She wanted to repay Daniel Lennox's hospitality – she'd buy a good bottle of wine for Deirdre and Rory in the local *caveaux* as a present instead of the vodka she'd intended for them. Before going downstairs to join Daniel and his sister, she gave herself one last searching look in the mirror.

'What a sweet ensemble, Madeleine,' remarked Sara when she emerged onto the balcony. 'It makes you look about sixteen.'

Daniel Lennox didn't say anything. He filled a glass with champagne from the bottle which was sitting in an ice-bucket on the table and handed it to her.

'Thank you,' she said. '*Santé.*'

'Welcome to Saint-Géyroux,' said Sara, raising her glass.

Maddie raised her glass back. Then: 'This is for you,' she said, handing a bottle of Absolut to Daniel. As he took it from her, she noticed too late that the nectarine he'd dropped into the carrier bag earlier had got squashed, and some of the fruit was sticking to the bottle.

'Designer vodka. Thank you, Madeleine,' he said, unfurling the napkin that had been wrapped around the neck of the champagne bottle and using it to wipe away the lumps of nectarine. *Designer vodka.* Had she imagined a sneer in his tone? For God's sake – what did he expect from a hurried visit to an airport shop? Genuine Russian Stolichnaya? Polish bloody Wyborowa? From the billiard room beyond came the sound of a phone ringing. 'Excuse me,' said Daniel. 'I'll have to take that. My agent's due to telephone this evening.'

'Has he clarified those dates?' asked Sarah.

'Yeah,' said Daniel with a world-weary air as he shambled through into the billiard room. 'But the director of that joint in the rue du Seine wants television coverage of the *vernissage.* I'm drawing the line at that.'

Pompous ass! *My agent . . . television coverage . . . vernissage . . .* Hell. Why was she allowing the geezer to annoy her? She was here to chill. She was here to escape. Determined to relax, Maddie took a sip of champagne and moved to the wrought-iron railing. A song came into her head, and she found herself humming. *La la – La Vie en Rose* . . . Funny. The last time she'd heard that song had been on the night of Josh's birthday party. Someone had been singing it tunelessly. Who? Nuala from the accounts department in her old job, her past life. The past is another country . . . who had said that? And how did the rest of it go?

From the street came the sudden sound of a car horn, and then angry voices soared over the high wall of the garden.

'Not road rage in Saint-Géyroux, surely?' she remarked to Sara over her shoulder.

'No. It sounds like Mme Poiret telling the Renard boy to get lost. He's been sniffing around her youngest daughter, and there's no love lost between the two families.' Sara stood up and stretched and then joined Maddie, leaning against the railing with her back to the garden. 'I can't imagine there could ever be road rage in this village – the pace of life here is far too laid back.' She was looking at Maddie with her brother's eyes, and Maddie felt self-conscious about her bruises again. However, if Sara noticed anything, she didn't betray it by her expression. 'What are you going to do to keep yourself amused while you're here, Madeleine? I know you said you were bent on peace and quiet, but you could go stir crazy. I mean, there's *nothing* here – no night life, no cinema, even. There's only one café, and it's decidedly unhip. The biggest social event of the week is market day.'

'I don't want a social life. I'm just going to take things easy for a while. Swim, read, go for long walks.'

'There's a bicycle in the shed at the bottom of the garden. Use that to get to and from the river.'

'Thanks. Daniel mentioned that I could borrow it. Gignac's a manageable cycle, is it? I might go there to eat some time.'

'It's manageable, yeah. You might have to rest *en route*, though, if the sun's very hot – and remember to take water with you everywhere. It's easy to dehydrate.'

Maddie leaned against the railing and breathed in the scent of lavender. The noise from the street had abated, and there was no sound except the low murmur of Daniel's voice in the adjoining room, and the cooing of doves from a dovecote at the end of the garden. 'This is a magical place,' she said. 'I wasn't sure about coming here, but I'm glad Maeve suggested it.'

'You haven't been sure about things for some time, have you, Madeleine?' remarked Sara.

'What do you mean?'

'I got that impression from you when we did the session. It's amazing what you can see through the lens of a camera. Very often you see stuff that the person who's sitting for you isn't even aware of themselves. Have a look at this.' Sara Lennox reached for a hard-backed envelope that was lying on the table next to the ice-bucket, and handed it to her.

Maddie opened the flap and drew a photograph from the envelope. It was a close-up of her which Sara had obviously taken when she'd been setting up the shoot on the beach that Thursday evening, a whole lifetime ago. It showed her looking out to sea, to where a pale moon was floating just above the horizon. The collar of her robe was pulled tight around her ears and under her chin, and she looked very young and very vulnerable. She also looked inexpressibly sad. The contrast between this photograph and the ones taken of her later, as she laughed and clowned on the sand, could not have been greater.

'The eyes are the windows of the soul,' said Sara Lennox.

For some absurd reason Maddie felt a great lump come into her throat. For a while she didn't say anything. Then she said: 'Do you mean for me to keep it?'

'Of course. But not if it's going to make you cry every time you look at it.'

Maddie managed a smile just in time. Daniel Lennox was strolling back through the balcony doors, looking at his watch and yawning.

'What time is it?' asked his sister.

'Nearly eight o'clock,' he replied.

'We should go,' Sara said. 'I know Bianca won't expect you to be on time, Daniel, but the sooner we get there the sooner we can leave. I have to be up at the crack of dawn tomorrow.'

'What time's your flight?'

'I check in at eight.'

'Shit. I hope you don't expect me to drive you to the airport?'

'It's all right. I wouldn't dream of overtaxing your fraternal feelings. Sam's taking me.'

Daniel draped an arm around her shoulders and gave her a kiss on the cheek. 'I'll miss you, Sara,' he said. Then he drained his glass. 'I'm starving. Let's go and eat.'

*　　*　　*

Bianca's house was a short stroll away. It was still warm, and it felt good to walk through the narrow streets without a coat on. Daniel stopped and exchanged small talk with some local men who were playing *boules*, nodding gravely every time the *poubelle* situation was mentioned. People looked twice at Maddie, trying to mask their curiosity with polite smiles. In such a small village a stranger would be a first-class source of gossip.

A church bell was marking the quarter hour with tinny rings as they arrived at Bianca's. Their hostess answered the door with a flurry of kisses, looking so gorgeous in a white slip dress that Maddie almost wished she'd worn her cheongsam.

'What a beautiful house,' she said as she was ushered through the door, realizing it was the second time that day she'd uttered those words. This time, however, the remark had none of the spontaneous awe she'd felt when she'd walked into Daniel Lennox's entrance hall. This was the kind of house that made you feel that you were under obligation to comment on how tasteful it was.

'Thank you,' said Bianca, shutting the door behind them. 'Actually, it's really more of a love affair than a house. I've spent the last decade of my life refurbishing it.' She linked arms with Maddie in a cosy way as they crossed the tiled vestibule. 'As soon as I saw it, Madeleine, I knew it was the one. It had no roof, no water and no electricity. Everybody told me I was crazy to buy it – even though I got it for a song – but the more people advised me against it, the more determined I was to do it. I'm a pigheaded kind of person, and when I decide I want something nothing can put me off.' She gave Daniel a sideways look. He raised an eyebrow at her and smilingly inclined his head. 'Would you like a guided tour, Madeleine?' asked Bianca.

'Oh – yes, please. That would be fascinating.' Maddie remembered what Daniel had said to her earlier about guided tours, and she took care to avoid his eyes in case she might let slip an inadvertent smile.

Bianca escorted Maddie up a wide staircase and in and out of half a dozen rooms, pointing out details of architectural interest as she went.

'The terracotta tiles in the bathrooms were hand-made by local artisans,' she explained. 'I had to replace all the floorboards in the main rooms – can you believe it? I used original oak boards, of course, reclaimed from a farmhouse just outside the village, and some of the doors came from there too. I used reproduction stuff only where it was absolutely unavoidable – I wanted the house to retain as much of its original character as possible. I think I succeeded in making it rather *simpatico*, don't you?'

'Yes. It's quite stunning.'

'I *love* my *trompe-l'oeil* shutters – aren't they amusing?' said Bianca, pulling out the shutters on her bedroom window to reveal a painted landscape. A nude figure was reclining on a chaise-longue in the middle of the landscape, and Maddie realized that it was a likeness of her hostess. Bianca didn't wait for Maddie to reply, but continued with her running commentary. 'I wanted Daniel to do the portrait, but I got fed up waiting for him to get round to it. I commissioned a rather struggling local artist instead. I like to think that I'm a supporter of local industry – not just a blow-in who gets some interior designer to tart up their house in Colefax and Fowler. Do you know what I mean?'

Maddie mm-ed a polite affirmative.

'I got a local carpenter to make the bed, too. I was going to buy an antique four-poster, but the ones I saw were all too state-roomish. I wanted something light and airy for the bedroom. The lace is antique, of course.'

Bianca's bed was beautiful. Four slender white columns rose ceiling-ward from each corner, and it was festooned with web-like lace. An embroidered silk kimono was draped with elaborate casualness across the foot of the bed. It was a stylist's dream.

On the landing Maddie picked up a curiously carved object displayed on a side table. 'What's this?' she asked.

'Oh – it's a Tibetan trumpet,' said Bianca casually. 'It's made from a human thigh bone.' Maddie overcame the impulse to ask her when she had last played on it.

Her hostess propelled her through a set of double doors into a vast drawing room. 'Behold!' she said.

Maddie looked in the direction of Bianca's out-flung arm. Above the fireplace hung a painting which was obviously the work of Daniel Lennox.

'I'm sure you've been asked what would be the first thing you'd rescue from your home if it went on fire? Well – this would absolutely be it in my case. My magnificent Daniel.'

Maddie looked at the painting. Again it represented water, but unlike the one hanging in Daniel Lennox's hall there was very little movement in this painting, and the colours were more delicate. There was a wonderful sense of calm about it.

'He painted this shortly after Molly was born,' said Bianca, with a little sigh.

'When did he paint the one that's hanging in his hall?'

'Just before he and Marie-France split up. Couldn't you tell?' Bianca looked at her with the expression of a person who possesses superior knowledge.

'I don't know much about Daniel.'

'Very few people do,' said Bianca. 'Daniel is a very private individual. *Very* private, and very deep. I've known him a long time, and sometimes I think he'll never come to terms with himself. I call him my tormented soul.' There was a long pause as Bianca looked becomingly thoughtful. Then she shook her head and gave a little laugh. 'Sorry! It's just that I'm concerned for him, you know? Let's go down.' She preceded Maddie through the double doors and started back down the staircase. 'We're terribly informal tonight – I hope you don't mind? We decided to eat alfresco since it's such a lovely evening. Nothing fancy – just some seared tuna steaks and char-grilled vegetables.'

'That sounds delicious,' said Maddie. She followed Bianca across the hall and out into a courtyard where a dozen or so people were standing around, chatting and holding glasses.

'C'est cosy, n'est ce pas?' said Bianca brightly. 'I call it my outdoor dining room.'

A long table in the middle of the courtyard was surrounded with wrought-iron chairs. It was covered in a white cloth and set with painted earthenware. Lanterns burned, and there was a strong smell of some essential oil.

'Let me introduce you to some people.' Bianca descended on a couple who were both wearing white shirts and loose white trousers. 'How are you for Chardonnay, Roger? Gina? Oh! You naughty things, both dressed in pristine white! You're trying to outdo me – you know it's my signature colour!' The barely perceptible sideways look she shot her made Maddie aware that Ms Ingram had the monopoly on white when it came to sartorial matters in Saint-Géyroux. She made a mental note to wear something other than her white Marks & Sparks ensemble if she received another invitation to dine chez Bianca. 'This is Madeleine Godard,' fluted her hostess.

Maddie took a deep breath and stapled a smile to her face as she walked across the courtyard.

*   *   *

Half an hour later they took their places at the table. Maddie was relieved when Sam, who had obviously only just arrived, slid into the chair beside her. The couple she'd been introduced to had been perfectly pleasant, but small talk was hard work. She could be more relaxed around Sam.

'Hello, beautiful,' he said, giving her his wonderful smile. 'D'you think anyone noticed I was late? Dominic and Françoise and I shared a spliff before heading out.' He indicated a dark-haired couple on the other side of the table who were both wearing stoned smiles.

'God. I'm envious. I could have done with some of that,' said Maddie.

'I can oblige any time,' said Sam, sloshing wine into her glass. 'You'll just have to make do with Bianca's Chardonnay for now.'

A voluptuous girl with wonderful, tawny hair insinuated herself into the space between Sam and Maddie, and set plates in front of them. On each plate was a teeny-weeny *tartine de chèvre* resting on a bed of lollo rosso.

'Merci, Claudine,' said Sam. 'Mais que tu es belle ce soir!'

Claudine gave Sam a slow, sideways smile, and moved on with an exaggerated movement of her hips. Sam looked after her with a wolfish expression. 'Daniel's painting her soon,' he said. 'I hope she knows what she's letting herself in for. Eat up, Madeleine. Let's start on your weight-gain diet. Extra dressing for you.'

Claudine had drawn level with the head of the table where Daniel was taking the seat that Bianca had allocated to him. Maddie noticed a perplexed expression cross his face as he regarded the plate she put in front of him.

'Designer food,' said Sam in an undertone. 'Daniel doesn't understand it. He's more of a cassoulet man.'

'Like you.'

'Like me. I promised you I'd show you how to make it, didn't I? Drop by tomorrow and I'll give you a cookery lesson.'

'I might do that.'

'You might as well. There's really bugger all to do here apart from eating and swimming and taking photographs.'

'Why don't you go north with Sara, then?'

Sam sent her a little, stoned smile. 'Why do you think?'

She was at a loss. 'I really don't know,' she said.

'Because I heard that you were coming, Maddie Godard,' he said.

*　　*　　*

They left at around half-past eleven. Bianca saw them to the door, urging Daniel to come to her for supper any time. 'You mustn't neglect yourself now that Mme Thibault isn't around to take care of you. I know you, Daniel. You'll end up eating out of tins.'

'I shouldn't worry too much, Bianca,' said Daniel. 'I'm a hardy bugger – and anyway, Sam's promised to cook me something from time to time.'

Bianca turned her attention to Maddie. 'Good night, Madeleine. It was lovely to meet you. Do call in any time you're passing.' Then: 'Oh!' she

300

exclaimed, her hand flying to her mouth. 'I nearly forgot about your key! I'll fetch it for you now.'

'What key?' asked Sara Lennox.

'The key to the McDonaghs' house. They left their spare with me.'

'I don't really think it's such a good idea for Madeleine to stay there tonight,' said Sara, sounding dubious. 'It's very late, Bianca, and she doesn't know the place. It won't have been aired, and there'll be nothing to eat. She can stay put where she is tonight – all her stuff's at Daniel's. You don't mind putting Madeleine up, Daniel, do you?'

'Not at all.'

'Oh – I couldn't accept any more of your hospitality, honestly,' said Maddie. 'You've been far too good to me already.'

'Nonsense, Madeleine,' said Sara. 'It would be miserable to have to move into a strange house in the middle of the night – especially after travelling all day. Look at you – you're practically white with exhaustion.'

They were right, and she knew it. The prospect of walking into an unfamiliar house and having to acquaint herself with the workings of it was a grim one. She pictured herself fumbling about in the dark looking for the fuse box to turn on the electricity, and trying to locate bedding, and having no hot water and nothing for breakfast in the morning. What finally decided her was the ultimate horror of suffering a flashback to the rape while in a strange house all on her own.

She relented. 'Thank you,' she said. 'I'd be very grateful for a bed.'

Bianca's face went a bit stiff. 'I'll make sure you get that key tomorrow, then,' she said. 'I won't be here, but I'll get Claudine to bring it down to you. She tells me she's sitting for you tomorrow afternoon, Daniel?'

'That's right.'

'Well. Make absolutely sure she gives the key to Madeleine,' said Bianca. 'She's completely scatty, that Claudine.'

'I'll make sure she does it,' said Sam, suddenly. 'I'm bound to see her on the beach tomorrow. She's always there around lunchtime.'

'Well, you'll get yourself sorted out one way or another,' said Bianca, giving Maddie a too-polite smile. 'I hope you'll enjoy your stay, Madeleine.' Suddenly her expression changed. '*Now* I remember where I've seen you before!' she said. 'You're the girl in the photograph that Daniel has on his bathroom wall!'

Maddie looked at her uncomprehendingly.

'You know – the one hanging next to that photograph that Sara took of that actress – the one who came over to stay with Rory and Deirdre last year?'

'Maeve Kirwan,' said Sara.

Maddie froze. She'd forgotten that Sara had told her that she'd be sending a copy of the photograph to Daniel. She could think of absolutely nothing to say in response to Bianca's observation. Her hostess was looking at her now with eyes in which assessment was more evident than ever. Then she gave a little feline smile. 'Oh, but you wouldn't have been into Daniel's *sanctum sanctorum*.' She turned to Daniel and laid a hand on his arm. 'You might at least allow her into your bathroom, Daniel, so that she can have a look at her own photograph.'

Daniel didn't say anything, but Sara said quickly: 'That was a lovely evening, Bianca – a really pleasant way for me to spend the last night of my stay here.'

'You're welcome, Sara. Don't leave it too long before you come back and visit us again.'

Kisses and thanks and farewells were exchanged all round, and then Bianca shimmied back into her house.

Sara gave a little shiver as they started down the street. 'It's got cold,' she said.

'Come here, auntie.' Sam wrapped an arm around her shoulders, and then held the other one out for Maddie. 'Do you want to snuggle up, too, Maddie?'

Maddie shook her head. 'I'm fine, thanks, Sam. I'm not cold at all.'

She trailed behind a little, feeling very self-conscious as she walked beside Daniel, hugging herself for warmth.

'It was a clever idea of Sara's to do a companion-piece to that shot of Maeve. It turned out beautifully.' Daniel Lennox looked forbiddingly

303

tall as he strolled along beside her, his hands in his pockets. 'I'll let you see them if you like. I hung them side by side.'

'It's all right.'

'It's all right? By that I take it you don't want to see them?'

Maddie shrugged and made a noncommittal noise. The thought of Daniel Lennox looking at her naked body every time he went into his bathroom made her want to shut her eyes and die.

There was a pause. 'The photograph was intended as a present for your partner, wasn't it? How did he like it?'

'I don't have a partner.' He looked at her, and she wished she'd said nothing. They continued in silence. If he was waiting for her to elaborate, he gave no indication. Ahead of them Sara and Sam were leaning into each other as they walked, talking in low voices.

'How did you enjoy this evening?' asked Daniel after a while. 'Careful – there's a treacherous pothole on that side of the street – it's difficult to see it in the dark.' He reached for her arm and steered her to the left.

Maddie thought for a second or two. Had she enjoyed herself? 'Well, yes, I did enjoy myself, as a matter of fact, even though I wasn't really expecting to,' she said. Daniel put his hands back in his pockets and gave her a quizzical look. 'I was very tired to begin with. I didn't think I'd be able to string two words together, but I met some really – '

She suddenly realized she was going to use the word 'nice', and remembered how scathing he'd been about her vocabulary the first time she'd met him. 'Some really *simpatico* – ' Aagh! That was even worse! ' – people this evening. Gina and Roger invited me to a barbecue next week. And Sam made me laugh a lot. He's a very sweet boy.'

'I'd hardly call him a boy.'

'He's just twenty-one.'

'That's what I mean. I'd hardly call him a boy. I know several women who have expressed a not altogether matronly interest in Sam Newman, and they're a great deal older than you are, Madeleine.'

Maddie broke eye contact at once. 'Oh – look at that! Isn't it pretty!' she exclaimed, stopping on the pretext of admiring a church in a little square to her right.

'That church bell marks every quarter-hour. Which bedroom did you leave your bag in?'

'One on the very top floor.'

'Looking onto the street or the garden?'

'The street.'

'In that case I ought to warn you that you might want to sleep in another room – you can hear the bells quite clearly on that side of the house. Some people are driven mad by them, others love them.' He looked at her speculatively. 'I wonder which type you are?'

Just then the bells chimed the three-quarter hour as if on cue.

Maddie found herself smiling. 'I think I'll love them,' she said.

'Aha!' It was Sara's voice. Ahead of them she and Sam had come to an abrupt halt. 'Look where the *poubelle* has ended up tonight! Right outside Mme Poiret's front door!'

'Poor Mme Poiret. She won't have the strength to shift it. Give me a hand, Sam.' Daniel moved towards the bin and started pushing it down the street.

'Where are we going to leave it?' asked Sam.

'Outside my gaff, of course,' replied Daniel.

Sara looked fondly at her brother as he and Sam bowled the bin round the corner of the rue des Artistes. 'He's a pussy-cat, really,' she said. Then she turned to Maddie. 'Did you have fun tonight?'

'Mm. It was kind of Bianca to invite me.'

'You may have cottoned on to the fact that she's a bit of a dilettante, but she really is very good at organizing social activities. If it wasn't for her there'd be no social life in the village at all – or none with that slight edge of glamour that she contrives to pull off. It's good for people to have a sense of occasion from time to time. Even Daniel gets press-ganged into it occasionally.'

'They're obviously very good friends.'

'Bianca and Daniel?' Sara sounded surprised. 'What makes you say that?'

'She told me so.'

Sara Lennox laughed. 'She'd love people to

think so, but I wouldn't call their relationship intimate. Except in the physical sense, of course. They've come to a very civilized – if not altogether conventional – arrangement that seems to suit them both.'

'Unconventional, how?'

'Um. Maybe I shouldn't have mentioned it, but – oh, bollocks to that! Everyone knows about it. Bianca even boasts about it from time to time.'

'About what?'

'About the fact that she was a top-class hooker in a former life.'

This information made Maddie literally stop in her tracks. 'No way!'

'Mm-hm. And when I say top class, I mean *top*. Lords, politicians, movie stars – the lot. She earned so much money turning mean tricks that she decided to take early retirement – get out while she was still in her prime.'

'So – is Daniel – well – a *client*?' Maddie felt a bit prurient about asking the question, but she was fascinated by the story.

'God, no. She doesn't need the money. Her memoirs will be worth millions if she ever gets round to writing them. It's a purely recreational thing between her and Daniel.'

Maddie was sceptical. Recreational sex might be Daniel's main reason for consorting with Bianca, but she suspected that Bianca was intent on something more. She remembered the way she had looked at Maddie when she'd made the connection between Daniel's new house-guest and the photograph in his bathroom. There'd been jealousy as well as curiosity in those kohl-rimmed eyes.

They'd reached the house. Daniel was waiting for them so that he could shut the gate into the courtyard. 'I won't see you again, Madeleine,' said Sara. 'Not until you're back in Dublin, that is. Call me then and we'll meet up for lunch some time.'

'Oh – I'll get up and see you off in the morning.'

'You will do no such thing, sweetie-pie,' said Sam. 'We'll be getting up in about five hours' time.' They were passing through the entrance hall to the house. 'Anyone for a nightcap?' he asked as they started up the broad staircase.

Sara gave him an incredulous look. 'Don't be ridiculous, Sam. I'm going straight to bed. You should too if you're going to get up in time to drive me to the airport,' she added reprovingly. 'Or are you planning to stay up drinking all night?'

'Don't be such a disapproving old maiden aunt,' he responded, laughing at her unamused expression. 'I promise I'll be on the ball to chauffeur you. And I'll stop off on the beach on the way back and get that key from Claudine for you, Madeleine.' He turned to her with a cajoling expression. 'You'll have a nightcap, won't you? I know you're tired, but you're on holiday now.'

Maddie shook her head. 'No thanks, Sam. I

308

really am knackered, and I've still to make up my bed. Where will I find sheets by the way?'

'There's a linen cupboard on the top floor,' said Sara. 'Help yourself to anything you need.'

'I'll have a drink with you, Sam,' said Daniel, looking at his watch. 'We'd better make it a quick one, though. I want to get a couple of hours' work in before I go to bed.'

'It's a bit late to do any painting, isn't it?' asked Sara.

'I won't be painting. I just want to prime some canvases. I'm starting on something new tomorrow.'

'Another portrait?'

'Yeah. Of Claudine. And Madeleine said she'd think about sitting for me while she's here.'

Maddie shot a startled look at Daniel, but not before she saw his sister raise a warning eyebrow at him.

'I did tell her it would be hard work, so I'm not going to put pressure on her,' continued Daniel. 'But I'd love her to agree. The first time I met her I told her someone should paint her, and it might as well be me. You *are* thinking about it, aren't you, Madeleine?'

Maddie made a hopelessly ambiguous gesture which Daniel obviously interpreted as a 'yes'.

'Good,' he said.

'I think I will join you for a quick drink, after all,' said Sara suddenly. 'I'm not likely to see you in the morning, am I, Daniel?'

'Absolutely not. Good night, Madeleine.' Daniel moved off. 'Irish for you, Sam?' he slung back over his shoulder as he disappeared from view.

'Yeah.' Sam came over to Maddie and took her hands. 'Good night, Maddie,' he said.

'Good night, Sam.'

'I'll go to the supermarket in Montpellier tomorrow. Get the ingredients for a cassoulet so I can instruct you in *la cuisine pour grossir*. Bollocks to all that *nouvelle* crap. Sleep well.' He kissed her on the cheek, then followed Daniel through to the billiard room.

Sara gave her a last hug. 'I hope everything works out for you, Madeleine.' She held her at arm's length and gave her that penetrating look again. 'I've a suspicion that you've come here to escape from something, am I right? I can sense that you've been through a rough time recently. It's not just losing your job that's troubling you, is it?'

Maddie shook her head.

'He hated it, didn't he?'

'What? Who hated what, Sara?'

'Your lover. He hated the photograph.'

'Yes.' Maddie bit her lip. 'I'm sorry. It was a big mistake. How did you guess?'

'I read it in your eyes. The windows of the soul, remember? Have you split with him?'

'Yes.'

There was a beat before Sara spoke again. When she did, her words were measured. 'You remind me of an injured bird, you know, Madeleine. One that really shouldn't try to fly again too soon. Stay here for as long as it takes for your wounds to heal, won't you? Don't even think about coming back to Dublin till you're ready. Promise?'

Maddie nodded. She hugged Sara back, wishing that she wasn't going away in the morning. 'I promise,' she said. 'The next time you see me I'll be so robust you won't recognize me.'

The two women smiled at each other, and then Sara turned and went to join the men.

Maddie climbed the stairs very slowly, feeling dog-tired. At the top she was arrested by the sound of the church bell striking midnight. She stopped to look out through the window on the landing which opened onto the rue du Jujubier, leaning out over the windowsill and resting her elbows on the cool sandstone slab.

Beyond the roofs of the houses opposite, the spire of the church furled upwards, an elegant silhouette against the night sky. The last chimes of midnight rang out, and a dead silence fell. She stayed leaning out of the window for a few moments longer, then straightened up and turned back to the landing. Voices were drifting up from the rooms below, curiously amplified in the cavernous building. Sara Lennox was talking in an urgent tone, and Maddie could hear quite plainly what she was saying.

'Daniel – you've fucked every woman who's ever sat for you. What makes you think that it's going to be any different this time?'

'I didn't fuck Deirdre O'Dare.'

'That's because her husband would have broken your face if you did. Listen to me. Madeleine Godard is very fragile at the moment. I don't know exactly what's been going on in her life, but the last thing she needs is to be seduced by a dangerous bastard like you.'

'I never seduce women. It's always the other way round. And if Madeleine Godard is as vulnerable as you seem to believe, it's highly unlikely that she's going to want to seduce me.'

Maddie could hear Sara sigh. 'Just promise me you'll keep your hands to yourself.'

'Trust me. My conduct will be exemplary. She can even choose to keep her clothes on if I do get round to painting her. And I take grave exception to you calling me a dangerous bastard, Sara. I have a great deal of old-fashioned respect for women. The real problem is that most women seem to find that irresistible.'

'That's what I mean, you idiot. I'm going to bed. Please don't stay up too late, Sam, or you'll be of no help at all to me in the morning.' There was the sound of a smacking kiss. 'Ow. You give the hardest bear-hugs of anyone I know, Daniel. Good night, big brother. I love you.'

Maddie could hear the sound of Sara's feet crossing the terracotta flags of the parlour. As she took the stairs to her room two at a time the last words she heard were: 'Take care, little sister. I love you too. Have a safe journey tomorrow.'

* * *

The next morning Maddie was woken by plangent French accents floating up from the street below. She turned over in the bed, relishing the feel of the coarse linen sheets against her skin, and contemplated a cloudless blue sky framed by muslin curtains. The muslin caught in the light breeze that came through the open window and lifted a little. A bird was singing in the courtyard below, and a gang of them were bickering vigorously under the eaves. For a long while she lay completely still.

For the first time since Josh's birthday party she felt safe. She had escaped.

Stretching out a hand, she looked at the watch she'd left on the straw-bottomed chair by the bed. It was after eleven o'clock. She could hardly believe it – she'd slept for nearly twelve hours! No wonder she felt more serene than usual.

She slid out of bed, determined not to waste any more of the blue-sky day that beckoned beyond the window. She showered quickly, pulled on one of her cotton sundresses and made her way downstairs to the kitchen. There was no sign of Daniel Lennox.

The big kitchen was airy and warm, with light flooding in through the sliding glass doors that seemed to be the house's only concession to the twenty-first century. Pilot was snoozing on the paved terrasse outside, and he came to greet her, tail wagging, when she stepped out. The terrasse was scattered with cane garden furniture and big terracotta pots containing lemon and fig trees. Beyond the steps which led to the main body of the garden a wooden swing hung from an ancient-looking apple tree. Further down she could just make out a straggly line of fruit canes partially concealed behind an overgrown box hedge.

Somewhere above her a door opened. Looking up, Maddie saw Daniel emerge onto the wide balcony which ran the width of the house. She stepped back quickly into the kitchen. She didn't like the idea of him seeing her mooching around in his garden.

There was a cafetière with dregs in on a work-top, and two cups containing the remains of thick black coffee. There was no evidence of breakfast dishes – Sara and Sam probably hadn't left themselves enough time to eat. Hunting through the cupboards, she found foil packs of coffee, but no herbal tea. She sluiced out the cafetière and put on the kettle. There was half a baguette in a crock, and butter and jam in the fridge in the pantry.

She took her breakfast out onto the terrasse, checking first to make sure that Daniel wasn't still on the balcony above. As she sipped her coffee she leafed through the local guidebook that Maeve had lent her, pronouncing the French place names with enjoyment. Saint-Saturnin. Jonquières. Saint-Bauzille-de-la-Sylve. Arboras.

The only other sound in the garden was the

droning of the bees as they blundered about from flower to flower. It appeared that all the song-birds had retired to the shade, which was a pretty sensible thing to do. Maddie had plastered herself with sunscreen after her shower, but she could already see her skin turning a little pink.

When she finished her breakfast she dumped the dirty dishes in the dishwasher in the utility room, packed a backpack with swimming gear and a book, and set off down the garden to find the bicycle Sara had mentioned. Daniel Lennox's Harley was parked in a lean-to at the bottom of the garden, next to a creosoted garden shed.

The shed was bolted, but not padlocked. It housed an assortment of tools, some old garden furniture, a statue of a half-naked decapitated woman with her head neatly stowed on a shelf at her feet, and a lawn-mower. A straw sunhat trimmed with faded silk flowers was hanging from a hook, and there were a couple of bikes leaning against the wall. One was a child's, spattered with mud; the other was a lady's bike so gleaming that Maddie concluded it had rarely been used. It was well equipped with gears and had a carrier, as well as a padlock with a key stuck in it. It must have belonged to Daniel Lennox's ex-wife.

She pumped up the tyres and wheeled it along the garden path, manoeuvring it in through the sliding glass doors of the kitchen and across the entrance hall. Getting it down the steps which led into the courtyard proved difficult, but she succeeded. She let herself out through the gate, wondering how on earth Daniel had managed to get his Harley into the garden. There must be a side entrance somewhere that she'd missed. Clumsily she mounted the bike – when was the last time she'd ridden one? A decade ago? – and took off down the narrow street.

There weren't many people about, but those she passed smiled and wished her 'Bonjour!' She returned their greetings self-consciously, certain that word would have already got around the village that Daniel Lennox had a strange woman staying in his house.

The street meandered downhill until it reached the main road which would take her to the river. There the road forked. A signpost to Saint-Jean-de-Fos told her which direction to take, and she knew to go straight from there on.

Not more than half a dozen cars passed her as she covered the six kilometres that lay between the village and the river. It was blissfully quiet, apart from the sound of the water sloshing about in the bottle she'd stowed in her backpack, and the occasional distinctive rusty call of a cicada. As she bowled along past olive groves and vineyards with the warm breeze on her face and her skirt flapping against her bare legs, she remembered Maeve's over-the-top description of the rural idyll awaiting her in Saint-Géyroux, and she almost laughed. Maeve might not have been too far off the mark after all. What had she said? Something about strolling through olive groves and vineyards with the sun on her face. *Doing all that country shit –* that's how she'd put it.

Just outside the village of Saint-Jean-de-Fos the road curved steeply down towards the bridge where she and Daniel had stopped the previous day. Maddie stopped pedalling and freewheeled down, enjoying the rush of air that sent her hair flying about her cheeks. She dismounted and padlocked the bike to a post at the top of the path to the river before making her way down the steep, sandy incline.

There were fewer people on the shore than the day before, and Maddie realized it was because she had chosen the hottest part of the day to sit out. Most people would have retreated indoors at this hour. She found a place in the shade of a scrawny oak tree to spread out her towel and unpack her bag. She'd taken care to put her one-piece on under her dress that morning so that she wouldn't feel self-conscious about changing in public, but looking around made her feel self-conscious anyway. All of the women her age and younger were bare-breasted – only the older women wore swimsuits.

This was the first holiday she'd ever taken when she'd packed a one-piece instead of just the bottom half of her bikini. She remembered the proprietorial pride that Josh had displayed every time they hit the beach on holidays in the past, and the way he used to look sideways at other men, checking out their reaction to her when she removed her clothes.

She rubbed suncream into her exposed skin – glad to see that the bruises on her thighs were barely noticeable now – and then sat back and observed the other sunbathers from behind her dark glasses. There were three or four family groups, an elderly couple with skin the colour of dark fudge and the texture of leather, and a group of young people flaunting their golden physiques for each other's benefit. Maddie envied them their lack of inhibition. They were as comfortable with their bodies as sleek animals, and very obviously aware of how beautiful they were. Any time the eyes of the young men slid in Maddie's direction, one of the girls would preen or give a flagrantly sexy laugh to draw attention back to where it belonged.

She took out the book that she'd bought at the airport and read for a while before realizing she'd read it before. She'd been so abstracted before her journey that she'd picked a title at random. She'd root around in Daniel Lennox's library when she got back, for something light, escapist, un-demanding. There was bound to be something that would fit the bill among all those thousands of books.

The elderly couple had gone down to the water and waddled slowly out until their shoulders were immersed and only their heads were left sticking up, sunhats and spectacles still in place. Maddie's skin was looking dangerously pink. She decided to join them. She put her sunglasses in the pocket of her bag and walked down to the water, aware that she was the focus of several pairs of eyes. She kept her own eyes on the sand.

A couple of little girls were sitting together at the water's edge, plaiting each other's long, sun-bleached hair, and a toddler with an ice-cream was paddling in the water talking toddler-speak *en français*. He picked up a handful of pebbles and threw them into the creek, cooing when they hit the water. Looking up at Maddie with eyes the colour of dark chocolate, he pointed to where the pebbles had disappeared. She smiled and clapped her hands in admiration at his feat. Then: 'Phut!' he said gravely before continuing on his way.

She tested the water with her foot, then waded in. It felt like cold silk as it slid up her legs to her waist, and she gave a little gasp as she pushed herself off and struck out for the opposite shore. It didn't take long for the temperature of her body to readjust, and after swimming quite hard for a couple of minutes she turned over onto her back and floated with her eyes closed. When she opened them again she was looking into a smiling, tanned face. 'Fancy meeting you here,' said Sam Newman.

'Oh! Hi!' Treading water, Maddie smiled back. 'Where did you come from?'

'Over there.' He indicated the far shore. 'I'm sitting with Claudine and some of her mates.'

'Did you see Sara off safely?'

'Yeah. She sends her love.' Sam looked at her appreciatively. 'You're a strong swimmer, aren't you, Maddie? Elegant, too.'

'Thanks. I did a lot of competitive swimming when I was at school. I miss it. The gym I go to has a pool the size of a teardrop.'

'The gym I go to doesn't have a pool.'

'There's a gym in Saint-Géyroux?'

Sam laughed. 'No. I mean my gym in Dublin. It's pretty rundown, but it has the advantage of being really cheap.' He twisted his body in the water so that he was floating on his back, and kicked up a spray of water. 'There's a gym in Gignac if you need an exercise fix.'

Maddie considered. Back in Dublin she felt guilty if she didn't manage at least four sessions a week. 'Nah,' she said. 'I came here to get away from all that kind of stuff. Anyway, I'm going to get loads of exercise if I cycle here every day. It's uphill nearly all the way back to the village.'

'You can stick your bike in the back of the deux-chevaux if you want.'

'It's all right, Sam. I enjoy the cycle.' She began to swim leisurely back in the direction she'd come.

'Are you getting out?' he asked.

'Yes. I've had enough for now. I might get in again to cool off before I head back, but right now my priority is to soak up some sun. I feel embarrassingly white.'

'May I join you?'

She hesitated fractionally. 'Sure.'

'I'll go and get my stuff. See you in a minute.'

She padded back across the hot sand to sit on her towel and wait for Sam. On the opposite shore she saw him gathering up his beach paraphernalia and taking leave of a group of people his own age. On his way round the perimeter of the creek he stopped off at the counter of a shack that was selling ice-cream and cold drinks.

'Sam!' One of the golden-skinned girls in the group further down from her got to her feet and waved at him. 'Viens ici, mon beau mec!'

He paused as he drew near to them and chatted for a couple of minutes, laughing at some remark made by one of the youths. Then the girl who'd called him over took him by the hand and made as if to lead him off, but he shook his head and gestured up the shore to where Maddie was sitting. The girl shrugged and sat down, and again Maddie could feel curious eyes turn in her direction as Sam continued up the sand towards her.

'Here,' he said, handing her a choc-ice.

'Thanks.' She made room for him beside her on the big beach towel, and he sat down on her left, quite close to her. She resisted the impulse to edge to the right.

God, he was gorgeous! Half-naked, he was like some Botticelli demi-god – the Mars in *Mars and Venus*. His bathing trunks were slung low on lean hips, affording a demarcation line between a stomach that was washboard flat and tanned legs that were lightly covered in hair the colour of white gold. Maddie was aware of a line of darker hair running down his belly, but she wouldn't let her eyes wander there. What had Daniel Lennox said about him? Something about older women showing a rather unmatronly interest in Sam Newman. She really couldn't blame them.

'Cracker!' Sam was looking towards where the river flowed into the creek. A boy wearing Technicolor shorts had just hurled himself off the parapet of the bridge. He entered the water like a kingfisher.

'Ow.' Maddie gave a shudder. 'Daniel told me yesterday that someone ends up on the rocks every summer. Those boys are crazy.'

'I do it all the time,' said Sam.

'You don't! It's terribly dangerous, Sam!'

'I like to live dangerously,' he said, with a very boyish grin. 'I'm an Aries.'

He looked younger than his twenty-one years as he squinted up at the bridge to watch the next youth come hurtling, lemming-like, down towards the glittering surface of the river. 'Nice one!' he called, as the boy hit the water with a splash of sunlit silver. He bit into his choc-ice with the relish of a child, and the chocolate coating cracked. A sliver of cold chocolate landed on Maddie's bare arm, and she looked on uncertainly as he leaned his golden head down and retrieved it with gentle teeth, licking the place where it had fallen.

There was nothing remotely predatory in his

eyes when he looked back up at her. 'You're really very pretty, Maddie Godard,' he said, with quite disarming candour.

Maddie looked back at him and realized she was smiling. 'And you are far too young for me, Samuel Newman – as well as being an incorrigible flirt. I saw the way you were looking at Claudine last night. Are you two an item?'

'We were last summer,' he said. 'She's got herself a new boyfriend since then. She gave me the key to the McDonaghs' gaff for you, by the way. I have it here.' He stood up and reached into the pocket of his swimming trunks. Then: 'Oh shit,' he said.

'What's wrong?'

'It's gone.' He turned the pocket inside out. 'It must have fallen out while I was swimming.'

'Shit!' Maddie banged her forehead with the heel of her hand. She felt utterly defeated. Was anything on this holiday ever going to go right? 'Oh, Sam! What am I going to do? I haven't a clue when Deirdre and Rory will get here. I'm really stuck without that key!'

'No you're not,' replied Sam equably. 'You can stay on with me and Daniel.'

There was something so inscrutable about the expression on his face as he sat back down beside her that Maddie was almost inclined to believe that the bad boy had dropped the key on purpose.

Chapter Thirteen

Daniel was completely unfazed by the prospect of Maddie staying on in his house. When she returned to Saint-Géyroux with Sam later on that afternoon he was in the kitchen, wearing paint-spattered overalls and spreading ripe Camembert on a hunk of baguette. 'You're welcome to stay as long as you like,' he said. 'As long as you don't mind foraging for food.'

'You're in for a treat tonight,' said Sam, dumping carrier bags on the table. 'There's cassoulet. I'm going to teach Madeleine how to make it.' He had picked up the ingredients in Montpellier on his way back from the airport.

'Excellent,' said Daniel. 'Keep some for me, won't you?'

'Don't you want to eat with us?'

'No. I'll be working late.' He looked at his watch. 'I'd better make tracks. My sitter's due.' He moved towards the door and then stopped. 'Oh, Sam? Give Bianca a ring this evening, will you?'

'What does she want?'

'She's got a job for you. She wants her drawing room redecorated.'

'*Again?*'

'Yeah. It's that time of year.'

'Shit,' said Sam. 'I thought I was going to be able to take things easy for a while.'

'You should have gone north with Sara while you had the chance. Bianca will make you work your arse off.'

Sam considered. 'I suppose I could do with earning a few bob. I badly need a new enlarger, and I've no way of paying for it.'

'Do you want a loan?'

'No. I still owe you for that lens, remember? I'd hate to think that I was taking advantage of the fact that my uncle's loaded. Got to develop backbone and all that.'

'Makes a change from developing photographs, I suppose,' said Daniel as the door closed behind him.

'Well,' said Sam. 'That joke was nearly bad enough to be included in *my* repertory.' He turned to Maddie. 'Bit of a shame, that, my having to work. I'd like to have been able to spend every morning on the beach with you. Maybe you'd come out with me in the evenings, instead? We could head into Montpellier, or hang out at the café in Gignac. A crowd of us congregate there most evenings.'

Maddie couldn't help smiling at the idea of her – erstwhile chief copywriter in a shit-hot advertising agency – hanging out with a gang of kids barely out of their teens. 'It's very sweet of you,

Sam, but I'm not feeling madly sociable. I'd really rather just chill with a book in the evenings.'

Sam made a rueful face and shrugged. 'Well. If you get bored, let me know.' He moved towards the long, scrubbed pine table where he'd dumped his carrier bags. 'OK. Let's commence your apprenticeship as a *commis-chef*,' he said.

Maddie started unpacking groceries. 'By the way,' she said. 'I'm not a total klutz in the kitchen. I can manage more than a boiled egg. How did you learn to make cassoulet?'

'Mme Thibault taught me,' he said.

'Daniel's housekeeper?'

'Yes. I spent a summer here a couple of years ago when the weather was appalling. They referred to it on all the news bulletins as *les conditions exceptionelles*. I was stuck in the house most of the time, and la belle Thibault insisted I do something to make myself useful. I found out I quite enjoyed it.'

'You're a man of many talents, aren't you? You take photographs, you cook, you decorate—'

'I wouldn't call what I do decorating. I just slap a bit of paint around. Bianca gets me to do odd jobs for her every summer. The income comes in handy. I'm a starving student, remember?'

'Nice nixer. I spent two summers chamber-maiding in a hotel in Waterford when I was a student. It was grim. How long have you been coming here to Saint-Géyroux?'

'Most summers since Daniel moved to France.

326

About ten years, I suppose.' Sam moved to a drawer in the kitchen dresser and produced an enormous Sabatier knife. 'Now, Ms Godard. Get chopping. And when you've finished preparing the vegetables, go into the garden and fetch a fresh bay leaf.'

Maddie smiled as she took the knife from him. She wondered if Sam realized that, in the language of flowers, he'd just offered her undying devotion.

*   *   *

Over the course of the next few days, a kind of routine evolved in her life. She spent a lot of time lying by the river, and floating in the water when it got too hot. She acquired a light tan, and felt fit from all the cycling she was doing. She spent her evenings devouring books that she borrowed from the library downstairs. She didn't see much of Sam, who obviously had a fairly active social life despite what he'd said about the pace of life in the village, and she saw nothing at all of Daniel Lennox. He'd been right when he'd said that the vastness of his house meant that you couldn't get in the way even if you tried to.

There were signs that he was around – dishes stashed in the dishwasher, bread left lying on the kitchen table, a wineglass abandoned on the terrasse or on the balcony – but otherwise she might have been living in that huge, echoing house all by herself, just as he'd warned her. *You could even live there and I wouldn't notice . . .* It was rather pleasant, drifting through the cavernous rooms in silence, under no pressure to be anywhere or do anything. Solitude was what she had come here for – but it was comforting to know that Sam was there to turn to if she ever felt the chill touch of loneliness.

On Tuesday morning she went to fetch the bicycle from the shed as usual, and then began the business of negotiating the steps down into the courtyard. She hoisted the bike up, hooking the saddle over her right shoulder, and started the descent badly, misjudging her footing. In order to save herself she let go of the bicycle. It went clattering down the steps and crash-landed at the bottom, upsetting a plinth with a pot that contained a lush maidenhair fern.

'What in hell's name is going on?'

She looked up and saw Daniel Lennox framed in a third-floor window. 'Oh – hello, Daniel. I'm sorry about this. Getting the bike in and out of the house is a bit of a nightmare.' She ran down the rest of the steps and straightened the plinth. 'Don't worry – there's no damage,' she said, putting the pot back and fluffing out the leaves of the fern.

'Why don't you use the side gate?'

She'd noticed the small side gate when she'd returned the bike to the shed the first time she'd borrowed it, but any time she'd tried the gate, it had been locked. 'I've no key,' she said.

'All you had to do was ask.' Maddie hadn't seen him to ask. 'I'll see if I can find a spare.' There was a pause as he looked at her. He had his hands in his pockets and was leaning against the shutter of the window. 'How are you getting on, Madeleine?'

'Fine, thanks. I spend a lot of time down by the pont du Diable.'

'You should try further upriver. There's a wonderful place to swim about two miles up, off the road to Gignac. Hardly anyone knows about it because it's not easy to find. I'll take you some day, if you like.'

'Thanks.' The idea of going swimming in some remote spot with Daniel Lennox held little appeal for her.

'I notice you went shopping yesterday. Thanks for stocking the fridge.' She'd visited the market before hitting the beach.

'You're welcome.'

There was another pause. Then Daniel said: 'If you're cooking something for yourself tonight, maybe you'd include me? I've been living on leftover cassoulet since Saturday.'

Maddie felt guilty that she hadn't volunteered to cook something for him before now. 'Of course I will,' she said.

He straightened himself, stretched and yawned. She remembered that he'd reminded her of a lion when she'd first met him. There was something very leonine about him now. 'See you later, then,' he said, turning away from her and disappearing back into the room. Maddie guessed that it must be his studio.

'Goodbye,' she called, uncertain whether or not he'd heard her. She gave the maidenhair fern a final once-over and headed towards the gate.

*   *   *

She thought hard about what she'd rustle up for dinner that evening. She wanted to make some kind of an effort since Daniel had been so generous to her, but she didn't want to try anything too ambitious in an unfamiliar kitchen. In the end she decided on sundried tomatoes and pine-nuts to start. There were chicken portions in the freezer, and she'd spotted some fennel in Mme Thibault's vegetable garden. Lettuce grew there too. She'd do a salad as well.

At around seven o'clock she moseyed into the kitchen. She slid back the glass doors to let some air in, poured herself a glass of cold white wine and then kicked her sandals off, enjoying the feel of the smooth, cool flags under her bare feet.

The phone rang as she was preparing the starter. She let it ring for quite a long time, not sure whether she should pick up or not. After the seventh ring she reached for it.

'Hi, gorgeous.' It was Sam's voice.

'Hi, even more gorgeous. Have you finished work?'

'Yes.'

'Then why don't you come back here? It's ages since I've had a decent chat with you, and I'm cooking something special this evening.'

'Oh – hell, Madeleine. I was phoning to see if you fancied coming into Montpellier this evening. Bianca got hold of tickets to the Manic Street Preachers gig.'

'*Merde!* I'm sorry, Sam, but I really can't. I promised Daniel I'd cook for him. It's the first opportunity I've had to repay him, and I'd feel like a total ingrate if I let him down.'

'Bad timing,' said Sam.

'You'll get someone else to go with you, won't you?'

'Sure. No problem. But it would have been nice to go with you.'

'How's the decorating going?'

'Slowly. She wants me to do her study as well.'

Madddie's forehead creased in a little frown. 'Sam? A thought just struck me.'

'Yeah?'

'What's Bianca doing with tickets for Manic Street Preachers? I wouldn't have thought they were her scene at all.'

'She knows the promoter,' said Sam.

'Ah. That makes more sense. Well – enjoy it. Maybe I'll see you tomorrow?'

'Definitely. Gina's barbecue, remember?'

'Oh, yes. I'd forgotten about that. It's a date.'

'Good night, then, gorgeous.'

'Good night, even more gorgeous.' She hung up, smiling, and went back to her starter.

She finely chopped garlic and parsley and mixed them with a little excellent olive oil and the pine-nuts. Then she divided the mixture between the sundried tomato halves and arranged them on two plates. The chicken and the fennel went into the oven, and she made a dressing with oil and lemon juice. As she closed the oven door she realized she was humming 'La Vie en Rose', again.

By half-past eight she'd finished. It was starting to get dark. She wondered if she should light the candles that were stuck in wax-encrusted candelabra on the kitchen table, and then decided against it. Daniel Lennox might think that she was trying to create some kind of intimate vibe. She poured herself another glass of wine and sat down at the table. Maybe he'd forgotten that she was cooking dinner this evening?

After ten minutes had passed she decided to take her wine into the library and explore the bookshelves again. She wasn't in the mood for French chick-lit this evening. To judge by the quantity of volumes, Marie-France Lennox had been a big fan. Finally she opted for *Jane Eyre*. An old black-and-white version had been shown on television a couple of months ago, and she'd promised herself that she'd reread it. She'd devoured it at least three times when she was at school, but hadn't opened it since.

There was still no sign of Daniel, and the silence in the house was starting to unnerve her. On previous evenings she'd sat out on the terrasse or on the balcony, reading or scribbling in her note-book. Then she'd found the nocturnal sounds of the garden soothing, but this indoor silence was dead and oppressive.

She moved across to the grand piano, sat down on the stool in front of the keyboard and opened the lid. Where she had touched it, clear marks were left in the dust that blanketed the mahogany. She pressed a key with an experimental finger and the note rang out loud, reverberating in the vast, empty room and sounding ominous, some-how.

'Do you play?'

Catching her breath, she swung round with her heart somersaulting. 'Shit. You gave me an awful fright, Daniel,' she said.

'Sorry,' he said, ambling across the room and not sounding sorry at all. Pilot was at his heels. 'Well? Do you play?'

'A little.'

'Play something for me.'

Maddie was unwilling. 'I'm too rusty. The last time I sat down at a piano was in my parents' house over five years ago. I haven't played since.'

'Why not?'

'There's no room for a piano in my flat.' Pilot put his big head in her lap and looked up at her with a request in his intelligent eyes. Obligingly, she rubbed the velvet of his ears, and his tail moved on the floor.

'Why don't you play your parents' piano any more?'

'My parents are dead.'

'I'm sorry to hear that.' He put his head on one side and looked hard at her. 'Play for me. Please. I don't know how, and I love the sound. This piano isn't played often enough.' He reached down and took Pilot by the collar. 'Lie down, boy,' he said. The dog obeyed instantly, tucking his nose between his paws.

Reluctantly, Maddie racked her brain for something she could play. The only melody that came back to her with any real clarity was the 'Moonlight Sonata'. She ran her fingers up and down the keys a couple of times before starting. 'What's the point of having such a magnificent piano if you can't play?' she asked after a minute or two.

'My ex-wife played beautifully,' he said. 'And my daughter inherited her mother's talent. I keep the piano for Molly.' He ran his shirt sleeve across the top of the instrument, clearing a pathway through the dust. 'Look at that,' he said. 'I'm going to have to get someone from the village in to clean for me while Mme Thibault's out of commission.'

Maddie looked at him curiously. 'You don't strike me as a house-proud kind of guy,' she said, then added: 'Ouch. Sorry,' as she hit a bum note.

'I'm not,' he replied. 'I couldn't give a damn.

But my little girl's coming to stay next month, and I'll have to get the place into some kind of shape for her. Eight-year-olds are extraordinarily conscious of how their homes look to their peers.' He was tracing a spiral pattern in the dust with his finger. 'Molly has a tough enough time having a father who doesn't do normal things like DIY, or golf on a Sunday. I can't have her inviting chums back to a house that looks like something out of *The Addams Family*.' She came to the end of the piece. He looked down at her. 'You were right,' he said.

'About what?'

'You can play – a little.'

She gave a half-smile to acknowledge the truth of his remark and shut the lid of the piano. 'Are you hungry?' she asked.

'As a lion,' he said.

'Then let's eat,' she said, getting to her feet. 'Everything's ready.'

Daniel stood back to let Maddie and Pilot precede him through the library door. In the kitchen the first thing he did was produce a box of matches from a drawer and light the candles on the table. Maddie got the bottle of white wine from the fridge and went to fill a glass for him, but he covered the glass with his hand. 'I'll have red,' he said.

'We're having chicken,' she said. 'It's customary to drink white wine with white meat.'

'Do you always do what's customary, Madeleine?'

he said, looking at her with amused eyes. 'It must make life very dull for you. You told me earlier that I didn't strike you as a house-proud kind of guy. You don't strike me as a *comme il faut* kind of gal.'

Maddie shrugged. 'I used to be. My ex-partner was a very *comme il faut* kind of guy. House-proud, too,' she observed, remembering the way he'd tidied her flat after he'd raped her.

Daniel swung a big plastic flagon off one of the shelves and sloshed wine into his glass. 'This will do me.'

'Is that the local wine?'

'Yes. They fill this for me at the *caveaux*. They have tanks there full of gallons of the stuff. I only bother with good wine on special occasions, and then I make sure it's seriously good.' He looked at her and added: 'That's not to imply that this isn't a special occasion. It's not often that I get food served to me by a beautiful woman. Mme Thibault may be a demon cook, but she's not especially easy on the eye.'

Maddie stripped away the cling-film she'd wrapped over the plates laid out with their starters, and set them down on the table. Then she sat down opposite him.

'What's this?' he asked.

'Sundried tomatoes and pine-nuts,' she said.

Daniel Lennox started to laugh. 'Sundried tomatoes and pine-nuts!'

'Do you have a problem with sundried

336

tomatoes?' asked Maddie, putting down her knife and fork. 'Are you perhaps allergic?'

'No. Oh, no. This looks very good, really it does. Don't look so offended, Madeleine. It's just not the kind of stuff I'm used to, that's all.'

'Haven't you ever tried sundried tomatoes before?'

'Oh – I'm sure I have. I think I had them at Bianca's once.' He knocked down the little tower of tomatoes that she'd carefully constructed on his plate and started forking them into his mouth. 'Very good,' he said finally, smiling at her and wiping his mouth with a big linen napkin. He'd finished his starter before she was halfway through hers.

Just then the phone rang. 'Excuse me,' he said, pushing his chair back from the table and reaching for it where it lay on the dresser beside him.

'Bébé!' he said in a delighted voice. 'Comment ça va? Oui? Bien, bien. Alors, bébé, tu parles à ton père, maintenant. Il faut que tu parles en anglais. OK? Good girl. I know, I know. You always speak French when you're excited.' He leaned back in his chair listening with his right arm crooked behind his head, and an indulgent smile on his face. Maddie could hear a faint voice prattling away on the other end of the phone. Then she saw him frown. 'Uh-oh. When? *Tomorrow?*' There was a hiatus. 'Of course I can't wait to see you, but I wasn't expecting you quite so soon. You'd better let me talk to your mother, sweetie-pie. Yeah. Me too. Don't worry. We'll have fun. I love you lots. Bye, baby.'

Daniel tucked the phone between his jaw and his broad shoulder, broke off a hunk of the baguette on the table and mopped up the oil on his plate. Then he got to his feet and wandered out through the open doors onto the terrasse, followed by Pilot. It was quite a long time before he said anything else, then: 'Marie-France? Qu'est ce que tu fais? Tu sais que c'est très, *très* difficile pour moi. Marguerite, naturellement. Tu la connais – c'est la fille de Mme Thibault. Non. Elle ne retourne pas avant août. *Merde.*'

Maddie quickly finished her tomatoes and then started clearing plates and busying herself with the main course. She didn't want Daniel to think that she was earwigging – though it was difficult to hear what he was saying now, despite the fact that his voice was raised in anger. He had wandered further down the garden and had aimed a kick at the little wooden swing, sending it spinning. Maddie poured more wine for both of them and watched Pilot disappear into the shadows.

After a few minutes he came back into the kitchen, muttering under his breath and directing black looks at nothing in particular. 'Selfish fucking bitch,' he said, slamming the phone back onto its cradle.

Maddie wasn't sure what to say. She could

338

hardly ask him who the selfish fucking bitch was. 'Bad news?' was what she finally decided on.

'Yeah.' He sat back down at the table. 'My wife has just informed me that she's putting Molly on a plane to Montpellier tomorrow. Nearly a whole month earlier than we'd arranged.'

'Oh.' Maddie wasn't sure what the ramifications of this were. 'Is that a problem?'

'It's a huge fucking problem. I've no-one to look after her.' He took a long swig from his glass.

Maddie wasn't used to talking to men about their child-minding arrangements, but she assumed that someone as wealthy as Daniel Lennox could afford a nanny. 'Couldn't you hire a nanny for her?'

'I could, but I won't. The nanny Marie-France employed in Paris was an evil bitch. She could have fucked up Molly's mind bigtime if she hadn't been rumbled. You wouldn't believe some of the stuff she told that little girl. Molly's a great kid – full of confidence and optimism – but by the time that woman had finished with her she was practically gibbering. I knew nothing about it until it was all over and the damage was done. Thanks.'

Maddie had set his main course in front of him. She resumed her place opposite. 'Who usually looks after her when she's here?' she asked.

'Mme Thibault's daughter, Marguerite,' he answered, rubbing his eye with a finger. 'Molly's crazy about her – and about Mme Thibault, too. That woman's like a granny to her. Spoils her rotten.'

'So why can't Marguerite look after her this time?'

'She's working in her uncle's perfumery in Grasse all this month. His staff take holidays at this time of year and she covers for them.' Daniel picked up his knife and fork. 'Fuck it. I'll think of something. This looks good, Madeleine. What is it?'

'Chicken with mascarpone and fennel *alla parmigiana*.'

'Sounds impressive. You're something of a foodie, are you?'

'I was, once upon a time. This is just an easy dish to remember.' There was silence for a while as they ate. Then: 'Are you going to Gina's barbecue tomorrow?' she asked.

'Yeah – I'll come. It'll be good for Molly to meet up with Aoife again, and Gina does excellent grub.'

'Who's Aoife?'

'Deirdre O'Dare's little girl. They got on really well together last summer.'

'Deirdre and Rory will be at the barbecue?'

'Yeah. They're arriving tomorrow. Or so Bianca tells me. And it wouldn't be like her to get it wrong – she has her finger firmly on the pulse of the social goings-on in this buzzing metropolis.'

'So I'll be moving out of here.' She felt a sudden and totally unexpected pang of regret. 'It's funny – I'll miss my room under the eaves. I love the way the locals gossip in the street in the mornings.'

'You're very welcome to stay put. I've already told you that. You're a wonderfully unobtrusive guest. I'd almost forgotten you were in the house until your bicycle crashed down the steps this afternoon.'

'Sorry about that.'

Daniel helped himself to a heap of lettuce and drizzled dressing over it. 'In fact, the longer you stay, the better as far as I'm concerned – if you continue to throw food in my direction occasionally.' The smile he sent her back was wolfish, and she lowered her eyes and started folding her napkin. 'Is there anything else to eat?'

'There's cheese,' said Maddie, putting her knife and fork together on her empty plate.

'Why don't you take your wine out onto the terrasse and I'll bring the cheese and coffee out?' he suggested.

'Thanks,' she said. 'I'll load the dishwasher first, though.'

'Forget it. You've done enough. I'll do it while I wait for the kettle to boil.'

She wandered out onto the terrasse and down into the garden, breathing in air that was fragrant with night-scented stock. There was no cicada serenade tonight – as there had been most other evenings when she'd sat there alone – and no sound from the dovecote. She pictured the doves nestling up together inside, heads under their wings. Far overhead, the blinking light of a plane moved through the purple sky. A rustle from the

341

bushes on her right made her turn, and she saw Pilot bounding towards her with a tennis ball in his mouth.

'Hi, boy!' she said, reaching out her hand for the ball. 'Good boy – give me the ball, Pilot. Come on – give!' He dropped it at her feet, and she picked it up. 'Fetch!' she said, lobbing the ball down the garden and smiling as the big dog loped after it. He was back immediately with the ball in his mouth, and this time she didn't have to ask him to give it to her. 'Go again, Pilot!' she urged.

Maddie threw the ball for him over and over again, but on the dozenth throw he didn't come back. She waited for a minute or two, listening to him panting and lumbering around in the shrubbery as he searched for his toy, and then she gave up on him. She turned and strolled back up the garden, pausing to stoop and inhale the scent of a red rose. Its perfume mingled with the smell of French tobacco drifting towards her on the balmy air. She looked up. Daniel Lennox was sitting on a wicker chair on the terrasse, smoking a cigarette. There was a cafetière on the table beside him, a cheese dish, cups, and two brandy glasses. She wondered how long he'd been sitting there, observing her.

'It's a beautiful evening,' she said as she joined him.

'What do you do with yourself in the evenings, Madeleine?' he asked, putting out his cigarette and cutting a slab of Camembert. He spread the cheese on a hunk of bread and offered it to her. 'Want some?'

'Thanks,' she said, taking it from him. 'I read, mostly, out here. And I scribble a bit.'

'You sketch?'

'No. I just jot down ideas. Sometimes I mess about with bits and pieces of poetry. Nothing serious.'

'What kind of poetry?' He depressed the plunger on the cafetière and filled the cups. 'Help yourself to cream and sugar,' he said. Then he looked at her. 'What kind of poetry?' he asked again. 'Don't be shy, Madeleine.'

She stirred cream into her coffee, taking her time. Then she tucked a strand of hair behind her ear. 'You'll probably think this is a bit batty,' she said, not looking at him. 'I'm trying to write a series of sonnets.'

'I don't think that's batty at all. I think it's endearingly old-fashioned.' He helped himself to cheese. 'Why sonnets?'

'It's an excellent discipline. It makes you think very hard about each word you choose.' It was also a form of therapy for her, but she wasn't going to let him know that. She looked up at him with a rather defensive expression. 'They're probably execrable sonnets.'

'I don't see why they should be. You're a wordsmith by profession, after all. Even if your chosen *métier* is a stonkingly superficial one, if you don't mind me saying so.'

343

'I don't mind in the least,' she retorted carelessly. She was used to people's preconceived notions about the advertising world. 'Everyone who doesn't know anything about advertising thinks it's superficial. Anyway, my sonnets are superficial, too.'

'Why?'

She looked away from him. He'd touched a nerve. 'I couldn't write anything profound.'

'Oh – I'm sure you have hidden depths that you could plunder, Madeleine, if you wanted to. Everyone who works in advertising is just waiting for that definitive novel to finish gestating in their soul before it's unleashed on an awestruck but grateful public, isn't that so?' He broke off another chunk of bread, and then leaned forward, regarding her with uncharacteristic concern. 'Are you all right?'

Her heart was palpitating and she had stiffened involuntarily. It had taken just a sliver of a second for the image of Josh forcing her mouth open to rise in front of her mind's eye. It wasn't the first time she'd suffered a flashback since she'd come to Saint-Géyroux, but the nauseating vividness of the replay always took her by surprise. 'I'm fine,' she said raggedly, swiftly submerging the image in the sea of her subconscious. She could feel Daniel's eyes on her as she reached for her brandy glass. 'I'm fine,' she repeated, trying to regain control of her breathing. The flashback was threatening to surface again, and she downed an unwisely hefty slug of cognac in an attempt to prepare herself for the onslaught.

Just then a bird started to sing in the darkness. It was the most indescribably beautiful sound that Maddie had ever heard, and it had an extra-ordinary effect on her. The flashback that had been about to replay in Technicolor close-up in front of her mind's eye suddenly receded into pinpoint long-shot, then vanished entirely. She sat up straight in her chair, remaining perfectly still as she listened with undisguised wonder to the bird's song, gazing towards the garden. The aria went on for several minutes. She looked at Daniel with a question in her eyes. 'A nightingale,' he said in a low voice, putting a finger to his lips. The little creature was singing as if its heart would burst. 'Pouring forth thy soul abroad in such an ecstasy!' – Keats's words came back to her. Then there was silence.

She smiled and shook her head. 'I've never heard one before,' she said in an awed whisper.

'You were in luck tonight. It's a rare privilege to be serenaded by a nightingale.' He took a drink from his brandy glass. 'And a rare privilege for me to witness your response. You looked utterly spell-bound.'

Just then Pilot came galloping up the garden, wagging his tail in victory. He dropped the ball at Maddie's feet and she laughed. The brandy had made her lightheaded. Or was it the reprieve from the flashback that had lifted her spirits? 'You clever thing,' she said, crouching down on her hunkers and caressing the dog's ears. 'You found

345

it at last!' She looked up at Daniel and smiled. 'I'll take him for a walk some day soon if you like.'

He looked back at her for a long minute without saying anything. She was suddenly aware that the strap of her sundress had slipped down over her arm, and that part of her left breast was exposed. She averted her eyes immediately and hooked the strap back up over her shoulder. Then Daniel got to his feet and drained the brandy in his glass. 'If you like.' He put the glass down and looked at his watch. 'I told Bianca I might call by,' he said. 'I'd better move.' Then he turned and strolled through the glass doors into the kitchen. 'Good night Madeleine,' he added, almost as an after-thought. He didn't look back at her.

She watched his departing back. 'Good night, Daniel,' she said. *Thanks for dinner, Madeleine,* she prompted inwardly, but the kitchen door closed behind him and the words were left unsaid.

At the bottom of the garden the nightingale began to sing again.

*   *   *

On returning from her swim the following day she was greeted by the sound of a piano. Music was flooding through Daniel Lennox's entrance hall. She followed the sound to the library, and paused in the doorway. Molly was sitting at the piano with her back to her, her small hands dancing on the keyboard. The melody she was playing was unfamiliar to Maddie. When the little girl finished, Maddie broke into a patter of applause. The child twisted round on the piano stool. 'Hello,' she said. 'Who are you?'

'My name's Maddie Godard, but if you like you can call me Madeleine. I met you once before, do you remember? At your aunt's exhibition in Dublin.'

'Oh yes.' The child jumped to her feet and crossed the room towards Maddie. 'You're the one who couldn't decide whether your favourite girl singer was Christina Aguilera or Britney Spears. Have you made up your mind yet?'

'No. I've changed it. It's Samantha Mumba.'

Molly jumped up and down. 'That's a real coincidence!' she said. 'She's my favourite now, too! And she's Irish, like you.'

'I saw her in Dublin once.'

'On stage?'

'No. Walking down Grafton Street. She's just as gorgeous in real life.'

'Oh! You are *so* lucky!'

'What was that tune you were playing just now?'

'It's called "The Satin Gown".'

' "The Satin Gown"? I've never heard it before.'

'That's because I made it up.'

'You made it up? Honestly? But it sounded brilliant!'

'Yeah. It's one of my favourites. I'll do a concert for you some time if you like. I've made up loads of others.'

'Wow. An infant prodigy. Like Mozart. Before you know it Samantha will be asking you to write songs for her.'

Molly squirmed with pleasure. 'Would you like to see my room?' she asked.

'I'd love to. Do you keep it tidy?'

'No,' confessed Molly. 'It's tidy now because I've only just arrived, but it's usually a tip.'

She led the way out of the library and up the stairs, veering right at the divide.

Maddie stopped. 'Oh – I can't go through there, Molly. That's your dad's private apartment.' One of the tall, panelled doors was open wide enough for Maddie to see a long dark corridor with more doors off it. Through an archway at the opposite end a spiral staircase rose to the floor above. A jewel-like pattern glimmered on the stone floor at the foot of the staircase. At first Maddie thought it was a miniature Persian rug, but a second look told her that the pattern was projected through a small stained-glass window set into the far wall.

'He won't mind. Come on.' Molly took Maddie's hand and started pulling her up the stairs.

Maddie resisted. 'I'd better not, sweetheart. I don't want to upset him.'

'It's OK, Madeleine.' Daniel Lennox's voice came from behind them. He was standing in the doorway of the billiard room. 'It's only out of bounds to people I don't trust. Just don't go into the studio. I don't like people looking at my work before it's finished.'

'Yay! Merci, Papa!' said Molly, dragging Maddie up the stairs.

The little girl's room was much the same as any eight-year-old's. There were shelves untidily crammed with books and games; Barbies and stuffed toys poked their heads out of storage boxes. A giant whiteboard was covered with childish representations of witches and princesses and pop divas – obviously the work of Molly herself – and a pinboard crowded with family photographs hung above the child's bed.

What made the room unique were the paintings. Virtually every flat surface was covered in decoration. There were tropical fish swimming on the aquamarine painted floor, fabulous animals prancing through a forest on the walls, and birds of paradise soaring across the ceiling. The wooden furniture had been painted to represent treasure chests, and pink roses climbed over door and window frames. Looking closer at the murals, Maddie could see that there were human figures in the landscape, too. A woman who had to be Molly's mother was sitting side-saddle on a unicorn, holding a pomegranate in her hand.

'What a wonderful room!' said Maddie. 'Oh – you're a lucky girl, Molly! I would have loved a room like this when I was your age. I still would, come to think of it.'

'My dad did all the paintings,' said Molly with manifest pride. 'Can you find me anywhere in them?'

Maddie's eyes scanned the walls. 'Yes! There you are – riding on the back of a tiger! Oh, and look – there's your father!' Daniel Lennox had painted a likeness of himself sharing a banana with an orang-utan.

'And look,' said Molly. 'There's my mum, and there's Marguerite and Aoife – she's the one playing with the lion cubs – and that's Régine feeding the dragon.'

'Who's Régine?' asked Maddie.

'Régine Thibault. She looks after Daddy, but she's hurt her shoulder and has to have a rest.'

So that was the famous Mme Thibault! She was depicted as a stout, middle-aged woman wearing a no-nonsense expression and a glittering, be-jewelled crown trimmed with ermine.

'Dad puts in a new person every year as a surprise for me.'

'Who's the new one this year?'

'Bianca. Look.' Molly pointed to Bianca who was sitting on the branch of a tree wearing a flowing white dress with a garland of white flowers in her hair. She made a face. 'I don't know why he put her in. I don't really like her. I think I'll ask him to rub her out and put you in instead.'

Maddie laughed. 'Oh – that would be too much of an honour, Molly.'

'Look.' Molly hopped across the room on one leg. 'This is the cupboard where I keep all my secret things. And here's my collection of Barbies.

It's cool fun to dress them up and do their hair. Would you like to?'

'Yes, I would.'

'Ace! Is it OK if I have Gymnast Barbie?' Molly took the storage box full of Barbies and emptied them out on the floor. 'Now I'm doing gymnastics at school I like Gymnast Barbie the best. Which one would you like?'

'What's this one called?'

'Oh – that's Irish Barbie. She used to be my favourite. She's a bit battered, I'm afraid.'

Maddie found herself laughing. 'That's all right,' she said, looking at the doll with a kind of rueful irony. 'I know exactly how she feels.'

*   *   *

Half an hour later they heard footsteps in the corridor and Daniel came through the door. Maddie and Molly were both sitting on the floor surrounded by Barbie outfits. He looked down at Maddie with a perplexed expression. 'What are you doing?' he asked.

'Playing Barbies of course,' she said, smiling up at him.

*   *   *

The three of them went to Gina and Roger's barbecue together, but as soon as Molly got through the gate she let go of Maddie's hand

351

and dashed off to look for her pal Aoife.

It seemed as if the entire village had congregated in the couple's garden. Maddie recognized several faces that she passed on the street every day on her way to the beach, and exchanged smiling *bonsoirs*. She followed Daniel through the crowd to a long trestle table that had been set up under the shade of a balcony dripping with wistaria. Quiches and baguettes, enormous bowls of salad and countless bottles of wine from the local *caveaux* were crammed together on paper tablecloths. Daniel helped them both to plates of food, and poured wine into paper cups.

'Wow,' said Maddie. 'This wine is excellent. It's hard to believe it's *vin ordinaire*, isn't it?'

'It's ridiculously cheap,' said Daniel. 'I get through gallons of the stuff. Rory!' He raised his hand to salute a man with two days' growth of blond stubble and a spiky, vaguely military haircut. He was carrying a little girl of about five on his shoulders. She was laughing and swaying to the rhythm of a song she was singing, and as Rory McDonagh turned and angled his way towards them her swaying grew more precarious. She didn't appear remotely fazed by this, and carried on singing her Björk song with brio.

Rory reached up and swung her down when he drew even with them. 'Hi, Daniel,' he said, extending his hand. 'Good to see you.'

'Likewise. How are things?'

'Never better.' He took off his sunglasses and

smiled at Daniel with eyes that were as green as his daughter's. Then something caught his attention. 'Look, Aoife – there's Molly – over there by the front door. Run and grab her, quick!'

The little blond girl raced off to join her friend, tapping her on the shoulder when she caught up with her. When Molly turned round she gave a shriek of delight. Then the pair of them just stood there looking self-conscious and squirming with embarrassment.

'They're very coy, aren't they?' remarked Rory. 'I'd say that'll last about two minutes. Aoife's up to ninety about seeing Molly again. She talked about nothing else on the flight over.'

'When did you get in?'

'Midday. We plan to party away our jet lag.' Rory looked down at Maddie and smiled. He cocked his head curiously. 'Introduce me,' he said to Daniel.

'Forgive me,' said Daniel Lennox. 'I thought you two knew each other. Madeleine Godard, this is Rory McDonagh.'

'Hi,' she said, shaking his hand.

'You were meant to be our house-guest, weren't you?'

'That's right.'

'Sorry about the leak. You organized somewhere else to stay, obviously.'

'The leak?'

'Yes. The one in the spare room ceiling.'

'Oh. Well, actually, I wasn't able to get into the

house at all. The spare key got lost. I've been staying at Daniel's.'

'It's probably just as well. The place is a complete washout.'

'Not much of a welcome back to Saint-Géyroux for you,' remarked Daniel. 'How bad is the damage? There was a lot of rain last month. The usual *conditions exceptionelles.*' He produced a pack of Gitanes from the breast pocket of his shirt and deftly lit up with one hand.

'We'll be getting the builders in again. Half the roof will need to be replaced. We won't be having visitors for a while.'

'Better make sure the terracotta tiles are *simpatico,* McDonagh, or you'll have Bianca on your case.'

Rory laughed. 'They'll be so *simpatico* they'll look seamless.'

Daniel turned to Maddie. 'You'll have to stay put under my roof, after all then, Madeleine. I dare say I could get used to sundried tomatoes after a while.'

She gave him a scathing look. 'I don't know why you're so disparaging about sundried tomatoes,' she said. 'I bet you wouldn't say no to them if I served them up with the Hafners sausages I saw in your freezer.'

Rory raised an eyebrow. 'Am I missing something?' he said.

'Madeleine does a mean line in designer food.'

'I wish my inamorata did a mean line in any

354

kind of food. Ah. Here she comes, as if on cue. Her degree in theatre studies wasn't such a waste of money after all.'

'Daniel! How lovely to see you!' A woman with laughing eyes descended upon Daniel Lennox and gave him a great bear-hug.

'Deirdre O'Dare. Beautiful as ever.' He took her hand and kissed it.

'Hi, Deirdre,' ventured Maddie. Deirdre looked uncertain. 'Maddie Godard,' she prompted.

'Maddie Godard! Wow. I wouldn't have recognized you! I mean – sorry, I don't mean to be rude, but you've really changed since the last time I saw you. You look great.' Deirdre clapped a hand over her mouth. 'Oh yikes – that sounds awful – I don't mean that, either! It's just that you look so different.'

Rory winced and slung an arm around his wife's shoulder. 'She's a bit challenged in the diplomacy department, my missus,' he said, pulling her towards him and depositing a kiss on her mouth, then another. 'Kissing her's the only way of shutting her up,' he said. 'But unfortunately I'm the only person who's allowed to do that. The rest of you have to listen to her.'

Deirdre tried to look as if the idea of Rory McDonagh being the only person in the world entitled to kiss her was earth-shatteringly boring, but she couldn't manage it. Instead she laughed up at him, took hold of his other arm and wound it round her.

'You're still sick-makingly in love, aren't you, you smug bastards?' Daniel Lennox was looking at them with an expression of most un-Daniel-Lennoxish indulgence.

Deirdre sent him an apologetic smile. 'Yeah,' she said. 'Sorry about that.' Then she turned her attention back to Maddie. 'How did you cope?' she asked. 'The spare room's like a swimming pool.'

Maddie explained again.

'Oh – it's a much better idea for you to stay at Daniel's. His house is vast and gorgeous. Ours is only little compared to his, and it's not even that pretty yet. We haven't spent enough time here to get round to doing it up.'

'How long can you manage to stay this time?' asked Daniel.

Deirdre made a face. 'Only about a month. Rory's off to Jamaica to shoot some bodice-ripping epic.'

'You do a lot of that kind of stuff, don't you, McDonagh?'

'Yeah,' he said complacently. 'I love it.'

Deirdre gave him a dig in the ribs. 'Meursault me,' she said.

'There's nothing as grand as Meursault here,' remarked Daniel.

'Will *vin ordinaire* do for you, my little oeno-phile?' asked Rory, disengaging himself and moving towards the table.

'Oenie meeney miney whatever,' said Deirdre. She took the paper cup he proffered her and tasted the contents. 'Oh bliss,' she said. 'Now I know I'm not dreaming and I really am back in Saint-Géyroux. Come with me,' she said, turning to Maddie. 'We'll leave the boys to their wine and smutty jokes.'

'And what rarefied pastime are you going to indulge in?' asked Rory as Deirdre linked arms with Maddie. 'Croquet?'

'No. We're going to drink wine and tell smutty jokes, of course,' she said over her shoulder to him as she shimmered away through the crowd.

*　　*　　*

An hour later they ran into Daniel and Rory in another part of the garden. Deirdre and Maddie had filled each other in on what had been going on in their respective lives since they had last met. Maddie had been understandably economical with the truth, but Deirdre had waxed lyrical about her new life writing screenplays in a beach house outside LA. 'And Rory's just made a shit-load of money playing a naval admiral on some silly mega-budget movie – that explains the haircut. You should have seen him in his uniform, Maddie! Hell's teeth, was that sexy! I think I might buy him one, come to think of it . . . What else? Oh, yes! I'm pregnant,' she'd added with satisfaction.

'Oh – wow! How pregnant – and do you know the sex?'

'About four months, and yes, it's a girl.'

'Are you happy with that?'

'Ecstatic. And so's Rory. He wants all girls.'

'How many more do you plan to have?'

'I dunno. Not that many. I hate being pregnant. Hello, *mon beau mec*,' she said as they drew abreast of her husband. He and Daniel were still talking. 'Take me home now, will you?'

'What about your plan to party through your jet lag?'

'Aborted. I can't stick the pace. And my feet are killing me.' Deirdre kicked off her sandals and slung them over her shoulder.

'The ideal wife,' said Rory, with manifest pride.

'Me?'

'Yeah. Barefoot, pregnant and out of the kitchen. Come on then.' He put a protective arm around her. 'You must come for an aperitif some evening soon,' he said to Daniel and Maddie. 'I won't invite you to dinner, though. I wouldn't inflict my wife's cooking on you.'

'You could do scrambled eggs,' suggested Deirdre. 'You're good at them. Or we could get a maid.'

'We'll get a maid,' said Rory.

'Oh, really, Rory? I'd love that!'

'As long as she's French, wears one of those short puffy dresses and a dinky white apron, shows too much cleavage, has frilly knickers and carries a feather duster.'

'No maid,' said Deirdre sadly. 'Good night, Maddie. It was lovely to see you again. Sorry about the mess-up with the house, but you really are better off where you are.'

The couple wandered off through the garden, pausing from time to time to exchange words with friends. When they reached the gate Deirdre laughed at something Rory said, and swatted him with the thongs of her sandals. Rory pinioned her arms and kissed her deeply for a minute before releasing her, then held her at arm's length so that he could look at her. She reached up a hand to touch his face, and Maddie suddenly felt a hellish tug of envy. She had never seen a couple look so utterly content.

She turned away to see a woman observing the pair closely. For some reason she looked familiar, but Maddie couldn't place her.

'Do you know that woman, Daniel?' she asked.

'Can't say I've had the pleasure,' he returned.

She was distracted from her efforts at trying to put a name to the face by the arrival of Sam.

'There you are,' he said. 'I've been looking all over the place for you. Look – I nicked a bottle of *Mas de Daumas Gassac* and some excellent hash from Daniel's stash at home. Oh. I didn't see you there, Daniel! I'll replace it. Promise.'

He flashed Daniel a smile and then took Maddie by the hand in a proprietorial fashion and led her to a remote corner of the garden where a huge, drooping cedar tree grew. They sat on the grass beneath it and polished off the bottle between them, exchanging the most juvenile jokes they could think of. Maddie was particularly chuffed that her one about the squirrel being locked out of his tree made Sam almost inarticulate with laughter. She didn't know where the joke had come from, or how she'd managed to remember it. She hadn't told it for years.

An hour and a couple of joints later she was feeling very mellow indeed. A warm dusk had settled around them, obscuring them from the rest of the party. When Sam leaned over and kissed her lightly on the lips she didn't stop him. He drew back and smiled into her eyes. Then he kissed her again, and this time his kiss was more meaningful. This was the first time she'd been kissed sensuously since Josh, since before the rape. The kisses that had been forced on her then had been cruel, lurid, brutal. She stiffened a little, remembering, half-expecting a demon to visit her again, but no flashback happened. After a moment or two she found herself relaxing, leaning into Sam, kissing him back. Some instinct told her that this was the right thing to do, that this was another step towards reclaiming normality in her life. What harm could there be in kissing a beautiful boy under a tree in a crepuscular garden in the South of France? Sam's tongue was circling her mouth languorously, and then she felt his hand slide from her shoulder to her breast. She tensed as he started to undo the buttons on the front of her dress. Then his hand was warm against her bare skin.

She broke the kiss. 'Stop now, Sam.'

He sat back reluctantly, looking at her with his lips parted and his eyes half closed. His breathing was shallow. 'Oh, Maddie,' he said. There was urgency in his tone. 'Where shall we go? Back to Daniel's place?'

'You don't understand, Sam. I'm sorry – I'm just not ready for this.'

'Don't you want to?'

'No – it's not that.' She was confused herself, now. 'It's just that I don't – I don't feel I know you well enough. Oh, God – this sounds so uptight and stupid.'

'Maddie – you know I'd never hurt you or take advantage of you, don't you? I practically worship you, for Christ's sake!'

'Oh, Sam – please try and bear with me,' she implored him. 'Maybe I should have said that I don't know *myself* well enough. I find you incredibly appealing, honestly I do, and—'

'Appealing? I'm insulted, Maddie. *Puppies* are appealing.' He took hold of a strand of her hair and toyed with it. 'Don't you find me sexy at all?'

'Oh God, yes.' She gave a rather ragged laugh. 'You're that too – of course you are. And another time I'd have loved to have taken you to bed. But not now. Please don't ask me to explain. I'm just not ready for you yet.'

'Shit. The same can't be said of me.' He drew his legs up, looking very morose.

'I'm really sorry, Sam. I shouldn't have let you kiss me.'

There was a pause. Then he ran a hand over his blond crop and smiled at her. 'I'm glad you did,' he said.

The intimate mood was fragmented by the precipitate arrival of Aoife and Molly, bold-eyed and giggling.

'What are you doing here, Aoife O'Dare-McDonagh?' said Sam. 'I saw your mum and dad going home ages ago.'

'They allowed me to stay on,' said Aoife. 'Daniel said I could stay with Molly tonight as a special treat because we haven't seen each other for so long.'

The little girls shuffled and nudged each other. Then: 'You say it,' said Molly.

'No, you say it,' returned Aoife.

'No, you say it.'

'No.' Aoife looked stubborn. '*You* say it.'

'I know! We'll say it together.' Molly waved her hand like a conductor preparing an orchestra. 'One, two, three!'

They looked at each other, then: 'We saw you kissing!' they chanted. Molly squirmed, hiding her grin with her hands, and Aoife burst into fits of giggles and danced away back up the garden.

Sam and Maddie exchanged an oblique look and smiled at each other.

Molly sat down beside them on the grass and snuggled against Maddie. 'Why were you kissing?' she asked.

'Because it feels nice,' said Maddie. She pounced on the little girl and covered her face with kisses, tickling her at the same time. 'Doesn't it?'

'No! No! Stop! I'll do anything!' screamed Molly, rolling around on the grass in an unconvincing attempt to escape from her torturer's embrace.

'Anything?'

'Yes! Yes! I promise!'

'Will you let me have Gymnast Barbie next time?'

'Yes! Yes!'

'All right, then.'

Maddie finally released her and they both fell back on the grass, laughing.

'Time to go, Molly.' Maddie looked up, shading her eyes with a hand. Silhouetted against the setting sun, Daniel Lennox was smiling down at them, his hands in his jeans pockets.

'Aw – Dad! It's not even nine o'clock!'

'I don't care. You and Aoife have both had a busy day travelling, and you're over-excited. It's time you were in bed. Come on – up you get.'

'Bum,' said Molly, getting to her feet with bad grace.

Sam stood up and then put out a hand to help Maddie up, too.

'Thanks,' she said, shaking bits of dry grass out of her hair. 'Maybe I'll see you at the beach tomorrow, Sam?'

'You're not leaving too, Maddie, are you?' he asked. 'It's far too early. Why don't you stay for a little while longer?'

She shook her head. She had been seriously disturbed by Sam's kiss. She knew that if she stayed he would kiss her again, and she hadn't a clue whether she badly wanted him to kiss her again, or badly didn't want him to kiss her again. 'I told you before, I'm not a madly sociable animal,' she said.

'Go and say thank you to Gina and Roger, Molly,' said Daniel. The little girl turned round and started trudging up the garden. 'And tell Aoife I'll take the pair of you on a picnic tomorrow if you're good,' he called after her.

'Oh – thanks Dad!' She sent him a brilliant smile over her shoulder and skipped off up the path.

'Good night, Sam.'

'Good night, Daniel.'

'Good night, Sam.'

'Good night, Maddie.' He looked at her with entreaty, but she just gave him a small, regretful smile and turned away to follow Daniel up the garden.

'Sorry about Molly being over-excited,' she said. 'That was my fault.'

'No problem. I was looking for an excuse to leave, anyway.' He gave her an amused look. 'I

364

don't imagine she's the only one you over-excited. You might like to know, Madeleine, that the front of your dress is open.'

With her face flaming, Maddie did up the buttons on her dress. When she looked up again, Daniel was taking his farewell of Gina and Roger with an arm slung around Molly's shoulders. A smiling woman was part of the group. She was looking up at Daniel with a fascinated expression, batting heavily mascaraed eyelashes. It was the woman who had been watching Deirdre and Rory with such interest earlier.

With a sudden, blinding flash, Maddie remembered where she'd seen her before. At the opening of Sara Lennox's exhibition, of course! She was the tabloid journalist who had stitched up her cousin. The woman Maeve had called Darina Maguire.

Darina's lizard eyes swivelled towards Maddie as if aware that she was being observed, and Maddie waited for a spark of recognition to ignite. But the woman gave no indication that she knew who Maddie was. It wasn't surprising. Deirdre O'Dare hadn't recognized her either. Well, she thought. This business of reinventing myself seems to be working. Maddie Godard, copywriter, the Complete Works is dead: long live Madeleine Godard.

But what on earth was Darina Maguire doing in Saint-Géyroux? She was unlikely to be here on holiday. Maddie suspected that the hackette's holiday destination of choice would be a bit more

night-lifey – no – make that *nite*-lifey – than a
mountainy French village. Hers was no beneficent
presence, that was for sure. Maddie Godard knew
that Darina Maguire's presence here could only
mean one thing. It meant mischief.

Chapter Fourteen

The next morning when she came downstairs she found Molly sitting at the big kitchen table looking mournfully at a bowl of cornflakes. Daniel was standing at the range poking at something in a frying pan. There was an appalling smell of burning sausages.

'Hi, Maddie,' said Molly. 'Dad's burnt the sausages and the cornflakes are stale. They're the same ones that were in the cupboard last time I was here. I recognized the special offer. What are you going to have for breakfast?'

'Oh. Maybe I should run out and get a baguette?'

'I've already done that. Look.' The little girl pointed to a fresh baguette that was sticking out of a jug.

'Where's Aoife?' asked Maddie.

'Gone home to get her swim togs. Dad took her back on his motorbike. She looked so *sweet* clinging on! And now Daddy's taking us for a picnic.'

'Fucking sausages,' said Daniel Lennox, scraping them into the bin.

'Language, Dad,' said Molly cheerfully.

'Sorry, baby. I think we'll have to forget about a traditional Irish breakfast this morning. Won't bread and jam do?'

'OK.' Molly hopped down off her chair and disappeared into the pantry. 'I *love* the clothes you wear, Maddie,' she said on her way past. 'You remind me of someone from the olden days.'

'Do you want me to cook them?' Maddie picked up the packet of sausages that had been left lying on the worktop.

'Would you, Madeleine? I'd really appreciate that.'

'I'll give it a lash. Believe it or not, I've never cooked sausages before.'

'Too pedestrian for you, I suppose?'

'I'm afraid so,' she admitted with a self-deprecatory smile. 'You don't find a lot of imaginative recipes for pork sausages in designer cookbooks. Would you like mushrooms and tomatoes as well? I'll even do fresh tomatoes instead of sundried ones,' she added, slanting a sideways look at him. She saw his mouth curve.

'I'd love some,' he said. 'But don't bother doing mushrooms for Molly. She won't touch them.'

'What won't I touch?' asked Molly imperiously, coming back into the kitchen with a jar of apricot preserve.

'Mushrooms,' said Maddie, throwing butter into a pan.

'Are you having some?'

'Yes.'

'Then I will, too,' said Molly, with decision.

'You'd better bloody eat them, Molly,' warned Daniel. 'If Madeleine's going to the trouble of cooking them for you.'

'Don't worry. I will.' Molly emptied her cornflakes into the pedal bin and rinsed the bowl under the tap.

Daniel looked at her suspiciously. 'You're being unusually helpful,' he said.

'It's my new leaf that I turned over.'

'Oh? When did you turn it over?'

'This morning. Sit down, darling Daddy, and let me get you another cup of coffee. Would you like one, Maddie?'

'Yes, please.'

'Would you like to come swimming with us today?' said Molly, pouring coffee into cups. 'Me and Dad are going to make a luxury picnic.'

'Where are you going?' asked Maddie.

'To the river, by the Labadou.' Molly set a brimming cup of coffee down on the wooden worktop. 'We can build sand castles there, and the Labadou does the best ice-cream with toppings. I even made up a song about it. Listen. Labadou, Labadou, Laba, Laba, Labadou—'

'We are *not* going to the Labadou, Molly,' said Daniel firmly. 'I already told you that.'

'Aw – Dad!'

'Molly – I've tried to explain to you. There are

369

too many people there. It's July now – there'll be hordes of holidaymakers descending on the joint. No. If we're going swimming it'll have to be further upriver. I'll treat you to *crêpes* in Saint-Jean-de-Fos afterwards as a reward for compliance.'

'What's compliance?'

'Doing as I tell you.'

'*Crêpes* with ice-cream?'

'Sure.'

'OK. Will you come, Maddie? Please say yes. We can bring the Barbies and you can have Gymnast Barbie like I said.'

Maddie laughed. 'It's OK, Molly. I don't mind being Irish Barbie again. Yes – I'd love to come.' A thought struck her and she turned to Daniel Lennox. 'That is, if you don't mind?'

'Why should I mind? Of course you can come. God, that smells good.'

'It'll be another five minutes. Will you set the table, Molly?'

Molly rooted around for plates and knives and forks. '*Laba*dou, *Laba*dou, Laba, Laba, *Laba*dou,' she sang, in a reedy, melodic voice. 'Their chocolate ice-creams are so good they'd get anyone out of a bad mood. Even stinking crosspatch Daddy and sometimes sad-looking gorgeous Maddie – Ow!' as Daniel threw a mock punch. Then: '*I'll get it!*' she squawked, pouncing on the telephone almost before Maddie had even registered it was ringing. 'Hello. The Lennox residence. How may I help you? Oh – hi, Rory! Yeah. Yes, thank you. Tell

Aoife to bring her Barbies. Yeah. I'll get him for you. Dad? It's Rory.'

Daniel Lennox stretched out a paw for the phone. 'Hi, Rory. No problem. They were knackered – fell asleep without the usual palaver. Yeah. Really? Hell – that's good of you – I was kinda dreading that. Yeah. We'll drop by in an hour or so, OK? Oh – and can you put in enough grub for four? Madeleine's coming too. Thanks. See you then. Bye.' He put the phone down, then said: 'I'm off the hook.'

'What hook, Dad?'

'Since we're taking Aoife for the day, Rory and Deirdre have kindly volunteered to do the picnic.'

'Bum,' said Molly. 'I was looking forward to making it. I wanted chocolate spread sandwiches. Do you like chocolate spread sandwiches, Maddie?'

'I don't think I've ever had one.'

'I'll do them next time.' Molly came over to where Maddie was standing at the range and peered into the pan. 'Oh. I don't mean to alarm you, Maddie, but I think those mushrooms might be poisonous.'

'What makes you think that?' Maddie smiled down at her.

'Because she's decided she doesn't want them after all,' said Daniel Lennox. 'You will eat the mushrooms, Molly.'

Molly adopted an expression of extreme apprehension. 'But I might die!' she said. 'They have an evil look about them!'

'It's OK, Molly. You don't have to eat the mushrooms. Your dad and I can share them.'

'Good,' the child replied happily.

'So you've no qualms about whether Madeleine or I die of mushroom poisoning?' asked Daniel.

'Oh, no. You are adults. You have a much more robust constitution than I.'

Maddie was impressed. 'Do you know something, Molly? You have an excellent vocabulary for a child of eight.'

'I'm eight and a half, and my dad says he forks out a fortune to send me to an excellent school so that I get a good education. That's why I have an excellent vocab – what is it, again?'

'Vocabulary.'

'Vocabluary. Aoife's only five,' she added in a confidential voice. 'But she's pretty cool for a five-year-old. I don't mind playing with her. We had a really cool game of spies last night.'

'Yes, you did, didn't you?'

A private smile crept across Molly's lips, and she gave Maddie a disingenuous look. 'Sam's really nice, isn't he, Maddie?' she asked, picking crumbs off her plate.

'Yes, he is.' Maddie went back to the range and started to turn the sausages.

'I wish Bianca didn't make him work so hard – then he could come on the picnic with us. He's really handsome, too, isn't he? He's kind of like the Beast in the Disney *Beauty and the Beast* when he turns into the handsome prince. Daddy's more like the Beast – only joking, Dad. But Sam really is the split and image of the handsome prince.'

Maddie assiduously turned over more sausages. 'Is he?' she shrugged. 'I haven't seen that film.' She reached out a hand for her coffee cup and accidentally met Daniel Lennox's eye. He was looking at her in that way he had – that analytical, *painter's* way. She looked away again immediately, flushing when she remembered what he'd said to her last night. *You might like to know that the front of your dress is open.* What must he think of her? 'Bring me the plates, Molly, will you? This is just about done.'

'I've got all the Disney films on video. We could watch it some evening if you like.' Molly set the plates down on the worktop at the side of the range and peered into the pan again. 'D'you know something, Maddie? I think those tomatoes might be poisonous, too,' she said.

*　　*　　*

They picked up Aoife, who was waiting for them at the front door of Deirdre and Rory's house with a cool-box. Deirdre shambled yawning out of the door with a sheet wound round her to wave good-bye, and then the deux-chevaux headed in the direction of Saint-Jean-de-Fos. Daniel drove over the pont du Diable and continued for several kilometres along a road that followed the course of the river. It was another hot, cloudless day. The Hérault meandered below them like a broad green ribbon, the sunlight that danced invitingly on the surface of the water making it look like a lane swimmer's paradise.

When they reached a place where a number of other cars were parked by the side of the road, Daniel pulled over. 'Shit,' he said. 'I hope they've all kept to the bottom path.'

'What do you mean?' asked Maddie.

'There's no access to where we want to go from the bottom path – the bank's too over-grown. You can only get to it by a path higher up that runs parallel to the river. Not many people know about it. I hope you don't mind a bit of a hike?'

'I don't mind.'

They collected their paraphernalia from the boot of the deux-chevaux and set off: Molly and Aoife dawdling behind, holding hands and sharing secrets; Pilot racing ahead, pausing every now and then so that they could catch up with him. It looked as if he knew exactly where they were heading.

The path took them along the left bank of the river, past family groups lounging on the rocks and splashing in the water, until they came to where it forked. This path soon dwindled to what Maddie took to be a dead end, but then she saw Pilot disappear under the overhang of a massive oleander bush. Daniel took hold of a branch and held it up, gesturing for Maddie to go on in front of him, then waited for the girls.

Maddie found herself in the middle of a tangled thicket; she looked back at Daniel, uncertain as to what to do next. 'Duck through there,' he said, indicating a low, leafy tunnel ahead of her. Oleander flowers gleamed like beacons in the verdant gloom. She did as he told her, feeling clumsy as she pushed foliage out of her way, and taking care to keep her head down in case she got a branch in her face. She emerged into a clearing where a high bank of red earth blocked her way. 'Wait there,' said Daniel. He had followed her out of the undergrowth, and was pulling back treacherous suckers that might trip unwary feet. Molly and Aoife came through the passageway he'd cleared for them, still gabbling ten to the dozen.

'Up here.' Daniel nodded at the steep bank in front of her. 'I'll go first.' He climbed the bank with ease, making footholds in the earth with his boots, and using the protruding roots of trees to hoist himself up. When he reached the top he turned and looked down at her. 'Hand me the stuff first,' he said. 'And then help the girls.'

She passed up the cool-box and all their bags, and then pushed the squirming, giggling girls up the bank by their bums while Daniel pulled them up by their hands. Once both children had reached the top, Molly cried: 'Last one there's an eejit!' Maddie heard the scurry of feet, and their chattering, excited voices receded into the distance accompanied by the faint barking of Pilot.

Daniel leaned down towards her, reaching out his hand.

'I'm not sure I can do it,' she said.

'Of course you can. Just grab hold of my hand. I'll take all the weight – you just need to gain purchase with your feet. Like abseiling in reverse.'

Maddie took his outstretched hand and made an ineffectual kind of hopping motion. Daniel Lennox laughed, and she laughed back. 'You're a bit of a wimp, aren't you?' he remarked.

'That's what living too long in the city does to you.'

He reached down his other hand, and she took hold of that too. She remembered when they'd first shaken hands at Sara's exhibition, and how she'd winced at his grip then and wondered that a painter should have such strong hands. Suddenly she was at the top of the bank, without quite knowing how she'd got there.

'Thanks,' she said, brushing dry red earth off her dress. They were on a very narrow, overgrown path with the river some metres below.

Daniel slung his bag over his shoulder, picked up the cool-box and headed off down the path. 'We're nearly there,' he said.

She struggled into her backpack and followed him. Long grass brushed against her bare legs, and she registered a pungent smell of wild thyme.

Molly and Aoife were already unpacking their

bags on a broad outcrop of sandstone. Maddie deposited her backpack on a boulder and went over to where the slab of rock descended smoothly, like a slipway, into the river. Crouching down, she dipped her hand into the water. It was colder than at the creek, but for some reason it looked even more seductive.

She raised her head and looked around her. On either side of the river steep escarpments covered in dense greenery rose to a cerulean blue heaven. The river itself moved slowly through the gorge, taking its time, sinuous and calm. She had never seen water that colour before. It was impossible to put a name to it. Somewhere between dark emerald and jade, she thought, though it changed colour even as she looked at it.

There was no-one else around. The only sounds were birdsong and the incessant light chittering of the girls' voices. She was so used to their chatter now that she felt as if she had a very mild, quite bearable form of tinnitus. She looked back up the smooth slab of rock. The two children had stripped naked, and Daniel Lennox was taking off his clothes. For one hellish moment she thought she would be expected to go starkers, but Daniel caught her uncertain look.

'It's not a great idea to strip off completely, Madeleine,' he said. 'Although we're off the beaten track, canoes go up and down the river. Youths used to gawk at Marie-France and make ribald remarks. It didn't bother her, but I wouldn't particularly like Molly to overhear any of the appreciative remarks that would be sure to come your way.'

Maddie walked back over the rockface and started to unpack her bag. She located her sarong and her sunhat, her suncream and her water bottle, and spent ages looking for her sunglasses, before remembering that she'd left them in the car. Shit. She wasn't going to go all the way back for them, but she hated the idea of not having her black lenses to hide behind. She spread a towel out on the warm sandstone, and then lifted her dress over her head, trying hard to look relaxed. She hadn't brought her Ladyshave with her to Saint-Géyroux, and had had neither the time nor the inclination to shave her underarms or bikini line before leaving Dublin. For some reason this hadn't bothered her when she'd bathed at the creek under the pont du Diable – a lot of the women on the shore there didn't shave, in the continental fashion – but she felt self-conscious about it now.

'When can we have the picnic?' Molly was tip-toeing across the rocks towards them on small, elegant feet, trying not to step on the cracks in the sandstone.

'After your swim.'

'Aw – *Dad* – can't we have it now?'

'No. It's too early, and you know you're not allowed to swim on a full stomach. Come here and put some suncream on. You too, Aoife.'

The girls made faces, but did as they were asked. Daniel squirted a lavish amount of suncream into the joined palms of both children and instructed them to rub it carefully over every inch of their skin.

'I can never reach all of my back,' complained Aoife, contorting herself into a series of awkward shapes.

'Come here,' said Maddie. 'I'll do it for you.' She dribbled the cream down Aoife's spine, making her wriggle and squeal, and then Molly insisted that she do it to her, too. When the job was done to Daniel's satisfaction, he told them they could go ahead and swim.

'What about you, Madeleine?' he asked, as the girls stepped gingerly into the water, clinging to each other and shrieking. 'Are you going for a swim?'

'I think I'll leave it till a bit later,' she said, sitting down on her towel. 'When I get too hot in the sun.'

Daniel had stripped down to a pair of cut-off denims and was stretched out on a beach towel, leaning back on his elbows. He wasn't in bad shape for a man of his age, although Maddie noticed that he was carrying a bit of avoir du poids around his middle. She also couldn't help noticing a jagged scar on his left side, just underneath his ribcage.

He saw her looking. 'Good scar, isn't it?' he said. 'That was the work of my ex-wife. I think it was

379

probably the first time in her life that Marie-France had ever picked up a kitchen knife. Luckily for me she had a lousy aim. *Un*luckily, she happened to choose one of Mme Thibault's razor-sharp Sabatiers.'

Maddie was embarrassed that he'd caught her looking. She felt obliged to say something. 'Why did she do it?' she asked.

'We were having a tiff.'

'It must have hurt like hell.'

'Yes, it did. There were oceans of blood. Marie-France fainted.' He smiled at her.

'How long were you married?' she asked, encouraged by the smile. She had found herself wondering about him, recently, as she'd begun to realize that the reclusive painter wasn't really as reclusive as she'd been led to expect.

'Too long,' he said. 'We split up just after Molly turned five.'

Screams came from the river as Pilot bounded down the bank into the water, showering the two cowering children with droplets that glittered in the sunlight like diamantine. They had only advanced up to their knees, and still had their arms wrapped tightly around each other.

'Get on in, Molly,' called Daniel. 'You're a gibbering, craven girl's blouse.'

Molly stood up straight and looked back at him with her head held high. 'No, I'm not,' she said, before flinging herself off the slab of rock into the river. Her head emerged immediately, the mouth open in a wide O to let the mandatory scream out. Then Aoife took a deep breath and followed her example. Their screams harmonized, climbed through a crescendo, then subsided. A couple of seconds later they were swimming around happily, without a trace of post-traumatic stress.

'Shall I see what's in our picnic?' asked Maddie, reaching for the cool-box.

'Knowing Rory, there'll be an excellent bottle of wine.'

Maddie opened the lid. Inside was a baguette broken in half to fit the box, butter, smoked salmon wrapped in tinfoil, a lemon, *saucisson*, figs, peaches, a bunch of grapes and a punnet of strawberries. There were also tuna sandwiches, crisps and a packet of biscuits. There was a bottle of Orangina and one of chilled Meursault, a cork-screw, a couple of knives, a bunch of paper napkins and a little tower of plastic cups. Paper plates had been slipped down the side.

'Wow. Epicurean!' said Maddie. 'Will you open this?' she said, handing the wine and the cork-screw to Daniel. She laid the food out on the paper plates and then called to the girls, who were trying to drown Pilot in the river.

Daniel handed her a paper cup and poured, and she sat back on her towel. 'Santé,' she said.

'Santé,' he returned. Then: 'Hey! Leave Pilot alone, you wild Saracens, and come and have lunch.'

Reluctantly the children stopped trying to

drown the dog, and left him swimming by himself in the river. He looked a bit miffed at being abandoned.

'Pilot loves being drowned,' explained Molly as she and Aoife dried themselves with Barbie towels. 'Hey, Dad – can we take our picnic up to the cave? See, we're pretending that we're pirate princesses trapped on a desert island and Pilot's the evil Sea Wolf, and we have to hide from him, and we've only enough rations to last a few more days and then we're going to have nothing but sick wild fennel and mushrooms to eat but then we find this old abandoned vineyard with really sweet ripe grapes and loads of olive trees and wild strawberries and stuff growing in it and—'

'Yes, Molly – you may take your picnic up to the cave. Have you your watch with you?' Molly nodded. 'Good girl. Put it on – and some clothes, please, and check back here at three o'clock sharp, OK?'

'Yay! Thanks, Dad.' She and Aoife quickly started getting into their clothes. 'Do you want to come, Maddie?' asked Molly. 'You could be – what could you be? You could be this kind of mysterious old crone who lives in a grotto on the island and who only comes out at night and who kind of sneaks around the bushes and gives us frights. Do you want to be that?'

Maddie laughed. 'I think I'll take a rain check on that, Molly.' She had broken off a hunk of the baguette and was spreading it thickly with butter.

'All right,' said Molly, equably. 'But if you change your mind you can come and give us a fright, OK?' She paused fractionally, furrowing her brow. 'Only do warn us when you're going to give us a fright, OK? Otherwise it's not fair.'

'Fine,' agreed Maddie.

Molly had got into her shorts and T-shirt, and was now checking out the picnic. 'Right. We're off,' she said, shoving packets of crisps and the iced biscuits into her swimming bag.

'No, you're not,' said Daniel. 'The crisps and biscuits are for later. You can take sandwiches with you, and fruit.'

'Aw, Dad! Can we not even take one packet of crisps to share?'

He considered. 'Yeah. All right,' he said. 'But eat them *after* your lunch, OK?'

'OK,' said Molly happily.

'Oh – *Pilot*!' screeched Aoife. The dog had come out of the water and was shaking himself dry, sending drops of water cascading all over her. 'You stinking, smelly, horrible Sea Wolf—'

'Aaaagh! The Sea Wolf!' screamed Molly, and took off like an arrow, clutching the bag of rations.

'Aaaagh! The Sea Wolf!' echoed Aoife, following her friend hotfoot up the bank. Pilot gave himself a last shake and trotted after them, barking mildly.

Smiling, Maddie watched them go. Then she turned to Daniel. 'They'll be all right by themselves?' she asked.

'Safe as houses. The cave where they like to play is just around the next bend of the river, and when I tell Molly she's to check back with me, she knows I mean it.'

'She's a sweet kid.'

'Yes, she is.'

'Where does she go to school?'

'In Paris. She lives there for most of the year with her mother, but she usually comes to me for the holidays. I wasn't expecting her until the beginning of August – she took me a bit off guard this time, as you know. I've a *vernissage* coming up in Paris later this month, and I really didn't want to have to drag Molly up there with me.' He looked at her and raised his eyebrows. 'A *vernissage* is an exhibition opening – or did you know that already?'

'I knew it already. I'm not a total philistine, you know.'

'Philistine. How do you say that in French?'

'*Philistin.*'

He laughed, and Maddie smiled up at him as she laid thin slivers of smoked salmon on top of her baguette, and squeezed lemon juice over it. She bit into it, and crumbs fell onto her bare thighs.

'Shouldn't you put suncream on?' asked Daniel. 'Your skin can't be used to this kind of heat.'

She tensed. She put out a hand to brush the crumbs off her thighs, and then changed her mind, unwilling to draw more unwanted attention to her bare flesh. 'I put it on before I left the house,' she said stiffly. She didn't want him volunteering to do her back.

Pilot had returned sharpish from the torture chamber of the cave; now he settled down beside his master, looking up at him with beseeching eyes. Daniel Lennox had polished off his smoked salmon and had started on the *saucisson*. 'You have no pride, have you, dog?' he said. 'But you do have manners. I suppose if you could talk you'd say "please". Here you are, then.' He broke off a chunk of *saucisson* and gave it to the dog. Pilot wolfed it down, and then resumed his posture of entreaty. 'Do you want some?' he asked Maddie.

'I haven't tasted it for years.'

'Try it. See if it conjures childhood memories.'

He handed her a lump of thick, densely packed sausage, and she bit into it, tentatively at first, and then with more enthusiasm. 'Mm – it's good,' she said, forgetting her manners and speaking with her mouth full. 'And it does bring back memories. The last time I had *saucisson* was when I visited my grandfather in Montpellier.'

'Have you any relations still in France?'

'No.'

'So you're all alone in the world.'

'I have my cousin Maeve. She's sterling.' A yellow butterfly landed on Maddie's hip, attracted by the bright pattern on her swimsuit.

'It thinks you're a flower,' Daniel said with a smile. The butterfly basked for a minute or two, spreading its wings to display orange markings before lifting itself into the air and fluttering away. He leaned over and refilled her paper cup. She saw the way his gaze gravitated towards the valley between her breasts, and didn't like it. Her thank you when he finished pouring was curt. Daniel sat back and let his eyes travel back up to her face. She kept it immobile. 'I've to go to the art supplier's in Montpellier soon,' he said, pouring wine into his own cup. 'I'll drive you in if you like, and you can indulge in a nostalgia trip.'

'It's OK,' she said, mutinously, and then wished she hadn't. She actually *would* like a trip into town, to see how much had changed since she was last there.

'It's OK,' he repeated. 'You say that quite a lot, don't you? What exactly do you mean by it? That it's OK, yes, you do want to come, or it's OK, no, you couldn't be bothered?'

'It's cool, yes, I would like to come.' She backtracked fast. She didn't like the idea of being beholden to him, but it sure as hell beat the prospect of driving into the city on her own in a left-hand drive on an unfamiliar road.

They ate in silence for a while, Daniel abstractedly feeding Pilot bits of *saucisson*.

Maddie had finished hers. She surveyed the remains of the picnic and decided to round off her meal with a fig. The one she selected was so ripe it looked as if it might burst open. She split it in two with her fingers and started to pull at the soft fruit with her teeth. There was no need to pull hard – the flesh yielded easily. She needed only to coax it gently away from the skin before sucking it into her mouth.

'I must try one of the figs in your garden,' she remarked, wiping away the juice that was trickling down her chin. It was about time to embark on a conversational gambit. The silence that had grown between them had started to feel awkward, and it didn't seem likely that Daniel was going to instigate small talk. 'They look almost as good as this.'

'You can't eat the figs in my garden.'

'Why not?'

'The tree they grow on is a male tree. The figs it produces are inedible. They're shrivelled up and dry inside, and full of blastophages.'

'What are blastophages?'

'Parasitical insects.'

'Yeuch!'

'They coexist with the fig and help it to reproduce – it's an extraordinarily complex process. The tree and the parasite are mutually dependent. But if you were to help yourself to one of my figs and bite into it the way you've just done to the one you're eating now, you could end up with a mouthful of larvae or little black flies.'

'Jesus, Daniel. I think you've just succeeded in putting me off eating figs for ever.'

'That would be a pity. You look good eating figs.'

She didn't answer, but set about clearing away picnic things. 'What do the flies look like?' she asked. 'Would I have seen them in your garden?'

'No. They live inside the fig. The females only fly once – to other figs on the male tree where they lay their eggs. The eggs hatch in the summer, and this generation of blastophages bugger off to pollinate sweet-smelling female trees. Those are the figs that are good to eat – the ones that appear in late August.'

'So the fig I just ate was forced?'

'I guess.'

'What happens to the male blastophages?'

'They stay at home and shag the females. They can't fly anywhere.'

'Why not?'

'They don't have any wings.' He finished his wine and stood up. 'That concludes the biology lesson,' he said. 'I think I'll swim now. Are you coming in?'

'Yes. It's about time I cooled off.' The sun was high in the sky, and very, very hot. The heat and the wine had combined to make her feel slightly muzzy, and she decided that she'd better stick to the shade when she got out of the water.

Daniel strolled down to the edge of the river and dived straight in, without bothering to test the temperature first. Remembering what he'd said about her being a bit of a wimp, she was determined to prove him wrong. She stood as tall as she could on the edge of the rock, and then executed an elegant dive. The water was so cold that she gibbered when she surfaced.

'Shit, shit, *shit*!' she said, shaking her head. 'It's a lot colder than the creek.'

'That's because the ice on the mountains has melted and flowed all the way down here. But I'm not about to start lecturing you on geography now as well as biology.' They swam together for a couple of strokes, and then he said: 'You're a good swimmer, Madeleine. Swim across with me.'

They struck out for the opposite bank and then rested in the shade of the overhanging trees, Maddie supporting herself on a fallen sapling. Branches trailed in the green water like the graceful, slender arms of dancers, and a dragonfly scudded lightly over the surface. A loud droning noise made Maddie look up, and she saw a big, cumbersome-looking insect descend on the branch just above their heads.

'Oh, look! How beautiful!' she exclaimed. It was some kind of beetle with diaphanous wings and a carapace of iridescent green. It looked as if it had been coated in the kind of shiny cellophane Cadbury's Roses come wrapped in. 'It would make you want to pick it up and wear it as a brooch!'

'More becoming than jewellery,' said Daniel. 'How gorgeous if women could adorn themselves with living things, like beetles and bees and butterflies. Real flowers, not silk. Marie-France had a passion for antique jewellery and silk flowers.'

'Why did she leave Molly with you earlier than you expected, Daniel?' She knew it wasn't any of her business, but it was something that had intrigued her since the night she'd heard him arguing with his ex-wife on the phone.

'Because she wanted to fuck off to the Caribbean with her latest meal ticket, that's why.' He plunged back into the water and swam across to the other bank with powerful strokes.

Maddie wished she'd left the question unasked. Hell. What did she care about Daniel Lennox's private life, anyway? It was a matter of complete indifference to her. She stayed on in the water for another ten minutes or so, diving and turning somersaults and kicking her legs hard so that water sprayed up in cascades around her. Then she rolled over onto her back and floated, letting the current take her where it wanted. Above her a vapour trail crossed the bright blue sky like a dry white brush-stroke on a painted heaven.

The cold got to her in the end. When she emerged dripping from the water Daniel was lying on his stomach, reading. She picked up her towel and rubbed herself dry, glad that he was immersed in a book. It meant that she could get hers out too, without looking rude, and she wouldn't have to rack her brains for more things to say to him.

She towelled her hair and coiled it loosely on her head, securing it with tortoiseshell jaws. Then she got her book out of her backpack, draped her cream-coloured sarong over her shoulders to protect them from the sun and settled back against a comfortable, cushion-shaped boulder to read. She was cross with herself for forgetting her sunglasses, because the sunlight bouncing off the page made reading difficult and she knew her eyes would soon get tired.

After several minutes had gone by, Daniel sat up and helped himself to grapes. 'Want some?'

'Please.'

He detached a small bunch and threw them across to her. 'What's the book?' he asked.

'It's *Jane Eyre*,' said Maddie. 'I got it from your library – I hope you don't mind.'

'Not at all. They're there to be read.'

'I noticed that your dog and Mr Rochester's have the same name.'

'Yes. That was Marie-France's idea. We got Pilot at around the same time as she was playing Jane in Paris.'

'She's an actress, then?' This was news to her.

'Well deduced. A bloody talented one, actually, but she doesn't work often enough.'

'Through choice?'

'No. People are reluctant to cast her. She has a reputation for being temperamental.'

'Oh.' Maddie couldn't prevent her eyes from sliding in the direction of the scar on his flank.

'But then, she doesn't need to work. She does a great line in wealthy consorts.'

Just then Molly and Aoife burst out of the bushes on the bank above, making Maddie jump. 'Boo! Boo!' they shouted. Molly descended the bank in a rush. 'We decided that since you weren't going to give us a fright, we'd come and give you one instead,' she announced. 'Look, Dad,' she added, showing Daniel her watch. 'Three o'clock on the button.'

'Good girl.'

Molly sidled up to Maddie, holding something behind her back. She planted a big kiss on her cheek, and tucked a red oleander flower into her hair.

'Aren't you sweet! Thank you, Molly,' said Maddie, kissing her back, and then giving Aoife a kiss, too, as the little girl solemnly presented her with a trailing length of flowering bindweed.

'Can we have our biscuits now, Dad, and then go back to the cave?' Molly started skipping from foot to foot. 'You see, in the game, Aoife's been kidnapped by the Sea Wolf and – oh.' She put both her hands to her mouth. 'Oh-oh, Maddie. I completely forgot that you wanted to play Barbies. You don't mind, do you, if we go off to the cave? I promise we can play Barbies another time. It's just that we've got to this really exciting bit and—'

'Of course it's OK, *ma puce*. I'm quite happy here with my book, I promise.'

'Good.' Molly turned to her father. 'OK, Dad. What time?'

'Four o'clock, sweetie-pie. You can have another hour.'

Molly saluted her father in the manner of a soldier standing to attention, and then set off up the bank with Aoife.

'Not a minute more!' threw Daniel at the child's

departing back. Then: 'Perpetual motion,' he said with a sigh, reaching for the water bottle and draining it before resuming his reclining position on the outstretched towel.

The French put it so much better, thought Maddie. *Se coucher.* To recline. She heard in her head the classroom chant: *Je me couche, tu te couches, il se couche, elle se couche, nous nous couchons* . . .

She had put her book aside and was gazing at the river, toying with the length of bindweed Aoife had given her. She could discern traces of sapphire blue in the water now, merging with the green. Her limbs felt heavy and relaxed, and she knew that if she had been on her own she would have dropped her defences and fallen asleep.

'Did you ever visit the Musée Fabre when you stayed with your grandfather in Montpellier?'

'The Musée Fabre?' Maddie furrowed her brow, trying to remember. The question had come out of the blue and fractured her reverie. 'Um. Is that the art gallery on the esplanade?'

'Yes.'

'I'm not sure. It's possible.'

'Visit it again when I take you in next week. There's a painting there you should see.'

'Oh? Which one?'

'It's called *Albaydé*. It's by Alexandre Cabanel. He was a nineteenth-century painter with a penchant for neo-classicism.'

'What's so special about it?'

Daniel had raised himself on his elbows and was

393

looking at her. She couldn't see the expression in his eyes behind the dark lenses of his glasses, but there was something about him that reminded her of the way he'd looked when he'd first approached her in the Demeter Gallery all those weeks ago. How many weeks? Five, she supposed, or thereabouts. She'd lost all track of time.

'Remember I said I'd like to paint you?'

She nodded stiffly.

'This is how I'd like to paint you. The way you look now.'

'What's that got to do with the Alba – ' She couldn't remember the name of the painting he'd mentioned.

'*Albaydé?*'

'Yes.'

'The way you are now is the way she is. That sleepy look.'

'It's a painting of a woman?'

'Yes. She's reclining against cushions – much the same way as you are against that boulder – and she's wearing the exact same expression as you had on a minute ago. She has a red flower in her hair – which is piled up like yours – and she's holding a strand of that bindweed. Morning Glory, I think it's called. That's how I'd like to paint you. After Cabanel.'

Maddie was on guard again. 'Why do you want to paint me, Daniel?' she asked, trying to sound careless.

'Because you have a quality. You're paintable.

394

Sara saw it in you too. Why do you think she wanted to photograph you?' He reached out a hand and broke another cluster of grapes off the bunch. 'Paintability's not easy to define, and it has nothing to do with beauty. The world is full of women much more beautiful than you, of course, but I wouldn't necessarily want to paint them.' He slid a grape into his mouth, and she found herself looking. She hadn't noticed till now that he had a sensual mouth. She looked back at his eyes. 'My style has nothing in common with Cabanel's – as you'll see when you visit the Musée – but he did have an uncommon gift for conveying sensuality. Will you allow me to paint you, Madeleine?'

'Sure,' she said with a little shrug. The shrug was supposed to indicate that it was no big deal, but when she tried to relax the muscles in her shoulders, she found that they remained tense. She sat there looking at Daniel with her shoulders hunched defensively for a moment. Then she looked back at the river.

*　　*　　*

An hour later the girls had returned and they started to pack up their things. Further conversation between Daniel and Maddie had been desultory and confined to banalities, and they had slid back into their respective books.

'Dad?' said Molly as Daniel put the last of the picnic rubbish into a plastic bag and tied the ends together. 'Who's going to look after me when you go to Paris?'

'I don't know yet, sweetie-pie.'

Molly looked at him sideways. 'Can Maddie do it?'

'No.'

'Aw – why not, Dad?'

'Because it's not her job.'

'But she doesn't have a job. She needs one – she told me so. Didn't you, Maddie?'

'Just drop it, Molly, will you?' said Daniel.

Molly scowled at him, but it was obvious that she knew by his tone not to push the issue any further.

They picked up the last of their bags and climbed up the bank. 'When do you have to go to Paris?' asked Maddie.

'Next Tuesday.'

'How long for?'

'Three or four days. I aim to get back by Saturday.'

'I don't mind looking after Molly.' Beside her she could see the little girl stiffen with excitement and exchange delighted looks with Aoife.

Daniel looked at her. 'I can't ask you to do that for me, Madeleine.'

'You're not asking me. I'm offering. I'd like to feel that I'm repaying your hospitality somehow. Please let me do it. I'd enjoy it.'

He looked uncertain. 'You'd be getting me out of an awful bind if you did. Are you sure you wouldn't mind?'

'I wouldn't offer if I minded. Believe me.' She smiled down at Molly, who was practically bursting with anticipation. 'I reckon Molly and I could have some fun. What do you think, Molly?'

'Oh, yes – oh, yes! Oh, please, Dad, let Maddie look after me. I promise I'll be good. Please say yes?'

Daniel Lennox looked from one expectant face to the next. 'OK,' he said. 'But if you cause Madeleine any trouble, Molly, I'll confiscate your beloved teddy.'

Molly looked at him with scepticism written plainly all over her face. 'You wouldn't do that *ever*, Dad,' she said.

'No, you're right,' he admitted, conceding defeat with a shrug. 'I wouldn't.'

'You're the *best* dad!' she said, giving him an enormous hug. 'And you're the *best* . . .' She hesitated. '*What* are you the best of?' she asked Maddie, looking perplexed.

'The best baby-sitter?' suggested Maddie.

'No, no – baby-sitters don't live with you. And I am *not* a baby.'

'The best nanny?'

'Nah. We don't have any truck with nannies, do we, Molly?'

Daniel had intervened quickly, and Maddie turned to him with a look of enquiry. He gave her a barely perceptible frown and then Maddie remembered with horror how Daniel had told her that Molly's Paris nanny had been the nanny from hell. 'I know,' she said quickly, inspired by the book she'd just been reading. 'You could call me your governess.'

'But governesses are kind of olden days and really strict, aren't they?' said Molly.

'Well, you did say that I wore olden days clothes, didn't you?' said Maddie. 'And I promise you I won't be too strict. I'll be a perfect pussy-cat of a governess.'

'OK.' Molly seemed quite intrigued by the idea of having a governess. 'I think I'll ring Ghislaine tonight and tell her I've a governess. Can I, Dad?'

'Who's Ghislaine?'

'My best friend at school, remember?'

'The one with the Danish mother?'

'Yeah.'

'I remember.'

Suddenly Pilot, who had disappeared, emerged panting from a bush.

'Aaagh – the Sea Wolf!' shrieked Aoife.

'Aaagh – the Sea Wolf!' shrieked Molly. And the two of them ran off down the path together.

Daniel Lennox turned to Maddie. 'Thanks, Madeleine,' he said. 'I owe you.'

'I'm happy to do it,' she replied. 'I like your little girl.'

It was true. But there was another reason why she was happy to do it. It meant that she was no longer quite so beholden to him.

Chapter Fifteen

Later on that evening Maddie wandered up the rue des Artistes to the *alimentation* to get pasta for dinner. She'd promised to make Molly pasta with Neapolitan sauce, and had told Daniel she'd demonstrate the recipe so that he could do it himself some time. He'd looked mutinous at first, but relented when she told him that the Neapolitan sauce came out of a jar.

On her way up the rue des Artistes she said 'Bonsoir' to an elderly woman who was sitting on her doorstep having a conversation with a neighbour leaning out of an upstairs window. She smiled to herself when a young man pushing a baby in a buggy 'accidentally' caught her eye. She paused to watch the old men of the village playing *boules* in the little square where Daniel parked his car. The sound of a cello was drifting from one of the windows open onto the street, and for some reason it made Maddie feel peculiar. She hadn't felt this way for a long time, she realized. She was feeling happy.

After she'd bought the pasta she decided to visit the *caveaux* and pick up a couple of bottles of *Mas de Daumas Gassac.* As she strolled past the little café she had been told about but never visited, she heard a woman's voice call out her name. Deirdre O'Dare was sitting by herself at a table on the terrasse of the café. 'Come and have a coffee,' she suggested. 'Encore un café, Maurice, s'il vous plaît,' she called to the waiter, who was gathering up empty glasses from a nearby table.

'Mon plaisir,' said Maurice, responding instantly to her dazzling smile.

Apart from Deirdre, the terrasse was deserted. Maddie stooped down and gave her a kiss. 'You look radiant,' she said.

'That's because I'm feeling happy,' said Deirdre. 'And for your information, you're looking radiant too.'

'Oh! Thanks.' Maddie sat down and set her carrier bags on the ground. There came the clinking sound of bottles. '*Mas de Daumas Gassac* for Daniel,' she explained. 'He's been very generous to me.'

'He's a very generous man,' said Deirdre. 'It's funny – he has this reputation for being an ogre, but it's totally unwarranted. He just appreciates the value of privacy. We all do.'

'Maybe that's why he was so rude to me the first time I met him,' said Maddie. 'He thought I was eavesdropping on a conversation he was having with his sister. Actually, when you come to think of it, I suppose I *was* eavesdropping. He was probably justifiably rude.' The waiter put her coffee in front of her. 'Merci,' she said, trying to copy Deirdre's smile, and feeling pleased when she got quite a good smile back. 'Where's Rory?' she asked.

'Gone to pick up Aoife. He'll probably stay for an aperitif with Daniel. I'm quite happy here on my own – as long as he doesn't stay for more than two. Then it starts getting serious.' She stretched herself contentedly. 'Sometimes I try to fool myself that I'm reading when I sit here, but really I'm just revelling in doing bugger all. You're allowed to do that in Saint-Géyroux. That's why we come here. To escape from all that real-life shit.'

'That's why I came here too.'

'Oh?' Deirdre turned disconcertingly candid eyes on her. 'What were you escaping from?'

'A relationship that had gone wrong.'

'How had it gone wrong?'

'He tried to turn me into someone I wasn't. He very nearly succeeded.'

'No shit!' said Deirdre, leaning forward in her chair. 'I was in that place once upon a time. It stinks, doesn't it?'

'Yes,' said Maddie with a smile. 'It really does.'

Just then a very smart car with two women in it pulled up outside the café. Bianca was in the driver's seat. The woman in the passenger seat gave a friendly smile as she opened the door and started moving across the road towards them.

'Who's that with Bianca?' said Deirdre in an undertone. 'I've never seen her before.'

Maddie was flooded with dismay. 'Oh, hell. Why didn't I think to tell you earlier! Her name's Darina Maguire, and you are going to have to be as circumspect as you can, Deirdre, because—'

'But I'm completely crap at being circumspect! And why does the name Darina Maguire sound so familiar?'

'She's a hack,' Maddie hissed under her breath as Bianca and Darina descended on them.

'What?'

It was too late.

'Deirdre! Welcome back to Saint-Géyroux!' Bianca deposited three kisses on Deirdre's cheeks and misjudged a fourth. 'You and Rory have been sorely missed by our little community! Hello, Madeleine.' Maddie got two kisses. 'How on earth did I manage to miss you both at Gina's barbecue last night? I saw Rory in the distance, but he skulked off somewhere with Daniel, and I didn't get a chance to talk to him.' She settled down on a chair and beckoned to the waiter. 'Deux Perriers,' she said. Then she turned back to Deirdre. 'Let me introduce you to Davina Costello-fFrench.'

Deirdre opened her mouth as if to say something, and Maddie kicked her ankle under the table.

The woman Bianca had called Davina smiled ingratiatingly. 'Hello,' she said. 'It's wonderful to meet you, Deirdre. I didn't believe Bianca at first when she told me there was a celebrity couple living in such a remote place as Saint-Géyroux.'

Deirdre smiled back wanly, but didn't say anything.

'Davina's a writer,' said Bianca. 'She's here to do some research on provincial French village life. She contacted me because she'd heard I was an authority, and she'd seen pictures of my house in a magazine. Well! I was frightfully chuffed, I can tell you! She asked me which was the best *pension* to stay in while she was here, and I had to laugh! "Davina," I said to her. "There are no *pensions* in Saint-Géyroux. It's far too small to attract any kind of tourist element!" And do you know what she said to me? She said—'

' "It sounds like just the place I'm looking for," ' finished Darina/Davina obligingly.

'So, of course I volunteered to put her up.' Bianca beamed all round the table.

'I can so absolutely understand the appeal of a place like this for people like you and Rory,' said Darina/Davina, engaging Deirdre in eye contact and looking sage. 'It must be so relaxing after the rattle and hum of Tinseltown. Does your little girl like it here?'

Deirdre shot a look at Maddie. 'Yes,' she said.

'You've only the one, haven't you?'

'Yes.'

'Deirdre,' said Bianca, twinkling at her. 'A little bird at Gina's barbecue said something to me last night . . .'

'What?'

'I believe there's another one on the way?'

'Well. Congratulations,' said Davina/Darina. Her eyes were gleaming with interest. 'You're pregnant, are you?'

'I didn't say that—' began Deirdre.

'Oh, hell!' said Maddie suddenly, looking at her watch and jumping to her feet. 'We were meant to have dinner on the table by eight o'clock! Excuse us, Bianca, we have to dash. Deirdre's cooked a cassoulet for Rory and – um – Sam and me. Nice to meet you, Davina. Come on, Deirdre.'

Deirdre picked up her book and Maddie grabbed her carrier bags. They went through the kissing ritual again, and then set off up the road at a brisk pace.

'What was all that about?' asked Deirdre in a tone of absolute incomprehension. 'Me, cook cassoulet!'

'That woman's not called Davina Costello-ffrench. Holy shit!' Maddie laughed. 'Imagine dreaming up a moniker like that! Costello-ffrench!'

'Who is she then?'

'She's a tabloid journalist from Dublin. She used to write a column for the *Sunday Satellite*. It was called—'

Deirdre stopped in her tracks. 'Who The Hell Do They Think They Are?' she intoned.

'That's right.'

'She's the one that wrote that vile stuff about Maeve!' Deirdre was open-mouthed with indignation.

'Yes.'

'What the fuck is *she* doing here?'

'Well,' said Maddie slowly. 'I know she approached Maeve about contributing to an unauthorized biography of Irish celebrity couples—'

'I don't believe you!' There was a fierce light in Deirdre O'Dare's eyes. 'She's doing me and Rory! Isn't she? That's why she's here in Saint-Géyroux!'

'I've a suspicion you're right,' Maddie agreed. 'It seems a plausible enough reason, doesn't it? I mean, what else would a hackette from Dublin be doing in a place like this?'

'Holy shomoly. Holy fucking shomoly.' Deirdre shook her head. She took a few more slow steps up the street, looking thoughtful. Then she stopped again, looking even more thoughtful.

'What's up?' asked Maddie.

Deirdre smiled. The smile got broader. Then she began to laugh. She turned to Maddie. 'I'm having a totally brilliant idea,' she said.

'Oh? What is it?'

'I'm going to invite her round for aperitifs.'

*　　*　　*

The following evening Maddie and Molly knocked on the door of Rory and Deirdre's house, which was on the other side of the village to Daniel's. Deirdre came to the door wearing a stunningly beautiful, antique Chinese gown. It was in floor-length heavy silk, patterned with rich pink flowers, and the central panel was hand embroidered. Its mandarin collar was fastened high at the neck with intricately wrought frogging.

'Hurry up, Sam and Dad!' shouted Molly down the street to where they were standing examining some architectual feature, presumably debating its photographic or artistic merit. 'Come and see what Deirdre's wearing!'

'Wow,' said Maddie. 'Where did you get the stunning *gúna*?'

'Rory brought it back from some promotional trip to China. You should see what I'm wearing underneath. He brought me *that* back from Agent Provocateur. He has impeccable taste – don't you, darling?' she added, as Rory joined them at the door. 'I confess I had a scary near-miss once, with a French man who was into catalogue stuff. His preference was for a brand called Scandalous Scanties. Agh!' She grimaced at the memory.

'Now there's a thought,' said Rory. 'That tacky catalogue stuff could be quite a turn-on, actually. Maybe I should start shopping there instead of those upmarket joints you tend to frequent. I'd save myself a fortune. Hello, beautiful,' he said to Molly, crouching down so that he was on a level with her. 'Will you marry me when you grow up?'

'No.'

'Why not, you heart-breaker in miniature?'

'Because you're already married and I'm going to marry Prince Harry.'

'Clever girl,' said Maddie. 'You've got your destiny all mapped out.'

'All right, Mrs Windsor-to-be—' began Rory.

'I'm keeping my own name!'

'All right, Ms Lennox – run on up to Aoife's room. You can both pretend you're the kind of children you see in the advertisements.'

'Pah. I don't believe those kind of children exist,' said Molly scornfully. 'I think they're probably some kind of CGI.'

'You're probably right,' remarked Rory as Molly went up the stairs like a shooting star in reverse. 'And their mothers and fathers are too.'

Daniel and Sam rolled up, and admired Deirdre's outfit volubly. Daniel was carrying a bottle of wine, Sam had flowers for Deirdre. 'Is she here yet?' he asked, handing her the bouquet.

'No,' she said, kissing him on the cheek. Then she flinched. 'Oh, God, I shouldn't have done that. It's never advisable for me to kiss devastatingly attractive young men.'

'In that case it's safe enough to kiss me,' said Daniel, proffering his cheek.

Deirdre gave him a speculative look. 'I don't think so, somehow,' she said. The smile she gave him was foxy. 'Now, come on in, all of you, quickly. My neighbour across the way is giving me some very strange looks.'

'Can you blame her?' said Rory, leading the way through into the house. 'She's obviously fascinated by your sartorial unpredictability. You walked out of here with the shower cap still on your head this morning, remember? Now – who wants a drink? We're going to need all the Dutch courage we can grab if we're really going ahead with this preposterous charade.'

'Trust me, darling,' said Deirdre. 'Just think of the exquisite pleasure it will afford me.'

'I can think of better ways of enjoying exquisite pleasure,' said Rory, opening a cupboard and extracting half a dozen champagne flutes. 'You can keep that underwear on when we go to bed tonight, sweetie-pie.'

Maddie took the glass he offered her and looked around. Deirdre's house was much smaller than Daniel's, but obviously just as old. The sitting room she found herself in had rough plaster walls washed in pale rose. There were two big armchairs on either side of a fireplace which was a replica in miniature of the one in Daniel's hall. A smaller armchair had been plonked between the two bigger ones, and Maddie was reminded of the three bears. A blue jug on a side table was crammed with marguerites, and a gold-painted plaster angel guarded the double doors that led through to the garden. One wall was covered in paintings which were obviously the work of Aoife, another boasted a large nude portrait in oils of the lady of the house – which was obviously the work of Daniel Lennox.

'We'll go through to the garden,' said Deirdre, leading the way. 'Come on Daniel,' she said, taking him by the arm and looking at him coquettishly. 'I bet you've never done anything quite as daft as this in your life.'

'I have. But it was a long time ago. By the way, I ran into Bianca earlier. She was rather miffed that she wasn't invited to your soirée. I told her that you just wanted to help her friend with her research. That mollified her a bit.'

'And it's true,' said Deirdre.

'What's this hackette's name again?' asked Sam.

'Darina Maguire,' said Deirdre.

'No, no,' Maddie corrected her. 'Davina Costello-fFrench is her *nom de plume*.'

'*Nom de guerre*, more like,' said Deirdre darkly.

'You mustn't use her real name, Deirdre, or she'll know something's up,' said Maddie, reaching up a hand to flick something off the back of her neck.

'Careful, Madeleine – there's a wasp on you,' said Daniel.

'Oh.' She lowered her hand and stiffened. 'Get rid of it, Daniel, would you?'

He brushed her neck with gentle fingers and she felt a tingling sensation as the insect took off. 'There you go,' he said.

'Thanks.' Maddie found herself concentrating very hard on the wasp's flight path. A champagne cork popped.

'Oh – I've just had an excellent idea!' said Deirdre.

'Oh, no,' said Rory.

Deirdre disappeared into the sitting room and came back almost immediately with a weighty volume bound in dark red leather.

'What is it?' asked Maddie.

'It's the *Erotica universalis*. Take a look.' She handed the heavy book over to Maddie.

'Wow,' said Maddie, leafing through the pages. 'What raunchy stuff.' It was a book of erotic drawings and paintings, but there was nothing remotely seedy or prurient about the illustrations of the sexual acts. They were unashamedly exuberant, sensuous and joyous. There were even representations by such redoubtables as Picasso and Miró.

'Hee hee,' said Deirdre, reclaiming the book and carefully positioning it in a prominent position on a small garden table. 'I'm dying to see her face when she gets a load of that.'

'Ah, but is it enough to make a hardened hackette blush?' asked Maddie.

'I'll fucking well make sure it does,' said Deirdre, with feeling.

'Hell's teeth,' said Daniel. 'The lengths women go to to extract revenge! You're like a pair of harpies.'

'You didn't see the stuff she wrote about Maeve,' said Deirdre, giving him a reproachful look.

'Was it that bad?'

'It was pretty savage all right,' conceded Rory, pouring champagne.

'And you know Rory is the master of understatement.' The doorbell went. 'Yikes – she's here!' Deirdre laid claim to a garden chair and started to arrange the silken folds of her gown. 'You answer the door, Rory. She'll be madly impressed by that debonair manner of yours.'

'Go for it, baby,' said Rory, dropping a kiss on her shoulder. Then he saluted the rest of the company with a relaxed hand. 'Good luck, comrades,' he said before strolling in the direction of the door.

Maddie sat down on a garden swing beside Sam. He trailed a finger down the length of her arm and smiled at her. 'This will be a jolly jape, won't it?' he said.

'Yes.' She smiled back. 'I don't think I've played a practical joke since I was at school.'

'You know I have an incredibly juvenile sense of humour. And you can't pretend to be that grown-up, Madeleine. You laughed at every single one of my jokes the other evening. Even that one about the interrupting cow.'

'It was the way you told it. I'm crap at telling jokes. Even juvenile ones.'

'Juvenile people have more fun,' said Daniel. 'Look at Deirdre. She laughs more than any woman I know.'

'How dare you imply I'm juvenile, Daniel!' protested Deirdre. 'I just like playing games, that's all.' She raised her eyebrows and gave him a disingenuous look.

Across from her, Daniel settled down in a wicker

armchair, stretched out his long legs, and gave her an indulgent smile. 'Stop flirting with me, O'Dare,' he said.

'I can't help it,' she said. 'You're very sexy, Daniel. You were designed to be flirted with. Look at the effect you have on Bianca.'

Voices came from beyond the french windows, and Deirdre got languidly to her feet. 'Ah! Davina! Bonsoir!' she fluted, as Rory appeared with Darina Maguire by his side. Darina and Deirdre observed the air-kissing ceremony, and then stood back from each other. A rather uncertain expression crossed Darina's face as she surveyed her hostess, and Deirdre registered it expertly. Her acting talent was certainly going to come in handy this evening, thought Maddie with amusement.

'You're admiring my *chinoiserie*, I see? I'll let you into a secret, Davina. I'm researching nineteenth-century China for a forthcoming film project. I like to *inhabit* the characters I create – d'you know what I mean? I wear their clothes, behave as they'd behave – *live their lives*! I think it has a lot to do with my old life as an actress.' She gave a merry little trill of a laugh. 'If you'd come yesterday you'd have found me in a school uniform, and if you come tomorrow you'll find me in dominatrix black leather.'

'I must remember to drop by tomorrow,' said Sam.

'Bad boy, Sam!' scolded Deirdre, giving him a meaningful smile. 'Now, Davina – let me introduce

you to everyone. You've met Maddie Godard – '
the two women exchanged courteous nods.
'That's *beautiful* Sam Newman over there.' More
nods. 'And this is Daniel Lennox.'

Daniel rose to his feet and took Darina's hand.
Maddie noticed that the nail polish – metallic
green this time – was still chipped. 'Enchanté,
Mademoiselle,' he murmured, executing a little
bow and grazing the back of her hand with his
lips. Wow, thought Maddie. Well done, Daniel!
She wouldn't blame Darina Maguire for swooning
after that little display.

'Daniel Lennox?' said Darina, clearly impressed.
'Well – it's a real privilege to meet you! Bianca's
been telling me all about you!'

Daniel gave her an urbane look.

'Do sit down, Davina,' said Rory, indicating a
chair. 'Would you care for some champagne?'

'Champagne? Lovely, Rory!' she said, gushily.
He poured with a flourish and handed her a flute.
'Thank you, Rory.' She was obviously delighted to
be able to call this shit-hot Hollywood star by his
Christian name. 'It's a beautiful evening, isn't it?'
Weather talk, observed Maddie. The universal,
anodyne opening gambit that makes everyone feel
at ease.

'There's bad weather on the way,' obliged Rory.
'The forecast for the next few days is grim,' he
said. 'We're thinking about leaving the place to
the builders, buggering off somewhere for a while
and letting them get on with it.'

'Are you having restoration work done?' asked Darina politely.

'In a manner of speaking. The roof is in dire need of repair. The *bateau lit* in the spare room looked like a lifeboat when we arrived the other day.'

The small talk petered out, and people took genteel sips of champagne.

Then: 'You said something about a school uniform, Deirdre?' said Darina, turning glittering eyes on her hostess. 'Is one of the characters you're researching a schoolgirl, then?'

'Oh, no,' said Deirdre brightly. 'She's just into kinky sex.'

'Ah,' said Darina Maguire.

First point of the evening to Deirdre O'Dare, thought Maddie.

'She's having an affair with a British peer who's into playing sex games – did you know that I was married to a British peer once? Well, he wasn't actually a peer when I married him, but he is now. You may have heard of him? Lord Gabriel Considine.'

'Oh, yes. I read somewhere all right that you'd been married to a British peer. Is the peer in your screenplay based – maybe a *little* – on him?'

'Lordie, no. I'd be letting myself in for libel if I gave away any of Gabriel's peccadilloes. We weren't married for long, but it was long enough for me to find out that the marriage was most certainly not made in heaven, even though we'd had a wildly romantic wedding – in Murrisk Abbey in the West of Ireland.' Information was positively spilling out of Deirdre now.

'Murrisk Abbey? How lovely! I didn't know that.'

'There are lots of things that people don't know about me. And Rory. Don't believe everything you read in *Hello!* magazine.'

'That's rich coming from you, O'Dare,' remarked Rory, reaching for the champagne bottle and topping up glasses.

'No more for me, darling,' said Deirdre, putting her hand over the glass. 'I'm not going to run the risk of our son developing foetal alcohol syndrome.'

'You're expecting a boy?' asked Darina.

'Yes.' Deirdre smiled sweetly at her. 'Isn't it nice after our little girl?'

'I thought your daughter was Gabriel Considine's child?'

'Oh no – she's definitely Rory's.'

'Oh.' Darina Maguire looked confused again. 'I must have been misinformed. I thought I read somewhere . . .' she trailed off vaguely.

'Misinformation's a dangerous thing,' said Deirdre. 'Remember that incident when someone let slip to the papers that you and I had split up over some fling you were meant to have had in LA, Rory?'

'Wasn't it true?' asked Darina.

'Good God, no,' said Rory. He and Deirdre exchanged amused smiles.

'Careful of that book, darling,' said Deirdre, as Rory went to put the empty bottle on the small table next to the *Erotica universalis*. 'It's a rare first edition.'

'How interesting – may I have a look?' Darina Maguire picked the book up off the table.

'It makes excellent bedtime reading,' remarked Rory. 'Have a gander at page sixty-nine.'

'Goodness,' said Darina, turning a gratifying shade of vermilion. She leafed through a couple of pages with a kind of stilted casualness, trying hard not to look fazed. Then she put the book down and said, in the smarmy, confidential manner of an inveterate gossip, 'Hardly the kind of stuff you'd want your little girl to get her hands on, is it?'

'Of course not,' returned Rory. 'We keep all our erotica under lock and key. Along with the thesis I wrote on pornography at college.'

'You wrote a thesis on pornography at college, Rory?' said Darina, leaning forward with interest.

'That's right. It was great fun doing the research. I went around with a permanent hard-on for the best part of a year.'

'Ha ha ha,' went Darina, looking flustered. 'Do you know, for some reason I understood that you studied veterinary science before going into the acting business.'

'Rory's a dark horse,' said Sam. Maddie tried not to snigger.

'Well, really, Rory! Are there any other talents

you're hiding under your bushel?' Darina smiled at him encouragingly.

'Under my what?' asked Rory.

Darina looked disconcerted again. 'Your bushel,' she said.

'What's a bushel?'

'Well – it's a – a kind of measurement. You must have come across the phrase "Don't hide your light under a bushel"?'

'No.' Rory looked blank.

'I haven't either,' said Maddie. 'How do you spell it?'

'B-U-S-H-E-L,' said Darina Maguire. 'Surely you've heard of it?'

'I've heard of it,' said Maddie helpfully. 'But definitely not in that context. The only bushel I know is to "bushel" your clothes. You know – as in "to mend". "The seamstress bushelled the man's trousers" – that kind of thing. For instance, I got this dress in a second-hand shop and I had to bushel a buttonhole before I could wear it.'

'Well. That's a new one on me,' said Darina, looking confused. 'Are you sending me up?'

'Not at all,' said Maddie. 'You'll find it's in the dictionary.'

'And Maddie should know what she's talking about,' remarked Daniel. 'She has an excellent "vocabluary".'

Maddie smiled at him. 'Thank you, "Dalien",' she shot back.

'Fetch the dictionary for Maddie, Rory, darling,'

said Deirdre. 'And some fresh champagne for our guests.'

Rory rose obligingly to his feet.

There was a wonderfully embarrassing hiatus. Deirdre stretched herself in her chair. 'Ow,' she said, rubbing her neck. 'This rig-out gets dead uncomfortable after a while.' She undid the tight frogging at her throat, then stood up and proceeded to undo the elaborate little catches all the way down. 'It's also a bit bloody warm to be wearing in weather like this,' she announced, sliding her arms out of the heavy silk sleeves and removing the offending garment with a dramatic flourish. Underneath she was wearing a delicious confection of rosebud-trimmed bra and matching knickers, and a pair of high-heeled mules trimmed with fluffy pale pink marabou feathers. 'That's better,' she said, slinging the kimono over the back of her chair.

Beside her, Maddie could feel Sam stiffen. 'Sweet Jesus Christ,' he muttered under his breath, as Rory came back out carrying a dictionary and another bottle of champagne. He evinced absolutely no surprise at seeing his wife in her underclothes.

'You'll keep those mules on when we go to bed tonight, darling, won't you?' he said in a disarmingly conversational tone. 'I love having sex with you in them. I'm something of a fetishist,' he added, turning to Darina, who went as pink as Deirdre's mules. 'Oh – sorry,' he continued. 'I

418

forget that some people tend to get embarrassed about other people's sexual preferences. You didn't strike me as the easily shockable type.'

'Oh – I'm not really,' said Darina quickly. 'I'm not afraid to talk about people's sex lives.'

Rory gave her a knowing look. 'It's just as well. Saint-Géyroux's a hotbed of vice.' He started peeling the foil off the neck of the champagne bottle.

Darina gave a little laugh, and Rory looked up at her again. 'I'm not joking,' he said. 'Ask Daniel. A lot of car keys get swapped in that café late at night, don't they?'

Daniel gave Darina an enigmatic smile. 'What an extraordinary mouth you have,' he said. 'Like a crushed flower. Someone should paint you. Maybe you'd consider sitting for me while you're here?'

Darina didn't know whether to look cynical or flattered or a bit of both. She looked away with a half-smile stapled to her face.

Daniel looked across at Maddie and gave her a slow wink. Stiff with the effort of trying not to laugh out loud, she concealed her expression by taking a sip of her champagne as she leafed through the pages of the *Concise Oxford*, looking for 'bushel'. She suddenly found herself remembering how she had once wondered when she'd ever feel enough like celebrating to drink champagne again. When life got back to normal, that's what she'd concluded. *This* was *normal*?! 'Found it!' she called. She cleared her throat and read from the dictionary. 'Bushel. To mend or alter clothes. From "bosseln" – to do odd jobs. Hey! That's what you do, Sam, when you go round to Bianca's!' Maddie was giddy with the relief of being allowed to laugh at last. 'You *bosseln*.'

'I'd *bosseln* you, given half the chance,' said Sam, sliding a finger under the strap of her sundress.

'Wasn't there *anything* there about hiding your light under a bushel, Maddie?' asked Darina.

'I dunno,' she said, setting aside the dictionary. 'I didn't bother to look.'

Rory poured champagne.

'Thank you,' said Darina, taking a sip before continuing her offensive. 'So,' she said, forcing an unconvincing little laugh, 'what else do you keep under your bushel, Rory?'

'Well,' he drawled. 'I ride. Like a demon.' He gave her one of the lazy, interested looks he did so well, and Darina went pink again.

'Rory and Deirdre have to be the most enviably talented couple I know, Darina,' supplied Maddie. 'They're a bit like the new Hugh Grant and Liz Hurley of Hollywood.'

'That's an interesting comparison.' Darina fastened on the fascinated expression she did so well as she returned her attention to Deirdre. She's bigtime into eye contact, thought Maddie. Eye contact and that soothing trust-me-you-can-tell-me-everything voice. 'Liz Hurley gave up acting to concentrate on film production, and you gave it up to concentrate on screenwriting. Your screenplays have certainly taken off, haven't they,

Deirdre? Can you tell me anything more about the one you're working on at the moment?'

'Yes. But it's very hush-hush. Maddie's the only person who's read it so far because the plot's based on something that actually happened to her cousin.'

'Oh? Run it by me, please? I won't breathe a word.'

'Promise?'

'Promise,' said Darina in a wonderfully sincere voice.

Deirdre feigned coyness by biting her lip and lowering her eyes. 'OK. Steven Spielberg has commissioned me to write this one.'

Darina looked as if all her Christmases had come at once. 'How wonderful! Any stars in mind?'

'Julia Roberts, George Clooney, Cameron Diaz, Robert de Niro, Brad Pitt, The Rock and Buster Keaton.'

'What?' Scepticism was plainly scrawled all over Darina's face. 'You really *are* sending me up this time. Buster Keaton's been dead for decades.'

'*Nobody* stays dead now we've CGI,' replied Deirdre imperturbably. 'A million movie stars will soon be rolling in their graves.'

Darina narrowed her eyes, considering. Then: 'I suppose you're right,' she conceded, but her demeanour was definitely guarded now. She knew something was up. 'Nothing stays sacred in Hollywood for long, does it?' She turned to Rory. 'No part in it for you, Rory?' she asked.

'I turned it down. Too much screen nudity, even for me.'

There was a pause before the journalist spoke again. 'What's it about?' she asked, in a much more careful tone.

'I don't much like talking about my work,' said Deirdre with more uncharacteristic coyness. 'You run the plotline by Davina, Maddie, and I'll see if I can spot any holes in the narrative.'

Deirdre had graciously handed over the baton, and Maddie accepted it with a smile. 'Well,' she began. 'First I'd better fill you in a bit on that cousin of mine who inspired Deirdre with the storyline, Davina. She happens to be an actress, so she's a sitting target for the tabloids. You know the way some tabloids paint pictures of actresses as divas or sex-crazed, or both? Well, Maeve hasn't a temperamental bone in her body, and she's been in a blissfully happy relationship with the same partner for years. The only slightly unusual aspect of her private life is that her partner is another woman. Maeve's life was nearly ruined when a journalist got hold of this classified information about her.'

Darina Maguire had blanched visibly.

'This is where Deirdre's screenplay starts,' continued Maddie without missing a beat. 'The actress's friends decide to get revenge on the journalist – she's a woman, incidentally – by spinning her a massive spiel: a web of lies with some truth thrown in as a double-bluff.' Maddie tucked her knees up under her and sent Darina her most dazzling smile. 'The information they feed her has a delicious potential for scandal of the lowest, most prurient kind, but it's so full of contradictions and untruths that it's completely worthless to the journalist. And the fact that this journalist had sought to procure information by a form of entrapment has *serious* damage potential. If the material is ever published, a huge libel action will be taken against her and whoever is foolish enough to print calumny. Or is slander the more accurate word? I must look it up. You see how careful I am about the words I use, Davina?' Maddie cocked her head to one side as she reached for the dictionary again. 'I have to be – I'm a copywriter by profession. But then, you're a wordsmith too, so you'd know all about that, wouldn't you? You'd never knowingly write anything that might mess up someone's life, would you?' Maddie smiled at Darina Maguire with genuine pleasure. Revenge *was* sweet, she thought with a small, illicit thrill. 'More champagne?'

The journalist put down her glass. 'No, thank you. I'll go now,' she said. From the minute Maddie had referred to Maeve she'd been looking more and more uncomfortable. The colour of her face had gone from shocked white to mortified red as Maddie delivered her speech, and great patches of sweat had spread under her arms. 'All I can say', she mumbled, as she rose to her feet, 'is that a girl's got to make a living. And if I hadn't written that piece, someone else would have.'

'But you *did* write it, Darina.' Maddie looked at her unsmilingly now. 'And all *I* can say is "shame on you".'

Darina tried very hard to look dignified as she made her way across the terrasse, but it didn't work. She practically radiated humiliation. Maddie would have felt sorry for her if she hadn't remembered the phone call she'd received from Maeve when Darina had stitched her up in 'Who The Hell Do They Think They Are?' It was the only time in her life she had ever heard her cousin distraught.

'Rory? Would you show Ms Maguire – I beg your pardon – Ms *Costello-ffrench* to the door?' said Deirdre.

'It's all right,' replied Darina, giving her a black look. 'I can find my own way out.' She practically dived through the french windows.

'Wow,' said Sam. 'I'd love to see you pitch for an account, Maddie. You handled her admirably.'

'Thank you,' said Maddie, feeling very chuffed indeed.

'Well.' Deirdre sat back in her seat and gave a little chirrup of pleasure. 'That was fun! What'll we do now?'

'I know,' said Maddie. 'Let's write our own piece. How about this? "Lounging on their sun-drenched terrace in the South of France, Hollywood screenwriter Deirdre O'Dare and her devilishly handsome husband, the actor Rory McDonagh, sip champagne and discuss literature with famous recluse, the internationally acclaimed artist Daniel Lennox, while their beautiful, fragrant children frolic in the nursery upstairs . . ." '

'Hey, Dad!' Aoife sprinted onto the terrasse. 'A horse just went down the street and did this deadly poo right outside the door. It's *ginormous* – the biggest one I've ever seen, and Mme Tuvache is shouting her head off! Come and see, quick!'

Rory rose to his feet with a sigh. 'Well. Welcome back to real life,' he said.

Chapter Sixteen

Bianca graciously gave Sam a breather from his decorating work that weekend. 'Let's hit the beach,' he said the next morning, swinging into the kitchen. Maddie was sitting with her elbows on the table and her hands wrapped round a big blue breakfast cup, and Molly was beside her, drawing a picture of a spotty horse with a sea-green mane and wings. The horse that had pooed in the street had acquired mythological status. 'Come on, Molly – pack your gear and we'll pick up Aoife on the way through the village. Will Daniel want to come, do you think – or is he already ensconced in his studio?'

'He's ensconced,' said Maddie. They'd passed each other fleetingly in the kitchen earlier.

'Good. That means I'll have your undivided attention,' said Sam, looking at her wickedly. 'I want to drizzle ice-cream onto your thigh and lick it off.'

'Why do you do that, Sam?' asked Molly, getting up and fetching her swimming togs from where they'd been hung to dry on the sun-lounger on the terrasse. 'I saw you doing that to Florence on the beach one day.'

Maddie shot him an amused look. 'Oops,' he said, and then he gave her a wicked smile. 'I will confess that I didn't confine myself to just her thighs,' he added in an undertone. 'But I'll only drip ice-cream on the bits of you that you allow me to.'

Maddie laughed. 'You are a seriously naughty boy,' she said.

'Punish me, then.'

'I will not. You can bloody well ask your ice-cream queen to punish you. Ring Aoife, Molly, and ask her if she wants to come to the beach.'

Deirdre decided to come as well. She wanted to escape from the noise of Rory drilling into a wall upstairs. 'He's trying to put up shelves that fell down when the plaster came away in the spare room,' she told Maddie, as she clambered into the back of the deux-chevaux with Aoife twenty minutes later. 'I wish he wouldn't. He's crap at it. If only we had someone to *bosseln* for us. Bianca's bloody lucky to have you, Sam.'

'I'm bloody lucky I'm not *bosseln*-ing for her this weekend. I wouldn't have fancied the idea of running into Darina again.'

'I'd say it's more likely that she wouldn't fancy the idea of running into *you*, Sam,' remarked Maddie. 'Anyway, she'll have made some excuse to Bianca and disappeared back to Dublin with her tail between her legs by now.'

'Bianca would feel a right eejit if she knew

she'd been harbouring a hackette,' said Deirdre.

'Mm,' agreed Maddie. 'It's probably as well not to let on.' She stretched herself in the passenger seat, and smiled a cat-who-got-the-cream smile. 'I can't wait to tell Maeve, though.'

*　　*　　*

The first thing Sam did when they hit the beach was to head off to the Labadou to buy ice-cream. Maddie and Deirdre laid out towels and stripped off. When Deirdre removed her bra, Maddie took a deep breath and did likewise. She knew her knickers were pretty enough to pass for bikini bottoms. It was the first time she'd sunbathed topless since coming to France, and she was conscious that her breasts were very white compared to her arms and legs.

'Want me to do your back?' asked Deirdre, indicating a tube of suncream.

'Yes, please.'

Maddie lay down on her tummy and Deirdre drizzled suncream between her shoulder blades. 'Wow. There's a lot of tension there,' she remarked as she massaged the cream into Maddie's skin.

'Not as much as when I first arrived here, I can tell you,' replied Maddie.

'Oh? You were really that uptight, were you? Something to do with your ex?'

'Yes.'

428

'You know what you should do while you're here, then?'

'What?'

'Take a lover,' she said, matter-of-factly.

Maddie looked up at her.

'I'm not being facile,' continued Deirdre. 'Making love is the best way I know to really loosen up.'

Maddie smiled. 'I suppose you're right.' She laid her cheek back on the pillow made by her forearms. 'It's been a while,' she added, ruminatively.

Suddenly she heard Sam call her name. She looked towards the snack bar, but he wasn't calling from there. He was on the rampart of the bridge, waving both his arms to attract her attention.

'Maddie Godard! I love you!' he cried. Then he launched himself into the air. Maddie hid her face immediately.

'Ow. Tell me when it's safe to look, Deirdre,' she said.

'A perfect swallow dive!' exclaimed Deirdre. 'Elegant execution, clean entry. I'd give him nine out of ten.'

Maddie looked at Deirdre through her fingers. 'Why does he lose a point?'

Deirdre raised an eyebrow. 'Indiscretion. Rumours of his declaration of love will be circulating in Saint-Géyroux within the hour. Will you do my back, now?'

Deirdre stretched out on her towel, and Maddie dotted suncream along her spine. She looked up

429

and saw Sam coming back up the beach, moving with that indolent grace of his. He paused momentarily to talk to a group of his friends, and she saw the eyes of the dark-haired beauty she now knew was called Florence slide in her direction. Then Sam turned, flashed Maddie his great smile, and started to stroll towards her.

'There. You're finished,' she said to Deirdre, snapping the cap back on the suncream.

'I suppose I'd better put some of that girly stuff on too,' said Sam as he drew level with them. 'Hey – you kids!' Molly and Aoife were making sand castles further down the beach. 'Run up to the shop and bring back ice-creams for us.' He reached into the pockets of the jeans he'd discarded, threw a wad of francs at them, and they scampered off in the direction of the Labadou. Then he looked down at Maddie. 'That's Florence over there, Maddie.'

'Yes. I guessed.'

'*She* thinks I'm sexy. She's dead jealous of you.'

'You *are* sexy, Sam,' said Deirdre.

'Sexier than him?' Sam indicated a photograph of a sulky bronzed youth who was modelling jeans in the magazine Deirdre was reading.

'Absolutely.'

'D'you know what Maddie called me the other night, Deirdre? She called me "appealing". Bloody awful word, isn't it? At the very opposite end of the spectrum to sexy.' He dropped down on the towel beside Maddie, and before she could stop him, he was kissing her. It wasn't a long kiss, but her lips had parted instinctively as his mouth made contact with hers.

'Why do you pull that stunt, Sam?' asked Maddie as she broke away, trying to ignore the triumph in his eyes.

'Why do I kiss you? I would have thought the answer to that was pretty obvious.'

'No – I mean why do you dive from the bridge? You scare the shit out of me when you do it.'

'For the adrenalin high. There's nothing to beat it. Well, almost nothing.' He smiled at her obliquely. 'It's actually quite safe, as long as you know what you're doing. The first time is the scariest because you're not quite sure of your trajectory. But once you've done it and know exactly where to aim for, it's a piece of piss.'

'I think you're mad.'

'I am mad. With love for you. Mad about Maddie. I meant what I said up there, you know.'

She gave him an indulgent smile. 'At your age you fall in love at the drop of a hat.'

'Did you ever?'

'Did I ever what?'

'Fall in love at the drop of a hat?'

'Yes, I did, as a matter of fact.'

'How many times?'

He had called her bluff. 'Once.'

'What about you, Deirdre?'

Deirdre considered. 'I used to think I was in

love with other men all the time, but there really was only ever one. Coincidentally, here he comes now.' She raised herself on her elbows and looked towards where Rory was walking across the beach with Aoife and Molly, carrying half a dozen ice-creams. 'Hello, darling,' she said as he approached. 'How did the DIY go?'

'It didn't,' said Rory, plonking a kiss on her bare shoulder. 'Life's too short to wield a Black & Decker.'

'Or a Moulinex,' observed Deirdre.

Rory handed out ice-creams. Sam peeled the paper off, and leaned over Maddie. 'Where should I start?' he asked, looking hungrily at her. He let his eyes graze briefly over her white breasts, and when he raised an eyebrow she felt a wonderfully unexpected sensation somewhere deep inside. The last time she'd experienced this feeling had been with Josh when it was good, before the rape. She recognized it at once as the first fluttering of sexual desire.

*   *   *

On Sunday night Sam took Molly to stay over at Aoife's. Maddie decanted some of the local red wine into a *pichet*, and took *Jane Eyre* and her notebook out onto the balcony.

For some reason it was hard to concentrate on reading this evening. The house-martins were soaring and diving through the darkening sky, their white underbellies gleaming in the last light of the low-slung sun, and sparrows were staking claim to dormitories. A bee visited a lavender bush in a pot on the windowsill, its drone unexpected at this late hour of the evening. She stretched herself luxuriously, feeling contented and sublimely comfortable in her own skin, and then she ran a hand down her bare arm. Her skin felt satiny to the touch. It was golden now from days of lying lazily on beaches, and fragrant with the sun-balm she'd rubbed into it after her shower earlier.

She opened her notebook, reread the sonnet she'd written earlier that day, and then leaned back in her chair again, hoping that the nightingale might sing this evening.

The sound of a cork being pulled in the billiard room made her jump. Quickly she drew her feet up under her and arranged the folds of her dress, then picked up her book and opened it at random. The crushed petunia blossom she'd been using as a bookmark fell to the ground.

Daniel Lennox wandered out, dressed in the ripped T-shirt and faded jeans he often wore when he was painting. He seemed to get almost as much of a surprise at seeing her there as she had done when she had heard the bottle being opened. He had a brandy glass in one hand and a bottle of Calvados in the other, and he looked tired.

'Oh. It's you,' he said. 'Well. I could use some company. Where's Sam?'

'He hasn't come back from leaving Molly at Deirdre and Rory's,' she replied, shutting her book.

Daniel yawned and settled down in a chair beside her. 'Poor little Moll. It's nice for her to have the occasional break from being stuck here with her boring old dad.'

'Come on, Daniel! What makes you think she finds you boring?'

'She finds me brain-numbingly boring when I sequester myself in my studio every morning.'

'Can't you take some time off?'

'Not right now. If I take time off when I'm in the middle of a series I find it hellishly difficult to get back into my stride again. Marie-France's timing was woeful this summer. Usually I make sure to have four weeks free before Molly goes back to school in September. The month of August is exclusively Molly's. Unfortunately, she can't help resenting the fact that I can't devote my undivided attention to her right now.'

'Do you manage to spend much time with her during the rest of the year?'

'Yeah. Two weeks at *Toussaint*, two weeks at Christmas, and two weeks in April. Even though she doesn't live with me all year round I probably manage to spend more time with her than most fathers might.' He looked at her levelly. 'I really love my daughter, Madeleine.' He pronounced the words with quite a disarming candour.

'It shows. She's a very happy little girl. You've

434

even managed to put manners on her. That's unusual these days.'

'Thanks.' He stretched and yawned again. 'Haven't you finished that book yet?'

'No,' she said, 'I've been having too much fun during the day, and sometimes it's difficult to concentrate at night.'

'Why's that?'

He'd made her feel shy. 'Well. Every time I start a page the garden calls to me to look up and admire it, and I go off into a kind of trance.'

He smiled at her. 'I know the feeling.'

'I've even become an expert in the nocturnal habits of house-martins since I've been here. It's better than soap opera. There's one pair in particular that fascinates me. They're the Chris Evans and Billie Piper of the avian world. That is – I can't be sure it's the same pair, but I like to think it is.'

Daniel stood up and moved to the balustrade, and as he looked out over the garden the tired lines around his eyes relaxed. A house-martin darted past so close to him that if he'd reached out a hand quickly enough, he might have caught it. 'I'm going into Montpellier tomorrow. Do you still want to come with me?'

This time she didn't say 'I don't mind.' She said: 'Yes, please. I'd like that.'

'We'll head in around lunchtime.' He turned back and looked at her. 'You've filled out a bit since you've been here, Madeleine. You've lost that haggard look you had.'

She looked down at her wineglass. 'I've been sleeping better, too.'

'No nightmares?'

'No nightmares.' How did he know she'd been suffering from nightmares? She was quite sure she hadn't mentioned it to him. She gave a shiver. An evening breeze had got up.

Daniel noticed. 'The weather's due to change, according to Mme Poiret. I hope you have something warm to wear. You're going to need it if you want to sit out here in the evenings.'

She hoped Mme Poiret had got it wrong. She had packed no warm clothes at all. She'd forgotten that it could be wet and windy and cold in the South of France in early July, just as it could be in the West of Ireland. 'If we're in for really bad weather I suppose I could always cut my stay short.' As she said it, she realized she didn't want to cut her stay short. She wasn't ready to go back to Dublin yet.

'You can't do that, I'm afraid. You promised Molly you'd be her governess. And you agreed to sit for me, remember – to be my *Albaydé*?' He uncrossed his legs and stretched himself. 'It's not inconvenient for you, is it? You did say you had an open-ended ticket.'

'No – it's not inconvenient.' She was actually relieved to have an excuse to stay on. After all, what was waiting for her in Ireland? Real life, unemployment and the ruins of a relationship. She felt safe here. She should be glad of the opportunity of extending her holiday. 'I'll ask Deirdre to lend me something warm to wear.'

'Don't worry about getting cold while you're sitting,' said Daniel. 'There's a wood-burning stove in the studio.'

You've fucked every woman who's ever sat for you. Suddenly Sara Lennox's words came back to her and she stiffened. What if Daniel Lennox had no real interest in painting her at all? What if sex was item one on his agenda? Maybe she was inviting disaster. Maybe she should try and back out now, before things went any further.

'You're having second thoughts, aren't you, Madeleine?' he said. He was watching her carefully.

'About what?'

'You're not sure you want me to paint you after all. Of course you can say no. I warned you it was tedious.'

I never seduce women. The words he'd used to rebuff the accusation Sara had levelled at him came back to her. *It's always the other way round.* The likelihood of her seducing Daniel Lennox was so remote as to be laughable. Hell. Why was she behaving like such a wuss? She should be thrilled at the prospect of sitting for a major artist!

Daniel was still looking at her as if he could read her mind. 'Maybe you should go and have a look at *Albaydé* in the Musée Fabre tomorrow. That should make your mind up for you.' He finished his brandy and got to his feet. 'I'm going downstairs for a swim. Do you want to join me?'

She shook her head. 'No, thanks. By the way, Daniel – is it all right if I make a phone call?' She'd deliberately left her mobile in Dublin and had talked to Maeve only once since she'd arrived. 'I'll be sure to keep a record of all my calls, and I'll settle up with you before I leave.'

'Be my guest, Madeleine. Use the phone as often as you like. I think I already told you that I owe you. If you weren't here to look after Molly for me next week I'd have been in a real hole. Sweet dreams.' He ambled back through the billiard room.

Maddie sat on for a while, watching the darkening garden. She finally found the energy to pick herself up and trail into the den to call Maeve. She got the answering machine. 'Hi – it's me,' she said when the tone sounded. 'Nothing urgent – I'm just feeling a bit lonely tonight, for some reason. I wish you were there to talk to. I'll try again tomorrow. Much love to you both.' She put the phone down and hesitated for a moment, wondering if she should phone someone else. In another life she'd have rung Josh to tell him she was feeling lonely, and she would have felt reassured and comforted by his voice on the line.

She wandered back out onto the balcony to finish her wine, still hoping that she might hear the nightingale sing before she went to bed, but the birds had all dispersed. The only sound she could hear was the dull, one-note call of a sparrow who hadn't yet managed to find a bed for the night.

*   *   *

The following morning she was making coffee in the kitchen when the door opened and Daniel came through.

'Letter for you, Madeleine,' he said. 'May I take some of that coffee?'

'Sure,' replied Maddie, pulling her robe tighter around her as she put out her hand for the letter. 'Thanks.'

She took her coffee over to the kitchen table and looked at the envelope. She half expected the handwriting on the front to be Josh's, and was relieved to see Maeve's elegant script.

Daniel had poured himself a very large coffee. There was black liquid slopping over the side of his mug as he padded on bare feet to the kitchen door and shut it behind him without once looking in her direction. She tore open the envelope and took out a sheet of vellum.

'Dear Maddie,' she read. 'I hope you are chilling to perfection in beautiful Saint-Géyroux, and all demons are exorcized. I tried to reach you on the phone a couple of times, and when I eventually got hold of Deirdre she told me that there'd been a foul-up and that you were still staying in the Lennox place.

I have been called off to the States this week for advance publicity on that television series I did last year. It's been sold coast-to-coast, which is excellent news. Anyway, in the meantime I hope you don't mind, but I've let a visiting actor chum of mine from London use your flat until he can find somewhere more permanent to stay. His name is Nick Fielding, he's absolutely sound and there will be no parties. I know it would have been preferable to run it by you first, but I had no way of contacting you, Nick was desperate, and I owed him a favour. If you want a more detailed character reference, do give Jacqueline a buzz.

I'll be in touch when I get back. I think about you a lot. Give Rory and Deirdre big kisses from me.

Much love,

Maeve. XXX

PS: I just couldn't resist packing your cheongsam. Afterwards I wondered if I'd done the right thing. I hope you didn't mind?'

Maddie read the letter twice. She knew there'd be no need to contact Jacqueline. Maeve's testimonial was enough – she would never allow anyone remotely dodgy to stay in her apartment. There was no problem. This Nick Fielding was welcome to stay as long as he wanted, or until she needed it back. She poured herself another cup of coffee and headed towards the bathroom. On the stairs she met Daniel coming out of his rooms with his mug in his hand.

'Is there any more coffee, Madeleine?'

'You might get half a mugful.'

'That'll do,' he said, continuing down the stairs. 'I'll be heading into Montpellier in a couple of hours, by the way,' he threw back over his shoulder at her. 'Will you be ready?'

'I'll be ready.'

'Don't expect too leisurely a visit. I intend to skedaddle once I've got my business out of the way. It's grim at this time of the year.'

'Oh, God. Is it?'

'Tourists. How do you say that in French?'

She was just about to oblige with a translation, when she realized he was laughing at her. She obliged him with a smile instead. 'Oh, piss off, Daniel,' she said.

*   *   *

He was right. Montpellier was not fun. It was crowded and hot, and Maddie felt stressed for the first time since her arrival in France. It was hard to believe that barely an hour earlier they had driven out of a village so quiet it could have been a ghost town. Daniel put her down in the Place de la Comédie, and they arranged to meet at one of the cafés there at four o'clock. That gave her a couple of hours to 'do' the capital of Languedoc.

As she wandered round the streets she realized with a kind of despair that she could have been in any city in the world. Here were acres of malls housing the very same shops she had left behind in Dublin – Habitat, Body Shop, all the usual suspects. The narrow lanes leading off the Place de la Comédie were more interesting, but she didn't feel much like shopping, and most of the boutiques here were too expensive, anyway.

She trailed down a side street, narrowly avoiding being run over by a man on a bicycle who was dragging his dog behind him on a lead, and emerged onto a tree-lined esplanade to find herself standing in front of the Musée Fabre. She looked at her watch. It was just half-past three. She had thirty minutes to kill before she was due to meet Daniel.

It was cool in the gallery, and quiet. She wandered through the rooms feeling tension lift from her shoulders. She admired Raphael and Delacroix and Matisse, and paused in front of a painting by Bourdon, struck by its title. *The Curing of a Man Possessed by a Demon*, she read. Had Josh been able to rid himself of the demon that had possessed him the night he'd raped her? She recalled the first sentence of Maeve's letter. *I hope you are chilling to perfection in beautiful Saint-Géyroux, and all demons are exorcized* . . . Were they? They certainly weren't as clamorous as they'd once been – she hadn't had a single visitation since the evening the nightingale had sung during *l'heure bleue* – but she knew that they were lurking, hoping to catch her unawares. She sensed too that there was a way of exorcizing them for good, and that it had a lot to do with Sam Newman.

Something told her that she needed to take things a stage further. She needed to know if she could make love again without feeling fear or panic or disgust. Sam was far too young for her – younger by nearly six years – but somehow, when she thought about it, the age difference might be a good thing. He wouldn't feel it incumbent upon himself to make demands of her sexually, and he was unlikely to suffer from that macho arrogance that refuses to allow a woman to guide the proceedings. When would she be likely to come across such a man again, a man who would be biddable and gentle and unthreatening? She wandered thoughtfully away from the Bourdon, continuing her quest for *Albaydé*.

She was downstairs. Maddie recognized her immediately. She was reclining on a couch, looking unsmilingly into the eyes of the man who had copied her likeness onto canvas for posterity. Maddie calculated from the date on the catalogue that Cabanel had been quite young when he'd painted the portrait – only twenty-five. Had they made love? she wondered. The girl in the painting had a sleepy look about her – a look that was resonantly post-coital.

The muse that had inspired Daniel to paint Maddie Godard as Albaydé had clearly been something of a visionary. The attitude of this sultry, exotic-looking creature who wore a red flower in her tumbling coiffure and who was absently toying with a length of Morning Glory was identical to the

443

attitude Maddie had adopted that afternoon by the river, when Molly had tucked the scarlet oleander blossom into her hair.

And one aspect of the painting Maddie found infinitely reassuring. Albaydé was not nude. She was wearing a loose robe of fluid cream silk. It had been arranged so that while a generous amount of décolletage was exposed, the sitter's nipples were concealed. The other thing she noticed was that despite Albaydé's air of inscrutability, her eyes were very calm – even mildly stoned-looking. Maddie stood in front of the portrait for a long time, coveting the sense of serenity that emanated from it. If Daniel Lennox did paint her as Albaydé, how could she possibly replicate that serenity?

A glance at her watch told her it was time to go. She'd spent longer than she'd intended in the gallery, and she didn't want to keep Daniel waiting. She hurried back along the Esplanade Charles de Gaulle towards the Place de la Comédie and the café where they had arranged to meet.

He was sitting on the terrasse already, looking much the same as he'd looked the day he'd picked her up in Gignac. His eyes were invisible behind his dark glasses, and he was perusing another back-issue of the *Irish Times*. This time a glass of beer stood alongside his pastis on the table. He took off his sunglasses as she sat down rather breathlessly beside him.

'Sorry I'm late,' she said. 'Have you been waiting long?'

'Not long. You look hot. Have some beer.'

'Thanks.' The beer was gratifyingly cold. 'God, that's good,' she said, sitting back in her chair and smiling at him.

'You look great when you smile, Madeleine. You should do it more often. Although, having said that, I've noticed, you're smiling a lot more these days. You were the picture of misery when you came here first.'

'It's the company I'm keeping that's making me smile,' she said. 'Rory and Deirdre and Sam are such fun. And Molly, too, of course.'

Daniel Lennox raised an amused eyebrow. 'I notice I'm conspicuous by my absence,' he remarked.

'Oh!' Maddie flushed. 'I didn't mean that—'

'That I'm an irascible old fart? I don't take offence when somebody says to my face what they're probably saying behind my back.'

Was he an irascible old fart? Now that she'd bothered to think about it, she realized that he was nowhere near as thorny an individual as she'd first supposed. Laid-back was a better word to describe him, and he had as wicked a sense of humour as any of her new friends. The outrageous evening they'd spent at Deirdre and Rory's had proved that. She hadn't had such fun in years. She smiled at him again, and he reached out and picked up the Musée Fabre carrier bag she'd plonked on the table. 'I see you've been to the Musée. May I have a look?' he asked, sliding her catalogue out of the plastic bag. He leafed through the pages, pausing to admire a fleshy Courbet nude, until he came to the reproduction of *Albaydé*. 'What do you think?' he said.

'She's much more beautiful than I am.'

'That depends on one's definition of the word. She's different.'

'She's far more serene than I am, that's for sure.'

'You had that same look that day by the river. She's sexy, isn't she?'

'Yes. She is.'

'I like to think that she and Cabanel rogered each other rotten every time she sat for him.'

Maddie laughed a little awkwardly. That had been her first impression when she'd looked at the portrait, too.

'Don't worry, Madeleine – I won't expect you to be that obliging.' He drained his glass and set it down on the table. 'Drink up,' he said. 'I'm homesick already. This town is hellish today.'

He was following the progress across the terrasse of a very beautiful, heavily pregnant woman, looking as though he found the sight anything but hellish. Maddie noticed the woman's mouth curve in a half-smile when her eyes slid in his direction and she saw Daniel smile back at her, admiration evident on his face. 'How gorgeous,' he said, as if to himself. Then he leaned down to pick up the stack of carrier bags which rested at his feet. *Société Artissimo, Montpellier*, read the legend on most of them, but Maddie also noticed that one bore the name of an exclusive-looking lingerie shop which she'd passed in the rue de l'Argenterie earlier.

'The lingerie's not for me,' he said, in response to the curious expression she couldn't conceal. 'I'm not into cross-dressing. I've a suspicion I'd look a tad ridiculous in ladies' underwear. Take a look,' he added, handing her the bag.

What a strange invitation! She peered in, feeling a bit uncomfortable. Inside was some kind of garment wrapped in layers of tissue paper. 'Go ahead. Take it out,' said Daniel.

A heavy length of burnished silk unfurled from the nest of tissue paper. If water were malleable, this is how it would feel, she thought, as the garment took shape between her hands. It was a cream silk kimono. 'Oh! What a beautiful thing!' she exclaimed. She couldn't resist rubbing her cheek against the smooth fabric. 'Bianca's a lucky woman.'

Daniel Lennox laughed. 'It's not for Bianca.'

'Oh? Who is it for?' She cringed as she heard herself ask the question. It was absolutely none of her business who Daniel had bought the garment for.

'It's for you, of course. Can't you make the connection? It's Albaydé's gown. Shit – that *flic* is going to give me a ticket. Get ready to give him your best smile for me, Madeleine, will you?' He strode off to where he'd abandoned the Harley in the middle of the Place de la Comédie, leaving

Maddie holding the silk kimono. She looked down at it and then started to pour it slowly back into the glossy carrier bag.

As she walked across the terrasse to Daniel, who was negotiating with a graphically gesticulating gendarme, she passed the table where the beautiful pregnant woman was sitting. She smiled at Maddie as she walked past, and directed an eloquent look at Daniel. 'Vous êtes une femme qui a beaucoup de la chance!' she said. 'Quel beau cadeau! Votre amant est un homme très généreux.' She indicated the expensive carrier bag with a little incline of her head and smiled again.

There was no point in explaining that Daniel wasn't her lover. Anyway, she knew the woman wouldn't believe her. Only a lover would buy a robe like the one she'd just handled. She smiled back at the woman and gave a little shrug of her shoulders to acknowledge that yes, he was indeed a generous man, and then she continued across the square. Daniel seemed to be pointing out some feature of the Harley which was of extreme interest to the traffic cop. Remembering what he'd said, she made her smile warmer.

Ten minutes later Daniel and the *flic* were swapping Harley stories and Maddie was still smiling.

Chapter Seventeen

The following day was the first day of Maddie's new job as dedicated governess. It was also the first day of the weather Mme Poiret had predicted. It had changed dramatically. Maddie and Molly waved goodbye to Daniel as he set off gloomily for his *vernissage* in Paris, and then they dashed straight back into the house to avoid getting soaked. There was no prospect of going swimming in the river, so they messed about indoors all day. They played pool in the den, and water polo in the pool. They watched videos and painted each other's faces and grazed on junk food. In the evening when Sam came back from Bianca's, Molly entertained them with a piano recital in the library. Maddie and Sam curled up together on the chaise-longue with a bottle of the local red, and Sam wrapped one of the threadbare cashmere throws round her shoulders when he saw the goosebumps on her arms. Molly's rendition of 'Moonlight Sonata' was so much better than the one Maddie had attempted for Daniel that she groaned when she recollected the evening she'd played for him.

Molly didn't want to sleep by herself in Daniel's private apartments. 'Daddy hasn't rubbed out the picture of Bianca on my wall yet, and I don't like the idea of her looking at me when I'm sleeping,' she announced.

'OK, OK – you can sleep with me until he comes back,' said Maddie.

'Yay!' went Molly, jumping up and down, and Maddie felt absurdly chuffed by her reaction. She'd never had many dealings with children – none of her friends in Dublin had got round to having any yet – and it gave her a nice feeling to know that this small person was genuinely smitten by her.

Together they made up the double bed in one of the grander bedrooms on the first floor.

'I hope you don't snore, by the way,' said Maddie, plumping pillows.

'Oh no. I never snore. Sam does though, don't you, Sam?' He had come into the room with a fresh glass of wine for Maddie.

'How should I know? Nobody knows they snore until they share a bed with someone else. Do you fancy doing the research, Maddie?' He smiled and raised his eyebrows in enquiry.

Smiling back, she chucked a pillow at him.

He caught it, buried his face in it, and sent her a blissed-out smile.

'What are you grinning about?' she asked.

'The pillowcase smells of you,' he said.

*   *   *

Later that night, when the little girl had finally trailed off to bed and they'd finished clearing up the remains of their evening meal in the kitchen, she yawned and announced that she was going to bed, too. Sam looked at her with hot eyes and she shook her head. Putting a finger to his lips, he transferred the kiss to hers and then gently traced the outline of her mouth before kissing her properly. She let herself be kissed for a long moment, and then she put a hand up to his face to indicate that the kiss had gone far enough.

'Just once, Maddie? Just once?' There was yearning in his voice.

She shook her head. 'Not now. Not here.'

'When? Where?'

'I don't know, Sam. Maybe not ever. I'm sorry. I'm sorry – really I am. I just can't be more specific than that.'

Bowing his head, he conceded. Then he smiled. 'I can keep trying, though, can't I?' he said, looking at her with eyes which she found dangerously tempting. 'May I woo you, Maddie Godard?'

His use of the old-fashioned word made her smile back at him. 'Yeah. You may woo me.' The idea of indulging in a little flirtation was really an extremely attractive one. It was years since she'd flirted with anyone – pre-Josh, that was for sure – and she'd felt a pang of envy after witnessing the relaxed way Deirdre had flirted with Daniel

451

the other evening. 'But you're not to spend any money on me, Sam. Is that understood? Now. Go to bed.'

* * *

The following evening he arrived back from work with a bunch of tulips, a bottle of wine and a packet of *madeleines*.

'I told you you weren't to spend money on me,' said Maddie, folding her arms and trying to look cross.

Sam gave a dismissive shrug. 'It's hardly as if I'm showering you with diamonds. And I got the tulips from Bianca. She was all sniffy about them because her posh florist sent her variegated instead of her usual white ones. Hello, *pucelette*,' he added, as Molly came into the kitchen tripping over the hem of Maddie's green satin cheongsam. She'd spent the afternoon dressing up in her governess's frocks and pretending to be living in the olden days. 'I'd love to see *you* in that dress, Maddie,' said Sam, sitting up on the kitchen table and swinging his legs. 'Maybe you should wear it to Bianca's party next week.'

'Bianca's having a party?'

'Yeah. It's the highlight of the social scene in Saint-Géyroux. She always throws a big bash around this time of the year to celebrate her birthday. The amazing thing is that she seems to get younger each year.'

'I haven't been invited,' she said, indifferently, putting the flowers into a yellow jug.

'She sent it to Deirdre's. She was a bit put out when I told her you weren't staying there. It seems she's the last person in the village to be apprised of that particular nugget. She's been an awful sourpuss since.'

'Why?' asked Molly.

'Curiosity killed the cat,' retorted Sam, flicking the little girl's nose with a finger.

'But I'm *not* the cat. Bianca is.'

'Mind your manners when you're speaking of your elders.'

'But you just called her a sourpuss. And curiosity hasn't killed *her* yet. She phoned up yesterday and asked me when Maddie was going home.'

Sam laughed. 'Bianca must have nine lives,' he said.

'And she asked when Dad was coming home.'

They'd had a phone call from Daniel earlier that day to say that Paris was grim. The gallery in the rue du Seine had lined up too many interviews for him, he was fed up talking about himself to the press, and he missed Molly like mad.

'I'm bored. I'm going to make buns,' announced Molly, opening a cupboard and extracting a packet of banana-flavoured My Little Pony cake mix. 'D'you want to help, Sam?'

'Sure,' he said. 'As long as I don't have to eat any of them. And it would be a good idea to take that frock off. I'm sure Maddie doesn't want it to get covered in bun mixture.'

Molly slid out of the dress. 'Why haven't you worn this ever?' she asked.

'There hasn't really been a special enough occasion,' replied Maddie.

'Bianca's party will be a special occasion.'

'Mm,' said Maddie, realizing that she sounded rather too pensive. She left Sam and Molly pouring yellow cake mix into a bowl and went upstairs to transfer some of her stuff to her new bedroom. She was about to hang the cheongsam back in the wardrobe where the cream silk kimono now hung alongside her collection of second-hand frocks, when something made her hesitate. She moved to the mirror and held it up against her, studying her reflection. The last time she'd worn the dress had been at a rather staid dinner party held by the marketing manager of an insurance company whose account had been handled by the Complete Works for years. That evening Josh hadn't been able to wait till they got home before making love to her. They'd ended up having urgent and extremely good sex in the marketing manager's downstairs bathroom.

She ran her hands down the green satin, enjoying the smooth feel of it as she draped it on a hanger. Then she put on the Aran jumper Deirdre had lent her when the weather changed, knowing it looked hick over her cotton frock, and not caring. Her priority was keeping warm, not looking good, she thought as she skipped back down the stairs to join Sam and Molly in the kitchen.

*   *   *

Towards the end of the week she started to feel a bit lonely. Some cousin of Sam's who was backpacking round Europe had phoned to say he was in the vicinity, and could he stay for a couple of nights? 'Bloody hell,' said Sam. 'Trust Donald to descend on Saint-Géyroux when neither Daniel nor Sara are here. He won't be able to hack it – he'll want to spend all his time in Montpellier. What a life! I work my ass off all day *bosseln*ing at Bianca's, and then I have to work my ass off entertaining my wussy cousin in the evening, when all I want to do is woo Maddie Godard.'

'We might all go out for a meal together in Gignac?' suggested Maddie.

'Oh, no. I wouldn't dream of inflicting my cousin on you, Maddie. Donald's the most boring arse on the face of the planet. You'd end up snoring like the dormouse in *Alice in Wonderland*, with your face in your soup.'

She had taken his advice, and kept a low profile for the duration of Donald's stay. She remembered how Daniel had said it was possible to live in his house and never encounter another individual. She saw Donald only once – engrossed in a computer magazine at the kitchen table one morning. She had backed out of the room on silent feet and escaped to Deirdre's kitchen for her morning coffee instead.

She didn't see as much of Molly, either. Because the weather was so bad, she and Aoife had taken to disappearing off into the den every afternoon to play computer games, and on two evenings in a row Deirdre had invited Molly to stay overnight. 'I know how grim it is trying to keep a single child entertained when they can't go outside to play,' she'd said. 'I've had experience of *conditions exceptionelles* when I lived in the West of Ireland, remember? They can keep each other busy here. It's easier when there are two of them.'

So Molly had gone off with her toothbrush and her teddybear called Small Claude ('Clawed, Maddie! Do you get it?') looking guiltily at her over her shoulder. 'You're sure you won't be too lonely? I hate to think of you all by yourself in that big bed. Maybe I should leave Claude here so that you have someone to cuddle at night?'

'It's OK, *ma puce*. I've got Bassa.'

It was a strange feeling – not unpleasant – to have the house to herself. During a dry spell on Friday afternoon she wrapped herself up warmly and sat out on the *terrasse* with her notebook. For a couple of hours she worked on a sonnet inspired by the tulips Sam had bought for her, quite oblivious to the gathering storm clouds on the horizon. In her notebook, after lots of scribbling out and false starts, the following words finally took shape:

456

My friend brought me tulips, the unruly kind.
Those tousle-headed ones that quite disdain
To be arranged. They suit themselves. Constrain
Them, their demeanour will at once remind
You that they're having none of it. Confined,
Their loveliness diminishes. They attain
Perfection when they thumb their noses. Vain,
Glorious, self centred, unrefined.

I'd like to be like them. My inner child
Still kicks against convention, still breaks rules,
Still tingles with the impulse to run wild,
Still questions the authority of fools.
Real life's the stumbling block. In dreams we
   may assume
The unconcerned abandon of those blooms.

Some of the lines didn't scan properly, but she didn't care. She was happy with her poem the way it was, warts and all. In fact, she decided, she rather liked the fact that she'd flouted a literary rule. Hah! Maybe she was learning how to thumb her nose a little. Maybe she could break a few more rules.

When she'd completed the fair copy, she left pen and notebook on the terrasse and went for a swim in Daniel's pool. She cut the swim short. She felt self-conscious, somehow, floating on her back under the mosaic scrutiny of Daniel's former wife. Marie-France Lennox seemed to be telling her that she had no right whatsoever to be there.

When she returned to the terrasse to retrieve her sonnet, heavy rain had come and gone. The ink had run, the pages were saturated, and the words she'd worked so hard on were obliterated for ever.

*　　*　　*

That evening there was an electric storm. Maddie had finished supper – *feuilleté roquefort* from the village *pâtisserie* and *pistou* which Bianca had sent round for Daniel – and was sitting reading in the billiard room. There had been ominous rumbles in the sky all evening, but nothing prepared her for the crash that sounded above her head. She dropped her book and leapt to her feet. White light bathed the room, and lit up the smiling face of the merchant's wife above the door. Maddie stood absolutely still for another minute, waiting for the next crash, and laughed out loud when it came. Rain was coming in sheets from the sky. As she made her way across the room to throw open the french windows onto the balcony, the phone jangled. It was Sam.

'Are you all right, Maddie?' he said. He sounded worried.

'Yes, I'm fine. Why?'

'I thought you might be frightened by the storm.'

'Oh, no. I love storms,' she replied happily. 'It used to be my favourite thing when I visited my grandfather. I always used to pray that there'd be a storm while I was there. Wow! Listen to that!' The sky outside sounded as if it was being torn apart, and the room was flooded with uncanny light again.

'Damn it,' said Sam.

'Damn what?'

'I thought it would be a good excuse to dump Donald in Gignac and come home early to comfort you.'

Maddie laughed. 'That won't be necessary, Sam. Oh – it's so beautiful out there!' she exclaimed. 'I'm going to stand on the balcony in the rain before I go to bed.'

'What are you wearing?'

'My pink silk dress.'

'No jumper?'

'No. It's not as cold tonight.'

'Shit.' At the other end of the phone he groaned.

'Why do you have such a sudden interest in my sartorial affairs, Sam?'

'I'm just picturing you standing in the pouring rain with pale pink silk clinging to you.'

'Good night, Sam. Take a mind-improving book to bed with you when you get back.'

'I'll have to take a cold shower too. Good night, Madeleine. And by the way – the cousin from hell's leaving in the morning, so my style won't be cramped any more. I can begin wooing you in earnest.'

She was smiling as she put the phone down.

Outside on the balcony it was glorious. The instant she stepped through the french windows she was drenched. Stretching her arms out, she closed her eyes, threw back her head and let rivulets of rain run down her face. When she opened her mouth she could taste it, cool and clean on her tongue. Her hair was plastered to her cheeks and the silk of her dress clung so closely to her skin that she might as well have been naked.

At the same time as the lightning flashed again she heard a noise from the room behind her. She spun round to see a figure standing in the middle of the den. Lightning illuminated his face before she could draw breath to scream. It was Daniel Lennox.

'Sorry to disturb you, Madeleine,' he said. 'I decided to come home early.'

*   *   *

The next day Rory phoned. 'We've had it,' he said. 'Another section of the roof's gone. The builders are here, the house is a mess and we're fucking off to Paris in the morning.'

'Oh, well,' said Maddie. 'That means you can spoon and moon and do all those things that people are meant to do in Paris.'

'Hardly. We're not doing the young lovers in Paris thing. We're doing the sad bastards in Euro-

Disney thing. Does Molly want to come?'

'Wow. I'm sure she'd love to. I'll check that it's cool with Daniel.'

'It'll be cool with Daniel.'

It was cool with Daniel.

That afternoon Maddie helped pack a bag for Molly and dressed Small Claude the teddy in one of Barbie's safari outfits. Daniel spent the afternoon painting over the image of Bianca on Molly's bedroom wall, so that Molly could go back to sleeping in her own bed, but Molly was adamant that she still wanted to sleep with Maddie.

'Please, Maddie? You know I don't snore, and your bed smells so nice.'

'Molly – I am not going to allow you to get out of the habit of sleeping in your own bed,' said Daniel with authority. He wiped his paintbrush on a rag and gestured to the wall: Bianca had been magically transformed into Samantha Mumba. 'Look. Bianca's gone now. You've no excuse.'

'When are you going to put Maddie in?'

'There's gratitude for you.'

'I don't mind if Molly wants to sleep in my bed,' said Maddie.

'Thanks, Maddie!' The little girl flung her arms round Maddie's neck and gave her a big hug. 'You're the best governess in the world. Aoife's really jealous. She wants a governess too.'

'I haven't heard you say thank you to me for turning bloody Bianca into Samantha Mumba, either. That took some doing, I can tell you. And if you say anything to Bianca I'll have your guts for garters, sweetie-pie.'

'Thanks, Daddy!' Molly turned and launched herself into her father's unprotesting arms. 'Oh – I can't wait until tomorrow! I know – I'll bring Barbie's picnic tent for Small Claude. Doesn't he look brilliant in his safari outfit, Dad?' She flung herself off her father and started rummaging in one of her toy-boxes. 'What are you going to do next week, Maddie? You'll be dead lonely without me around, I expect.'

'Madeleine's going to be too busy to be lonely, baby.'

'Oh?' Molly turned curious eyes on Maddie. 'What are you going to be doing?'

'She's going to be sitting for me.'

Molly's grimace was eloquent. 'You poor thing, Maddie,' she said. 'You're in for a really boring time.'

*　　*　　*

Molly departed early the next morning in a flurry of excitement. Daniel and Maddie watched Rory's jeep disappear down the street, its wheels sending water slooshing over the gutter. Molly and Aoife were waving wildly from the back seat, and Deirdre was waving rather glumly from the passenger seat.

'Let's hope the weather's better in Paris,' said Daniel, holding the gate open for Maddie. He looked at his watch as she slid past him into the courtyard. 'D'you mind getting changed now, Madeleine? I'd like to get to work as soon as possible. Come on up to the studio when you're ready.'

She twisted her hair. 'Where is your studio?' she asked.

'I'm glad you asked that question. It means you weren't tempted to sneak a look while I was in Paris.' He smiled at her. 'Do you know that one of Marie-France's friends once smuggled a camera into my studio and then showed the photographs she'd taken around the table at dinner parties in Paris? She thought it was a social coup to be able to boast that she'd visited the *atelier* of a famously reclusive painter. Can you believe that people behave like that?'

Maddie *could* believe that people behaved like that. She'd met people like that in her other life, in Dublin. She shuddered when she thought of the name-dropping that had gone on at some of the dinner parties she'd been invited to, and realized rather ruefully that she hadn't been totally innocent of it herself.

'The studio', continued Daniel Lennox as they passed into the house, 'is on the third floor. There's a door that leads to it on the top corridor beside your old bedroom but it's locked and I can't be bothered hunting for the key. You'll have to come the long way round – up the spiral staircase at the end of the passage.' They had reached the divide in the stairs. 'How long are you likely to be?'

'Do you want me to wear make-up?'

'Good God, no.' Then he looked at her and reconsidered. 'Do you have any kohl?'

'I think so.' She'd flung bits and pieces of Shu Uemura and Mac into her cosmetics bag before fleeing Dublin, but now she was unsure about the contents because – apart from the concealer she'd used to camouflage her cuts and bruises – she had worn no make-up at all since arriving in France. In Dublin she wouldn't have dreamed of setting foot outside her apartment without having painted her face.

'Rub a little kohl around your eyes. It'll help give that sleepy look Albaydé has. Jesus! That woman knew what she was doing.' He smiled to himself, and then gave Maddie a look of appraisal. 'Let's see – what else . . . Do you have a comb or something to hold your hair up?'

'Yes.'

'Good. About five minutes, then?' he said, taking the stairs to his apartment two at a time.

'Five minutes,' echoed Maddie.

She continued on up the stairs, thinking how bizarre it all was. Once upon a time Josh would have been smug as hell at the prospect of Maddie having her portrait painted by a shit-hot artist. She imagined him at openings, talking art-speak and making ostentatious reference to the fact that his partner had sat for the famous Daniel Lennox.

Poor Josh! All the blatant posing was a cover up for how insecure at heart he must have been. And all the time she had believed that he was the chief whip in their relationship. How strange to think that she'd spent the past five years of her life living in a gilded cage, blindfolded.

The gown felt like a caress against her skin as she slid it on. She applied a smudge of kohl to both top and bottom eyelids, bundled her hair onto the top of her head in an approximation of the style favoured by Albaydé, and padded back down the stairs on bare feet.

She had never been farther into Daniel Lennox's apartments than the corridor where Molly had her room. All the doors off it were closed this morning, and it was very dim. The only light was the faint glow which filtered through the small stained-glass window at the end of the corridor, where the spiral staircase led up to Daniel's studio.

She climbed the staircase rather awkwardly, holding up the trailing folds of the silk gown, and found herself on a windowless landing. There was only one door to try. She knocked, feeling horrifically self-conscious suddenly.

'Come on in, Madeleine,' came his voice.

She blinked as she stepped into the room and was hit by the powerful smell of linseed oil. The studio was vast and flooded with light which streamed in through a series of massive skylights. It must run the entire length of this wing of the

465

house, she realized, as she looked round with surprised eyes. At least three big rooms must have been knocked into one to create the floorspace, and the walls were covered in an acreage of canvases whose vibrant colours jumped out at her. The unanticipated bombardment of her senses almost made her reel.

Daniel was standing at the far end of the room with his back to her. He had changed into a pair of ripped denims and a T-shirt so paint-stained it looked kaleidoscopic, and he was mixing something in an aluminium can. He turned as she started to move across the floor. 'Very nearly perfect,' he said, running his eyes over her perfunctorily before taking down a postcard reproduction of the Cabanel portrait which was pinned on the wall above a trestle table laden with more aluminium cans. Then he handed her an old Artissimo bag. 'I hope you won't mind if I'm perfectly blunt with you, Madeleine, and ask you to take off the underwear you have on? There's very little more offensive to a painter's eye than visible panty line.' He shot a look at the postcard and then said: 'We're going to need cushions, of course. Excuse me while I get some from the drawing room.'

Maddie waited until he left the room before sliding out of her white cotton pants. She rolled them into a ball and slipped them into the bag Daniel had given her, feeling a bit insecure without them. Then she told herself to wise up. It was considerate of him, she thought, to leave the room so that she wouldn't have to strip off in front of him. Anyway – didn't models sit for painters all the time with no clothes on at all? A glance around the walls of the studio confirmed that. Hell – she herself had posed nude for a photograph not a million years ago. She remembered with some embarrassment that the photograph in question was at this very moment hanging on the wall of Daniel Lennox's bathroom somewhere below.

She wandered around the room, enjoying the feel of the silk as it brushed against her naked body. It felt as cool as the rain she'd stood under two nights ago when Daniel had discovered her on the balcony. He hadn't seemed remotely fazed by the sight of a mad woman prancing around outside his french windows in the middle of an electric storm. He'd just asked her if there was anything to eat in the kitchen and then wished her good night before heading downstairs.

Maddie explored his studio with curious eyes. Landscapes and riverscapes predominated, but there were portraits, too. The one he'd recently finished of Claudine showed the girl standing by a window in Daniel's studio looking pensive and wearing nothing but a string of amber beads. There was a portrait of Molly too, done in thick oils. It has been hung in a prominent place on the studio wall. The little girl was looking un- characteristically serious and was clutching Small Claude on her lap. It was a younger Molly. Maddie estimated that it had been painted when the child was about three or four.

She wondered idly how many thousands of pounds' worth of Daniel Lennox's paintings were hanging on the walls and stacked in corners. His surroundings certainly gave no indication that this was the workplace of a seriously wealthy man. The serried ranks of aluminium cans which contained his paint were old household tins with the labels peeled off. Shelves were coming down with bottles and tubes, spray cans of fixative and paper bags of pigment bearing the name *Sennelier. Paris.* A cardboard box overflowed with rags, and paint-spattered workman's overalls hung from a hook on the back of the door. Pages torn from sketchbooks – most of them displaying views of the Hérault executed in watercolour – were stapled on a notice-board, and a selection of well-worn tools hung from a rack. Some rough-cast sculpture figures – obviously abandoned at a fairly early stage in the execution – huddled together in a corner.

She moved to a shelf and ran her eyes along the bags of pigment, reading the labels out loud and enjoying the sound of the words: 'Titanium White. Monestial Blue, Cobalt Blue. Payne's Grey. Leaf Green, Sea Green. Burnt Umber. Rose Madder, Crimson Lake, Cadmium Red.'

'Vermilion. Permanent Magenta.' It was Daniel's voice. 'Amazing names, aren't they?' He'd come back into the studio and was striding across the floor carrying a pile of rugs and cushions. She recognized the paisley-patterned cashmere throw which Sam had wrapped around her shoulders the other night when Molly had played the piano for them in the library. Daniel threw the exotic bundle down on a low day-bed which was positioned directly under one of the skylights. An easel set up in front of it supported a pristine canvas. He looked her up and down briefly before moving to the trestle table. 'That's better,' he said. 'Come and sit over here. Lose the sash, if you don't mind.' She walked across the floor towards the bed, unknotting the sash from around her waist and taking care to keep the silk wrapped around her as she moved. She glanced towards Daniel, but he wasn't looking at her. He was concentrating on pouring linseed oil into a tin.

'It's a great smell, isn't it?' she said in as conversational tone as she could muster, dropping the sash over the back of a paint-spattered wooden chair and lowering herself onto the bed. She was feeling clumsy and awkward, and she knew that she must look nothing like gorgeous, languid Albaydé.

'Yes, it is. For me it's the smell of bliss. I'm at my happiest when I'm up here, working in my studio.' It was true that Daniel looked relaxed – tranquil, in fact. He strolled towards her and handed her the postcard reproduction of the Cabanel portrait. 'To refresh your memory,' he said. Then he leaned closer and tucked a red oleander blossom into her hair before moving away again.

Maddie studied the postcard, then sat back on

the bed, stretching her legs out along its length and draping her right arm over one of the big Turkish cushions, hoping the tension in her limbs didn't show. *Je me couche, tu te couches, il se couche, elle se couche, nous nous couchons . . .*

'What is she thinking?' asked Daniel suddenly.

'Albaydé?'

'Yes.'

She's thinking about the last time she made love, thought Maddie. But she said: 'Oh – I couldn't hazard a guess,' in a careless kind of voice.

Tendrils of Morning Glory spilled out from a jug on a side table. Daniel helped himself to a length of it and studied her with a critical expression. 'Not bad,' he said. 'Here's your prop.' He took the postcard from her, then laid the trailing stem carefully across her belly. 'We'll need to loosen your hair a little, Madeleine.'

She reached up to do as he suggested, but he pre-empted her by laying his hand over hers. 'Stay as you are, please. I'll take care of the details.' He teased a lock of hair away from the mass she'd piled on her head and let it fall over her shoulder. Then: 'Excuse me,' he said, as he parted her robe and arranged its folds. His hand made fleeting contact with her bare skin as he positioned the silk over her left breast, taking care that the nipple was concealed. To her acute embarrassment she felt her nipple harden. She avoided looking at him as he straightened up and took a step backwards.

He looked down at her and smiled. 'Molly was

470

right. This will be boring. But it just might be worth it when you go back home. You can indulge yourself in one of the most enjoyable forms of narcissism known to man.'

'Oh? What's that?'

'Hanging a portrait of yourself above your bed.'

She laughed. 'I wish.'

'Why the sceptical tone?'

'I couldn't possibly afford it, Daniel. Your work's way out of my reach financially.'

'I'm not asking you to buy it.'

She looked at him in disbelief. 'You'd *give* me the portrait?'

'Yes. You may remember I told you once before that it amuses me to give presents. I don't need any more money.' His gesture took in the paintings all around him. 'I could translate all of this into hard cash tomorrow if I wanted – but what would I do with it? I'd just stay here and go on painting. I imagine you'd get a kick out of owning a portrait of yourself, wouldn't you, Madeleine? Most people seem to. And I'd get a kick out of letting you have it.'

'I couldn't accept it, Daniel.'

'Why not?'

'It's far too generous of you.'

'What a load of crap. How can anyone ever be *too* generous? The spirit of altruism is a splendid thing and should never be undervalued. There are too many people in this world with mean minds and ungenerous souls.'

'Honestly, Daniel—'

'The matter's closed.' He moved to the trestle table and selected a brush from an assortment sticking out of an old paint can. 'Let's get to work,' he said.

*   *   *

Later in the week Bianca's redirected party invite arrived for Maddie in the post. As she made herself comfortable on the day-bed in the studio that morning, she asked Daniel if he intended going.

'I'll have to,' he said darkly. 'She went into a major sulk when I didn't show last year. I'll make my escape early, though. I can't hack occasions like that. Will you go?'

'I think so,' she answered. 'I'm feeling a lot more sociable than when I first arrived in Saint-Géyroux. It might be fun.'

This was the fourth day in a row she'd spent sitting for him, and she was finding the experience nowhere near as boring as he had warned her it would be. Some days they talked, about nothing much. About books they'd read and films they'd seen – nothing earth-shattering, nothing revelatory. The only thing she learned about Daniel was that his star sign was Leo. That didn't surprise her at all. Some days they listened to music – laid-back jazz mostly, with some classical stuff thrown in. He was knowledgeable about music – much more knowledgeable than Josh, who'd boasted continually about his classical CD collection. She cringed when she remembered how he used to drive around Dublin in the summer with the soft top of his Beamer down, Wagner blaring from the speakers of the CD player.

Sometimes – if Daniel was involved in working on some detail of her skin tone or her robe and she didn't need to concern herself about her facial expression – he would allow her to read. She would lose herself in the story and then look up and feel vaguely surprised to find his eyes on her. The expression he wore while he painted was quite unguarded and disturbingly intense. She could almost feel the brush strokes.

He worked every day until quite late in the evening, when he'd join her and Sam around *l'heure bleue* for an aperitif and something to eat on the balcony or on the terrasse outside the kitchen. The fine weather had returned the day after Molly had gone to Paris, and the evenings were balmy once more. Initially she had been puzzled that Daniel could continue working on the portrait without her actually being there in front of him, but he'd told her that a lot of the time it was easier to capture something of the essence of the sitter without having them there physically. 'The expression goes dead after a couple of hours,' he said. 'The eyes glaze over and you can't see the soul behind them any more.'

When Sara had remarked, 'The eyes are the window of the soul' on the evening of Bianca's

473

dinner party, Maddie's very first evening in Saint-Géyroux, she had wanted to cry. Now she found herself smiling as she heard Daniel say: 'Your eyes are looking more serene every day, Madeleine. It's becoming difficult to distinguish which soul is looking out at me – yours or Albaydé's.' He leaned over and poured more red wine into her glass.

'I'm feeling very content. I'm glad you asked me to stay on.'

'So am I,' said Sam, with a meaningful smile. He was peeling a clementine, and the smell mingled with the usual night-time smells of Daniel's garden, making their surroundings seem as exotic as those in the Cabanel painting.

'You might think about staying even longer. The more I work on your portrait, the more detail I want to add. If I'm going to finish it as I'd like to, I could do with more time.'

She couldn't stay longer, even if it meant leaving the portrait unfinished. She'd been here for three weeks now, and she'd really need to start thinking about getting a job soon. She couldn't stay on indefinitely in the South of France drinking good wine and eating good food and lounging around in the sun. She needed to start facing up to things again. 'I don't think I can stay,' she said, with a sense of enormous regret.

'So you're ready for real life?'

She looked at him, taken aback. His ability to tune in to her mindset was uncanny sometimes. 'Yes. I think I am,' she said.

'In that case, maybe I should just try and work harder.'

'Oh, please don't! Not just because of my time constraints. You work too hard as it is, Daniel.'

'He enjoys it,' said Sam. 'I wish I could say the same of my *bosseln*ing at Bianca's. The closer the day of her party gets, the more she wants me to do. I was there till eight o'clock this evening.'

'Isn't it funny?' said Maddie. 'I used to work really hard too, and I thought I enjoyed it. But I didn't, really. I can see that now. I've discovered that I rather enjoy being lazy.' She smiled at them and stretched in her chair.

'Maybe it's Albaydé's influence.'

'You think so?'

Daniel smiled back at her. 'Well, she's got the laziest eyes of almost any woman I know. There's only one physical activity I can imagine her indulging in.'

Maddie took a sip of her wine.

'Here's your clementine, Maddie,' said Sam. 'Peeled and ready to eat. Will I do you some grapes, next?'

'Don't be ridiculous, Sam. Life's too short to peel grapes.'

'All the vamps used to demand that their *beaux* peeled grapes for them. Look at you reclining on that lounger! You look so gorgeous that you deserve to have Nubian slaves feeding you mountains of peeled grapes.'

There was a beat, and then Daniel rose to his

feet. 'Time for my swim,' he said. It was the first time ever that he hadn't politely extended an invitation to Maddie to join him, and for some reason she felt slightly miffed. '*A demain, jeunesse dorée.*' He saluted them with a relaxed hand and then sauntered out through the kitchen.

Maddie actually *would* have loved a swim this evening. Even though it was late, it was still warm on the terrasse, and there was no whisper of a breeze to ruffle the air.

'How's the portrait going?' asked Sam. He had plucked a blossom from a petunia in a container on the windowsill next to him, and was idly rubbing the petals between his long, elegant fingers.

'I don't know. Daniel won't allow me to see it.'

'He never allows people to see their portraits before they're finished. I actually meant how's the *sitting* going?'

'Oh – it's OK,' she said, licking clementine juice from her fingers. 'It's not as boring as I thought it was going to be.'

'That's because Daniel's good company.'

'Yes, he is.'

Sam was studying her closely. 'Have you felt tempted to go to bed with him yet?'

She sat bolt upright. 'No, I haven't, Sam! Jesus – what a question! What on earth makes you think I might be tempted to go to bed with *Daniel*?'

He gave a little shrug. 'Because Bianca says that he's the most sexually charismatic man she's ever met. And she should know. Also, I know for a fact that he sleeps with most of his models.'

'Well, for your information, he has behaved like a gentleman. He's been perfectly charming, and he hasn't laid a finger on me.' That wasn't quite accurate, she thought, as she reminded herself that Daniel was in fact obliged to touch her quite intimately every time he arranged her pose before a sitting. She was playing with the strand of hair that he had coaxed loose for her earlier. 'Anyway, what makes you think I'd jump into bed with Daniel when I haven't jumped into bed with you? You're infinitely more attractive, you know, even though you're only a baby.'

'Jump into bed with me, then.' He slid swiftly off the recliner he'd been lounging on, and was by her side. 'Here,' he said, sliding a grape into her mouth. He followed it with another one, looking directly into her eyes. 'Oh shit,' he murmured. 'I'm doing this all wrong.'

'What do you mean?'

'I forgot to peel them.' She gave a ragged little laugh. He was rubbing the petunia blossom against the skin of her forearm. 'And now you're laughing. Didn't someone once say that if a man can make a woman laugh spontaneously he's half-way towards getting her into bed?'

'Did someone say that?'

'I don't know. I was just chancing my arm. There! You're laughing again.'

'Don't you think it's about time we changed the subject?' she said, suddenly realizing that she didn't much want to change the subject. She was enjoying this.

'Whatever you wish, princess. What do you want to talk about if you won't talk about when exactly you're going to invite me into your bed?' He took her left foot between his hands and gently trailed the petunia blossom along her instep and up to the concave area below her ankle.

'God, you're persistent, Sam.'

'Well – you know what they say?'

'Persistence pays off?' She smiled into his eyes.

'Amen to that, I say.'

Sam pushed the skirt of her dress up over her thighs. She could feel the light touch of the flower on the back of her knee, and then again on the inside of her thigh as it travelled higher. Maddie felt almost as languid as Albaydé looked. It wouldn't hurt to play with him, just a little. 'What do you think I should wear to Bianca's party, Sam?'

'Jesus, Maddie! That satin dress, for sure.' She laughed low in her throat. She hadn't laughed like that for weeks. Months. She could feel Sam's fingers exploring the very top of her inside thigh. The heel of his palm was pressed hard against her clitoris. 'Stop laughing like that,' he said. 'It's doing things to me.' It was doing things to her, too. She'd better say good night. She swung her legs off the recliner just as his phone rang. He picked it up. 'Oh. Florence. Ça va?'

She could see his mouth soundlessly form the word *merde*.

478

'Good night, Sam. I'll see you tomorrow,' she said, getting to her feet and smiling at his pleading expression.

He put his hand over the mouthpiece. 'I'll be stuck at Bianca's until late – she's got a million last-minute things she needs doing. Will I see you at the party?'

She nodded. Then she plucked a petunia blossom and wandered through the kitchen into the hall, rubbing the waxy petals between her fingers. There was something incredibly sensual about the feel of it. It reminded her of the silk of Albaydé's robe. She trailed the petunia flower across the bare skin of her neck, then held it to her nose and inhaled its scent. It smelt vaguely pungent.

She didn't see Daniel standing at the fork of the stairs until she nearly collided with him. He had been leaning against the newel post, looking down at her. She was momentarily stuck for words, and then he spoke. 'You had a very pensive look about you just then, Madeleine. Your dreams will be sweet tonight, I don't doubt. Sleep well.' Then he continued down the staircase and the door to the swimming pool swung shut behind him.

*   *   *

Maddie climbed the stairs to her bedroom with a sonnet simmering in her head. It had been taking shape all day, since she'd read her horoscope in a magazine Deirdre had lent her. The only aspect of the poem that had been posing problems had been the all-important last two lines. Now she thought she had them. She took her notebook and pen to bed with her, and in very little time she'd scribbled the following:

My horoscope's too silly. It says here
A blond man's keen. Perhaps it's darling Sam?
'*Water's significant.*' Touché! I swam
Yesterday and this morning too. It's clear
The planets have got something right. Three
   cheers
For stellar forecasts! Do I give a damn?
Quite frankly, no. I *think*, therefore I am:
I am no plaything of some batty seer.

Water's significant. It's helped ease my pain.
The baths I took after the hellish rape,
The waters of the Hérault, teeming rain,
The copious tears I've shed since my escape.
Tonight the starshine bathes a motley trio.
Young Aries. Pisces. And an ageing Leo.

When Maddie went shopping early the next morning she went to the *charcuterie*, the *caveaux* and the *pâtisserie*. Then she went to a shop in the village she had never before had occasion to visit. She went to the local pharmacy.

Chapter Eighteen

She didn't spend as long as usual sitting for Daniel the next day. She had too many preparations to make.

Bianca's birthday party was due to start at six o'clock. At around five she ran a bath, adding a generous amount of the bath oil she'd picked up in the pharmacy along with her other purchases. Then she poured herself a glass of wine and soaked for a while, realizing as she lay in the warm water that she hadn't had such a sybaritic bath since the night of Josh's birthday. She had discovered some days ago that she could think of that night quite dispassionately now, as if it had happened to someone else. Someone had once written words that described exactly how she felt about Josh and the rape and her old life in Dublin. She recalled those words again as she sipped her wine. *The past is another country.* How did the rest of it go? It annoyed her that she couldn't remember. *The past is another country . . . They do things differently there.* That was it. She knew it wouldn't be long now before she would have to go back, re-enter that past. But tonight she planned to do something that she hoped would make the journey easier for her.

When she had soaked for half an hour she showered and shampooed her hair and rubbed herself with a body lotion that smelt vaguely of petunia. She applied a little very discreet make-up and then opened the wardrobe door and took out the cheongsam. She hesitated before slipping it over her head. If she wore this dress tonight there would be no going back. It was a statement of intent.

The sea-green satin accentuated every curve of her body. She had certainly filled out since she last wore it. She wondered why she didn't care. Josh would have been horrified. Her ass was rounder, and her breasts, while far from page three dimensions, strained against the silk-embroidered buttons. When she looked down she could see the convex line of a belly that had once been concave. There was a word to describe how she looked. What was it, exactly? Feminine? No. That was way too weak an adjective. Womanly. She recalled how that had seemed to her to be the adjective that best described how Maeve looked in her Sarah Lennox portrait. What else had struck her that evening of the exhibition opening at the Demeter Gallery? The photographic image of her cousin floated in front of her mind's eye – or was it her own image she saw emerging from the sea? Maeve had looked as if she'd just made love, that's what she'd thought – *and was already looking forward to making love again.*

Maddie regarded herself in the mirror with calm, almost solemn eyes before slipping the condoms she'd bought that morning into the little matching satin purse that Maeve had pinned to the gown. Then she walked downstairs and out through the lush green courtyard.

Bluesy saxophone music floated from the open window of Daniel's studio three floors above. She looked up, but there was no sign of him. He was expecting a phone call from the director of his gallery in Paris, and had told her not to bother waiting for him.

The walk to Bianca's took her five minutes. She was the focus of admiring eyes as she walked up the long main street, and there was a fracas of compliments from the elderly men playing *boules* in the square. She smiled at everyone she passed, and tucked one of the white gardenias she'd bought for Bianca behind a toddler's ear.

Bianca's door was opened by the voluptuous Claudine. She widened her eyes when she saw Maddie, and gave little 'oohs' of approval. Maddie smiled back, looking at the girl with new knowledge. She remembered the nude painting of Claudine that she'd seen in Daniel's studio, and Sam's words of the previous night came back to her. *I know for a fact that he sleeps with most of his models* . . . Had Daniel added Claudine's name to the list of those he'd bedded?

Although it was barely half-past six, Bianca's party was already buzzing. The birthday girl met her with a flurry of kisses, accepting the white gardenias graciously and informing Maddie with a genuine smile that she'd put on weight since she last saw her. Bianca ordered her to find some champagne at once, and then tore herself away to greet more arrivals.

Maddie negotiated the crowd of chattering guests with a glass in her hand, pausing only briefly to exchange pleasantries with the few individuals she knew, aware as she did so that her eyes were roaming the crowd. She hated that awful habit some people had of looking over your shoulder hoping to find another person more amusing to talk to, and could barely tolerate it when people did it to her, but for her plan to work tonight she needed to find Sam Newman, and she needed to find him urgently. She was uncomfortably aware that she was beginning to get cold feet.

The girl she often saw by the river – the one called Florence who'd phoned him last night – drifted by, looking like a sleek, snooty cat and ignoring her ostentatiously. Maddie ignored her back and made her way through the dining room out onto a balcony which overlooked the garden, exchanging her empty glass of champagne for a fresh one of Dutch courage.

Sam was in the garden. She heard his easy laugh before she saw him. He was standing next to a pretty blond girl she didn't know, talking with relaxed intimacy. She studied him – the wonderful, lazy, taken-for-granted youthfulness of him – and she suddenly felt old beyond her years. Josh O'Regan had stolen her youth. He'd appropriated it for himself, and then he'd spat on it and ground it under his foot. She wanted some of it back.

Sam looked up, and as she read the expression on his face she felt her lips curve in a slow smile. He turned immediately to make his excuses to the petite blonde, but before he could race up the steps of the balcony towards her she experienced the most peculiar sensation. It was the feeling she sometimes had when she was sitting for Daniel – the feeling she got when she looked up and found his eyes on her. She knew that somewhere in the party he was standing watching her.

He was behind her.

'You look elegant tonight, Madeleine,' he said as she turned to him. He wasn't smiling, and neither was she. She didn't acknowledge the compliment because she couldn't. She couldn't say anything at all. Something incendiary was happening inside her, and in a blinding flash she was certain of only one thing in her life. She didn't want Sam Newman. She wanted Daniel Lennox. She wanted him with every fibre of her being, and she knew by the look in his eyes that the desire was reciprocal. Something intense and unspoken passed between them before Bianca materialized as if in a dream, and smilingly drew him away from her. Then she felt Sam's hand on her arm. 'I could prostrate myself in front of you,' he said. 'You're no princess tonight. You're a goddess.' He breathed her in. 'And – oh, wow – you smell of petunia!' And as she turned uncomprehending eyes on him, he gave her the sweetest, most disarming smile she had ever received.

She went through hell at that party. She saw little of Daniel, but when their hands accidentally brushed as they simultaneously went to lift champagne glasses from the tray being circulated by Claudine, she flinched as if she had been burned. He apologized immediately, provoking a curious look from Bianca, who was obviously determined not to let him leave her side all evening. From then on they avoided each other assiduously.

Sam danced attendance on her, bringing Maddie food which she couldn't eat, and champagne which she drank too fast. He was puzzled by her reluctance to get involved in their usual silly banter, and looked hurt when she kept engaging other people in conversation. She didn't want to be alone with him – she wouldn't be able to bear the bewildered look in his blue eyes when she told him that she would never, ever go to bed with him. She wanted to cry when she thought of the way she'd led him on. After tonight Sam Newman wouldn't be calling her princess or goddess any more. He'd be calling her a cock-teasing bitch from hell, and she wouldn't blame him.

She didn't know how much hazy time had passed before she became aware that Daniel didn't seem to be anywhere in evidence. She tried to sound casual as she asked Claudine if she'd seen Monsieur Lennox around, and didn't quite know what to feel when the girl told her that Monsieur Lennox had gone home about an hour ago. Her mind whirled as she cast around for what to do next. Sam had gone off to chat up the blond girl she'd seen him with earlier, and Maddie knew it was because he was upset and confused by her behaviour, and was trying in vain to make her jealous. It seemed ironic that only yesterday he might have succeeded. She stood there at a loss, twisting her hair. Then she turned and ran down the stairs to the hall.

She could hear the beating of her own heart as she let herself out through the front door of Bianca's house and walked down the garden path to the wrought-iron gate that led to the village square. Her nails were digging hard into the palms of her hands. Could she do this thing? Could she initiate proceedings? Could she see it through, or would she back off at the last moment? Her thoughts inevitably veered towards the last time she had had sex. It had hurt then. Would it hurt again? Would her body tense up so that the act would become impossible? She'd read of such cases. But that wasn't the worst thing that could happen – that could be overcome. Maddie knew that the worst thing that could happen to her would involve her demons. Would they come back to her? Would they reclaim her? Or was this a way of banishing them for ever? She shook her head, as if physically trying to cast them out. No, no, no – she didn't want to think of them. She'd think of something else.

Hell. *How* could she do it? How could she let Daniel know that she wanted him to take her to bed? She remembered the first time she'd met him, in her other life in Dublin, and how prickly she'd been with him then. She thought of all the times she'd frozen him out, and of all the times she'd sought out Sam's company in preference to his. She knew there could be nothing subtle about her seduction of Daniel Lennox. She'd wasted too much time already. She would simply have to be brazen.

She moved through the deserted streets of the village like a sleepwalker, but Madeleine Godard knew where she was going. She reached the heavy gates and passed through them into the courtyard, up the steps and into the cavernous entrance hall. She didn't even pause on the threshold when she pushed open the door to the staircase that would take her down to Daniel's swimming pool.

He was just finishing a lap. He stopped when he reached the shallow end and shook the wet hair back from his face, sending droplets spinning. They glittered in the beam of the spotlight that hit him from above. He lifted a hand and dashed the water from his face, and, as he did so, Maddie turned the dimmer switch lower. Daniel paused, one hand still on his jaw, and looked up at where she stood at the top of the stairs. He remained completely still as she descended the steps. She took them slowly, with one hand on the wall for support and with a very careful, measured tread. She didn't want to look where she was placing her feet because she didn't want to lose eye contact with him for a second. At the side of the pool she stood motionless for a moment or two. In the water, Daniel too was motionless. They were frozen, as if in eternity, as if in a painting. Then Maddie took a deep breath, and did the bravest thing she had ever done in her life. She slid out of the sea-green satin to show him that she was naked underneath.

She heard him suck in his breath, and she smiled at him. The smile felt shaky.

'For me?' he asked uncertainly, as if unable to believe that this was really happening.

'For you,' she said.

The smile of admiration he sent her made her want to melt, and suddenly this was the most natural, glorious thing in the world to be doing. She slid easily into the silken water of the deep end of the pool and swam its length with slow, strong strokes until she reached him and they fused. Winding her legs around his waist and her arms around his neck, she kissed him very deeply and very languorously. His mouth tasted faintly and deliciously of wine and French cigarettes. He supported her hips with one hand and let the other explore her until she orgasmed once, then twice. 'You're beautiful,' he said in her ear as he felt her surge the second time. 'You know what you are, Madeleine? You're like a sea-cat.'

'A sea-cat?' she murmured after a while, feeling blissfully confused. 'Isn't a sea-cat some kind of ferry?' Her voice sounded as if it was coming from a long way away.

'Not the kind I'm thinking about. A sea-cat is a current that can draw even the strongest swimmer out to sea.'

'Come inside me, then, Daniel,' she said, looking down and tracing the scar on his belly with a finger.

'Not without a condom.' He licked her neck.

'Please.' She licked his neck back. She was aching with want for him.

'You're pushing me to the limit, Madeleine.' He had taken her earlobe between his teeth and was circling it with the tip of his tongue. 'But I like to think that I'm responsible enough not to be seduced without being sure that there's a packet of Durex within arm's reach.'

'There is,' she said in a smallish voice. She hauled herself out of the pool and moved on wobbly legs to where she'd dropped her dress, dripping water all over the green satin. She fumbled with the catch on the silk purse, and finally managed to extract the condom she'd intended for Sam. Then she returned to where Daniel was waiting for her. 'I think I'm suffering from narcosis,' she murmured, as she lowered herself back into the water and pulled open the sachet. 'You know what I mean? That state known as rapture of the deep. Divers get it when they venture out of their depth.'

He lifted himself out of the pool as she pulled open the sachet. 'How do you feel, exactly, Madeleine?' he said. 'Tell me.' Maddie took the satiny rubber between her fingers, rolled it slowly over his cock, then invited him to enter her.

'Euphoric. Like I've just smoked the most delicious hash. Oh! They say that when narcosis hits you, your ability to make rational decisions is impaired. Oh, God – Daniel! This has to be the most irrational, rational thing I've ever done in my life. Oh, dear Jesus!' Maddie let out a sigh that seemed to go on for ever.

Below them Marie-France Lennox looked on with amused, anthracite eyes as her ex-husband and Madeleine Godard made blissful, exquisite, rapturous love in the mosaic temple he'd built for her ten years earlier.

*   *   *

The next morning when her dreams receded she found herself lying in Daniel's bed, feeling gorgeously blurred at the edges. She looked at his face as he slept on beside her until she could no longer resist the temptation to coax him awake with her hand. Then she mounted him and rode him, letting him feed on her breasts and wishing there was more of her to give him.

Afterwards he brought her breakfast and made her laugh by insisting that she eat figs for him.

'Daniel?' she said, as she stirred cream into her coffee.

'Yes, Albaydé?' He was lying back against a mountain of pillows, leafing through one of the glossy art books that were piled up beside his bed.

'Remember Bianca mentioned that you'd hung Sara's photograph of me on your bathroom wall?'

'Yeah?'

'Well, when I went in there for a pee last night I couldn't see it.'

'That's because I took it down and put it away in a cupboard.'

'Oh.' She was surprised to find that she felt incredibly disappointed. 'Why did you do that?'

'Because I could tell that you weren't comfortable with the idea of me keeping a photograph of you with no clothes on on my bathroom wall, and I knew it would be the first thing you'd see if you ever had to visit my bathroom while you were sitting for me.'

'Oh!' She gave him a delighted smile. 'Aren't you considerate?'

'Yes, I am. It was a desperately difficult thing for me to do, as you can imagine. I kept wanting to go to the cupboard where I'd stashed it to sneak a look.'

'You can put it back up now, if you like.'

'Thanks. I will. Christ – Brit Art's a pile of shite. Literally, sometimes.' He flung the book aside with a disdainful gesture. 'Look at you,' he said. 'Have another fig at once.'

'No,' she said, rolling over on to her tummy and wriggling her toes. 'I'll be farting all morning if I eat any more figs.'

'Ah. Then maybe figs aren't such a good idea. I'll need you to keep especially still for this sitting. Emphatically no farting today.'

She took a sip of her coffee and smiled at him over the rim. 'Why today especially?'

'I want to paint your eyes today,' he said, looking back at her with an expression that made her want to lean over and never stop kissing him. 'I think I'll have to make love to you again first, though,' he added contemplatively. 'Put that coffee cup down and come over here at once, Madeleine Godard.'

Madeleine had never felt more obliging.

*   *   *

When they eventually made it to the studio, much later than usual, they both had to work very hard to keep their minds on the job in hand. Her body felt as if an electric eel was brushing against her skin every time he touched her. She shuddered and closed her eyes when he trailed the Morning Glory across her belly, and when he draped Albaydé's robe over her bare breasts she opened her eyes again and looked at him beseechingly.

'Stop it, Madeleine,' he reproved her, kissing

her lightly. 'We're here to work. And I couldn't make love to you again just yet. I'm older than you are, remember? I need breathing space, unfortunately. Now give me that look again from a safe distance,' he said, moving away from her and picking up his brush. 'Look at me with Albaydé's eyes. Do you know what she's thinking yet?'

'Yes. I do.'

'What is she thinking?'

'She's thinking about the last time she made love.'

'And she's looking forward to making love again?'

'Absolutely,' said Maddie.

She held the pose for as long as she could while he worked in silence. Beethoven's Seventh was playing on the CD player – the slow, sensual movement – and the smell of petunia and oleander mingled with the all-pervasive linseed oil. It was hot again, and the electric fan did little to move the air around.

After a while he could sense that she had had enough – even though she felt blissfully relaxed. He pulled a bottle of Volvic from the fridge and took a long swig from it, before flopping down beside her on the cushions. 'That's better,' he said, as the light breeze from the fan hit him. He handed her the bottle and she drank thirstily. Then he added: 'You can uncover yourself now. And let me look at you.' He parted the robe and slid it down from her shoulders. Then he laughed.

'It's ironic, that. I usually say exactly the opposite to my models.'

'What do you mean?'

'I usually tell them they can cover themselves when they take a break.'

She didn't want to think about his other models. She imagined that most of them didn't bother to cover themselves when he told them to, anyway. 'When will you be finished on the portrait, Daniel?' she asked, changing the subject.

'I'm not sure. It could take me another four or five days.' He took another swig from the bottle. 'Have you thought about staying on for a while?'

She could almost have cried with relief. 'Yes. I think I can manage it,' she replied. There was no harm – was there? – in postponing real life for a while longer. 'I'd better make some phone calls, though. I'm going to have to start putting out feelers for a new job in Dublin.' The prospect of making those phone calls filled her with dread.

There was silence between them for a while. He had draped an arm over her shoulder and was idly rubbing his finger against her nipple, making it grow under his touch. She rested her head on his shoulder.

'Dublin,' he said. 'There's going to be an exhibition of my new stuff there in a couple of months' time. I'll have to travel over for meetings with the gallery people.'

Once again she could barely stem the sense of

relief she felt when she knew that she might see him again.

'How do you feel about going back, Madeleine?'

He'd done it again. Tuned into her mindset. 'I'm not sure what you mean,' she said. She could hardly bring herself to hope. Was he going to ask her to stay on here with him in Saint-Géyroux? What would she say if he did? Would 'Oh – yes please!' make her look too keen? It would have to do. It was the only response she could think of.

'You were running away from something when you came here, weren't you?' he asked.

She was very still. He had stopped playing with her nipple and was stroking the back of her neck instead. 'Yes, I was,' she said.

'Something or someone?' His voice was careful.

'Someone.'

'Your ex?'

'Yes.'

'What did he do to you?'

'He beat me up and then he raped me.'

Daniel said nothing. He just sucked in his breath, then released it in a long sigh. He laid his hand on her head in a gesture that was infinitely tender, but she saw the muscles in his neck go stiff. 'I suspected from the bruises that you'd been beaten, but I didn't like to conjecture any further than that. You poor sweetheart – oh, poor injured mavourneen.' He began to stroke her hair. 'No wonder you needed to escape.'

'I really had no choice. He had started to stalk me. I was in shreds.' She lifted her face from his shoulder so that she could look at him. Then she smiled, leaned forward and kissed him on the cheek. He smiled back, but the expression in his eyes told her that he was in agony for her. 'I'm so much better, now, Daniel. I wouldn't have done what I did last night if I wasn't. It was the right thing to do. Thank you for being such a considerate lover.' She settled her head back down on his shoulder. 'And thank you for giving me the most delicious orgasms I've ever had in my life.'

'There's such a thing as quid pro quo, you know. The pleasure wasn't entirely yours.' He was stroking her hair very gently with a finger. When he spoke again there was no smile in his voice. 'Was your partner that geezer who came to claim you at Sara's opening?'

'Yes. That was Josh.'

'He had cruel eyes,' said Daniel.

'Yes – I suppose he had,' she replied. 'But he did look after me, you know, Daniel. For more than five years. I was very confused after my parents died. I felt emotionally bonsai'd, if you know what I mean.'

He nodded.

'The night he raped me I grew up.'

Daniel took her face between his hands. 'Let's not do any more work today,' he said, stroking her cheek. 'We should be celebrating the discovery of our outstanding physical synergy. Let me take you into Montpellier and buy you dinner somewhere classy.'

'I've nothing to wear to a classy joint, Daniel.'

'Jesus. Women. Marie-France never bothered to learn any language other than her native French, but she could say "I've nothing to wear" in ancient Egyptian if necessary. What's wrong with that green thing you had on last night? That was pretty special.'

'You might recall that it's lying in a crumpled heap by the side of your swimming pool. Hanging my clothes up before I went to bed last night wasn't high on my list of priorities.'

'Stick on that old pink one, then, for the time being. I love the way it billows around your legs when you sit astride my Harley.'

She laughed. 'You are an incorrigible satyr, Lennox.'

'Yes, I am,' he said happily.

'And while that pink dress may look sexy at ninety miles an hour, I wouldn't describe it as classy.'

'You can change out of it in Montpellier. I'm going to buy you something gorgeous to wear in Marie-France's favourite boutique. Whatever else about that woman, she knew how to dress, that's for sure. She even looked chic when she was sticking a kitchen knife into me.'

She wasn't sure she liked the idea of Daniel buying clothes for her.

'Don't be daft, Daniel. Anyway, the shops will be shutting soon.'

'I'll phone to say I'm on my way. They'll know it's worth their while staying open for me.'

'I can't let you buy me a dress, Daniel.'

'Why not? I'm being "too generous" again, am I? Don't be half-witted, Madeleine. If the famous reclusive painter is going to be seen in public with a doxy on his arm, that doxy had better look pretty damn special. And although you wear pink silk beautifully, my dear – especially when it's clinging to you in a downpour on a balcony – I think it might be interesting to see if we can find you something as elegant as that green Chinese thing you wore to seduce me, OK?'

'I didn't wear it to seduce you,' she said indignantly.

'I know you didn't, Madeleine. You wore it to seduce Sam Newman.'

She coloured. 'How did you know that?'

'It's hard to keep secrets from artists. I can see your mind working as I paint you.' He unleashed a lethal, leonine smile. 'Now get your kit on before I decide to make you come all over again.'

*   *   *

As they drove through the village with Maddie's brown legs on display under the fluttering pale pink silk, they passed Sam heading in the direction of the pont du Diable with a girl sitting in the passenger seat of the deux-chevaux. It was the little blonde he'd been chatting up last night at Bianca's party. On her way up to her room to fetch Albaydé's gown that morning, Maddie had passed Sam's bedroom and had heard a girl's light voice coming from behind his closed door. Now their eyes met fleetingly as they headed in opposite directions, and both of them had the decency to flash each other extremely guilty smiles.

In Montpellier Daniel parked the Harley in an area full of horrifyingly expensive-looking shops. 'You will let me choose the dress, Daniel, won't you?' Maddie said as they walked through the streets. She was unpleasantly reminded of the way Josh had always had the final word on her clothes any time they'd gone shopping together.

'What on earth are you talking about? Of course you can choose it.'

'But it's your money I'm spending.'

'It may be my money, but you're the one who's going to be wearing the damn thing. You've got to feel comfortable in it. And don't dare look at the price tag.'

'Why not?'

'A: because it's extremely bad manners, and B: because the price will frighten you so much that out of misguided consideration for me, you'll pretend that your outfit of choice is the cheapest one in the shop. And that means you'll wear it because you feel you have to, not because you want to. And if you don't enjoy wearing it, Madeleine, I won't enjoy watching you wear it.' He slung an arm around her shoulder. 'There's nothing worse than watching a woman wearing clothes she thinks look wonderful on her, but are actually way off the mark. I'll never forget the first time I saw you. You had on some kind of tailored black thing, and you looked as if you had a poker stuck up your bum.'

Maddie laughed. 'Yeah – I remember that too. And you're right. I didn't feel comfortable.' She slid her hand into the back pocket of his jeans. 'You were terribly rude to me that time, Daniel.'

'I was tired, I was in a bad mood, and I fancied the ass off you.'

'Did you? You had a peculiar way of showing it. I didn't fancy you at all. I thought you were a complete pig.'

'I know you did.' He looked sideways at her. 'You see, Madeleine, I couldn't reconcile myself to the fact that I found some smart copywriter bitch so fiendishly fucking attractive. The realization that the sentiment was plainly unreciprocated was what spurred me to be rude to you.' He grabbed her suddenly and kissed her on the mouth in full view of the people passing by.

'Daniel!' she protested unconvincingly. 'We're in public, remember?'

'Don't be thick, Madeleine. When you're in France and you're lovers this kind of behaviour's *de rigueur*, for Christ's sake!'

This time she kissed him back.

They finally arrived at a little shop whose

ambience murmured exclusivity, and whose female staff were vociferous in their delight at seeing Monsieur Lennox again. They scolded him for not having come near them for so long, and they were clearly intrigued by his mysterious new companion, though they tried hard not to show it. There was a faint smell of incense in the air.

The clothes hanging on the racks were exquisite. Maddie had never seen such a magical array of dresses. There were gossamer-light gowns trimmed with lace and delicate beading, there were wonderfully sensuous gowns constructed from yards of jewel-coloured devoré velvet, there were amazing bias-cut silks scattered with hand-painted roses, there were sequins and feathers and embroidered buttons, and even the humblest garment in the shop – a little crêpe de Chine bustier trimmed with scraps of velvet and marabou – made her want to rub her face against it like a cat.

She finally decided on an eau-de-nil dress in silk chiffon. It had a wonderful, crumpled look about it, and was appliquéd on the bodice with shimmering sequined flowers. Triple layers of silk floated down to rest just above her ankles. An abalone shell choker was produced, along with a pair of green silk pumps so light that she still felt barefoot when she put them on.

She enjoyed seeing Daniel's reaction when she emerged from the changing room. He didn't go into over-the-top panegyrics the way Sam would have done, or shake his head dismissively as Josh would most certainly have done. He just sent her that same heart-stopping smile of approval that he'd given her the first time he'd seen her naked.

The *vendeuses* prattled away as they packed her old pink silk frock and her sandals into a glossy carrier bag, telling her that she'd made an excellent choice. They were obviously also highly satisfied at the amount of money that had changed hands. As the inanely smiling couple made their farewells, the *vendeuses* warned Daniel that he wasn't to leave it so long before coming back again. He kissed their hands – to their manifest delight – and assured them he'd be back soon. Maddie's heart skipped a beat. Don't be daft, she told herself. He's just saying that to keep them happy. It's not as if he's going to be dashing in and out of Montpellier every other day buying frocks for you, Madeleine Godard.

She felt as if she was floating when they left the shop. The pale green chiffon caught in a light breeze that made it drift around her legs. 'I'd love to do a twirl,' she confessed to Daniel. 'I'd love to feel all this stuff billowing out around me.'

'Do it, then. I'd love to see it billowing out all around you too, especially since I know you have particularly pretty knickers on.'

'I can't do that, Daniel. It wouldn't be fair.'

'On whom?'

'On all these bad-tempered-looking, overheated commuters. It would look as if I was showing off.'

'Showing off?'

'Yes. Showing off how happy I am.' They had emerged onto the Place de la Comédie, and the square was full of people on their way to buses and trains. Everyone they passed looked sweaty and bad-tempered, striding out with cross self-importance or scuttling along miserably. Beeping mobilettes navigated the crowd like angry insects. The only other person on the square who looked genuinely happy was a roller-blader who had hooked onto the back of the little tourist train full of sightseers and was sailing blithely along in its wake. 'Nobody has any right to feel as blissed out as I do right now.'

'Are you going by the same rule that decrees that people shouldn't be too generous? Tell me – what sub-imbecile came out with that utterly fatuous line – how does it go? "A woman can't be too rich or too thin?" It should be changed to "A woman can't be too happy or too generous." Anyway, I think the sight of your swirling skirts would probably cheer all these stressed-out buggers up considerably, Madeleine. Go on – do it.'

'No. I'll do it for you later in the privacy of your bedroom.'

'Is that a promise?'

'It's a promise.'

'Good. I'll look forward to that.' He gave her that smile again.

'By the way, Daniel,' she said, after they had walked some distance in contented silence.

'Your bedroom won't be that private any more after tonight. Don't forget Molly's coming home tomorrow.'

'That doesn't mean we'll have to discontinue our liaison, does it? Unless you want to, that is?' He looked at her and raised an interrogative eyebrow.

'Oh – no!' She was almost embarrassed by how hastily she'd replied.

'Good. I rather hoped you'd say that. It just means that we'll have to be a little more discreet about the way we conduct ourselves, that's all. Kiss me again, please.' He pulled her closer to him.

'This is hardly what I'd call discreet behaviour.'

'I don't care about what people think, Madeleine,' he said. They had turned into one of the laneways off the square. He backed her up against a narrow gate, leaned his hands on either side of her, then lowered his mouth to hers and drank her in. When he eventually broke the kiss her head was spinning.

'But I care about what Molly thinks, Daniel,' she continued, after she'd regained a degree of equilibrium.

'And so do I.' He considered for a moment or two. 'OK. For the meantime what I suggest is this. You move back into the room you slept in when you first arrived – the one at the top of the house. I can visit you there after Molly's gone to sleep. I'll use the door in my studio – the one that accesses the top corridor – and I'll leave the same way before she wakes in the mornings. That way I'll be less likely to disturb her.'

Maddie felt bereft at the prospect of not being able to spend the whole night in her lover's arms. She was also intrigued as to what he meant by 'for the meantime', but didn't dare ask. 'I thought you'd no key for that door, Daniel,' she reminded him.

'I'll turn the studio upside down to find it. I've an incentive now,' he said.

*   *   *

The restaurant they dined in had been established at the turn of the century, Daniel told her. It was smallish, L-shaped and rather dim. The only natural light came through high, horizontal windows, but each of the tables had a lamp with a leaded-glass pendant set into the wall above it. The dining tables were of dark stained oak, as were the high-backed chairs, and each table was covered with an embroidered linen runner on which arrangements of dried gypsophila had been placed in pewter bowls. The ambience was one of old-world discretion.

Afterwards, Maddie could hardly remember what the food had tasted like, although she knew it was the most delicious meal she'd ever had. She'd had mussels to start, followed by wood pigeon with button onions and Lyonnaise potatoes. Daniel had had fish soup, and *bou lin blanc* with onion gravy. Maddie didn't dare meet his eyes when their main courses were set in front of them with a courteous: 'Bon appetit, Madame. Bon appetit, Monsieur Lennox.' Daniel's *boudin* was the most phallic looking thing she'd ever seen. 'What's wrong Madeleine?' he'd asked with an amused smile when he saw her shoulders start to shake. Then he'd looked down at the sausage on his plate. 'Remind you of anyone?' he'd asked.

'I'm sorry,' she managed finally, wiping tears of laughter away from her eyes. 'I don't know what's got into me. I'm not normally this juvenile.'

'I told you once before – juvenile people have more fun.'

The rest of the evening passed in a rosy haze. She drank most of the wine because he was driving, and ended up feeling very giddy. Fortunately, Daniel seemed to find even her most infantile jokes amusing. She told him the one about the squirrel who got locked out of his tree, and the one about the interrupting cow. After she had scoffed a small mountain of profiteroles with chocolate sauce she had an amaretto with her coffee while he stuck to a double espresso.

Maddie glided out of the restaurant on Daniel's arm, flashing radiant smiles at the staff as she went. She felt as if she hadn't stopped smiling all evening. It was starting to get dark, and a chill had crept into the air. Daniel wrapped his jacket around her as they made their way unhurriedly back to the Harley.

The road between Montpellier and Saint-Géyroux unwound like a ribbon under the wheels of the machine. This time Maddie didn't sit pressed against the backrest. She leaned forward and eeled her arms around her lover's waist, loving the feel of his cotton shirt against her breasts as he drove. The skirts of her gossamer gown streamed out behind her like a pennant.

There were few people on the streets when the Harley purred into the village. They turned into the rue du Jujubier and dismounted at the side gate. Maddie waited for Daniel to produce a key, but he just pushed the gate open with a foot. 'Yikes,' she said. 'Did you forget to lock it?'

'I often forget. It's not a problem. People in the village leave their doors open all the time.' He glanced back down the street. 'Look – there's Pilot off on the skite. There'll be interesting-looking cross-breeds up for grabs soon. He's been in hot pursuit of Mme Poiret's poodle for the past week.' Maddie saw a fluffy white dog disappearing round the corner of the rue des Artistes with Pilot loping determinedly at its heels. 'I notice the Poiret girl has changed the colour of the bulb in her bedroom,' he added, as he manoeuvred the bike through the gate, taking a last look up the street as he did so.

'Is that significant?' Maddie followed the direction of his gaze.

'Yes. It's a signal to her boyfriend that the coast is clear. Joel Renard used to hang around under her window for months making little cooing noises until Mme Poiret decided she'd had enough and threw a bucket of water over him one night. That's when the devious child introduced the coded light-bulb system.' He shut the gate behind them, took the key from his pocket, and locked it.

'How do you know that, Daniel?' she asked. 'I'd never have thought you'd take much interest in the courtship rituals of your neighbours.'

'I don't. She told me one day.'

Maddie felt an irrational stab of jealousy. 'Has she sat for you?' she enquired casually.

'No.'

She tried not to show her relief. 'So how come you know such intimate details about her love life?'

'She told me about it in the local bar one night. She works there.'

'And she confided this in you?'

'Yes. Don't ask me why.'

'Don't you think you're being a little naïve, Daniel?'

'What do you mean?'

'Are you sure it wasn't just a subtle way of letting you know she was interested?'

'Don't ask me. I've never been able to understand the machinations of the female mind.' She gave him a sceptical look. They were strolling up the garden towards the open kitchen door. The sky was a wonderful inky blue – the same dark blue as the cover of a Gitanes packet – and there was a cicada concerto playing. 'I can't say I blame Joel,' he continued, looking at her sideways. 'She's pretty bloody gorgeous, that girl. Maybe I should get around to painting her soon, before the first bloom of youth is gone. What do you think, Madeleine?'

'I think she's rather ordinary looking, actually,' she retorted, with a snooty shrug of her shoulders. She tripped as she crossed the threshold into the kitchen.

He laughed, and put out a hand to steady her. Then abruptly he swung her round and kissed her very hard indeed until she thawed. 'Maybe you're right,' he said. 'Maybe the next portrait I do should be another one of you. With no clothes on at all.'

'That might be a problem, Daniel,' she said.

'Don't you like the idea?'

'I love it. I just don't know how much actual work you'd get done.'

He laughed again and took her by the hand. 'Come on,' he said. 'I could do with a nightcap after showing such admirable restraint in that restaurant. We'll have a brandy in the billiard room.'

He pulled her into the hall and took the stairs with his usual two-at-a-time stride so that she was forced to run a little to keep up with him. In the billiard room the answering machine light was flashing three times. Daniel pressed playback and went over to the sideboard to pour their drinks while Maddie drifted out onto the balcony. The first message was from Molly to say that she'd had a 'blinding' holiday but that she missed them both and was looking forward to seeing them tomorrow. The second message was from Bianca to chastise Daniel for leaving her party without saying goodbye and to remind him that she was supposed to be cooking for him on Monday evening. Maddie bit her lip when she heard this and stole a look at him. He looked quite unperturbed and just continued to pour brandy into the glasses he'd taken from the cupboard. The third message was from Maeve, asking Maddie to ring her urgently.

Maddie bit her lip as the answering machine sounded its full stop. She carried on staring out into the dark garden with unseeing eyes. She didn't want to ring Maeve. Maeve was a reminder of her past – of that other country she'd fled from. She didn't want real life impinging on her *vie en rose*. Not just yet. She wished she hadn't listened to the message. It had put a downer on the evening. Suddenly she felt like crying.

'Here.' Daniel had come up behind her and was holding out a glass. He leaned against the balustrade and looked at her. 'Aren't you going to telephone your friend?' he asked.

Maddie took a sip of brandy and thought hard. She wanted to make this idyll last as long as she possibly could. She made a decision. She'd ring Maeve back first thing on Monday morning. She'd postpone real life until next week. She felt a bit bad about not getting back to Maeve straight away, but she knew that her cousin would understand. Maeve would be delighted to know that Maddie's demons had finally been exorcized.

She looked up at Daniel. He seemed guarded. 'No,' she said. 'I won't call her now. It's too late.'

His expression relaxed. He put an arm around her waist and then let his hand slide down her hip. He started to caress her ass through the layers of silk chiffon. 'Come upstairs then.'

'Why?' she asked, disingenuously.

'I imagine you're the kind of well brought up young lady who keeps her promises, Madeleine, aren't you?'

'Of course I am, Daniel.'

'You made a promise to me earlier in the evening that you'd show me how those skirts might look swirling up above your thighs. In the privacy of my bedroom.'

He gestured for her to precede him back through the french windows and she smiled over her shoulder at him as she did so. The answering machine was still switched on, she noticed with satisfaction. That meant that they wouldn't be disturbed by phone calls.

Its red eye glowed on in the darkness after Daniel had turned off the lights and shut the door behind them.

Chapter Nineteen

That night she dreamed that she was back in her flat in Dublin. She was hunting for her suitcase, but she couldn't find it. This was bizarre, because she knew perfectly well that she'd only just packed it. The phone kept ringing with people from agencies saying they were expecting her and asking why she wasn't there yet, and she kept telling them that she was on her way, and then she'd put the phone down and resume her hunt for the case. The last thing she remembered doing in the dream was struggling to take down the enormous Dufy print – *La Vie en Rose* – from the wall of her sitting room. She knew that when she found her suitcase she had to pack the print, and she found herself worrying about how on earth she was going to fit it in.

She woke up feeling vaguely anxious, and then realized that Daniel's eyes were on her. She smiled up at him. He was leaning on an elbow, studying her.

'What were you dreaming about, Madeleine?' he asked.

Her memory of the dream was vestigial already.

'I was dreaming about *La Vie en Rose*,' she replied, stretching herself like a cat.

He trailed a hand the length of her body. 'You had a tiny little frown on your forehead,' he said. 'I wanted to banish it.'

'Oh?' she said, pouting a little and furrowing her forehead. 'I know a good way of banishing it.' She reached up and pulled his head down to hers. 'There. It's almost gone,' she said, after several minutes had elapsed. 'You've kissed it away.'

He ran a finger along the inside of her thigh. ' "Almost" isn't good enough,' he said. 'Let's try a little harder.' This time he ran his tongue the length of her body.

*   *   *

An hour or so later he swung himself out of bed. 'Where are you going?' asked Maddie. Her frown had disappeared completely now.

'To the studio,' he said, pulling on his jeans.

She was lying back on the pillows with nothing covering her. 'Oh, Daniel, don't go,' she pleaded, holding out a hand to him. 'Let's not do any work today.'

'I'm not going to work. I just want to sit up there by myself for half an hour and inhale the atmosphere.'

'Inhale my atmosphere instead,' she said, sliding off the bed and giving him a provocative look.

'I've been doing that all morning, Madeleine. I'm intoxicated by you. I badly need a breather.'

She slung a backward smile at him as she wandered over to the window and leaned out, resting her elbows on the sill. Mme Poiret was depositing a bag of rubbish in a *poubelle* beneath, slamming the lid with a vehemence she obviously enjoyed. Through the window of a nursery in a house opposite she could see a baby pulling itself up by the bars of its cot. She smiled at it. A cat ambled through a door below and sat down in the precise centre of a pool of sunlight, blinking lazily.

There was the noise of a car engine approaching. Leaning out further, she looked towards the end of the street to see Rory's jeep rounding the corner. Her hands flew to her mouth as she turned to Daniel. 'Molly's back!' she said.

'Don't look so aghast, Madeleine,' he said, with an amused glance at her. 'Just go back to your own room and behave as normal. I'll go down and let the prodigal in.'

When Maddie opened the door of the bedroom she almost tripped over Pilot, who was lying on the threshold of his master's bedroom with his nose between his paws. He looked a bit morose when she emerged, but he thudded his tail stoically against the floorboards before getting up, stretching, and disappearing into Daniel's room. As she ran down Daniel's corridor and up the stairs to the room she'd shared with Molly, the doorbell rang.

Molly was delighted to be back, even though she'd had a 'deadly' holiday. By the time Maddie had finished showering and had dressed and gone downstairs, Molly had just finished telling Daniel all about the fun she and Aoife had had, and she was delighted to have an opportunity to repeat the entire saga to Maddie. Daniel poured Maddie a cup of coffee and she sat down beside him at the kitchen table with her chin in her hands, listening with an enraptured expression to Molly as she prattled on. Beneath the table Daniel's hand caressed her thigh. She felt supremely happy.

'Dad says we can go to the *pont* today, and have *frites* and ice-cream at the Labadou. *Sam*'ll be there, so you'll come, Maddie, won't you?' Molly gave Maddie a meaningful smile.

'How do you know Sam'll be there, Molly?' asked Daniel.

'We met him on the Square. He says he's mitching from Bianca's today. She wants him to start on her bedroom.'

Daniel suppressed a smile, but Maddie blanched at the prospect of meeting Sam. 'I'm not sure I can take time off to come to the beach, *puce*,' she said. Beneath the table Daniel's hand started to pull her dress inch by inch up her thighs. She crossed her legs.

'Of course Madeleine will come,' Daniel said. 'She needs a break. She's been working very hard while you were away, Molly – sitting for me every day.'

'Oh! Can I see the portrait?'

'No. It's not finished yet.'

'Oh, please, Dad. Just this once?'

'Absolutely not, sweetpea. You know it's my rule. Not even Madeleine has seen it yet. You'll just have to be patient and wait until it's finished, like you always do.'

'But it's of Maddie, Dad!'

'What difference does that make?'

'It's the first time you've painted a portrait of anyone I've really, really liked apart from Deirdre and Maman.'

'Sorry, baby.'

Molly lapsed into sullen silence for about a nanosecond. Then: 'When'll it be finished?' she asked.

'Next week some time, I imagine.'

Maddie didn't say anything. She didn't want to think about next week.

'But that's ages away!' complained the little girl.

'Molly. If you really want to go to the river today and stuff yourself with *frites* and ice-cream, then I suggest you shut up and go and get your swimming gear together.'

Molly got up from the table and shot him a cross look. 'Bum,' she said. Then: 'OK, OK,' she added hastily, as she clocked the expression on her father's face.

When the door shut behind her Maddie looked

at Daniel. Then she leaned back in her chair and uncrossed her legs.

* * *

It was crowded by the creek, but not unpleasantly so. Pilot was in irrepressible form now that Molly was back to play the Sea Wolf game with him, and he also seemed relieved finally to be able to spend some quality time with his master. They spread towels and mats out by the edge of the water and Maddie stripped down to her pants.

Looking around, she saw Sam almost immediately. He was sitting with the usual crowd of young Labadou *habitués*. 'I'd better go and have a word,' she said to Daniel.

'I'd say that would be requisite all right,' he said, lying down on his towel and opening his *Irish Times*. 'Oh, look – there's a photograph of Sara on the Arts page.'

Maddie squinted over his shoulder to see Sara's familiar face smiling back at her. 'It's a great photograph,' she said.

'You'd better bugger off pretty smartly, Madeleine,' said Daniel.

Maddie was taken aback. 'What on earth made you say that, Daniel?'

'Your breasts are brushing against my shoulder, *inamorata mia*, and if you don't disappear sharpish I'm going to get a massive erection. It's not easy to conceal a hard-on when you're wearing bathing togs, so run along, will you please, you sexy bitch?'

She stood up, laughing, and made her way across the beach to where Sam was. He met her halfway, probably sensing that she'd feel awkward around his friends. They kissed each other four times on the cheek, then wandered down towards the water and sat on the sand.

He was the first to speak. 'Where did you disappear to the other night?' he said.

'I'm sorry, Sam. I shouldn't have gone without saying goodbye to you.'

'It's OK,' he said. 'I kind of knew there was something up. You looked fan-fucking-tastic, Madeleine, but I'd a feeling you hadn't done it for me.'

He was tracing patterns in the sand with his finger, looking so mournful that Maddie reached out and touched her hand to his face. 'Oh – please don't, Sam. I'm sorry this all had to happen this way. It was just godawful timing, that's all.'

'It's Daniel, isn't it?'

She knew there was no point in denying it. 'Yes,' she said, feeling very foolish. She wouldn't have blamed Sam if he'd made some 'told-you-so-ish' remark. She had allowed herself to be seduced by Daniel Lennox just as the legion of sitters who'd preceded her had done. Or rather, she corrected herself – she had seduced him. She remembered how he had once stated quite categorically to his sister that he never seduced women – that it was invariably the other way round. She wondered if he'd said it with prescience, knowing that she'd eventually make a move on him, and if he felt smug now that he'd been proved right. Had he been playing with her when he'd dressed her up as Albaydé and told her how gorgeous she was and played sexy music on the CD player in his studio? Maddie shook her hair back from her face. She wouldn't allow herself to go there.

Beside her, Sam sighed. 'I can't be hypocritical, Madeleine,' he said in a serious voice. 'I've a confession to make to you, as well.' He turned his head and looked at her with a sheepish expression. 'You were right,' he said.

'Right about what?' she asked.

'Remember that time you warned me that I could fall in love at the drop of a hat? Well – it's happened. I've met someone. At Bianca's party. It was so weird. At first it was just to make you jealous, and then . . .' he trailed off apologetically.

'You mean you've *really* fallen in love this time, Sam?' Maddie was starting to smile.

'Yes. I mean, I think so. I'm sorry, Madeleine. Um – I like – I led you on a bit, I suppose, didn't I?'

'No. No, you didn't.' She wanted to laugh with relief. 'This is the most wonderful news I could have heard, Sam! It means the timing wasn't godawful after all. It was probably perfect! Oh – I'm so glad for you!' She gave him a big kiss on the cheek. 'Who is she? No – don't tell me –

I know already. That gorgeous blond girl. The one I saw you with in the car yesterday. Am I right?'

'That's the one. She's the daughter of some English friend of Bianca's. She's going into her last year at school in London, and she wants to study photography when she leaves. I suggested that she apply to Dun Laoghaire.'

Maddie threw her head back and laughed. 'A match made in heaven!'

'Oh God, Madeleine – you look so sexy when you laugh like that.' Sam leaned forward and spoke huskily into her ear. 'Can't I have another kiss – a proper one, not just a peck on the cheek? For old times' sake?'

'Sam! What a spectacularly bad line!'

'Sorry. Come on, Madeleine,' he crooned. 'I know you like it when I talk in your ear. It's worked before. Kiss me.'

She laughed. 'You're very nearly irresistible.'

'You're laughing. You know you want to kiss me. Do it.'

'I really don't think that's terribly wise, darling boy,' she said.

'Why not?' He was starting to nuzzle gently at her neck.

'Your new girlfriend's standing over there.' She smiled at him and Sam jumped to his feet as though he'd been stung.

'Thanks for warning me,' he said, looking like a guilty schoolboy. He turned and waved up the beach to a blond girl who was looking rather lost. 'Perdita!' he shouted. 'Hi!'

A big smile crossed Perdita's face, and she waved back.

'I'd better go and look after her,' he said, turning to Maddie. 'She doesn't know anyone here.'

'Tell her to watch out for Florence.' Maddie got up and smiled at him. 'And Claudine. And all the others.'

'Aren't you curious?' Sam was walking backwards up the beach.

'About what?'

'To know what you missed?' He flashed her an incredibly boyish smile before turning and starting to run to where his new-found love was standing with one leg wrapped rather gauchely around the other, waiting for him.

Maddie made her way back across the beach. Daniel was lying on his back with the *Irish Times* covering his face. She could hear a slight snore coming from underneath it.

She sat down beside him and watched a boy leap from the parapet of the pont du Diable. Her heart still somersaulted every time she witnessed the astonishing recklessness of the local boys, but nobody else around her paid any attention to it, or even seemed to notice. The toddler she'd seen throwing pebbles into the water on her first day on the beach trundled past, aiming more pebbles at a rather resigned-looking wading bird. The elderly couple with skin weathered to a deep shade of ox-blood were paddling in the creek. Sam and Perdita were sitting at a remove from the rest of his friends, and Florence was looking even more pouty than usual. This time next week, thought Maddie, all these people would still be here, enjoying the sun, diving from the bridge, skimming stones, conducting love affairs. And she would be in Dublin doing homework on potential employers, reacquainting herself with the *modus operandi* of the advertising world.

She reached into her backpack and took out her pen and notebook. 'Quel beau village!' she wrote. Then she put down the pen and thought for a minute before picking it up again.

Half an hour later the sonnet was finished and Daniel was stirring under the newspaper. 'What have you got there?' he asked, sitting up and looking at the notebook in her hand.

'A frivolous sonnet,' she said, putting it away.

'A completed one?'

'As complete as it'll ever be, I imagine,' she said, with a disparaging laugh.

'Give me a look.'

'No.'

'Go on.'

'No. You won't let me look at my portrait. Why should I let you look at my sonnet?'

'It's finished, isn't it? You spend a lot of time in my studio looking at my finished work. Why shouldn't I be allowed to cast a critical eye over your sonnet, Madeleine? It's only fair.'

'All right, then,' she said, extracting the notebook from her backpack and tossing it over to him. 'You've succeeded in making me feel churlish. It's the last written entry. I'd prefer it if you didn't read any of the other stuff, though.'

'Fair enough.'

She turned her face away and pointedly studied the people swimming in the creek. She was aware of him leafing through the notebook and then stopping as he reached the relevant page. 'Not bad,' he said, after a minute or two. 'And, by the way – I think you were wrong that time you told me you could never write anything profound. I think this sonnet says something quite profound about you, Madeleine, even though the tone is frivolous.' Maddie remained staring out across the water.

'Maddie Godard!' She looked up at the bridge to see Sam standing there, waving at her with a silly grin on his face. Before she could call back to him, he was in the air. She clamped her eyes shut until she heard the splash. At the edge of the water the blond girl stood lost in admiration as he swam across the creek to her with lazy, powerful strokes. Sam and Maddie exchanged a last smile before he slung a nonchalant arm around Perdita's shoulders, then ambled back with her towards his friends.

'What are you reading, Dad?' Molly's voice made her turn.

'It's a sonnet written by Madeleine.'

'What's a sonnet?'

'A sonnet, my little Saracen, is a poem with quite a complicated rhyme structure.'

'What's rhyme structure?'

'It's – oh, read it for yourself, *ma puce*. May she, Madeleine?'

Maddie smiled. 'Of course she can read it.'

Molly took the notebook from Daniel and cleared her throat. As she started to read the poem aloud in her reedy, childish voice, Maddie turned away again. She was suddenly scared that she might cry.

' "Quel beau village!" ' began Molly. 'Which *village* are you talking about, Maddie? Oh – I see – it's about us!' she exclaimed in a delighted voice before launching into the sonnet again.

'Quel beau village! That town of Saint-Géyroux
Where *artistes* strut their stuff on every street,
Where every second person that you meet
Is worthy of a *Newsweek* interview
Or better travelled e'en than Paul Theroux:
Where war is waged o'er *poubelles* in the heat,
Accommodation's more *château* than *gîte*,
Bidons are bottomless – *mais comme c'est fou*!

The memory of it haunts me as I sit
In sullen silence on the north-bound plane.
The pilot's just informed me that there's rain
In Gatwick. Oh, hell! Why must I quit

La vie en rose and head back to the pain
Of my real life? That pilot is a shit.

The end.' Molly handed the book back to her father. 'Sorry about saying "shit", Daddy, but it's written down here in black and white.' She smiled at Maddie. 'I like the bit about the *poubelles* best. Come with me and get an ice-cream, Maddie. Will you, please?'

'I'd love to.' Maddie got to her feet quickly and moved a little way up the beach. Then she paused to extricate a pebble which had lodged between her toes. 'Would you like an ice-cream, Daniel?' she asked, without turning round.

'No, thanks, Madeleine.'

Molly was skipping on the spot beside her. 'Why are you crying, Maddie?' she said.

'Ssh, Molly. I'm not crying,' said Maddie, grabbing the little girl's hand and running up the beach with her.

'D'you know something, Maddie?' said Molly as they reached the Labadou.

'What's that, *ma puce*?' said Maddie, smiling down at her. She'd surreptitiously managed to wipe away her tears.

'I think the pilot is a shit, too,' confided Molly.

* * *

That evening Maddie cooked omelettes for the three of them. Sam had asked to be excluded because he was taking Perdita out for supper in Gignac. Molly pronounced Maddie's omelettes the best meal she'd had since the spicy chicken wings she'd had in Disneyland, Paris, but Maddie suspected that this was a white lie. Molly was only saying it because she'd been feeling sorry for her ever since she'd spotted her crying on the beach.

'Can I sleep in your bed again tonight, Maddie?' Molly asked as they were drawing towards the end of the meal. She threw a winning smile at her. 'Even though Samantha Mumba's on my wall now instead of—'

'No you certainly cannot sleep in Madeleine's bed, Molly,' interposed Daniel before she could get any further. 'We agreed that last time was to *be* the last time – remember?'

'Well, actually, Molly,' said Maddie carefully. 'I'm going to move back into the room I had when I first came here.'

'But why? The room you're in now is much posher. I always pretend I'm a queen when I sit on that big loo in the *en suite* bathroom. I wish I could have an *en suite* bathroom in my room.' She got up and wound her arms around Maddie's neck. 'Your old room is so *bare*, Maddie.'

'I know, sweetheart, but on the top corridor I can hear the house-martins waking up under the eaves in the morning and I like that. And I can hear Mme Poiret complaining about the *poubelles*, and I can hear the church clock chime, and I like all of that too. I won't have many more chances to wake up that way.'

'When do you have to go home?'

'I'm not sure. Soon, anyway.'

'That pilot is a shit,' muttered Molly darkly, as she helped herself to a fig.

*   *   *

After dinner Daniel and Molly cleared up and sent Maddie off to relax on the terrasse. She couldn't relax. She kept thinking of the phone call she was going to have to make to Maeve in the morning, and the first tentative steps towards a *rapprochement* with her old life in Dublin. Daniel came out with coffee and brandy, with Molly in his wake bearing a dish of figs. The child set them down on the table and then lay back on the wicker lounger and started counting.

'What do you think you're doing?' asked Daniel.

'Seven, eight, nine . . . Counting stars, of course,' she replied happily. 'Ten, eleven, twelve—'

'Well you can cut it out. Deirdre told me you were all up at the crack of dawn this morning. It's time you were in bed.'

'Seventeen, eighteen . . . Aw, Dad. I'm not hardly tired at all. Can't I watch a video? Nineteen, twenty, twenty-one . . .'

'No, you bloody can't watch a video. Go.'

'Twenty-four, twenty-five, twenty-six—'

'Molly. *Now.*'

Molly looked sideways at her father. 'OK,' she said. 'There's no need to shout.' She swung her legs slowly off the lounger, keeping her face held up to the sky. 'Twenty-seven, twenty-eight, twenty-nine – can I have a fig?'

'No! You can't have a fig! You've had two already,' said Daniel, requisitioning the sun-lounger.

'I'll have interesting poos tomorrow.' She started to amble exceedingly slowly towards the kitchen door, still looking heavenward. 'Thirty, thirty-one—'

'Go to bed!'

'OK, OK – let me just get to thirty-five. Thirty-two-thirty-three-thirty-four-thirty-five. There! Night, Dad! Night, Maddie!' She plonked kisses on the tops of their heads. 'Will you come up and tuck me in later? I'm going to read for a while.'

'Yes, of course I will,' said Daniel, looking relieved that Molly had actually made it as far as the sliding doors.

'You too, Maddie?'

'Yes, sweetheart.'

'Yay!' And as she made her way across the kitchen and out through the door into the hall they could hear her piping voice recede as she climbed the stairs: 'Labadou, Labadou, Laba, Laba, Labadou . . .'

They looked at each other and smiled.

'Thank Jesus for that,' said Daniel.

'She's a charmer, all right.'

'Takes after her mother.'

'How long were you in love with Marie-France?'
It was a question she'd wanted to ask for ages.

'Not long. She had a cheating heart. That put
me off. Come here.' He held out a hand. 'I've
been having exceedingly lustful thoughts about
you all day, Madeleine Godard.'

She moved across the terrasse and settled down
beside him on the sun-lounger, curling into the
crook of his arm. They lay in silence for a while.
Then: 'You haven't moved your stuff back up into
the top bedroom yet, have you?' he asked.

'No.'

'Are you going to?'

'Yes. I'd like to,' she said in quite a small voice.
There was a pause. 'Have you located the key yet?'

'No. I'll go up shortly. I'm pretty certain I know
where to find it. If I don't, I'll simply jemmy the
lock.' He put a finger under her chin and raised
her face to his. They kissed leisurely for a long
time. Then she curled herself into his arms again
and rested her head against his chest.

'Madeleine?'

'Mm?'

'When I finish your portrait you'll have no real
reason to stay on here, will you?'

Her reply when it came sounded horribly final.
'I suppose not,' she said.

'In that case may I run something by you? How
about—'

'Papa!' They could hear the door to the kitchen

opening. Maddie jumped to her feet and moved across the terrasse on swift feet. She pulled a fig off the fig tree and split it open, pretending to examine it. The fruit inside was withered and dry. When she turned round again, Molly was standing on the step leading onto the terrasse. She looked very pale.

'What is it, *ma puce*?' Daniel had got to his feet also.

'Papa – Daddy – what's a *putain*?'

'Molly – I'm not sure you want to know. Why on earth do you ask?'

'Daddy – do you promise you won't be angry with me?' Molly's voice was trembling and she was on the verge of tears.

'I promise I won't be angry with you, baby.' He was trying to make his voice as reassuring as possible, but Maddie could tell that he was unsettled. 'Come and sit down beside me.' He crossed the terrasse and put his arms around the little girl. She had started to cry in earnest now. He picked her up and held her against him, then moved over to the sun-lounger and sat down on it with Molly on his knee. He rocked her to and fro for a minute or two until her sobs had subsided. 'OK, sweetpea – what's wrong?' he asked.

'I'm sorry, Daddy. I did a bad thing.' The little girl rubbed her eyes with her knuckles and sniffed. Then she rubbed her nose. 'You see, I couldn't wait to see Maddie's picture. I really like her – I think she's one of the nicest people who's ever sat for you, and I wanted to be sure that her portrait wasn't one of those kind of weird ones you do sometimes – like the one you did of Maman once, remember? Where the colours were all kind of dark and gloopy and it didn't really look like Maman at all?'

Daniel had rested his chin on the top of Molly's head. He was looking at Maddie and he was smiling now. 'It's OK, baby. I know what you're going to say. You're going to tell me that you went up to the studio for a sneak preview, aren't you?'

'Yes.' Molly's voice was tiny. She buried her face in her father's chest.

'It's all right, darling. I can understand that this time the temptation was just too much. You're forgiven.' He kissed the top of her head, and continued to rock her in his arms in silence for a while. Then he said, very gently: 'What has the word *putain* got to do with any of this, Molly?'

Molly sat up straight now and looked at her father with enormous, worried eyes. 'Well, when I looked at the canvas I got a really awful fright. There were big scratch marks all over the painting, and there were these letters – P-U-T-A-I-N – written at the top. What does it mean, Dad?'

Maddie could have told her what it meant. *Putain* was the French word for 'whore'. She sat down suddenly, and she knew her face had gone as white as Molly's.

'And there was something else, Dad. This was hanging on the easel on a piece of string.' She showed him something which glistered in the palm of her hand. Then she held her hand out to Maddie. 'Does it belong to you, Maddie?' she asked, in her high, curious, innocent child's voice.

When Maddie's voice finally made it out of her mouth, it didn't sound like her voice at all. It sounded like the old woman's voice she had found herself speaking in the night Josh had raped her. 'It used to belong to me,' she said, as she took the heart-shaped locket from Molly's slender little fingers. 'It doesn't any more.' She made her way into the kitchen and dropped the locket Josh had given her into the bin along with the dried-up fig. Then she bent over the porcelain sink and retched and retched.

Chapter Twenty

The following hour passed as if in a dream. Daniel took her up to the billiard room and poured her a large brandy. A video was produced for Molly, and then Daniel locked the door while he searched the rest of the house, and sent Pilot outside to recce the garden. He was concerned that Josh might be still around, hiding in the grounds or in one of those cavernous rooms. Maddie wasn't surprised when there was no sign of him. She knew that her ex wouldn't want to run the risk of a physical confrontation with Daniel any more than he'd want to confront a big dog.

When he'd satisfied himself that all was well, Daniel joined her where she was sitting on the balcony. He wrapped a rug around her and questioned her gently. She told him about the other photographs Sara had taken of her, and about the stalking, and about how threatened she'd felt. Then Daniel suggested that she telephone Maeve. He brought her the phone and sat down opposite her, studying her face with sad, watchful eyes.

Maeve picked up almost immediately. 'Maddie!

Thank Jesus it's you! You just got my messages, right?'

Maddie was confused. 'Messages? No – I only got one – last night—'

'I've been leaving messages all day. I've been frantic to reach you.'

Through the french windows Maddie noticed for the first time that the red light on the answering machine was flashing like a distress signal. It hadn't been checked for some time.

'It's about Josh, isn't it?' said Maddie dully.

'Yes it is.' Maeve sounded very grave. 'How did you know?'

'He's been here. He got in last night when we were out.'

'He's been in the house?'

'Yes.'

'Have you seen him?'

'No. But he – tampered – with my portrait. Daniel's been doing a portrait of me.'

'Jesus, Maddie. Get on to the police at once. The guards here already know about him.'

'The guards? Why?' Maddie's heart felt as if it was being clenched by a cold fist.

She could hear Maeve take a deep breath. 'I wanted to put off telling you this for as long as I could, Maddie. Josh trashed your car. That's why I suggested that Nick take your flat.'

'I don't understand.'

'Josh smashed your windscreen and sprayed graffiti all over your car. I reckoned he wouldn't go near your flat if there was someone living there – that's why I installed Nick Fielding. But Nick was called back to London for an audition a couple of days ago. Josh broke in and trashed the joint. That's how he knew where to find you. He must have found the travel agent's itinerary.'

'That only took me as far as Montpellier.'

'He put two and two together, Maddie. I talked to him about Saint-Géyroux on the night of his birthday party.'

'Oh.' Maddie imagined her ex-lover spying on her apartment, waiting through the night until there was no likelihood of Nick Fielding returning, and then breaking in and wrecking the place. He'd have done the same thing last night, too – observing them leaving for Montpellier on the Harley, making sure that the dog wasn't at home, and that Sam was out. How utterly craven. Josh was stooping really low, now – cowardly and abject at heart, like all bullies.

'Maddie? Maddie – are you still there?'

'Yes. I'm here.'

'Are you OK?'

'I'm OK.' Beyond the french windows she could see Molly smile at something on the television screen, and she was glad that the little girl had got over her fright. For now, anyway. She wondered if what Josh had done would have any lasting effect on her childish sensibility. How dare he! How dare he inflict his sick world-view on an innocent like

Molly! 'Really I'm OK. It's about time I re-entered, anyway.'

'Re-entered?'

'Real life. I've kind of been living on another planet.'

'I'm sorry to be the one to beam you up.'

'That's OK, Maeve. Thanks for ringing. You're a star.'

'Take care,' said her cousin.

'You too. I'll talk to you tomorrow and let you know what's going on.'

She put the phone down and drained her glass. She knew the brandy would do nothing to help clear her head, but she craved some kind of anaesthetic.

Daniel touched her face. 'D'you want another?' he asked.

She shook her head.

'OK,' he said. 'This is what I am going to do. I am going to give you one of Mme Thibault's tisanes. She suffers from bouts of insomnia, and she swears by this stuff. Then I'm going to put you and Molly to bed. I think it's probably a good idea if you sleep together in the same room again tonight. What do you think?'

'OK.'

'I've already phoned the gendarmes. I said I'd get back to them later with more details. I'll tell them that you'll be happy to help them with their enquiries tomorrow, but I don't think you should talk to anyone tonight. You look very shook up. How do you feel?'

She actually didn't feel much about anything. She just felt numb. The brandy was evidently having the desired effect. 'Tired,' she said.

He put his arm around her. 'The most important thing right now is that you try and get some sleep. And don't let yourself start imagining any horrific scenarios, OK? You are perfectly safe here, Madeleine. This house is like a fortress – as long as people remember to lock the gates.' He smiled at her and she managed a smile back. 'I wouldn't mind the idea of running into your ex-boyfriend, though,' he continued in a conversational tone. 'I'd break the evil bastard's fucking neck.' His arm tightened around her.

'Poor Josh.'

'I wouldn't waste any sympathy on him, Madeleine.'

'No – I mean that it's sad, really. He was OK, once. A posey git, but essentially OK. And he did love me a lot.'

'He sounds to me like a miserable, craven wretch of a man.'

Craven. The very word she'd used herself about him earlier. 'He's that now, all right. A craven wretch. He's crossed over into some scary, inhospitable no man's land of the mind – I can't bear to think of the person he's become. Hell, Daniel – he's going to need more help than me if he's ever going to return to real life.'

Real life. That's where she was now. She wasn't

running away any more. *La vie en rose* was over. She stood up abruptly, then moved to the balustrade and looked out across the darkening garden. It was a study in chiaroscuro, a dreamy nocturne. She remembered how she had once described Daniel's courtyard as a sanctuary. His courtyard, his house, his garden, his studio, his swimming pool had truly been that for her – she'd found serenity here, and love. And now Josh was somewhere out there, somewhere beyond those walls, waiting for her. 'I'm not frightened,' she said. She turned and looked at Daniel. 'I'm not frightened of him, you know. If Josh has become a different person, then so have I. He can't touch me now.'

'That's good to know.' Daniel held out a hand to her. 'Come with me, Madeleine. I'm going to tuck you into bed, and then I'll bring up that tisane. Molly might read you a bedtime story.'

She smiled at him as they passed through the french windows. 'I'd like that,' she said.

But it looked as if she'd have to forgo the bedtime story. On the big sofa in the billiard room Molly was fast asleep.

*   *   *

The tisane was as effective as Daniel had claimed it would be. Maddie woke early the next morning after a dreamless sleep, with Molly and Small Claude the teddy and Bassa the panda tucked in beside her. She felt strangely calm as she showered and dressed, and went downstairs. Daniel was drinking coffee in the kitchen.

'How did you sleep?' he asked. He crossed the kitchen floor and took her in his arms.

'I slept well,' she said. She raised her mouth to his and he kissed her lightly.

Then he said: 'Are you ready for this?'

'Yes.'

'Do you want some breakfast first?'

'No thanks. I'll just have a cup of coffee. When can we head into Gignac?'

'Whenever you like. Are you really feeling up to it?'

'I'm feeling surprisingly up to it.'

'I'm impressed. You're a brave girl. It's not going to be easy for you.'

'I'm not really brave. Just resigned. I'd forgotten that real life's full of shit things to do. It's about time I put some practice in. What'll we do with Molly?'

'I talked to Deirdre. She's going into Montpellier soon, but she's dropping Rory and Aoife off at the creek first. We can leave Molly with them.' There was a beat. Then Daniel said: 'I'd better go and wake her before I start wanting to touch you too much.'

'It's OK,' said Maddie. 'I'll wake her.'

It was a shame she never got to see the expression on Daniel Lennox's face as she left the room.

*   *   *

They pulled up by the pont du Diable an hour and a bit later. Daniel got out of the car and strolled over to the rampart to make sure that Rory and Aoife had arrived.

'Molly – have you got all your stuff together?' Maddie asked as Molly tumbled out of the back, spilling Barbie outfits onto the ground.

'Yeah yeah yeah,' intoned Molly. Maddie crouched down and helped her stuff the glittering garments back into her beach bag. Her face was on a level with the child's. 'Maddie, d'you know something?' she said. 'I think I love you.'

Maddie smiled at her. 'And I think I love you too.' She gave Daniel's little girl a kiss on the nose and then stood up and took her by the hand. 'Come on. Let's go and find Rory and Aoife.' They paused to allow a red Merc to pull over, then started to walk across the road to where Daniel was standing, surveying the beach below.

'Do you love Sam, Maddie?' asked Molly suddenly.

'No, I don't, *ma puce*. I'm very fond of him, but that's not really the same as love.'

'Who do you love, then?'

'I just told you. I love you.'

'No, I don't mean that way. I mean what *man* do you love?'

Maddie pondered for a moment. She could hardly say to her small friend: 'Actually, Molly, I love your father.' Instead she said: 'I love Santa Claus.'

Molly pondered too. 'Mm. Good choice,' she said.

They had reached Daniel by the rampart. 'They're bloody miles away,' he said. 'I tried waving, but they haven't seen me. I'll have to go down with you, sweetpea.'

'Aw, Dad! Can't I go down by myself?'

'No, Molly, you can't. You're not old enough to go anywhere unchaperoned. And that pathway can be treacherous.'

Daniel started striding towards the path that led down to the beach, trailing Molly behind him by the hand. She looked over her shoulder as Maddie sat down on the rampart. 'Aren't you coming, Maddie?' she asked piteously.

'No, *puce*. I'm going to have a little rest.' She wanted time to herself to sort out her head before talking to the police. Before shopping her ex-lover. Before revisiting her past: that other country.

The beach was comparatively empty today – Monday mornings were always among the quietest times. She remembered the spot further upriver where she'd gone with Daniel that time he'd been inspired to paint her as Albaydé. It had been one of the most peaceful times of her life. Far below she saw Daniel and a miniature Molly emerge onto the sand. Molly looked up and waved at her, and she waved back. Sunlight danced on the green water, a warm breeze moved her hair; nearby a bird was singing. She thought of the nightingale she'd heard in Daniel's darkening garden that night and suddenly realized that she loved this place more than any other place she'd ever been.

The great shadow of the pont du Diable straddled the riverbanks, and she could see her own shadow there too, tiny, insignificant. For some reason it struck her with whimsical detachment that it was the shadow of her former self, and something compelled her to raise a valedictory hand. As the shadow on the rocks below did likewise, it was joined by another dark shape.

Josh leaned his hands on the parapet beside her. 'So. Which one are you fucking?' he asked.

She straightened up very slowly and looked him in the face. He was wearing black shades and black cut-offs, and he had an unwashed look. His mouth was twisted in an unpleasant sneer.

'Don't dare touch me, Josh,' she said in a very even, toneless voice.

'Don't flatter yourself. I don't touch whores. Which one are you fucking?' he said again, conversationally. 'The young stud you shagged in Dublin? I saw him feeling you up on the beach yesterday. Or are you having a scene with the ageing, randy artist? Maybe you've had them both, Maddie. It wouldn't even surprise me if you'd had them both together.'

She turned her head away and took a deep breath. 'You are a sad, sad fuck, Josh. Get help, will you? Get help from somewhere. You're sick. You know that, don't you? You're not the person I once knew.'

Behind the black sunglasses she could see his eyes narrow. 'You never knew me, Maddie. Not really. You wouldn't have betrayed me if you'd really known me. Known how much I loved you.'

And suddenly the words he'd used after his unspeakable treatment of her all those weeks ago came back to her. *I'm sorry I had to slap you,* he'd said. *But you had it coming, Maddie. You deserved it, and I hope it's taught you a lesson.* Then he'd smiled at her. *You know I still love you, don't you? Jesus, Maddie, I love you so much. I love you so much it hurts* . . .

'Love! That was love!' She gave a mirthless laugh. 'You listen to me, Josh. You commandeered five years of my life! I spent five whole years in denial of the fact that the man I thought I loved and admired more than any other man in the world was a fake. *Love!* Hell's teeth, you don't know what love is! But *I* do. And I know that whatever it was I once felt for you certainly wasn't love.'

He curled his lip. 'Just because of a little rough treatment? C'mon, Mads. You can't still be—'

'You don't understand. I didn't stop loving you because you raped me. I couldn't *stop* loving you because I never started. *I never loved you,* Josh.'

He looked as if she'd slapped him. He looked very scared, suddenly, like a lost boy. Craven. The words Daniel had used came back to her. 'You are a craven wretch, Josh O'Regan,' she said lightly, as if making some casual, conversational observation. 'You are a craven wretch, you are a bully and you are a coward.' She smiled pleasantly at him, then took a step backwards and let the smile atrophy. 'Now fuck off, Josh. Fuck off and leave me alone.' She turned and started walking towards the path that would take her to the beach.

'*Craven*? Oh, I'm no coward, Maddie.' Something about the measured tone in his voice made her look back. He had stepped up onto the parapet of the bridge and was standing with his head held high and his hands on his hips. 'Your toyboy thinks he's pretty damn cool when he pulls this stunt, doesn't he? You wouldn't call him a coward, would you, or your macho artist with his dick extension motorbike? Well, I'm not a coward either, Maddie.'

She took a step towards him. 'Josh – don't be stupid,' she said. 'It's not as easy as it looks. Please don't try it.'

He took off his shades and dropped them. They bounced off the parapet and disappeared over the edge. Maddie recalled how Daniel had described his eyes as cruel. They weren't cruel now, just infinitely sad and infinitely vulnerable. Then, still keeping his eyes fixed on her, he raised his arms very slowly over his head.

She took another tentative step towards him. She was scared now, but instinct told her not to make any quick moves. 'Get down, Josh,' she said in a very level voice. 'Please get down now. I don't think you're a coward. I don't think you're a coward at all.'

'I love you, Maddie,' he said. 'I've always loved you.' She had never seen such tenderness in his eyes. Then he turned away from her and thrust himself out into the air beyond the parapet.

From far below came the sound of people screaming.

*   *   *

It rained at Josh's funeral. Afterwards she didn't know what to do. She didn't go back to the house with Josh's family. She couldn't have hacked that. So she just travelled back to Dublin with Maeve, and spent the car journey curled up asleep in the back seat. When they hit the suburbs she woke up, but she remained huddled in her ball of grief and shock, pretending to be asleep still. She didn't want to talk to anyone. She wanted to be somewhere peaceful by herself, but she could think of nowhere in this city that could give her the tranquillity she craved.

From the glimpses of passing landmarks, she gauged that they were in the Kilmainham area. Abruptly she sat up. 'Maeve? Can you drop me at IMMA?'

'The Museum of Modern Art? Why?'

'I want to be somewhere peaceful by myself. When I visited Montpellier the only refuge from the heat and the noise and the unpleasantness was in the Musée Fabre.' She looked out of the window. It was still raining, but it was easing off and there were patches of blue on the horizon. 'It'll do me good to wander round the gallery. I might wander round the grounds too, if the rain lets up. OK?'

'Of course it's OK. It's a great idea.' Maeve's mobile started to ring. 'Shit. Just let me pull over and get this, will you?' She slid into a side street and put the handbrake on before answering the phone. Maddie could see the cupola of the old Royal Hospital where the Museum was housed. She could walk it in five minutes.

'Hello?' said Maeve into her mobile. 'Uh-oh – you're breaking up. I can't hear you very well.' Maddie let herself out of the car. 'Sorry – can you hang on for just a sec?' Maeve covered the mouthpiece of the phone with her hand. 'Maddie?' she said. 'Where are you off to?'

Maddie pointed towards the cupola. 'I'll walk, Maeve. I feel like it, honestly. I'll see you back at your place, OK?'

'Are you sure about this?'

'Positive. I'll see you later.'

She strode out along the street with her hands dug into the pockets of her coat, glad to get out of the car. The rain was still falling lightly as she turned up the long driveway that led to the elegant old hospital building, but it was a relief after the sticky humidity of the past two days. It had been too hot in France, but that was preferable to the cloying, muggy heat that had hit her when she'd arrived in Dublin. Now the rain had cleared the air a little, and relieved the city of its coat of dust. Here in the grounds of the old hospital things looked clean and fresh.

She allowed her pace to slow a little as she looked around her. Maybe if she strolled round the gardens for half an hour she could start to make some sense of things. For the first time, she cast her mind back to the day of Josh's death. It was like trying to remember a bad dream. She couldn't clearly recall the sequence of events – the police procedure, for instance. The real life stuff. But she could remember with dazzling clarity tiny irrelevant details, like the burst blood vessel in the desk sergeant's eye, and the loose button on his shirt, and the resignation in his voice when he wondered aloud to his colleagues how many more lives the pont du Diable would claim this summer. She had never found out how Josh's body had been recovered, but she had a vivid memory of the sound of the ambulance siren. A gendarme had found a photograph of her and Josh in the glove compartment of the red Merc he'd hired, and had given it to her with a sympathetic smile at some stage in the proceedings. She remembered that she'd thought it was sweet that Josh had chosen that particular photograph to carry with him in his wallet. It had been taken on holiday in some sunny location – Italy, she thought vaguely – and it showed them both smiling and larking for the camera. 'Oh – look at that awful dress I have on!' she'd said, showing the photograph to Daniel and laughing before she'd suddenly burst into inconsolable weeping again.

Daniel had taken control of everything. He'd unravelled red tape, used influence, and showed her where to sign. He'd contacted Maeve, and Josh's family in Kildare, he'd booked her plane ticket and called in favours. He'd talked to the Irish embassy in Paris and he'd spent nights without sleep, stroking her hair and murmuring to her while she wept for the Josh she'd known and cared for before the demons had taken over. Mme Thibault had cut short her sick leave and had taken charge of the house, and Deirdre had taken Molly for the week until Marguerite could come home from Grasse to look after her. He'd made sure she was seldom alone. He knew that demons thrive in solitude. Deirdre and Rory had been frequent visitors. Sam had worked overtime at trying – sometimes even successfully – to make her laugh, and while Bianca had been too busy to drop in, she had sent white flowers. Lilies.

In Dublin Maeve and Jacqueline had taken charge. She hadn't been back to her own apartment yet. Her cousin had told her carefully that it would require a lot of work to put it right. Maeve had managed to have all the major repairs seen to, but hadn't had time for the more cosmetic stuff, like painting and replacing things.

Maddie couldn't let herself think about how strung out Josh had been when he'd trashed her flat. Nor could she allow herself to think of the state his mind was in when he'd defaced her portrait. She knew that Daniel had burned it. She'd watched him from a window one night when he had thought she was sleeping. He'd broken it and shredded the canvas and then he'd doused it with petrol and torched it. She had never seen it.

Often in dreams she pictured it. The serene eyes of Albaydé gouged and bleeding. The mad eyes of Josh blazing with demonic light. But then he would turn his eyes on her in the dream and they'd be the sad, vulnerable eyes he'd turned on her just before he dived from the pont du Diable, and she would wake up weeping again, with Daniel comforting her.

She turned into the quadrangle of the old hospital building and walked through the cloisters to the entrance. The heels of her sandals rang out on the tiled floor. There were few people around. It was nearly five o'clock – the gallery would be closing soon. She asked the woman at the reception desk if there were any Lennoxes currently on show. 'You're in luck,' she was told. 'There's a riverscape in the gallery upstairs. It goes back into storage next week.'

Maddie climbed the steel staircase and walked the length of the gallery like an automaton, moving past astonishing artwork with unseeing eyes. The Lennox painting was at the very end of a pristine white corridor. She stood for a long time looking at the swirling green paint strokes that Daniel had executed years before, during the turbulent time of his marriage to Marie-France. She was looking at the waters of the Hérault – the river that had caressed and soothed her battered body in the aftermath of the rape; the river where she'd dived and played before she and Daniel had become lovers; the river that had claimed her ex-lover's life. She remembered his studio, and the first time she'd sat for him, how she'd chanted the names of the pigments he used. She'd loved them so much she'd memorized them. Titanium White. Monestial Blue, Cobalt Blue. Payne's Grey. Leaf Green, Sea Green. Burnt Umber. Rose Madder, Crimson Lake, Cadmium Red. Vermilion. Permanent Magenta.

She chanted them now under her breath, like a mantra, and as she did so it struck her that they represented the colour palette of her past year. The route she had followed had taken her from sterile, empty white through a whole spectrum of blues and greys to a renaissance the shade of a new leaf. Thereafter, the colours had become more vibrant, vigorous – peaking, ironically, at the colour of passion. Was she now to return to the nadir of that spectrum, plunging from Permanent Magenta straight back down into dull Payne's Grey and the solitary, joyless blues of Real Life?

She heard footsteps approaching and brushed away the tear that was sliding down her cheek.

Then she braced herself to face the museum attendant who would politely inform her that they were closing now.

'You've been looking at that painting for a very long time.'

She turned round to find Daniel leaning against the sill of a tall window, looking at her. His lion's mane was backlit by the sun that had just cast off a cloud, and was now streaming in through the glass. 'Hello, Madeleine,' he said.

'What are you doing here?' she asked in an expressionless voice.

'I'm in Dublin to consult with my gallery about my exhibition. Remember? I told you I'd be coming over on and off until September.'

'No – I mean what are you doing here? In the Royal Hospital?'

'I rang Maeve on her mobile. She told me I'd find you here, and something told me which room you'd be in.' He moved towards her. 'How have you been, Madeleine? I imagine today was pretty ropy.'

She nodded. She couldn't speak.

He had reached her now, and he lifted his hand to caress her face the way he had done the very first time he'd met her. 'Will you come back to France with me, Madeleine?' he said.

Tears started to well up in her eyes again. 'What would I do there? Who would I be?' she asked stupidly.

'You would be my muse, my model, my mistress,

my friend, my châtelaine – my wife, if you fancied the idea. You could have my baby or not have my baby. That's for you to decide. You could travel into Montpellier to work every day in some shit-hot advertising agency. Or you could work freelance from my house. I'll even install a computer for you, Madeleine.' He put his arms around her waist and pulled her closer in to him. 'You could swim in the Hérault and in my swimming pool late at night. You could play on my piano – as long as I'm not around when you're inspired to wax musical. You could eat good food and drink excellent wine and make love all day long. Or for as long as I can keep it up.'

A spluttery little laugh escaped her, and she wiped her eyes with the sleeve of her coat.

'You could write frivolous sonnets and not feel embarrassed by them,' continued Daniel, extracting an oversized handkerchief from his pocket and instructing her to blow. 'You could read all the books in my library. Maybe you could write one. You could afford me the pleasure of painting your likeness onto Molly's bedroom wall. You could plant a fig tree in my garden that might one day produce female fruit. What do you say?'

She could say nothing. Tears were still streaming down her face. He wiped them away, and gently licked away a splotchy one that had landed on the back of her wrist. He turned her hand and kissed the palm; and then he pushed up her sleeve and kissed the crook of her elbow, and the dip made by her collarbone, and the curve of her neck, before starting to kiss her properly.

'Yes,' she murmured finally, into his mouth. 'Oh, God, Daniel – I say yes. Oh, yes!'

Rodin had made a kiss famous. So had Klimt. But even a painter as gifted as Daniel Lennox might have found it difficult to convey the tenderness, the passion, the sensuousness and the unswerving commitment implicit in the kiss he now exchanged with his own muse.

Some minutes later a discreet cough came from behind them. 'Excuse me, please. We're closing now.'

She found it difficult to stop kissing Daniel, so he broke the kiss for her. Then he took her arm and escorted her towards the door, smiling at the museum attendant as they passed through. 'Great painting,' he said, nodding his head in the direction of the swirling green river. 'Is it worth a lot of money?'

The attendant was pushing the door shut behind them. Maddie looked over her shoulder and saw the green waters of the Hérault disappearing behind the white panel. 'Yeah,' answered the man. 'It's worth thousands. That bastard Lennox must be loaded.'

And Daniel Lennox's ringing laugh echoed down the staircase of the Royal Hospital as he and Madeleine Godard wrapped their arms tightly around each other, and walked towards the exit.

Epilogue

She was sitting on the balcony, as she often did at this hour of the evening. Twilight was slowly creeping up over the garden below, drawing a soft, warm, indigo-coloured pashmina across the lawn. *L'heure bleue.* Her favourite time. Her notebook lay on the table beside the single glass of wine she allowed herself these evenings, now that she had the baby to nurse. Rosa had nearly finished her evening feed, and was dozing on Madeleine's breast. The way her eyelashes fanned out against her round cheeks gave the impression that they'd been painted on with the most feather-light, delicate brush-strokes. Earlier, Daniel had covered pages of his sketchbook with tiny, thumbnail sketches of his daughter, his pencil moving rapidly over the paper as Rosa fed. Maddie was certain no other six-week-old infant on earth had ever had so many likenesses made of her! Daniel had thanked God when she'd been born that the only physical gene of his she'd inherited had been the colour of her hair. The child had hair the colour of spun gold, which contrasted dramatically with her eyes. The wise, slate-blue gaze Rosa had been born with had just recently metamorphosed into the conker-brown shade gifted to her by her mother.

Below Madeleine, the garden was festooned with light. The men had come today and put up a marquee and erected a platform for the local accordion band, and had slung fairy lights and chains of lanterns across the branches of every available tree. Molly's swing was garlanded with silk flowers and real fruit, and looked fit for a princess. Madeleine was *so* looking forward to seeing her!

She heard Pilot's nails against the stone floor of the billiard room beyond. The dog approached and then sat at her feet and laid his head in her lap. He had one of Rosa's tiny vests in his velvet mouth.

'Thank you, Pilot. Good boy,' murmured Madeleine, rubbing his ears and taking the vest from him. His tail moved in response.

The faint smell of frying garlic mingled with the scent of lavender this evening, and through the open windows of the kitchen below came the sounds of laborious chopping. She heard some heavy object drop onto the stone-flagged floor with a loud metallic clang, and a flood of vociferous oaths ensued. It was Mme Thibault's night off, and Daniel was cooking. Madeleine smiled, wondering what culinary masterpiece would be set upon the dining table for her delectation an hour later.

Rosa finally relinquished her nipple. The child

was fast asleep now. Madeleine tucked the rose-pink cashmere blanket up around her cherub face. She couldn't take her eyes off her baby. She'd made her! She and Daniel had actually *made* her!

The sonnet she'd written earlier in the evening came drifting into her head, and as she gazed at the child she chanted it, as one might a prayer to ward off evil. She had called her poem 'A Sonnet to Celebrate the Banishing of Demons', and this is how it went:

My diary's full tomorrow. Molly's due.
(She's dying to meet her sister!) We've a team
Of caterers booked. The garden's all agleam –
Decked out for Rosa's christening barbecue!
That person that I once was – thought I knew –
Has gone for good. I've woken up! It seems
Life *is* for zestful living. In my dreams
I meet that girl called Maddie, say adieu . . .

I'm double-jobbing now – don't have much time
To write my poems – it's tough being mum
   and muse!
This sounds strange, but it's true: getting the
   rhyme
And reason right helped exorcize those blues –
Those hellish demons – helped me reclaim
   power.
Poems, and the blesséd light of the Blue Hour.

From the bottom of the garden came the first lush strains of the nightingale's aria. She was sure she saw Rosa smile in her sleep.

THE END

Heaps of thanks are due to the following: Ann Murray for checking out Madeleine's psychological profile. Grace in the Rape Crisis Centre. Dr John O'Keefe. Monica Frawley and Hilary Reynolds for trawling through an early draft (and more thanks to the same Ms Frawley for arranging my sojourn in that stunning house in the Languedoc). Eithne Jordan for allowing me to snoop around her studio. Jan Winter for her insider knowledge of the advertising world. Amelia Stein for her photographic expertise. Kevin Reynolds for kindly allowing me access to recordings in RTÉ. Mark Richards for carrying me pillion through the Wicklow Mountains. Emmet Bergin, whose shell photographs I stole. Ciarán Hinds for unfailingly dragging me back down to earth (bastard!). Timmy Cullen for his terrific piano playing. Sinéad Dwane in Euro-languages for that last-minute tweak. Beth Humphries for her eagle eyes. Diane Meacham for finding the right look. Sarah Luyens for encouraging me to re-conjure Deirdre, Rory and Maeve – and for being so damn sensible. Felicity Rubinstein and Susannah Godman for listening. Cathy Kelly and Marian Keyes, who have provided nonpareil support, and whom I feel dead proud and privileged to call my friends. All in Transworld: I marvel still at my luck in signing with you! Sadie Mayne – a star. Francesca Liversidge – a solar system all to herself. My family; my daughter Clara whom I won't embarrass by saying all the gushing things I'd love to say; Malcolm, my husband, my rock and my best friend. Final thanks to my guardian angels.